I0717686

FATAL PROMISE

DIANNA LOVE

Praise for
the Slye Team Black Ops Romantic Series

FATAL PROMISE

"Fatal Promise left me speechless and in awe."
~~Heathercm, Amazon

"It was a slam dunk in terms of guns, international travel, romance, killers and resolution."
~~ Goodreads

STOLEN VENGEANCE

"This is one of those books where your body tenses, you stop breathing and you just can't read fast enough."
~~ Amazon

"If you love romantic suspense, you will adore Dianna Love's latest Slye Team."
~~ IMHO reviewer

DECEPTIVE TREASURES

"This may be my favorite book in the series so far. I swear they just keep getting better and better."
~~Heather CM, Goodreads

"Complex. Ongoing series. Nonstop action. Romantic suspense."
~~ Madison Fairbanks, Amazon

KISS THE ENEMY

"A FREAKING AWESOME continuation of the Slye Team series by Dianna Freaking Love!!! She did not disappoint."
~~Goodreads

"Kiss the Enemy is a high octane thrill ride through the high stakes world."
~~ J. Cazares, Amazon

HONEYMOON TO DIE FOR

"It seems with each book this series gets better."
~~The Reading Cafe

"…constantly believable and packed with intrigue."
~~Single Title Reviews

NOWHERE SAFE

"The love story is tender, steamy, erotic, and full of electricity, and the action plot will satisfy the reader's thirst for danger."
~~IndieReads review

"Blending taut pacing with sizzling tension, a little bit of James Bond with an engaging personal drama, this is a story for suspense fans and romance readers alike."
~~Goodreads

LAST CHANCE TO RUN [prequel novel]

"I could not put this bookdown...Once again Dianna has thrilled my suspense taste buds with an extra dashof spicy romance."
~~After Hours Rendezvous

"Engrossing, thrilling and wonderfully steamy...a pitch-perfect suspense that will keep readers breathless from the first nerve-racking scene to the last shocking revelation."
~~The Romance Reviews

Dedication

This book is for all the men and women in the military who keep us safe and make it possible for those of us at home to have lives. Also, a special thank you to all the families of our military who sacrifice so much as well. There are no words that can truly convey how much I appreciate all that you do.

Chapter 1

NIGHTHAWK 1911 9MM, cocked and locked. *Check.*
PPSS bulletproof vest. *Check.*

Last will and testament updated. *Check*

Over accessorized for dinner? Maybe.

Sabrina Slye kept her eyes on everyone she passed along Baker Street near the Centennial Park area in downtown Atlanta. Sweat drizzled its way down her back, soaking her thin black T-shirt and sliding under the shoulder holster she'd hidden beneath a black windbreaker. A slight breeze swirled across her damp neck, offering some relief from the heat at twilight.

Welcome to the dog days of summer in Georgia.

July fourth had just passed in its usual dazzling glory.

She kept her stride easy and smooth, when she wanted to run to the restaurant where she'd make a trade for intel on the number one, most wanted man.

Maybe not for the FBI, but former CIA agent Len Rikker topped her must-die list. He had to pay for his part in selling out her team over three years ago in the UK, and for all the deaths he'd piled up since then.

She had the money for the trade tucked into a small shoulder bag, but that wicked sixth sense of hers warned she might not be spending a penny.

This could be a trap.

Okay, to be honest, in her line of work, any time she met someone covertly it could be a trap.

That's why rule number one was *Always Be Prepared.*

Whatever it took, she was not passing up a chance to finally end this hunt, especially if Rikker really was holed up somewhere healing.

Ziggie, a dependable snitch from her early days as a CIA contractor, had rubber stamped the contact wanting to meet with Sabrina. *Ziggie doesn't say a word for eight months, then calls ninety-eight minutes ago with news that he has a female willing to spill her guts?*

Yeah, like that didn't sound suspicious?

But... this information had a short shelf life.

Rikker had been hurt during a shootout with one of her Slye agents in California twelve days ago. She'd have thought he'd be out of the country by now. Evidently, the person he worked for had left him high and dry when, thanks to her people, he'd failed to get his hands on an ancient scroll from the Vatican.

What goes around comes around, you sorry dog.

He'd orchestrated the deaths of two people—*this* time. She'd need a calculator for a true count. He'd almost taken out the pope in California. As in *the* pope. Rikker was harder to kill than a cockroach strung out on crack. Anyone else would have died crashing in an out-of-control helo on a rooftop two weeks back, but Rikker managed to escape. She'd been concerned that the miserable excuse for a human might have bled out somewhere with no way for her to confirm his death.

The small fortune she'd spent hunting him over the past three years was finally paying off. She hoped.

If tonight's meeting turned out to be a bona fide lead, it would be worth every penny invested. Her team had barely survived a failed op in the UK a little over three years ago when they'd gone in to rescue Rikker. A terrorist group had captured him on foreign soil. The US government couldn't claim him, but Uncle Sam had wanted the CIA asset back, so they sent in Sabrina and her people.

Correction, Gage Laughton, her CIA handler at the time, had issued the contract for Rikker's extraction.

Going after the captured spook had seemed no different than any other high-risk contract she'd taken from the agency, but someone who knew the details had burned her team, trading all five of their lives for Rikker's that night.

She had mixed feelings about Gage, but Rikker?

Dead man walking.

Once she got her hands on him, she'd find out who pulled his strings. Who'd traded his ass for her team.

At the door to the restaurant she waited for a trio of happy women to enter ahead of her, then stepped inside, allowing her eyes to adjust. She searched for two empty seats at the very end of the bar.

Friday night packed house, but look at that. Two empty seats at the bar.

That did not happen by accident.

She'd like to hang back and force the contact to sit first, just to have a look at this unknown person, but that wasn't how these things went down. Nodding at the hostess that she was headed for the bar, Sabrina took her time strolling over so she could casually scope out everyone already inside.

The aroma of sizzling steak toyed with her senses.

She circled the end of the lacquered bar. It curved so the two vacant seats allowed an unobstructed view of the entire room, with a wall at her back. Mirrored.

Someone had done her homework, if Sabrina's contact really was a female.

Snagging the last spot, the best choice of the two seats, she left the one on her right empty. Once she met her contact and got what she needed, Sabrina would hook the thin strap of her purse on the chair back so the contact could slide it off without anyone noticing they'd made an exchange.

She angled her body in a way that allowed her to observe every waiter and waitress who swept past her to reach the cubbyhole used for the barback area.

Voices blended and turned into one indecipherable sound surrounding her. Pleasant, though. Wait staff hurried back and forth, smiling and nodding at appropriate times as they interacted with patrons.

She ordered a club soda and lime, which the bartender delivered with polished efficiency.

She'd just taken a sip when her skin tingled.

Someone watched her.

Slowly, she floated her gaze around covertly, observing everything in the restaurant again.

No one stood out.

The hostess led a group of five from the entrance. As she passed Sabrina's end of the bar, the last person following the group peeled off and took the empty seat next to her.

They had a brief stare down until she unlocked her jaws and asked, "What the hell are you doing here?"

Chapter 2

SABRINA SHOOK WITH the need to strangle Gage Laughton. He rested his elbow on the bar and turned toward her as if she'd agreed to meet him for drinks.

Had he really tapped her snitch just to arrange a clandestine meeting with her? Of course he had. He knew she'd jump at a chance to take down Rikker.

Still, the fact that he'd sink this low carved her up inside.

Gage started in, "We have to talk. I—"

She cut him off. "*You* might have to talk, but I've got nothing to say. I said it all this morning." That hadn't been a fun phone call. She'd left California two weeks ago with her insides twisted up. Everyone had a weakness.

Hers was staring at her hard enough to shove her off the stool.

Damn him for making her suffer more than she already did for being the strong one and cutting ties while they were still civil to each other.

It hadn't been easy.

And damn him twice over for tricking her into thinking she had a lead on Rikker tonight. Pulling this prank just so he could talk to her in person was classic CIA agent Gage Laughton.

He ordered a scotch on the rocks and sat quietly, allowing those whiskey-brown eyes to search her face for any tell. He could look all he wanted for something he could use to spin this conversation in his favor, but she'd locked down her emotions.

Okay, yes, her libido was doing a tango at the rush of having him so close. She missed running her fingers through his hair. Now maybe an inch long, it had grown out enough for red highlights to show in the rich brown. He had a harsh cut to his jaw. He was all man. Not a smooth edge on him when he showed his fierce side.

She missed touching the sculpted muscles hidden beneath the sport coat and T-shirt he wore with jeans. He pulled off that look like no other man.

What she *really* missed was the way this man took his time. When he focused on a woman, she was the only thing in his universe.

Gage never rushed into anything, well, except on the occasions that she'd taunted him sexually, determined to push that rigid control to snap. When it broke free, he'd rip her clothes off, then he'd pay her back with smoking sex.

Good times.

All in the past now.

She had to get her head out of yesterday and worry about today. Time to end this once and for all to keep Gage out of her way. Her heart seized at the idea of never seeing him again, but that organ didn't have a say.

It had a bad track record when it came to this man.

Flicking a look around the restaurant to check her surroundings out of habit, she parked her gaze on him. "What part of *we can't do this anymore* confused you? Tell me and I'll put it in shorter words this time."

Nothing showed in his face.

Not a hint of emotion. He had his game face on, which meant he'd come here with a plan in mind. Fine. She'd allow him to lay it out, then make him pack up and be on his way.

"I listened to you," he said just loud enough for her ears. "That doesn't mean I believe what you said."

"Believe it." She'd snapped that out sharper than she'd intended. "I allowed you, no not *you*, but us, to come between me, Josh and Dingo. I've never allowed that to happen in the past. I'm not going to deny that I enjoyed the time we had together before ... the UK mission. But all things come to an end, especially in our line of work."

Almost losing Dingo had brought that home with crystal clarity.

She caught Gage's flinch of pain at her reducing what they'd had to nothing more than sex, but dressing it up any other way would mean leaving a hint of possibility in her voice. The longer she allowed this to be dragged out between them, the more pain it would cause them both.

Gage had never wanted more than an easy-terms affair when they first hooked up, and she'd been fine with it at the time. She could admit to herself that he was special to her.

Even though they'd never have the bond she shared with Dingo and Josh ... she didn't want to watch Gage leave again with no idea when he'd return.

She was not adding one more person to worry about losing.

Undercover work had many faults and she didn't like her world much these days, but it was all she knew. One thing was for sure. She intended to find Rikker and stop him from ever threatening the people in her world again.

Once that happened, she'd have to figure out how to keep Josh and Dingo out of dangerous missions.

First, she had to finish ripping off this Band-Aid so her soul could start healing. Her heart never would. "There is no future for us, Gage. Not as long as we're in this business. Are you planning on leaving the agency?"

"No, but—"

"But nothing. This worked between us when I contracted with the agency and we partnered on missions. It worked because neither of us expected anything more than what we had, but ... that's changed for me. I'm not cut out for any life except the one I have and I now realize this life doesn't allow for a relationship, not a true one."

Pain filtered through his gaze.

Damn, she hated hurting him, but she was being honest.

Gage said, "Not true. You're cut out for anything you want to do ... if you want it bad enough."

She'd spent two long days alone once she got home, trying to make her decision, and kept coming back to one simple truth.

She and Gage had no common ground anymore. What they did have had created a rift with Dingo that she'd managed to repair.

Before she met Josh and Dingo, everyone who'd claimed to

care about her had always chosen something, or someone, else instead of her when things got real.

Gage had put the agency first in the past.

He still did and always would. She wouldn't hold that against him, but neither could she go back to living that way again. Even after what she'd gone through in the UK, Gage shielded the names of those in the agency who had been involved. In fact, he *still* blocked her from digging around to find the person who'd burned her team when they inserted to rescue that bastard, Rikker.

When the deal went bad, a local contact died and Sabrina almost lost Josh, one of two people in the world she considered family.

She'd trusted Gage beyond belief at one time.

But he'd interrogated Dingo in California, and in the process he tried to make Sabrina mistrust the man she considered a brother. Worse, Dingo had walked away. She wasn't losing Josh and Dingo. Not for anything. Especially not for a relationship that would never amount to any more than great sex.

Not true, whispered through her heart.

Stupid heart.

She drew herself up inside and put on her own battle face. "Okay, Gage. That was my nice attempt at ending this. You know why this is never going to work for us. I don't trust you and you don't trust me."

"I trust you."

If she'd trusted him, she wouldn't have spent two years out of touch after the UK mission.

And if he trusted her, he would have shared those names.

Leaning an elbow on the bar and propping her chin, she waited him out.

He shook his head and made a sound of disgust. "The fucking agency names. Why won't you let that bone go? That doesn't mean I don't trust you." He leaned in. "I told you in California that I've checked out everyone who knew about your UK mission and none of them sold you out. If I give you those names, either you're going to poke around and get killed by the person I haven't found yet or you're going to kill someone you'll regret later when you realize I've been telling you the truth. It's none of the obvious people."

She was done arguing about this. Trust was trust.

You couldn't talk it right.

She summed it up for him. "Oh, I see. I'm capable of putting my life and my team's lives at risk for the agency, but I'm not capable of protecting myself or controlling some unexpected urge to commit cold-blooded murder. Do I have that right?"

Gage cupped his forehead and washed the hand down over his face. "What possessed me to fall for a stubborn woman like you?"

Fall for her? Gage was a genius at strategy, but he had no idea that uttering three words would end this conversation faster than anything else he could say.

She'd learned better than to accept a man's claim of love after surviving childhood with a father who'd beaten her mother to death while proclaiming his love to both of *his girls*. Speaking of love, what had her mother done?

Chosen her monster of a father over protecting her daughter when Sabrina was too small to defend herself against a brutal beast.

She didn't place Gage—or any other man she allowed in her life now—in that category, but neither did she want meaningless words from him.

Sabrina forced herself to maintain a calm front and ignore Gage's persistence as he tried to put a chink in her emotional armor. She should be worried. He'd done it before.

His eyes lifted to hers.

The world saw little when looking at him because he was a master at concealing his real thoughts and feelings. But she knew him better than most, and she saw pain inch into that unyielding gaze.

Gage had not been the person who betrayed her, but someone in the CIA had and he protected them, which meant he was not a hundred percent on her side.

Just like others who had sworn they cared for her.

Words were the face of deceit.

He relaxed, acting as if he'd shaken off his irritation, but it continued to simmer just beneath the surface. "I'm sorry about what happened in California with Dingo. I stepped over a line with him. I promise you it won't happen again."

She appreciated the apology and heard his sincerity, but that wasn't going to fix this. She didn't hate him. She couldn't. In truth, she wasn't even angry anymore, just ... sad to give up what they had.

But it was either here and now, or a week from now, or a month later. It would happen no matter what.

She had to say something so she went with, "Thank you."

He waited and when she said nothing more, he said. "Thank you, as in, thank you, but no dice?"

She nodded.

"What's it going to take for me to convince you we can stay together?"

In that moment, she heard a longing so deep it twisted her heart. A man like Gage never exposed a vulnerability, but his was showing now and she had to clamp her lips shut to keep from giving in. She'd played that possibility out in her mind a hundred times.

It never ended well.

Taking a deep breath and sticking to her plan, she said, "You can't convince me to change my mind and you know me well enough to believe that, so please stop trying. Please don't make me keep repeating myself. I can't go back to the way it was before with us and I'm ... ready to move on. I mean it. I wouldn't jerk you around so stop punishing me by forcing me to say it over and over, and by showing up when I don't expect you."

He lifted his chin and looked away, but not before she saw how deeply she'd cut him.

Now she wanted to punch herself in the head for hurting the one man who had once brought warmth into her cold world. But that was back when she'd believed he was unlike any other man.

Back when she thought he would put her first.

Swallowing hard, he said, "Fine. If that's what you want, I'll ... honor it." He wiped his mouth, a tiny sign of his switching gears to business mode. "I had a second reason for finding you. You have to get off the radar."

"What?" She sat up straighter.

"Remember I told you that I have two people in the agency that I trust?"

"Yes. I bet *they* have the list of names you're keeping from me," she added tartly.

Ignoring that, his tone turned a shade dire. "Your name is surfacing in the wrong places. Someone is coming for you and it might be from inside our government. I can't protect you out here in the open. I need you to go to a safe house with me."

Was he serious? "Dream on," she muttered.

His eyebrows drew together in confusion. "I'm not joking, Sabrina."

"Good. Maybe the person looking for me is the one who sold out my team for some POS rogue agent, but why now?"

"I have no idea why now," he snapped, clearly unhappy she wasn't climbing aboard the do-it-my-way train. "It's intel, and you know that doesn't come with footnotes for clarity. If it is someone in the government, I don't think he or she is with the agency."

"So you say."

He muttered something dark, shook it off and said, "I don't know how much time you have before someone grabs you or what that person wants with you, so let's talk about what needs to be done to keep you safe."

"No."

His flint-hard eyes could stop a bullet, but it couldn't knock down her determination. He argued, "Yes."

"No. I can do this all night."

"Fuck. I knew you'd be this way."

"Oh, this way?" She pointed at herself. "You mean unwilling to go slinking away to some unknown location you pick? I'm not hiding from anyone. I'll hunt him or her, and when I get my hands on them—"

"What're you going to do?" he snarled with the force of a Rottweiler on attack, but not loud enough to draw attention. His hand gripped the edge of the bar top. "This could be anyone." His voice dropped even lower. "Hell, we could be dealing with those fanatical Orion Hunters who've infiltrated the government."

"Exactly, Gage." She leaned in, tapping her index finger on the bar as she said, "That group is behind most of the terrorist operations my teams have shut down this year. That alone puts *all* of my people on their radar. Len ..." She caught herself before she said Rikker's last name, then continued. "*That* person is neck deep in all of this and he was the reason we almost died in the UK. I'm not about to hide somewhere and leave my team exposed."

Hope jump into his face. "Not a problem. I'll find places for them, too."

She chuffed out a sarcastic laugh. "News flash. They don't trust you and that's just another reason you and I have no business trying to be together."

He sat back, defeat clear in his face. "You're a walking target and I don't know who the enemy is, but you think it's me."

Why did he have to say crap like that? "I don't think you're my enemy, Gage," she countered softly.

"Yes you do, Sabrina. You've spent your entire life operating with one set of criteria. Someone is either on your team or not. I'm clearly not, as far you're concerned."

It didn't help that he was right. Her insides had turned into a battlefield where her heart waged war against her mind and her other organs were quickly becoming unavoidable casualties.

She'd be sleeping with a sleeve of Tums tonight.

Gage cared for her.

She knew it logically and heard the sincerity in his voice, but those were just words. Dingo and Josh had grown up on the streets with her. They'd stepped into any fight and shared everything they'd had with her even if it was one slice of bread to feed the three of them.

Even all these years later, they'd never used the L word with each other because love was *only* a word. What they had was stronger than anything you could put into words.

Gage had never understood their bond and never would.

This was why she had to be the strong one right now. If not,

Gage would follow her home. If he did and she opened her door, they'd hole up without their clothes until the phone rang with a call to duty.

Then this vicious cycle would start all over again.

She'd watch Gage vanish or *she'd* vanish for days, weeks or months. One day, one of them would not come home.

She didn't want to be the one left behind, not by this man, and she couldn't continue half in and half out of a relationship any longer.

He reached over and grasped her hand. All her convictions wobbled on their unsteady foundation, but the truth pushed its way forward.

All they had were stolen moments here and there.

That wasn't a relationship. At least, not the kind she could live with now.

Standing up, she pulled out of his grip and slipped the purse strap over her shoulder, which reminded her why she'd come here to begin with—a phony snitch meeting that he'd set up.

All her unsteadiness fled. She put steel in her voice and said, "I'm through talking. Stay out of my way and don't *ever* screw with one of my snitches again."

He gave her a confused look. "What snitch?"

"Ziggie."

Gage shook his head. "Not following you."

Blood rushed through her so quickly the sound roared in her ears, blocking the noise of the restaurant. She took in the place with one sweeping scan then turned to him. "How did you know I was here?"

"Why?"

She dropped her head down and her voice came out in a low growl of warning. "Just *fucking* answer me for once."

He blinked at her rare curse. "I tailed your car from the airport. Picked you up leaving your office."

Her face chilled with a clammy feeling. "You didn't set this up with someone for me to meet you here?"

"No." He was stone-cold serious now. "What's up, Sabrina. Talk to me."

She wanted to swipe the glasses off the bar and knock him off that stool. He'd screwed up her meeting with the contact. Her anger rose with the power of a tidal wave, threatening to kill everything in its path.

Sucking in a deep breath, she said, "Don't call me. Don't come near me and don't you dare *ever* walk up to me uninvited again."

"Who were you expecting to meet here?" Gage was looking around, now up to speed on what he'd cost her.

"None of your damn business." She strode away, leaving him in a wake of her fury. He'd better stay the hell away before another word could be spoken.

If not, she'd say something she'd live to regret.

Outside, the street life had picked up with the approach of prime-time dinner hour.

Sabrina wove in and out of groups, then scooted through traffic against a *Don't Walk* sign. She picked up speed going downhill toward Peachtree Street, swinging into the parking deck before she got to the next intersection.

When she made it to the third floor, a middle-aged couple stepped onto the elevator as she hurried off and turned to the right. Her car was eight spaces down.

The lights on that end of the parking deck were out.

She'd arrived before they came on, so she had no idea if that was normal or not.

Drawing her 9 mm, she crossed her arms to keep it shielded as she walked toward her car. She watched and listened for any hint of threat, keeping to the middle of the lane between the lines of parked cars.

A raspy voice called out in a sharp whisper, *"Over here!"*

Damn. Sometimes she hated to be right.

She turned to find a hunched-over figure emerging from shadows where nothing had been a second ago. The plump, elderly woman in a gray blouse and stretch pants shuffled forward. She favored her left arm, holding it tucked against her body as though it were injured. Sabrina believed that *how much*?

Not one bit.

The woman kept her voice down and moved forward two

more steps, asking, "Who was that man? You were supposed to meet me."

Ziggie's contact.

Sabrina held her position where she'd stopped two spaces from her car. The hinky feeling that had crept along her neck from the moment she'd stepped into the parking deck cranked up a notch.

She got right down to business. "I understand you have a location for me."

"Yes. I ... need the money. He'll kill me if he finds out." The woman kept moving slowly, limping actually, with her back to the light, which kept her face silhouetted. Had this woman been with Rikker? Had he abused her?

Sabrina said, "Stop."

The woman complied, pausing ten feet away. She picked her head up and Sabrina could make out a plain face with dark-rimmed glasses.

When silence stretched too long in Sabrina's mind, she said, "I have the money. Give me the location."

Nodding slowly, the woman pulled her right hand away from where it had been hooked around her left arm, and lifted her head as she straightened her posture. She held a Walther PPK. Her voice was soft, but urgent. "Come with me quietly and nothing will happen to you."

And yet again, she'd like to not be right.

Who had set this trap? Sabrina hadn't been asked to hand over her weapon yet, so maybe this woman didn't realize she was armed.

Had Rikker sent her?

Sabrina wanted to find out more before she might be pushed to use her weapon. She said, "I hate to disappoint you, but you're leaving without me *or* the money. You can tell Ziggie he owes me for this."

The woman dropped her voice to a whisper as if she thought someone was close enough to hear her low conversation. "Listen to me. You're in dan—"

An explosion blasted.

The shock wave hit Sabrina in the back.

She flew across the parking deck and smacked into the windshield of a car. Glass cracked. She slumped down the hood.

She couldn't feel anything. Bad sign. Her world faded to black.

Chapter 3

SABRINA FOUGHT THROUGH a mental fog.

She had to ... she didn't know what she had to do. Muffled noises kept coming and going, like a bad transistor radio connection. She drew in a breath, and choked.

Her throat burned. Coughing hurt.

She ordered her eyes to open. Eyelashes fluttered. No luck.

Rough hands shoved her down on a hard surface. Ow.

Her eyes decided to open.

A blurred face stared at her, then something slammed shut and the light was gone again. A trunk? Was she in a car? She clawed her way to consciousness only to slide back down the slope into darkness.

The next time she woke to the feel of the vehicle moving. The air stunk of a burned odor. She lifted her arms. Everything ached. She touched the ceiling above her. Definitely a trunk lid.

What had happened?

She sorted through jumbled thoughts. A restaurant. Sitting at the bar. Arguing with Gage then walking. An explosion. A woman.

Who was that woman?

What about Gage? Had he been in the explosion?

The harder she thought, the more it wore out her aching head. She drifted to sleep again.

Cursing woke her the next time. She was bouncing as someone carried her, fireman style, up steps.

She peeked out and saw lights in a busted sign. Something ... motel. Who had her?

Her body went up and over, falling down to hit a mattress. Not a thick, fun mattress kids bounced on in television commercials.

No, this was the kind of cheap and lumpy support that had an hourly rate at night.

Probably why this place stank of Lysol and musty old stuff.

Hiding in a motel. Why?

Her arms were suddenly wrenched together, then a tight band wrapped around her wrists.

She allowed her eyelashes to flutter open. Too bright. She squinted.

He cursed.

She didn't recognize his voice.

Every breath she took tasted like smoke and chemicals.

She tried to open her eyes again, but the light glared them shut. "Who ... who are you?"

"It'll come to you, but not right now."

A rag covered her nose and mouth.

Sweet chemical smell. *Shit.* Ether. She fought, but quickly lost the battle and her world spun into darkness again.

Chapter 4

GAGE FLOORED THE accelerator on his sport utility, pushing the speed limits in south Atlanta, and peeled off the interstate before he reached the airport. His hands shook.

His hands never shook.

But fear for Sabrina rolled through his body.

Who had set that blast? He wanted to bellow in rage, but that wouldn't get her back. The need to make every second count forced him to snatch control back into his grasp.

He caught a green light and took two corners until he was on the dead-end street for the Slye offices. A simple, two-story, brick building came into view.

The main floor offices welcomed corporations looking for the best in skilled security, a business front for the underground bunker where Sabrina accepted covert operations in the interest of protecting national security.

Gage should have never given her that first contract.

He whipped his Tahoe around, sliding to a stop and blocking in three of the five vehicles parked in front. The building's interior, normally dark after business hours, was flush with lights.

Dingo Paddock stepped out with arms crossed and the threat of death in his cold gaze.

All that did was feed the rage monster gaining strength inside of Gage. It wanted out. It wanted blood. It didn't care who bled right now.

But he couldn't make the same mistake twice. Not now and not with Dingo or Josh. He'd made a promise to Sabrina. Even if they were never together again, he was going to prove to her that she could trust his word. He never wanted to face her disappointment again, but right now he'd take even that, just to see her standing here alive.

He inhaled a deep breath and reminded himself, *never lose sight of the goal.*

Opening his door, he climbed out, hands loose and ready to defend himself in case that Aussie's temper got the best of him.

Don't make me hurt anyone.

That sure as hell wouldn't earn him any points with Sabrina.

Dingo shouted, "We can't reach Sabrina. Where is she?"

Gage had called Sabrina's assistant, Amanda, and told her he was inbound with intel targeting Sabrina. He knew better than to tell them anything more over the phone. "Did you hear about the explosion downtown tonight?"

"Yes. What about it?"

Gage replied, "Sabrina was there at the explosion site."

"Where the fuck is she now?" Dingo demanded in a guttural Australian accent, moving forward with a take-no-prisoners attitude sitting on his shoulder.

But a thread of worry had crept into Dingo's voice.

"Gone." Gage's throat constricted with that word. A meteor could have struck the ground between the two of them and no one would have paid it any mind.

Gone. They all knew what that meant in their business. The worst kind of missing-person situation. His heart was beating his chest with the force of a prize fighter.

Dingo exploded with a flurry of curses, striding toward him, ready for a throwdown.

Gage lifted his hands. "Stop, dammit, unless you *want* her to die."

Dingo froze, but that momentary magic was good for about three seconds with this agent.

Gage jumped in while he had a chance at getting everyone on the same page. "I'm here to work with you. The less time we spend arguing, the more we can put toward finding her. Someone set an explosion in a parking deck where she'd left her car. They had to be close by so that they could detonate the bomb as soon as she was in the right spot."

Dingo took in a deep breath, but still looked kicked in the family jewels. "She's alive then?"

"I believe so." God, he hoped so.

"What happened?"

"I got there less than sixty seconds after the blast. I scouted the scene and found where I think she landed on a car, but she was too far from the blast point."

"What do you mean?" Dingo demanded.

"I don't think they intended to kill her or they'd have let her get inside her car before detonation." Gage's mind kept screaming *how would they have known it wouldn't kill her?*

"Was she meeting you?" Dingo wanted to know, every word pumped full of suspicion.

Gage rubbed his head, begging for patience with this guy. "Let's not get sidetracked. This is what happened. I saw her go into that parking deck. I took the stairs just as the explosion rocked the building. When I got to the third floor, I found the burning car, but her shoulder bag was sitting fifty feet away filled with money. She was gone. I found a cracked windshield and a few bloody spots around the car she must have hit, but no large pool of blood. I'm thinking a snatch and grab."

Dingo's eyes flickered with the calculations his mind was doing. "What the fuck were *you* doing there, Laughton?"

He might as well answer this or they wouldn't get any further along. "One of my people picked up rumors about a contract on Sabrina. Not a hit but a bounty to deliver her, which makes me believe that whoever put the contract out wants her capable of speaking. I went to talk her into going off the grid until I could find out who was pulling the strings. She wouldn't listen to me ... because of you and Josh."

Dingo jerked back as if he'd been slapped. He snarled, "Is that all you've got? If so, get the hell out of here so we can find her. Unlike you, we don't have ulterior motives when it comes to Sabrina and every resource we have is now assigned to finding her."

Gage kept breathing in and out slowly, the way he did when he'd faced torture in the past. Nothing he'd suffered then matched what he was going through now with Sabrina in someone's filthy hands.

He locked down his control and said, "I have intel. I know you and Josh don't like me—"

"Don't trust you," Dingo interjected.

"Right, but I don't give a shit. I'll bed down with the devil if that's what it takes to get her back. If you're not willing to work with me, say so now and I'll go put together my own team. But I believe the odds of getting her back will go up significantly if we can put aside our differences and join forces."

The Aussie took a moment, but anyone could see that he took every word to heart. "We'll work with you for now. If I find out anything you've said is a lie or that the agency is pulling strings in this, you'll never get another chance to screw with her. Literally."

Gage dropped into mission mode, willing to do whatever it took to be successful, even if it meant sucking it up to deal with belligerence. For now, he'd do what was necessary to maintain this tenuous agreement. "Fine."

Dingo asked, "What's your intel?"

"It's in the back." Gage pressed his key fob to open the liftgate on his Tahoe. He led the way to the rear, where interior lights spilled down over the woman he'd dragged from the scene. Her lumpy body was turned away from them and the air around her reeked of a burnt chemical odor from the bomb blast.

Her clothes looked as if she'd been dragged through the streets, but she was still breathing.

Gage explained, "I found this woman ten feet from the car that had blood on it."

"Could be her blood."

"Sabrina had been meeting someone her contact Ziggie set up. I thought this female was some vagrant the kidnappers ignored, but when I rolled her over she was clutching a Walther PPK. No serial number. She's either part of the plan and got left behind for dead, or she's another player."

"Shit," Dingo muttered.

Nicer than what Gage had said right before he hoisted the unconscious woman over his shoulder and carried her two floors down to his car parked near the stairs. When someone tried to stop him, he'd shouted that there were more casualties.

As the chaos mounted, he'd tossed this one into the back and driven out of the parking garage as sirens headed toward the area.

Gage said, "All those bulges are padding and she's wearing a silicone mask."

"Guess it's a bloody good indication the blast was not intended to kill since this wench survived," Dingo pointed out. Then he added, "Of course, Sabrina wouldn't have been padded like this."

Gage had considered that and didn't want to be reminded. "This woman needs a medic."

"Blade's downstairs. Let's get her to him." Dingo stepped closer, staring at the woman. He murmured, "Who the fuck was behind this?"

"There was another body at the scene. White male in his thirties. Had the Orion star pattern scarring."

Dingo froze. "Fuck."

The door to the offices opened and a man called over, "What's up?"

Dingo waved him to the back of the SUV.

Gage recognized this agent from the California mission. Tanner Bodine sounded as if he'd just come off a cattle drive in Texas most of the time.

Other times, there wasn't a hint of a drawl, like now.

Built like a linebacker and eyes sharp with tension, Tanner walked up to them. "What you got?"

Dingo blew out a breath. "The only lead we might have on finding Sabrina. She's been grabbed. We need this one awake ASAP."

The cowboy's jaw muscle flexed. "Does she need to be restrained?"

"I cuffed her," Gage told him, "but she's an operative of some kind so watch yourself. She might have a concussion. Got some cuts. I don't think anything's broken, but I didn't waste time looking closely."

Everyone backed away to let Tanner roll her over where her

wrists were still held with flex-cuffs. Gage had also made damn sure she had no access to a knife or any tool while behind him where he couldn't see her if she woke up and caught her second wind.

But she was still out cold. Her wrinkled face had made him pause at first, until he decided a second later that she'd put herself into this mess.

Then he'd realized her real face was hidden beneath a professional-level silicone mask.

Tanner picked her up and headed inside.

Gage followed and walked in to find Amanda at the desk that sat outside of Sabrina's private office. Amanda Talifero looked more like a fit, blond-haired, brown-eyed, college intern than a deadly former MI6 intelligence technician. From what he knew, Sabrina's assistant could find out anything on anybody, and could kill with the same precision she broke through firewalls.

Gage had created files on most of Sabrina's people back before the UK mission went down and updated his information as soon as she surfaced again.

He didn't know everything about all of them. He figured that was because Amanda would be just as good at burying intel as she was at rooting it out. But he knew enough on this group to get through this operation.

Amanda took him in from head to toe, and not in a flattering way. He'd seen that look many times when an adversary sized him up to decide the simplest way to kill him.

The same reaction he got the minute he faced off in enemy territory.

She waited until Dingo stepped inside, then said, "Nick's on the way."

Dingo nodded. "Good. What about Josh?"

"He should be here any minute. I caught him before he got to the airport."

"Call and fill him in anyway so he's up to speed by the time he gets here. Might give him time to call Trish."

"Oh, yeah. The wedding." Amanda was already punching numbers into her phone.

If not for the circumstances, Gage would be glad for the way this bunch was rallying to find Sabrina. But at the moment, he had nothing to be happy about.

Tanner took the woman downstairs where Slye kept an infirmary. Gage hadn't been there, but he knew how Sabrina operated ... when it came to business.

He clearly didn't know squat about the rest of her mind or he might have talked her into going with him tonight.

He'd suffered the entire two years she'd been missing and never wanted to go through that again.

Like now?

Exactly. Why couldn't she understand that he knew how to keep her safe and would not stand by and allow anyone to harm her?

Good intel wasn't worth shit if no one acted on it though.

Where had he gone so far wrong with her? Maybe by not admitting the truth, that he couldn't walk away with any hope of ever feeling the same way about another woman.

That she'd become too important to him.

Sabrina's words drifted back to him. "... allow for a relationship, not a true one."

He had no argument for that.

With no idea where the stairwell to the underground bunker was hidden, he stepped over and hit the button for the elevator to follow Tanner.

Dingo called out, "Yo! Over here. That won't work without one of us."

Gage turned back as voices rumbled from the front office.

Dingo walked away, heading for the rear area of the ground level offices.

Josh appeared with a phone at his ear and dressed in a tailored suit that had to run four figures. He belonged in Atlanta's financial district negotiating million-dollar deals, but Sabrina claimed looks were deceiving with that one.

Striding quickly, Josh tossed Gage a keep-up-or-stay-out-of-the-way look and vanished down the hall behind Dingo, who turned into a room on the right.

When Gage got there, he entered a refined conference room clearly designed with corporate clients in mind. He found a spot on the opposite side of a long conference table from Josh, who stalked up and down the other side.

Dingo was clearing a white board and saying, "Let's start with what we know."

Gage said, "Rikker. What intel do you have on him after California?"

Dingo and Josh turned to him. Dingo said, "The helo pilot was shot and somehow Rikker got out of the bird as it was crashing. He used a makeshift rope to get off the building roof. That was a rope I'd left after extracting Valene via the roof of that four-story building when Maxx Navarro captured her. That rope didn't go all the way to the ground. We only used it to reach the next floor down. I was surprised no one caught Rikker on foot after a two-story drop. He should have broken an ankle, foot, knee, something."

Josh snapped a question at Gage. "What have you got on Rikker, or are you keeping that close to the vest, too?"

These two had butted heads with Gage every minute since that fucked-up op in the UK. He understood, but it didn't stop him from getting pissed off every time that job was shoved in his face. He hadn't burned them and he still hunted the person who had, but arguing would only delay him from finding Sabrina.

He said, "Let's make one thing clear. Any intel I have that will help us find her is on the table. I expect the same from you two and the rest of your team." He allowed a brief pause for someone to get mouthy. When no one said a word, he added, "Rikker is still stateside. No sign of him leaving and he was definitely injured. We found a dead nurse in Charlotte, North Carolina, who I believe treated him. I'm guessing Sabrina knew about that and thought she was meeting someone else he'd gotten to for help."

"What makes you think that?" Josh asked. "We've had no intel on Rikker since California."

No point in skating around the truth.

Gage explained how he'd had Sabrina under surveillance and followed her to the restaurant on Baker Street. He pulled her small handbag out of his coat and dropped it on the table.

"There's thirty thousand in there. It was left on the ground."

The Aussie glared fireballs at him, but didn't say a word about Gage stalking Sabrina. He'd deny it if that didn't have a kernel of truth. He *had* been stalking her, while keeping his ear to the ground, since she returned from California.

Gage finished by explaining, "I had no idea she was meeting a contact. When she realized I wasn't the person she'd been set up to meet, she took off."

"What contact?" Tanner asked, walking in on the tail end of that. He plopped down in the first chair he found.

Scratching his forehead, Gage said, "Someone sent by a snitch named Ziggie. Add that to your board."

Dingo did, then he asked, "Anyone know that snitch?"

Gage mulled it over. "I don't know him, but I've heard his name once. Back before the UK job."

Tension crackled at the mention of the elephant in the room. Gage spent his days swimming in tension, so he pushed on. "I'll put someone on finding Ziggie."

"No CIA is in on this," Josh said and Dingo nodded.

Shit, what was it going to take to get these two to meet him halfway? "I'm only using two people I'll stake my life on."

"This is Sabrina's life."

"Even more important," Gage shot right back. He shared as little as possible in his world, but he'd hand over enough to get through to this bunch. "We need the information they can resource."

Tanner asked, "We need to know who you're talking about."

Evidently, Gage's answer hadn't made the cut.

Damn this group. Gage had survived a long time in a business with a limited life expectancy by not spilling everything he knew to anyone. "I'm not burning them. All I can tell you is these are two people who can be trusted."

"So you say," Dingo spit out.

Same words Sabrina had spouted earlier.

Gage wiped his mouth, buying time. What could they do if he refused to share the names of the only two people in the CIA he trusted?

Those two would die before giving Gage up.

Was he supposed to just hand over their identities without any hesitation?

Taking in the hard faces watching him, Gage said in a level tone, "We can argue about who is who, or we can work on finding Sabrina."

Dingo put the marker down and crossed his arms. "See, this is the problem we have with you, Laughton. We'll drag every snitch out of their holes to get what we need to find Sabrina, but you're still playing 'he who holds the most cards wins.' We don't trust you. Sabrina doesn't trust you. If she did, she would have considered what you told her tonight."

Just shove that dagger deeper into his heart.

Gage's chest muscles ached. He debated leaving and going after her on his own. One simple fact stopped him from making that leap.

Despite how much this bunch pissed him off, they were one hell of a team.

And every one of them would rush into a hail of bullets to protect Sabrina. He might not like it, but he needed them.

They needed him, too. Now was the time to build a bridge where none had ever been before. He had been Sabrina's handler and she was the person between him and her team.

Josh stepped around the table and paused next to the door. "Go, Laughton. If you're going to choose what you share, we don't fucking need you."

Dingo stepped up next to him and Tanner stood as well.

All three faces held an identical message.

Gage walked over to them and tried to reason in the face of hostility.

"Let's get this out of the way. I realize the three of you were in the UK with Sabrina," Gage started and pointedly said to Josh, "I know you lost a contact you had become close to during the UK job. Nothing can fix that or bring her back, but I did not burn your team." He took in all three when he added, "I'm not saying this to earn your friendship. I care deeply about Sabrina and I know all of you do, too. I wouldn't have put her in danger in the UK if someone had held a gun to my head. As for those two people who work covertly for me, I am not throwing them under the bus any more than I would have handed Sabrina and her team to a monster. I wouldn't ask any of you to expose one of your resources just to prove a point. Exposing my people isn't going to help find Sabrina. In fact, doing so will slow us down."

Dingo frowned, looking unsure what he should say. Josh's crossed arms flexed as he fought through some decision. Tanner had that unconcerned look that played so well for him in the field, but Gage knew he was just as invested as the other two.

He'd offered an olive branch, but was not going to beat his head against the wall to do this. Not when Sabrina was in the wind.

When no one said a word, he bit down on his disgust and gave them one last chance, then he was done. "Focus on the end goal, men. I'm not going anywhere. I'm not hiding intel. We have a better chance of finding her if all of us combine our efforts. But if this is going to be a constant pissing contest, I'll leave right now rather than waste seconds I need for hunting her."

Tanner, Dingo and Josh exchanged a look that Gage couldn't decipher.

Fuck it. They had one minute to make up their minds.

That would be one more minute Sabrina remained in the hands of a killer.

Amanda stuck her head into the room. "If you can put your dicks away long enough to question the woman, Blade says she's coming around."

Chapter 5

GAGE RUSHED OUT of the conference room to follow Amanda. She'd opened a door halfway down the hall that appeared to be a small storage closet at first. She pressed a remote button on a key ring and the back wall opened to a set of stairs.

He hurried down the brightly lit stairwell with Tanner at his heels. With no idea where anything was down here once he reached the bottom, Gage let Tanner take the lead down a long hallway. From there, Gage stepped into a room that smelled as antiseptic as any hospital triage area. Their medic, Blade, stood drying his hands. "We found a surprise under her silicone mask."

Blade had the woman on a raised hospital bed with her wrists cuffed to the steel bars running along the sides.

Good man.

Dingo and Josh were whispering as they came into the room, but stopped immediately.

Gage nodded at the medic, but the man just glared icicles back. Gage sighed. That's right. Blade had been part of the UK team and wouldn't trust Gage either.

Blade finally looked back at his patient and reported, "She's got a concussion, nasty gash on her back where the blast tossed her into something, and a rash of miscellaneous cuts, none of which are life threatening."

She might not die from the blast, but Gage made no promises on his part if she withheld information on Sabrina.

"She say anything yet?" Dingo asked.

Blade shook his head.

Her eyelashes flickered. A gash on her temple had been

bandaged, but it still oozed blood through the gauze. The mask had kept it from being worse. Bruises were turning dark all over her face and what Gage could see of her arms. She looked different without the bulges, facemask and ratty cloth that had been tied around her hair.

Attractive. Just another weapon in her arsenal.

Dingo studied her as if she'd climbed out of the garbage. He ordered, "Wake her up."

Her chest rose with a deep breath and her eyes blinked open. She licked her lips and croaked out, "I'm awake. Water, please."

Blade handed her a cup and raised the bed so that she could lean forward to drink. He stepped back with his face closed down, sharing nothing as he watched the interplay.

Josh asked the woman, "Who are you?"

Her gaze walked across the room, taking in one man after another. "*Where* am I?"

Gage had expended what little patience he had upstairs. He recognized her action for what it was, a delay tactic. He said, "You don't need to know where you are. Did you set the bomb downtown tonight?"

"No."

"I still want to know who she is and how she's involved," Josh pointed out.

"What was your role in the attack on Sabrina?" Dingo added.

She took her time and answered in an even tone. "I was not a part of any attack."

Tension shot back and forth across the room with the energy of a lightning storm. The Slye team men surrounding her were chomping at the bit for anything to put them on Sabrina's trail.

They could be a bunch of hardheaded jerks, but Gage couldn't deny their devotion to Sabrina.

As for this operative in the bed, he'd never seen a woman so calm under fire, especially after having just survived an explosion. This one had ice water in her veins.

And who else do you know just like that?

Yeah, but he didn't need the reminder that this woman and Sabrina were cut from the same cloth. That's why Sabrina was in trouble right now.

Dingo grunted out a sound. "Let's cut through the crap. You were in disguise and packing an unmarked piece. You were with Sabrina Slye when the bomb detonated. You can make it easy and tell us who was behind that bombing, what they want with Sabrina and who you are as well." He shrugged. "We *will* find out whatever we need to know. It's up to you how much trouble we go through."

"Torturing me will not produce the results you're hoping for," she said, fully confident of her statement and too calm for the precarious position she was in.

The monster clawing Gage's insides pushed at him to grab her and shake the words out of her. But this was the time to hold his control in a steel fist and show no weakness. That didn't stop him from warning her, "If you believe we won't use all methods of interrogation—and be successful at it—you're gambling on your life with a losing hand."

She turned her full attention to him. "You're gambling on Sabrina's life if you touch me."

There. She'd admitted knowing something about Sabrina.

Dingo jumped in, grabbing the steel bars on her bed with a tight grip. "Thought you weren't involved with the attack, but you clearly know who Sabrina is."

"I'm not and I do," she quipped.

Blade had a smooth doctor's voice that could calm a stressed patient, but he didn't seem inclined to help this one. "You should answer them, Miss ..." He waited for her to fill in the blank. Not happening. Blade shrugged it off. "No one in here would harm an innocent person, especially a woman, but every agent in this place will dismember someone who appears to be a terrorist and who played a role in harming Sabrina. If you're innocent, now is the time to cough up information on what happened and how to find her. I'm skilled with drugs and knives. I can heal you *or* encourage you to give up intel."

Damn. The medic surprised Gage.

When Gage stepped around to the other side of the bed, Blade moved back, giving him space to close in on the suspect. Gage said, "You're clearly trained. You could be a terrorist or a spook.

If you're a spook, I'm pretty damn sure you're not one of ours."

She arched an eyebrow at him that he took to mean *no shit, Sherlock.*

He continued. "You're on your own here and you know the rules of the game. Your country will not acknowledge knowing you. No one will send anyone to investigate. In our business, we live. We die. The rest of the world moves on. Do you think we're bluffing?"

"No."

"Start sharing what you know and you'll end up in a safe cell when this is all done. That's the best offer I'll make you."

She matched his gaze with a chiding one of her own. "How do I know someone here didn't set up Sabrina? I choose who I speak with and you're not it."

Gage chuckled, a sound Lucifer himself would be proud of for the edge in it. "Guess it's going to be the hard way."

Blade's voice cut like his name. "Not in here. My rules."

Gage slashed a look at Dingo. "Where's your interrogation room?"

Dingo tilted his head to the left then lifted his chin in Blade's direction. The medic pulled out a key and tossed it to Dingo, then lowered the bed closer to the floor.

Once Dingo had her wrists unlocked, he stepped back. "You can walk, or we'll drag you."

She pushed up, grimacing with pain, then slid her feet to the floor. Blade had put her in a hospital gown that tied in the front. Gage told her, "Turn around."

She did and swung her wrists behind her, not the least confused about what was going on.

Josh said, "I'll lead, Gage follows the prisoner, then Dingo."

They walked her down one hall, made a turn, then continued to the end of a hallway with only one door at the end. Inside was stark and gray, right down to the concrete floor. A metal table and four chairs had been tucked in one corner. Restraints at shoulder level were anchored to the wall on the opposite side. A twisted wire cable had been run through a block-and-tackle setup mounted to the ceiling, then attached to an electric motor mounted on a sidewall.

The free end of the cable ended in a heavy-duty carabiner that dangled over a drain in the center of the room.

Josh re-cuffed the woman, but in front this time, then hooked the carabiner to the cuffs.

Dingo ran the winch motor that lifted her arms until she was on her toes. She might be tough, but she was gritting her teeth. Gage would bet on shoulder pain based on the massive bruise he could see on her shoulder where the gown slipped down.

The door burst open and a six-foot-two, deadly, black-haired Italian barreled in. Nick Carrera pointed an FNX-45 semi-automatic pistol at them. "Let her down. Now."

Gage was speechless.

Hadn't this guy been Sabrina's lead agent in California?

Everyone stared at each other for all of three seconds, then Dingo's mouth fell open. He snapped it shut. "What the fuck, mate?"

Josh ping-ponged his gaze from Nick to Dingo to Nick. "Have you lost it, Carrera?"

"No." Nick repeated, "Let her down."

Dingo lowered the cable until her hands dropped in front of her. She'd kept her gaze locked on Nick, who ordered Josh to release her. Josh stood there a moment, too shocked to move, then finally took the cuffs off.

She walked with a slight limp over to Nick and said, "Was all that necessary?"

Nick's dark-brown, Sicilian eyes flicked to hers for only a second. "Seemed so at the time."

Gage told Nick, "You leave with her, I'll find you both and make you sorry you ever drew your first breath of air."

Nick shrugged. "Been sorry about that many times, but not right now." He looked over at Dingo and Josh. "Who did this to her?"

Dingo sighed. "She showed up that way. Got caught in a blast with Sabrina. Want to explain what the hell is going on with you ... and *her*?"

"It's all good." Nick let his gun dip down and Gage made a move.

The gun came back up, but in Gage's direction. Nick said, "You can thank me later."

This fucker was mental. Gage asked, "For what?"

"For convincing her to work with us."

"What?"

Nick looked down and some message crossed between her and him. She shook her head and glared as if she'd use that gun on him.

The big Italian said, "Sorry." Then he announced, "This is Chatton, no last name. She knows what happened to Sabrina, probably knows who has her and why she was grabbed. I suggest you offer her something decent to wear and get her a shot of really good whiskey."

Chatton seethed for a second then whispered sharply at Nick, but Gage heard her say, "I hope you've enjoyed your bloody balls. You won't have them for long."

What did Nick do? Grinned. He told her, "Had to, babe. They need something to convince them I know you. By the way, I like your real face." Then he waved his gun toward the door. "Let's get moving. I hate this room."

Gage waited as Dingo and Josh filed out behind Nick and Chatton with Dingo muttering something about never knowing what Nick would do.

Who the hell was Chatton?

Gage had never heard that name in the covert business. As the three Slye agents and Chatton returned to the infirmary, Gage shook his head and reminded himself he needed these wackos.

On his way back down the hall, Amanda stepped out of a room Gage had passed earlier. She asked, "Is Nick alive?"

"Yes."

"I told Blade he'd be okay." She twisted around and shouted toward the infirmary. "We in the war room down here?"

Dingo called back, "Yes. It's bigger."

"Got it. I'll bring in supplies." She stepped out of a conference room that was much larger than the one they'd used upstairs and equipped with electronics on all walls. She hooked her thumb toward the room on her way out and told Gage, "In there."

He picked a spot at the rear of the room where he could observe everyone.

Josh and Dingo entered, huddling up front to speak quietly while tossing annoyed looks at Gage. Blade, Nick and Chatton came in next with Chatton now dressed in warm-up pants and a short sleeved T-shirt two sizes too big for her.

Nick pointed out a seat near the front of the long table and across from the door. Chatton sat with her arms crossed loosely in front of her, but still shooting poison-tipped glares at Nick.

He ignored her and asked the room in general, "What happened?"

Dingo quickly filled him in.

Nick's gaze jumped to Chatton, then back to each of the agents in the room. "Just so we're clear, she's not our enemy."

"Then why did she have a fucking unmarked gun at the blast site?" Dingo argued.

Chatton said, "I was trying to get Sabrina to leave with me without exposing who I was. It was the only idea I had on short notice for getting her out of there alive, since my meet point was ... compromised." She tossed a glance at Gage.

Someone snorted and Josh said, "You want us to believe you were trying to *rescue* Sabrina?"

No takers on that explanation.

Nick asked Gage, "You said there was a dead Orion Hunter on scene?"

"Yes. Double tapped, but not through the eyes."

Chatton said, "That doesn't mean what you think."

"I don't need you to tell me what I think. It's time you tell us what you know."

Sending Chatton a patient look, Nick said, "Tell them what happened."

She said, "I want an agreement first."

"No," echoed around the room.

Gage pinged on something she'd said earlier. "You said you'll choose who you speak with. So you were waiting on him?" He hooked a thumb in Nick's direction.

"Yes."

Gage turned on Nick. "What do you know about her?"

She warned Nick, "Don't."

Gage watched the battle of wills. Sabrina had called Nick the unknown element when she assigned him to a mission. Nick came from money, lots of it, and connections, but where Sabrina meant Nick was resourceful, Gage's notes ran along the lines of crazy and out of control.

Nick smiled at Chatton with a tinge of sadness. "It's time to come clean. You and I tell them the truth, or Gage takes you somewhere I can't get to you and you won't walk out alive. I'll have to bloody him before it happens, but in the end he has more firepower than we do if he calls in his people."

"That's my risk to take."

"They need to know they can trust what you share," he argued, oblivious to the audience watching them.

A muscle in Chatton's cheek jumped. "This ends our alliance."

Nick took a long look at her. "Everything has a price."

Gage had no clue what they'd been discussing, but Nick had clearly taken his stand on Slye's side of this. Ten minutes ago, Gage would have cut the Italian to pieces for betraying Sabrina, but clearly, that would have been a mistake. Now his instincts were telling him this man was solid and his loyalty not up for question. Nick was destroying whatever had made him Chatton's ally, and he was doing it for Sabrina and his team.

That gave him Gage's vote.

Chatton's face shifted for just a moment, long enough to allow everyone in the room to realize she considered Nick's actions a betrayal.

Of what, though?

Nick leaned back against the wall. "This group isn't going to give you time to work a deal. We need to know what happened to Sabrina. Work with them and they'll work with you."

She had a look in her eyes that would freeze hot coals but it vanished, leaving a flat expression in its wake. "I know who has Sabrina."

Everyone started demanding she give up a name.

Everyone except Nick, who said, "Let her talk."

The room fell silent.

Dingo scrubbed a hand over his ragged hair. "Now, dammit."

Gifting him with a tight smile painted with vengeance, she said, "Len Rikker has her." She looked at Gage when she said, "The only reason Rikker wouldn't have killed the Orion Hunter with his signature shot through each eye was lack of time. Based on what you said, he barely had time to get her out of there, which means he has a reason for keeping her alive. Nothing you can do will get her back until he decides to make his move or contact you, which I wouldn't bet on. I believe he's in trouble and will use her to trade his way out of the jam all of you put him in back in California."

Gage swallowed hard to force the bile down his throat.

Rikker. That murdering bastard.

Chapter 6

RIKKER STARED OUT the window of the crummy hotel room at a ho strutting her stuff along a highway. Probably on her way to the closest dive for her usual Friday night stint. She'd give a blowjob for ten bucks.

He'd like one, but not from any woman in this part of Atlanta. He'd been here for almost two weeks.

Too fucking long. His gaze drifted over to the bitch who'd screwed his plans in California. Sabrina Slye wasn't bleeding anymore and should be waking soon.

She might be playing possum.

Didn't matter.

She had no clue that he'd saved her ass from that Orion Hunter. Wasn't that rich?

Miserable Orion Hunters had failed to do their job two weeks ago and now one of them thought he was going to kill Sabrina before Rikker got what he wanted. Like hell.

That fucker wouldn't get in his way ever again.

He punched in the numbers on his burner phone and waited as the connection went through. When the clicking sequence ended, the man who owned Rikker's life came on the line.

"I hope you bring encouraging news," Wayan said with a refined Asian accent, in what most people would take as his pleasant voice.

Those would be the idiots who failed to realize there wasn't a thing pleasant about this prick.

Anyone else would still be threatening to kill Rikker for not delivering a rare scroll Wayan had sent him to retrieve. California had been going so well, then in the matter of a day, everything he'd set in motion had turned into a goat rope.

Thanks to that bitch on the bed.

Wayan didn't threaten. It wasn't necessary. Spend a month around the man and most men learned quickly that merely disappointing Wayan could result in having your skin peeled off slowly so that you kept healing to prolong the agony.

Rikker wasn't most men, but he and Wayan had a deal, and he expected the Chinese egomaniac to make good on it.

That meant not mentioning anything that might trip him up later.

"Everything is going to work as planned." Rikker hadn't been excited about Wayan's end game, but as long as it went off as intended, Rikker would be free and have enough money to live on forever.

"But you have yet to deliver my scroll."

This guy was busting Rikker's balls. "True, but I'm working on it."

"That is not acceptable news. I have allowed you additional time to recover the scroll."

No, you left me here on my own with the Feds hard after my ass, because I didn't manage to get the damn thing before the Vatican got their hands on it again. Arguing with Wayan would not improve Rikker's situation. He'd dealt with much worse in the past. *Just suck it up for now.*

Rikker played to Wayan. "I appreciate the extra time. I've been making good use of it."

"My generosity has limits."

"What about a copy of the scroll? I have the photos taken of the original. I can have it reproduced." Just like the one he'd almost died trying to get out of Los Angeles, only to find out the artifact he'd gotten his hands on had been a fake.

"If a copy would have sufficed, I would not have sent you for the original in the first place. All five authentic artifacts are necessary for revealing Orion's Legacy. Copies are not artifacts," Wayan said as if talking to the mentally challenged. Rikker had heard it called both a legacy and a prophecy, but either way it was some crazy shit.

What did Wayan expect to happen when those five rare objects came together in the same location? Did he think some wild Indiana Jones magic would explode into the air?

That wasn't happening. Good luck convincing a man like Wayan, but Rikker would not be the person who told him he was a nutcase. This cold-blooded bastard hadn't reached a point of power so high inside the Chinese government that he was virtually untouchable by tolerating a wiseass.

Antagonizing Wayan would not get Rikker out of this country before someone found him.

Add in Wayan's crazy factor over Orion's Prophecy, correction, *Legacy*, and you had one scary son of a bitch.

"You have not located Soo Jin either," Wayan added, piling on the I'm-so-disappointed-in-you tone.

Rikker thunked his head against the window. He'd feel much better if he could shove Wayan's head through the glass.

Wayan demanded the impossible and expected Rikker to produce it.

Sabrina Slye's team had extracted two physicists from North Korea earlier this year. Soo Jin, another fucking scientist, had tagged along to get out of North Korea. Everyone thought she was basically an indentured servant in the North Korean Orion Hunter network of loonies who were also searching for the artifacts. Lo and behold, Wayan discovered that Soo Jin was the top expert on Orion's Legacy, and had been groomed to translate the specific message—aka the final conflict predicted by the prophecy—once all five artifacts came together.

Maybe she could give me a lotto number once she finishes unraveling the mysteries of the universe.

Wayan had sent Rikker after Soo Jin months back, but she vanished into thin air before he could get his hands on her.

Really. She'd been in an airplane that blew up midair, but Wayan refused to believe she was dead.

"Rikker?"

Man, he hated the way his neck muscles bunched when Wayan spoke his name like a curse. He kept telling himself that he was on short time. All he had to do was pacify Wayan a little longer.

Rikker said, "I'll have what you need in time for the big party."

"You *will* bring me the scroll?" Wayan asked, not masking the sliver of disbelief in his voice.

Sure, I'll send Peter Pan to fly into the Vatican, get the scroll and fly out. That would be easier than what Rikker had in mind, but no was not an acceptable answer.

He hedged his reply. "I'll have the scroll in time."

Now Wayan turned silent. That might mean he was calmly deciding whether you were telling the truth, or how long he could keep you alive while dismembering ...

Wayan sounded thoughtful when he said, "That would redeem you in my eyes."

Rikker couldn't give a shit about proving himself to Wayan or anyone else, but he had a sweet deal and soon this would all be done. "Great. That's what I want to do. Prove to you I'm worth what you spent to get me out of the UK. But I'm gonna need an exit plan out of the US soon."

"I am always willing to support those who produce for me."

"I understand," Rikker said when in truth Wayan had done anything but. Wayan had left him here to survive with no support when things got hot after Sabrina and her asswipes screwed him in California. He was lucky to still be alive.

Rikker almost dying in a helicopter in Los Angeles clearly did not prove any degree of dedication to Wayan.

"You will have whatever you need when the time comes to return as long as you guarantee delivery of the scroll, the panel from the Amber Room and Soo Jin."

What. The. Fuck? Does he think I'm a magician? Rikker clamped his jaw to keep from spitting out something that would end with regret when Wayan hung up and sent an assassin after his ass. Rikker had outplayed his enemies for years by being the best in the business, but he was savvy enough to realize you could hide only so long from a network of people the size of Wayan's.

Bottom line? He needed to stay on Wayan's list of people who were more useful alive than dead.

Hadn't Wayan said there were four panels rumored to be floating around from the famous Amber Room that Hitler had claimed? Or destroyed, depending on whose history you read.

Taking care with his words, Rikker asked, "What happened to the deal the big G had with trading gold coins for the one in Germany?" He wasn't going to give Sabrina The General's name or anything else of use just in case she pulled out another of her nine lives.

"The General delayed for so long that the panel was sold. When I located what was believed to be the same panel, I sent a retrieval team. Unfortunately, the one they found was not the correct panel."

Rikker translated 'retrieval team' as a small unit of assassins. Whether it was the correct panel or not, no one would have remained alive. "If the one in Germany's a bust, what about the others?"

"A second one was discovered in Argentina during a drug raid. I had local contacts inspect that one and determine it is also not the one."

"That's two off the list. I need intel on the other two."

"I was under the impression gathering information was part of your skill set. You will have transportation, but no later than thirty-seven hours from now."

Sunday morning? This guy was killing him. "What happens then?"

"You will return to China to coordinate the last steps if you have what I sent you to retrieve plus the remaining artifacts. If you do not succeed by then, our agreement will cease to exist. Do not fail me *again*."

Yeah, Rikker caught the menace in that warning. And no, he hadn't gotten his hands on the scroll from the Vatican.

He considered all of his options and the limited time frame. There wasn't a chance in hell that he could find all of that on his own.

His gaze danced around as he thought and he paused when it landed on Sabrina.

Wait a minute.

Scratching his chin, an idea began to form. He was still going to trade Sabrina, but her value had just jumped now that he needed more than he'd originally planned on.

This was his last chance at escaping everyone who chased his ass, from the CIA to spooks in different countries, to his current Chinese nemesis.

Wayan wasn't just one of the most powerful men in the Chinese government. He held the ear of their president. Of course, Wayan was also bat shit crazy, but Rikker had spent enough time around him to know this man expected a major world conflict from Orion's Prophecy.

Not only that, but Wayan intended for China to come out on top of the pile.

Your basic rule-the-universe ego.

Supposedly, no one person knew what all the legacy actually predicted, but the only people who would dare to argue with Wayan's interpretation were suicidal.

The more Rikker's idea gelled in his mind, the more he liked it, but he wasn't sure about one part.

He asked Wayan, "What if Soo Jin really is dead?"

"Then bring me proof."

I got as much chance of finding her body as Jimmy Hoffa's. But Rikker just sighed and let that go.

Wayan must have taken his silence as hesitation. "I am quickly losing interest in this conversation. If you cannot hold up your end of our bargain, say so now."

Sure, then I'll just slice my own throat and save you the trouble of having someone torture me. Loading his voice with plenty of confidence, Rikker said, "Oh, I'm absolutely holding up my end. In fact, I'll venture to say that when I call you back you'll be the one wanting me to hurry up and get home."

Wayan made a sound that might be a sigh, which Rikker ignored and explained, "I have a plan that will deliver all you've spelled out and more."

That brought on another wave of quiet on Wayan's end.

Rikker had to go big or go home. He wanted Wayan anxious to hear from him. He added, "Consider this a heads-up that I'll be calling for that ride home much sooner than Sunday. Probably in less than twenty-four hours."

"Very well. I look forward to your call." The connection severed.

Now he had to make good on his boast, but he'd spent his

life making up plans as he went along in some pretty damn dangerous situations. He cast another look over at Sabrina. Skin pale, breathing still shallow, but he'd bet his left nut that she was conscious and had been listening.

That was a-okay by him. All part of the new plan.

He took a couple breaths and psyched himself up to pull off this next call, then he fished out another phone that had only one number in it. He'd been given this burner phone two weeks back when the General thought Rikker was working directly for him.

The General and Wayan were both after the artifacts, but Rikker didn't believe for a second that The General, who was *not* a freakin' general, put any stock in that legacy-slash-prophecy. The General answered to five powerful families who kept a grip on his short hairs. He'd never admitted that, but Wayan had given Rikker enough intel to do The General's bidding when it suited Wayan's purpose.

From what Rikker guessed, when The General had joined up with Wayan in a secret alliance they called the Czarion, it was for one reason—to keep an eye on China's most dangerous man.

And not for the benefit of the US.

To be precise, The General cared about only one thing. Keeping his five wealthy, powerful families content.

Finding out exactly who pulled The General's strings might be of use down the road.

Blackmail could be *so* profitable.

Rikker tapped the window frame he leaned against as he waited for yet another series of clicks. This place stank of ammonia cleaner, the hallmark of crappy hotels. Just one more week and he'd be living on an island with obliging women and plenty of fresh air. No more shit hotels.

He'd miss the killing, but he could always take a quick contract when he needed a little exercise.

"Oh, now you're calling?" The General snarled. "Where the hell did you go two weeks ago? Do you realize the clusterfuck you left me with?"

No one was happy to hear from him today. "I barely got away in LA. Been too injured to call you." Rikker coughed. "Just getting back on my feet again. Shit, if the pilot in that chopper you sent had been any kind of a shot to back me up we'd have made it out of there. He took a bullet and died as the chopper was lifting off a building. I should have died, too, but I didn't and I'm still here."

Grumbling sounds came through for a moment, then The General said, "What do you want?"

"Actually, I'm calling about something you want. The way I see it, you got a mess on your hands and I can help you out."

"How're you going to do anything for me when you've been too hurt to make a fucking phone call?"

Rikker grinned. The muscles in his shoulders relaxed.

The General thought Rikker was *still* his pit bull.

Time to throw out some bait and set the hook on a big one. Rikker assured him, "Oh, I'm up and about. You have two problems sitting in jail cells and the contracts you put out on them aren't going to get the job done. I'm the one person who can take care of everything for you, but I want payment in full ready by twelve hundred eastern time tomorrow."

"You can take care of Perdido and Navarro in less than a day?" The General asked, clearly stunned. After a beat, he said, "I'm listening."

That flat tone was The General's happy sound.

Rikker glanced at Sabrina, who no longer tried to hide from him. Nope, she was tracking his every move.

He winked just to piss her off, then shifted his attention back to The General. "I've got one hell of a deal for you. First I'll remove those two thorns in your side, then I'll deliver on the Atlanta contract that I assume belongs to you."

"Sabrina Slye? You can get your hands on that bitch?"

Turning to face his captive again, Rikker said, "Guaranteed."

"Fuck. If you do all that ... shit, name your price."

"One. Coin."

The pause stretched until The General snarled, "You son of a bitch. Did Wayan put you up to this?"

"No. I'm just as invested in this Orion shit as you are," Rikker said truthfully, laughing to himself at that joke.

The General breathed deeply several times in between grumbling sounds, before he finally said, "Done."

Just as Rikker had thought, The General hadn't been able to get anyone close to the two people about to knock the foundation out from under his dirty little empire.

Rikker said, "When I send you a text, your man has twenty minutes to reach me. If he pulls anything or you try to screw me, I'll release documentation of who ordered the California hits. It'll go straight to the Feds."

The General grunted. "Where does my man need to be so that he's within twenty minutes of you?"

Rikker detailed a location in the middle of downtown Atlanta, adding, "I have photographs of every nick on that coin so don't dare try to fool me."

After ending the call, he shoved the phone in his cargo pants.

Getting his hands on The General's coin, a rare Greek stater which was one of the five Orion artifacts, would turn Wayan very cooperative. Wayan wanted The General's coin bad.

The General had one hell of a dilemma.

If he believed Rikker could deliver on his promise, The General would have to hand over his precious coin to a delivery person, who might just double-cross him. If he didn't believe Rikker and failed to send the coin, The General risked Rikker making good on his threat to expose him to US law enforcement.

Oh, the joy of screwing with powerful people.

Rikker had been planning to cut a deal for Sabrina and the two hits for money. He already had people in place to handle The General's first two problems. Eva Perdido and Maxx Navarro were both under heavy guard in different federal facilities. If they'd been in the same facility, it would have actually been more difficult to take care of them both within a short window of time.

This way, Rikker could put two groups into play concurrently and stay on schedule.

Sabrina shifted, probably stiff from being almost blown up, then tied up and dragged around in the trunk of a car.

She watched him, the prey studying the predator.

He strolled over, put a hand on the nightstand and leaned

down. "I know you know where Soo Jin is. I intend to deliver her, and on time. I'm sure you know why as well, but you don't know when. I could tell you, but you're on a need to know basis and all that."

Sabrina glared at him through glazed eyes.

"Fucking concussion makes you hazy, doesn't it? Guess I should have been waking you up and all, but you aren't my concern. Soo Jin is. Ready to talk?"

Sabrina's eyes never lost the cold stare of death.

He chuckled, then turned serious. "You've been a pain in my ass for too long. You should have died in the UK and stayed out of everyone's hair. In fact, you should be dead right now. I almost missed grabbing you. You had an Orion Hunter after you, the leader of the group in this country. He wanted to cash in on your contract. If that fat, homeless bitch hadn't stopped you from reaching your car, he'd have blown you to pieces the minute you sat down in it."

Realization slowly shifted her expression until she stared at him as if trying to figure out what planet he came from.

His mother had given him the same look when she found the cat he'd practiced his early skills on. He liked that look of revulsion on Sabrina's face and kept feeding it.

"Yeah, that's right. You have me to thank for saving your sorry hide. You're lucky I got there in time and actually had a narrow opening for a shot. Didn't have time to make my signature double tap, but pop, pop, and he dropped." Rikker sighed heavily. "I hadn't planned on the fucker holding a detonator though." He shook his head, recalling how annoyed he'd been at that little unexpected complication. "Shit like that drives me nuts, you know what I mean?"

She blinked once and her gaze narrowed. Oh, yes, she was finally coming back to the living. What a shame.

He smirked at her. "Yeah. I know you're on to the Orion Hunters. So do they. You and your bunch of half-assed agents cost the Orion Hunters big time in LA. They were coming for you anyhow. Grabbing you was just a bonus to pick up payment from ... my friend. If I'd let that Hunter kill you then, you would have been of no use to me."

"What do you want?" she finally asked in a voice that begged for water.

"Now that I have your attention, you screw me one more time and I'll make you pay in ways you can't even dream of, starting with everyone who matters to you like Josh and Dingo. I have someone even better in mind. I've been doing my homework while I was healing up. Let's talk about Gage Laughton."

Chapter 7

SABRINA'S HEAD THROBBED and dots swarmed through her vision every time she moved, but once she could stand she was going to kill Rikker.

Just as soon as someone stopped beating on the inside of her skull with a sledgehammer.

He better enjoy his moment of power, standing over her and taunting her with the people he'd hurt.

His face was thinner than the photos she'd seen of him back when rescuing this miserable scum had been her mission, but he still had a wiry build of six-one and brown hair that needed a good scrubbing. He still had a scar at his hairline, doing nothing to improve his bland face. That average combination of features was a strength, the perfect mix of a basic nose, narrow mouth and soft-brown eyebrows that was so easy to change.

The cargo pants and T-shirt he wore would blend in pretty much anywhere. He'd been a natural as a CIA chameleon.

He snapped his fingers in her face. "Back to earth."

What had he been asking about? Gage. Did he know about her and Gage? She had to shut down any speculation fast.

"Laughton?" she replied with a scowl. "He *was* my handler. That's old news."

Rikker stood up from where he'd been leaning over and crossed his arms. "No, I think there's more to it. I'd have thought you were smarter than to work for the agency again, but he was in LA. You wouldn't have found me if not for him. That means you two were working together. I wondered why you would have anything to do with the CIA after they fucked you over. Then I got it. You've been fucking Laughton, haven't you?"

Not in over three years, but arguing would only convince him he was on the right track.

She wouldn't touch a CIA contract with a ten-foot pole these days, but she *had* collaborated with Gage since then.

Right now, she needed to sway Rikker from thinking Gage mattered to her. "I don't know where you get your intel, Rikker, but you wasted your money. I'd as soon sleep with a terrorist eaten up with VD as you, Gage or any other CIA piece of shit. You're right. I'm *not* working with the agency. In fact, I'm hunting everyone involved with burning my team in the UK." Then she had a thought. "Tell me, who all was in on it?"

Rikker arched an eyebrow at her. "You don't know? Ask Laughton."

There was the opportunity she was fishing for. A chance to ding Gage. "I did ask. Son of a bitch blew me off." She could sell that easily since she'd spoken the truth and it still got under her skin.

"Shit, that's golden. Guess he either doesn't know as much as he thinks he does or he's playing you."

She paused at that. What was Rikker saying? Or was he just screwing with her because he could?

Rikker laughed then switched to serious. "If he's not fucking you blind, why was he in LA when you were there and why was he sharing information? I know more than either of you realize."

Gage would be as shocked as she was to learn that Rikker had figured out they'd been together. Rikker had someone inside the government to be so well informed. Was his person in the CIA ... or somewhere else?

She snorted with a load of derision and accused, "Now who's funny? Laughton was in LA looking for *you,* Rikker. He's half convinced that you and I are working together. So either he's a better actor than the average spook, or he was left out of the loop when you went off the reservation." She cocked her head at him. "On the other hand, maybe he helped you pull that whole thing off and he's on my ass to keep attention away from him."

"Be serious. That fucker wouldn't piss on me if I was on fire."

She made a chuffing sound of doubt.

"Sad, but true. Laughton reported me as a serial killer." Rikker shook his head. "You believe that crap? I had a sweet deal until he got all righteous."

You are a serial killer. Now was not the time to say that out loud.

When Rikker's gaze returned to her, she let all the hate she'd harbored for him over the past two years fill her eyes for her next statement. "Fucking Laughton. Hard to believe you and I have anything in common, but apparently we both hate that bastard."

Rikker studied her. She held her tongue while he watched for any hint of deceit.

Every word she uttered was intended to deceive him.

She'd do anything to keep from giving this maniac a reason to add Gage to the short list of people she didn't want to lose.

For as long as Rikker lived, he had to believe nothing was going on between her and Gage in case she survived this.

Good thing I told Gage we were done, huh? Sure, tell her heart that when all she could think about was how her last words to him had been so harsh. But maybe if Rikker heard about that meeting it would help convince him she was telling the truth.

This was a perfect example of why she and Gage had no hope of any future together. They'd been in this world built on lies, suspicion and death too long for any hope of building a real relationship.

She'd never have what others considered a normal life.

Rikker's face took on a sly look. "Maybe if I keep you, Laughton will come looking. Then I could get both of you out of my way."

Sabrina maintained her don't-give-a-shit composure. She had to play this perfectly. "Of course Laughton will come hunting me. He'd love nothing better than to find the two of us together. That's the benefit of me being tied up. It might make him hesitate before killing me. You, not so much."

Her smile soured Rikker's moment of happiness. "Enough about that prick. You ready to make this easy and tell me where Soo Jin is?"

When she didn't answer, he sighed. "No? Well, you're not going to like my other option."

She didn't even blink.

He whipped his hand up and leaned down as he slapped her head to the side.

Her ears rang from that and her banged-up head screamed with new pain. She drew fast breaths and turned back to him, tasting blood on her lip.

Scratching his head, he said, "Damn. This is one of those times you're gonna wish you weren't such a hard-ass."

Chapter 8

GAGE LEANED A hip on the counter at the rear of Slye's downstairs war room and struggled to maintain what patience he'd dragged out of storage. He could sit still for only so long waiting for Rikker to make a move.

He forced his mind to be quiet so he could sort through everything he'd heard. He couldn't look at Chatton without wanting to squeeze more out of her. She hadn't given them everything, but she would.

Amanda checked the coffee maker on the side then paused on her way out to speak with Josh and Dingo, but not loud enough for anyone else to hear.

So this was where Sabrina made her deals with government agencies in the interest of protecting national security?

Well, not all government agencies. She wouldn't touch a CIA contract.

He didn't blame her. She and her team had gone through hell, but that hadn't been his fault.

One day, she'd believe him.

Being stationary was eating up his insides, but at least the posturing had settled down.

While Dingo had added more notes to his whiteboard, Gage had sent a text to one of his two people to forward anything they found on Sabrina or Rikker immediately. He'd had his people searching traffic cams in the area of the bombed parking deck, but the one that would have gotten a shot of Rikker's vehicle had been disabled.

Short of taking over CIA headquarters, that was as much as he could do until Rikker made a move.

No one at the agency knew where Gage was right now, but he'd have to check in soon. First he'd have to come up with a good reason for downtime. He never took it. Asking on short notice would be suspicious.

If Chatton was right, Rikker needed Sabrina for something, which meant she was still alive.

Gage had to believe that. He couldn't function if he considered the alternative.

Sabrina's agents were just as on edge, and oozing suspicion in every guarded glance at Chatton.

Nice to know they agreed with Gage on that much.

Nick was doing his best to find a bridge between both camps, explaining to the team, "Chatton's been a silent resource on our side more than once. I don't believe she was in that garage to do Sabrina harm or this would be a very different conversation."

Chatton smirked, hiding any reaction to that.

Nick believed what he said, but that still didn't mean Chatton was on Slye's side.

She was on her own side.

Gage stood and that movement broke up the conversation. It'd been seventy-eight minutes since he'd walked into this building.

Felt like a week. He said, "You claim Chatton will play ball. She says Rikker has Sabrina, but he's working for someone else. Who is this other person and what do they want with Sabrina?"

All eyes shifted to Chatton, who had been nursing a shot of whiskey courtesy of Amanda. Sabrina's assistant had delivered all forms of drinks, power bars and sandwiches and left them on a side bar before she'd exited the room.

Not that Amanda was anyone's coffee girl.

She'd be upstairs by now, monitoring any incoming intel, coordinating more feet on the ground for this, and guarding the front door.

Chatton turned her glass slowly with her fingertips. "The man Rikker answers to has a complicated agenda and I'm not privy to it, but my guess is that Rikker's running on his own right now."

Gage noticed she dodged answering the part of his question

that involved the name of Rikker's superior, but he let it go while she shared other information.

Dingo asked, "Why?"

She directed her answer at Nick. "Rikker was sent here to retrieve Galileo's scroll, but he failed."

"Because we stopped him," Dingo pointed out.

"Exactly. He can't return empty handed. The man he works for does not accept failure. Rikker would be better off to slit his own throat than to show up without that scroll. To run would only delay the inevitable, so my guess is he's come up with some plan for getting what he needs."

Nick frowned. "The scroll's back inside the Vatican pretty much out of reach for anyone."

"Right. I'm just giving you what you asked for, which is information that might explain why Rikker grabbed Sabrina. He's got to be using her to get his neck off the chopping block. That's my best guess, but beyond the ultimate goal of making his owner happy, it's anyone's guess what he actually has planned. The bad news about that is it means there will be little intel available until he makes a move."

"You didn't give us a name for Rikker's boss," Gage pointed out.

"No, I didn't."

"Why are you holding out?"

She angled her head and studied Gage the way someone would to determine if they were capable of a task. "I'm not holding out, I'm helping out. If I give a name, it will result in Sabrina's death and Rikker will have no say in that. I have no reason to wish her dead or I'd give it to you."

What the hell did he say to that?

Gage couldn't accept that they were at a standstill. "How do you fit into all of this, Chatton?"

"I have my own agenda."

"That answer's not good enough."

"It's the best you're going to get from me," she said without blinking, defiant and confident she could withhold whatever she refused to share. "If you persist in trying to discover my secrets instead of paying attention to your number one objective, you will end up empty-handed on both cases."

The threat in her words came all the way across the room to thump Gage in the chest.

She watched each of them, attentive as a wharf rat in a room full of feral cats, waiting to see which one would jump first.

Gage took note of how the Slye agents were now leaning toward Nick's opinion of Chatton. So far, Nick had made it clear to Chatton that they only wanted Sabrina and, to be honest, Chatton had been forthcoming to a point.

Dingo checked his watch for the millionth time, then turned a look in Gage's direction with eyes that dared him to screw with this fount of information.

Like that look is going to stop me?

Gage said, "Keep your secrets. But if in shielding them we lose Sabrina, your secrets will go down with you."

Chatton lifted her chin in acknowledgement, her pale blue eyes hard as cast iron.

Nick asked, "Would Rikker's boss accept a really good copy of the scroll?"

Dingo slapped the table. "Good thinking, mate. We'll get another one created like the one we used in California."

"Unfortunately, his boss will accept nothing less than the authentic artifact," Chatton said, bursting Dingo's bubble and pushing the agent past his limit.

"What the hell is all this about?" Dingo shouted. "Who gives a fuck about artifacts and prophecy in the twenty-first century?"

"You're looking at this with western mentality," Chatton countered calmly. "Your agency has gone up against Orion Hunters. I'm sure you know they've infiltrated law enforcement and the government in your country, but you have no idea just how deeply, or how committed they are to discovering the secrets hidden by the prophecy. Everything is relative in this world. You care about finding Sabrina, but she's just a pawn to others. You would be wise not to dismiss the ardent belief the Hunters and Rikker's boss have in this prophecy any more than you would dismiss all the religious beliefs around the world."

She had a valid point.

Gage had come up against people who stepped into the line of fire for their belief without a second thought.

Having quieted Dingo with that point, Chatton kept explaining. "Basically, there's a race to find the five artifacts and Rikker's boss has a specific time frame, but I don't know what's driving it because I've not found anything in Orion's Prophecy research that points to any specific day or time."

"What schedule is he working on?" Gage asked.

"I think it's this week, but I don't know for sure. Rikker's boss is not happy with me right now. If I hadn't been blown up with Sabrina, I would have gotten my hands on Rikker and found out more."

"So his boss is an Orion Hunter?" Tanner asked.

"Not in the sense that you're thinking. There are three factions of Hunters. One is here. The other two are in Europe and Asia, one of which is the strongest of all three. Rikker's boss has been secretly aligning himself with the most powerful members of the two groups not in this country. Still, that hasn't stopped him from killing Orion Hunters in his lust for acquiring all five artifacts for himself."

Dingo grabbed his hair, but he didn't yell this time. "What does he want with all five?"

Chatton said, "He's convinced that once the artifacts come together they will reveal the final conflict, aka a third world war, and I believe he thinks the prophecy will show his country as the one to come out on top."

"A third world war? What if there is *no* war?" Tanner asked.

"If you ever meet the man who controls Rikker, you'll realize that isn't part of the equation." Having addressed Tanner's question, she moved on. "Let's call Rikker's boss the Fanatic. Of the five artifacts, the Fanatic has one, a man we'll call the Imposter has one, then there's the scroll you saved from Rikker and returned to the Vatican. There's also a specific panel from the famous Amber Room. The panel was in Germany at one time, but from what I understand it was picked up by a broker and ... has dropped out of sight."

Josh spoke up. "My wife works with antiques. She was part of a show that had an Amber Room panel in Miami last year. Was that it?"

"No." Chatton said, "The owner of the correct panel, at that time, would have traded it for the eight *Saint-Gaudens Double Eagle* coins that were reported stolen two years back, but those coins were recovered in Miami by the FBI, thanks to your fiancé's sister-in-law."

Chatton had managed to once again surprise everyone in the room except maybe Nick, who watched her with fascination as someone would a precocious child.

She ignored him and said, "The Fanatic intended to use the gold coins to trade for the correct panel. He was not happy when the Imposter failed to get his hands on the coins before they were moved out of reach, though the Imposter assured the Fanatic the gold would be safe until they needed it."

Gage's mind played through all the pieces of information she carefully shared. The Imposter could be someone in this country, based on the man's confidence in accessing the gold coins.

Stretching his legs, Tanner said, "I'm just a dumb old cowboy, but you only told us about four artifacts. What's the last artifact?"

Chatton said, "A Celtic cross from the sixth century."

"Who owns that one?" Dingo asked.

"That's not pertinent to this discussion," she stonewalled.

Gage was pretty sure he couldn't be the only one in the room who thought she owned the cross or knew where it was. "How is this going to help us find Sabrina?"

"I can't tell you. I'm merely sharing information that could be useful once you find out what Rikker has in mind."

Tanner frowned. "If Orion's Prophecy is predicting a world war, what's the chance the Fanatic and Imposter are setting the stage for one?"

"I don't think the two of them are working together in that way. I think they're circling each other much like two dogs not sure if they're going to fight."

Gage disconnected from the information and studied Chatton.

She was answering only as a tactic. He'd seen it done before. Answer questions without giving up much, but enough to keep everyone content.

Only one flaw with that. It wasn't working for him.

Any other time, he'd be far more interested in finding out who those two men were, but until Sabrina was safe again, new mysteries would have to wait.

If Nick had any thought of Chatton walking out of here, he was out of his mind. She had information that could affect national security and had yet to give one drop of proof that she wasn't an enemy of this country.

Gage's phone hummed. He scanned until he read the mistyped word within innocuous text, which meant the contact he'd given the handle Contact Papa had information. Gage had stopped using their names a long time ago. Thinking of his two best resources as Contact Papa and Contact Victor was automatic now.

He stepped out of the room through the rear door to return the call, waiting until it was secure.

Contact Papa said, "I've got news."

"On my missing package?" Gage asked. The less he used Sabrina's name, the better chance he had at keeping his head focused on the mission, and the less chance any breach in security could undermine what he was doing.

"Not exactly. Eva Perdido was found hanging in her cell today."

Gage cupped his forehead, not liking this news one bit. Eva Perdido had been part of the assassination operation in California that Sabrina and her people busted. Eva had also been the front-runner for Governor of that state. She'd been shot when an assassination attempt on the pope went bad. Ironically, she'd been part of the attempt on the pope's life.

Word was that the minute Eva was shot, she started babbling about how she wasn't supposed to have been shot. The Feds were sure she'd squeal louder than a stuck pig when she came out from under the morphine, but she'd clammed up. All she'd say was that she'd been out of her mind in pain after being shot.

She'd spewed too much, though, before the morphine took

effect. Investigators believed the minute she was arraigned at the end of this week, she'd finally realize it was time to cut a deal.

Evidently, someone decided to make sure she didn't utter the wrong thing even in her arraignment hearing.

Contact Papa said, "That's not all. Navarro started making noises like he'd roll over. He was found around the same time with his throat slit by a homemade knife. He and Eva were two states apart."

Gage surmised, "Suicide will be the official statement, but that's bullshit. Navarro couldn't have been in his facility long enough to acquire something he could turn into a weapon while they watched him."

"Right. Both had to be inside jobs. Maybe one of the suits."

Gage understood that he didn't mean the CIA but someone high in government. A dangerous plant that moved with autonomy.

"Sorry, but I've got nothing on your specific package. I thought you'd want to know this because of the connection," Contact Papa said, referencing Sabrina.

He was right. Sabrina and her team were the reason Eva and Navarro had been captured.

That jerked Gage back to the present. "Thanks. Stay in touch and watch your back. Connect with Contact Victor and let me know if there's anything new to report."

"Copy that."

Sabrina and her team had uncovered more about the Orion Hunters than anyone in the CIA or other government divisions Gage either worked with or tracked intel through. Could those two hits be connected to the Hunters?

Or am I just jumping at anything to have a place to start?

He ended the call and stepped back in.

The conversation paused and attention shifted to him.

Gage said, "Eva Perdido and Maxx Navarro are dead." He didn't have to explain. Most of this team had been on site in California when Eva and Maxx were coordinating assassinations.

Chatton asked, "How?"

"Perdido hung herself in a secret facility awaiting arraignment.

Navarro died at approximately the same time. Someone slit his throat."

"Under watch?" Josh asked.

Frowning, Gage nodded. "Both have to be inside jobs and the time coincidence is probably *not* a coincidence."

"Interesting. Now you have somewhere to start," Chatton said.

Gage perked up, sensing the hunt. "What do you mean?"

"Word on the street is that the person behind the contract on Perdido and Navarro is the same one who offered money for Sabrina. Figure out who that is or how you can get in on that contract and you have a chance at stopping Rikker, because my guess is he's using Sabrina to swap for something important, maybe even the scroll."

As Nick had said, the scroll was safe inside the Vatican.

Gage's heart thundered in his chest. What would Rikker do with Sabrina when he couldn't get what he wanted?

Chapter 9

SABRINA REFUSED TO look at her reflection in the occasional glass window front on buildings she passed in the Old Fourth Ward district, a historic area on the east side of Atlanta. Sun baked down at midday, steaming her skin and heating up the disgusting smell of smoke that clung to her from the bomb blast.

Just a Saturday lunchtime stroll with a psycho.

Her hair had reached the ratty stage from Rikker shoving her in the trunk, then slapping her around and grabbing a fist full to shake her head back and forth.

Before heading here, he'd used concealer to cover the bruises on what little of her face remained unhidden by stringy locks hanging past her shoulders.

Nope, if she wanted to know what she looked like, all she had to do was pay attention to the people who cringed as she walked by wearing a sandwich board that read: *I'm a mean mother and I deserve worse than this for abusing my child.*

Rikker smothered another laugh. "I'm enjoying this so much. Just wish I didn't have to keep a serious look on my face, but it's part of executing a plan. A great operation is all about beauty. In this case, the ultimate beauty is watching you suffer maximum misery. Maximum misery has a ring to it. I should trademark that."

He paused to nod at a teen who shied away, stepping in the street to pass Sabrina. Rikker was on a roll, boasting, "You have to admit this is pretty fucking brilliant. You're walking out in the open and you can't ask a soul to help."

She refused to look up at him when he angled his head to draw her attention.

That did not deter him from his ongoing effort to get a rise out of her. "Even if you did try to talk to one of these people, the women especially, they'd spit on you as soon as they read the sign. Oh, just in case you get a crazy idea to try to tell them you're handcuffed and walking to your death, I'll kill the person who even listens to you. Adult or child."

Sabrina blew a piece of hair off her nose and focused on how many ways she could kill him. She hated to admit he was right about anything, but no one would lift a finger to help her if she screamed at the top of her lungs.

Rikker stretched, smiling up at the sun. "Beautiful fucking plan. I could have handed you over in a dark alley, but I would have missed this humiliation treat."

She wouldn't say a word and risk him harming an innocent person. But nothing stopped her from trying to twist her hands out of cuffs he'd put on her that were hidden by the sign.

The arrogant bastard hadn't even set up the meeting in a different city, so confident that he could do this in Atlanta without any interference. Of course, it helped that he was wearing a pristine suit with a Georgia Human Resources button on his lapel. He spoke pleasantly to everyone he passed, giving the impression he was accompanying her in an official capacity.

He'd trapped her yesterday and now he was going to sell her to someone who had a contract on her head. Plus gain a coin that had to be one of the Orion Prophecy artifacts.

Soo Jin, who Sabrina would never admit was still alive, had educated the team on this insane prophecy business.

People would die over some event *predicted* by Galileo in the seventeenth century. She couldn't blame Galileo though, since his only fault had been writing down a vision that had come to him. Should have been a harmless scroll.

It boggled the mind just to think about people willing to kill for artifacts.

Rikker smiled and nodded at two middle-aged women who scowled at Sabrina. At the next corner, he turned to the right into an older residential area.

She perked up, mentally cataloguing everything she saw. On

her left, a chain link fence ran around the property for the closed David T. Howard High School where a young Martin Luther King, Jr. had once attended. The four-story structure stood quietly awaiting renovation and Sabrina had a bad feeling that was Rikker's destination.

She'd been checking for traffic cams along the eight blocks they'd walked. Not one. He'd mapped a perfect route.

Rikker pushed the gate open.

That hadn't been left unlocked accidentally. The chain had been cut.

"Keep moving," he ordered.

"What if I just stand here?" she asked, stopping in front of the opening.

"I'll grab the next kid that comes along and snap his neck, then I'll drape his body around your shoulders."

He would.

Rikker laughed. "All this time you and your band of idiots have been hunting me. It's a shame I won't get to watch them as I parade their fallen leader in front of everyone." He put his hand on his hip just to allow his coat jacket to flap open, showing off her 1911 in his shoulder holster. "Mine."

He'd better pray she didn't survive this, because if she did she'd get her weapon back and use his genitals for target practice ... and maybe hand him over to law enforcement *after* that.

Turning sideways, she stepped through the opening and he pulled it closed behind him. Her boots kicked up red dust. Dried Georgia clay beaten down by thousands of school children's footsteps over the years.

She took in the U-shaped structure as they walked into the open area surrounded by the three sides. Cracked concrete had settled unevenly. He maneuvered her over to a shady spot.

She twisted her wrists, hoping for some give in the handcuffs. No luck. "Who do you work for, Rikker?"

"You really think I'm going to tell you?" He lifted his phone as if to type a text.

"Why not? You're handing me off to someone who wants me dead. What's the harm in telling me what the hell this is all about? Are you really part of the Orion Hunter network?"

He lowered his phone and gave her an incredulous look. "You think I'm with *that* bunch of crazies?"

Like his form of crazy was any higher up the loony totem pole? Rikker had a reputation in the covert world for marking his kills with a bullet through each eye of a victim. He'd kept it from the CIA for a long time.

Crazy? That would be a mild label for a serial killer with Rikker's record.

Sharing that observation would only end in another backhand across her face. The last cut on her mouth was trying to heal.

She changed the direction of her questions. "Just tell me this. Who threw my team under the bus in the UK when we came to rescue you?"

His face brightened like a kid on Christmas morning seeing what Santa had left. "I love that Gage hasn't told you shit, but you're not fooling me. You two had hooked up. So much for your fuck buddy, huh? Guess you weren't that good in the sack."

Screw this prick.

She wouldn't rise to his bait. She'd play his stupid game until she could find a way to escape and warn Josh and Dingo. And Gage. She had to for any hope of surviving.

Was Gage looking for her?

Undoubtedly. If she lived to see him again, she'd cut all ties permanently. That was the best she could do to keep him safe. Lowering her walls to let Gage in again hadn't turned out well for anyone. He'd pushed Dingo and Josh in LA until he'd driven a wedge between her and Dingo, all because Gage had believed someone on her team was undermining her.

That one mistake could have cost Dingo his life when he walked away from her safe house.

Rikker started to lift his phone again.

Sabrina grabbed at the first idea to draw his attention back to her. "Why do you keep persisting that Gage and I are intimate friends? We aren't even social friends," she said, unable to shrug with this blasted board structure hanging on her shoulders. She didn't want to give Rikker anything he could use to hurt Gage. She'd cut Gage out of her life, not her heart.

Hard to do that even after all that had gone down between them.

Still, the less Rikker knew about them, the safer Gage would be. That would let her focus on Dingo and Josh.

Rikker snorted. "Weren't you the one who said spooks are good actors? Just because *you* act as if you two weren't an item, doesn't mean you never hooked up."

She caught another idea. "Never mind. Forget about it."

"Giving up so easily?"

"Sure. I just realized I'm wasting my time. You weren't around when we went wheels up. You wouldn't have any clue who knew about my UK mission."

Rikker scratched his chin and turned a calculating look on her. "No, I wasn't in the country. But three people had access to my mission besides Laughton and those three would have had to be informed about you and your team coming for me."

Three names. She had a number. Or everything he said was a lie. She pressed for more, just in case there was a kernel of truth in anything Rikker said. "What's the deal then? Are you protecting someone in the agency?"

"Me?" He laughed. "I don't give a rat's ass about anyone in the agency. I do think it's hilarious that Laughton has held out on you."

If there *were* three people, were they the same ones on Gage's secret list? She switched up the conversation to glean anything else she could on Rikker and his boss.

"What made you so special to your new employer, Rikker?"

"This is not my day to play fill in the blanks for you, but think about it. Can't be that complicated. Someone in our government owed a favor to the man who paid my way out of that mess. There's your prime suspect, which you'll never figure out. But me? I could have figured that out knowing less than you do." He chuckled. "Been great catching up. We'll have to do this again." He snapped his fingers. "Oh, wait, you won't be around."

"You're a barrel of laughs," she muttered.

He raised his phone and tapped buttons.

Another phone in his pocket rang. He took the first one he'd used to call the one in his pocket and stuck it to the Velcro on the board covering her chest.

The phone hung there as he stepped back six feet while speaking into his. "Testing, one, two, three."

His voice came through clearly on the phone hooked to her. She asked, "Any chance I could cut a deal with you?"

"For your life?" He shook his head. "You don't have what I need. You're just a valuable pawn. Now stand right there or I'll have to make someone pay if you so much as flinch. Take that toddler for example. The boy with funky suspender shorts we passed playing in his front yard. Make a move and I'll shoot him in front of his mother."

"Why should I believe you?"

Rikker laughed. "You don't have to, but if you move he definitely dies. If you don't, there's a chance he lives. The more still you are, the quicker my little trade will go down, keeping me too busy to waste a round on a rug rat."

He stretched his neck and said, "Five minutes until show time." Then he strolled away quickly, but not looking rushed at all.

After a minute, he'd exited the yard and vanished around the next corner.

Another minute later, five Asian men entered the schoolyard, all packing and heading toward her. Each one was around six feet in height, which would stand out in their own countries. The one in the center had a shaved head, tattoos of Chinese writing down one side of his face and feral brown eyes.

He carried an HK VP9 pistol in one hand and a shiny black box, four-inches square by two-inches deep, in the other hand.

That must be the coin.

But where had he gotten a high-dollar weapon like that? Not the norm for a gang member, so who funded this bunch?

When the leader reached her, he paused ten feet away as if he questioned what she hid beneath her sandwich board. His cohorts turned around and fanned out to protect his back.

"*Quon?*" Rikker's voice called out from the phone. "*I didn't expect you.*"

Quon, aka their leader, stared at the phone on her chest and stepped closer. "You had no reason to expect anyone, Rikker," Quon replied in choppy English. "This is a poor place to meet. Where are you? What are you trying to pull?"

"Whine, whine, whine. Why would I screw you, of all people?"

Quon didn't reply to his question, instead saying, "The *man* has received confirmation you completed your part of the agreement. I am here to make the trade, but I want no surprises."

The man? Not much of a clue about the person trading a coin for her.

"Where's the stater, Quon?"

"I have it. Show your face if you want it."

"Just hold your hand out with the coin in it."

"No." Quon's gaze jumped all around, suspicious of every window looking down on him. He pointed the gun at Sabrina's head. "Show yourself, Rikker."

"Shoot her and you'll have nothing to deliver. Do as I say and we'll conclude our business in less than sixty seconds."

Sabrina hoped Rikker was right about Quon having to deliver her alive. It should be clear that Rikker had eyes on Quon.

Quon finally opened the box and placed it on his palm. He lowered his gun hand and extended the box on his palm toward the phone on her chest. "Here. Now what?"

Sabrina hadn't noticed Rikker setting up the phone on her chest to send a video feed of Quon. How would he know if the coin was real or not?

The buzz of a drone approached until it was directly overhead. The drone hovered lower until a basket dangling from the underside stopped at eye level with Quon.

Rikker said, *"Put the coin in the basket."*

Quon said, "I could take your drone, the woman and the coin right now."

"Testing me is not a way to build friendship, Quon. Take a look at her forehead."

Quon's gaze jerked to her face.

Rikker said, *"There should be a red dot dancing around. I've had it on the back of your head since we started talking. So play nice. Put the coin in the drone and let's get this done or I'll kill you and all your men, and still have her."*

Sabrina remained still, hoping she'd have a chance at breaking loose once Quon removed her boards of shame.

Quon now had the cold eyes of a venomous reptile. He snapped the box shut and placed it in the basket.

The drone shot up in the air and flew back across the street, vanishing from sight.

Quon said, "You don't want to check the coin?"

"I know he wouldn't have sent you with anything but the real deal. If you swapped it, I'll find you before anyone else can."

"I swapped nothing."

"Wonderful. The key to her cuffs is taped on the back of the sandwich board. Yank the boards off and she's good to go."

With the box exchange completed, Quon lifted the boards over Sabrina's head, peeled the key off the back and tossed the boards aside.

A flash of black drew her attention.

That caused Quon to turn and look over his shoulder.

Two black GMC sport utilities burst through the chain link gate, roaring toward them.

Quon shouted at his men, who were busy firing at the vehicles.

She spun and kneed Quon hard in the groin. That trick worked best if they didn't see it coming, and he hadn't.

His knees gave out, but as he went down he swung his weapon up at her. She kicked his hand and dove away, hearing the bullet rip into the brick close to her head.

Rolling would get her only so far.

Gunshots blasted everywhere, sounding as if a war had broken out in the schoolyard. Men were yelling. She held her breath, expecting to be hit by a stray bullet any second.

Twisting around to see the battle, she noted Quon on the ground clutching his chest. That might take his attention off his crushed nuts.

Two of his men dove through windows in the building, escaping.

Then silence.

She wiggled around to see Gage, Josh, Dingo, Tanner, Amanda and Nick charging toward her. Sabrina shouted, "Rikker is in the wind, but he's transmitting to the phone on that sandwich board. Two of the gang members went through the windows into the building."

Dingo raced past her, yelling, "Got it." Then he climbed through the window with Tanner right behind him.

A horn blared.

Sabrina jerked around. A white van that looked like the one Rikker had used to reach this area squealed tires down the street in front of the school.

Rikker stuck his arm out and waved. His voice shouted through the phone on the board. *"I'll be back to get all three of you next time!"*

Why was he happy?

Gage shouted, *"Rikker's escaping in the van!"*

Josh twisted away and ran for an SUV. "I'm on it."

Sabrina shouted, "No!" But Amanda had jumped in to ride shotgun with him and Josh peeled out of the lot.

Nick pointed to Quon and told Gage, "This one's dead. I'll watch your back while you get Sabrina." Then Nick turned to face away from them.

Gage had already dropped onto his knees in front of her, eyes hard and deadly. "Are you hurt?"

"I'm good. Get the key for the cuffs off that one behind you. They're probably still in his hand."

Gage found the key and freed her wrists. Her arms burned as she stretched her muscles. He helped her to her feet.

The world swam around her. She hadn't had food or water since Rikker grabbed her. And she smelled to high heaven. She warned Gage, "Don't get too close, I stink—"

He had her up against him, hugging her. "You smell like you're alive and that's all I care about."

Gunshots rang out from the other side of the building. More shots popped.

She struggled. "Let me go."

Gage had his Beretta 92 out, ready to take down anyone who came near. "Stand back."

She pushed away. "Let's go. They need us."

He pulled her around to face him. "You're unarmed and barely able to stand. I'm not leaving you or taking you anywhere until it's safe to move."

"Give me a damn gun. I can protect myself."

"No."

Two more shots were fired on the other side, then silence.

She whipped past Gage and grabbed Quon's 9mm. He didn't need it. She headed toward the noise. Gage picked her up off the ground and swung her around. He dropped her on her feet.

She shoved the gun in his face. "Damn you. Get out of my way."

"Sabrina?" Dingo yelled, running around the building. "Are you okay?"

"Yes." She pulled her weapon down. "What about everyone else?"

"We gotta go. Amanda called. They ran into a trap. Someone wrecked them four miles from here."

Sabrina started shouting orders to load up. She snatched the phone from Dingo and heard shooting. She shouted, "Amanda?"

Amanda's voice shouted, *"Josh, no! Shit!"*

"What?" Sabrina ran to the car with Dingo and Gage right beside her. Shooting blasted in her ear again.

Amanda screamed. *"I'm hit ... hurry ... they ... took ... Josh."*

Sabrina stumbled and Gage grabbed her arm. She shouted into the phone, *"Amanda?"*

Silence answered her. Not even a gunshot.

Sabrina fought for air.

No, not Josh.

What about Amanda? Was she dead?

Chapter 10

SABRINA STARED AT the white doors, willing the surgeon to come out and tell her Amanda had made it through.

The ambulance Dingo called for had been one street away and got to the scene in less than a minute. They'd been racing away with Amanda as Sabrina pulled up.

That had been six hours ago.

Her assistant had been sheet-white when Sabrina reached the hospital in time to see her as they wheeled her in. Amanda had been with Sabrina for over a year and never hesitated to do anything asked of her.

How many people will I have to watch die before the blood stops running? Sabrina held in the agony when she wanted to scream and beat the walls.

She couldn't see Gage, but she could feel him, standing back to give her room.

He'd be right here by her side if she'd let him, but she couldn't face him right now. To his credit, he'd sent her ahead to the hospital and had dealt with local law enforcement. For that, she thanked him.

But he'd also been in charge of sending her team into a trap. Gage had thrown caution to the wind the moment they got a tip on Rikker making an exchange. He should have scouted the area and followed whoever took her from the schoolyard even if it had ended with the kidnappers eluding him.

No, he came roaring in with guns blazing, because he'd feared this would be his only chance. Where she'd never risk the life of one person on her team in exchange for hers, Gage had sent in everyone he could find the moment a lead popped up.

Sure, he did it because he cared, but he also did it because he had to run the show. He had to have final say on a mission and believed whatever he decided was the only way it would work.

He knew her people would do anything to get her back. He was wrong to run a half-assed mission on the fly.

Now Josh was gone.

She couldn't breathe every time she allowed that thought to pass through her chaotic mind.

Movement snatched her attention when a double door swung open. Out came the doctor she'd spoken to for only seconds before he'd hurried to the surgical ward. He peeled his mask off, revealing a man who reminded her of the actor Terrence Howard, whose smile could instill comfort.

But she got no smile from this man.

Her stomach hit her feet.

She'd lost Josh and, based on the apologetic look hanging on the doctor's face, Amanda might not have made it through surgery.

Dingo stepped up next to Sabrina, reminding her she wasn't facing this hell alone. He whispered, "Amanda's tough."

"Let's hope so."

The doctor let out a deep sigh and said, "She's alive. The surgery went as well as could be expected."

Sabrina forced her knees to stay locked and waited as the doctor continued.

"Due to the fragments that pierced her abdomen and bounced around, I had to perform a hysterectomy."

Sabrina took a breath to keep from breaking in half.

Amanda had told her in confidence that she might be leaving this business soon. She'd found a man worthy of being her husband and she was ready to settle down and start a family.

Dingo cursed and ran a hand over his disheveled hair, then reminded Sabrina, "She's alive."

The surgeon went on to explain that Amanda would be in ICU for the next twenty-four to forty-eight hours with no visitors except family, who were on their way from California. Amanda had been put into a medically induced coma.

Sabrina thanked the doctor for what he'd done. She forced her limbs to work and her mouth to tell everyone to return to Slye headquarters.

Gage walked up to her, his eyes traveling over her from head to toe as if reassuring himself that she was really in front of him.

His voice held a gruffness she tried not to notice when he said, "Ride with me."

She thought she was too numb to feel anything, but found she could manage cold anger just fine. "No. Stay away from me."

"I'm not leaving. I'll help you get Josh back."

She held his gaze so long that hope budded in his face. Then she shook her head and walked away.

Nick and Tanner rode back with Gage.

She rode with Dingo, who filled her in on what had happened since she'd disappeared. All she did was nod.

"We will get him back," Dingo said, sounding as if he was talking to himself as much as her.

If she didn't lock down her emotions and start thinking like a leader, she'd lose Josh. "Why would Rikker take Josh after he'd had me in hand? For that matter, if he wanted someone, why give me up?" she said, thinking out loud.

Dingo maneuvered through the light traffic of early Saturday evening. He frowned and mused, "Rikker grabbed you to pay a debt, so—"

"No, he didn't."

Dingo slashed a look at her. "Let's start with what you know then I'll tell you if anything we have fits with it."

"Rikker called someone and said he'd make two problems go away, plus he'd hand me over for a coin. The dead guy who showed up with his gang to deliver the coin and take me in trade was called Quon. From everything I saw and heard, he brought Rikker a very old-looking coin called a stater and Rikker referenced the Orion Prophecy in his phone call. That must be one of the artifacts. He didn't give up names."

"The two problems Rikker referenced might have been Eva Perdido and Maxx Navarro," Dingo said. "We heard about those hits before the tip came through that a contract on you was being closed out today." He looked over at her. "Listen, I hate Gage so much it's hard to describe."

Her chest muscles constricted. Before she could come up with something to say, Dingo added, "But to be honest, Josh and I were all for going after you the minute the tip came through. Nick argued that the lead was fortuitous, which it was, but ..." Dingo shrugged. "I share some of the blame for this today. Even so, I still would have gone after you on nothing more than that."

"No, if it's anyone's fault, it's mine." She finally gave voice to what she'd been holding inside.

"How do you see that?"

"I was ready to let Rikker go when we were back in California, to be done with vengeance. Then I heard from Ziggie, and he indicated a snitch had information about Rikker and that he was targeting Slye."

"Why'd you go alone?"

Sabrina sighed. "We meet informants alone all the time. I was fine with meeting a woman in a crowded restaurant and ... I just could not pass up a chance that maybe this would be the end of it. I'd planned on bringing the intel back, grabbing Nick, Blade and Tanner to put together an op and go after him."

She shook off the grief threatening to swamp her.

He reached over and grabbed her hand, giving it a squeeze.

"I know what you're thinking and you're right," Sabrina admitted. "I shouldn't have gone to that meeting without someone to watch my back."

"Why didn't you call us?" Dingo asked quietly, no accusation in his voice.

"First of all, Ziggie said this had a ninety-minute time limit." She'd tried reaching Ziggie. No answer. Because he was in the wind or because he was dead? She let that go and finished explaining, "But even so, Josh was supposed to finally be getting married after a million delays due to working with Slye." She swallowed, now thinking about what she was going to tell his fiancé, Trish. "And you were ..."

"I was what, Sabrina?"

She slid her gaze at him, staring into the eyes that had watched her grow up. Dingo and Josh were the closest to family she'd ever had and would probably ever have. "You were finally living your life. At one time, I felt the same about Valene as you do about Gage, but after you told me what she means to you and I could see how happy she makes you, I changed my mind. You were sitting in *handcuffs* waiting to find out what the FBI was going to do to you in LA, and Valene came over to sit with you. I'd never seen you so happy as you were when you looked at her."

Dingo shut off the engine and the silence sounded loud.

"You can always ask me to do anything," he grumped.

"I know." She let out a deep breath, ready to do something productive, anything that might save her sanity. "Finding Josh and getting him back takes precedence over everything from this moment on. No wild, off-the-cuff plans. I won't lose another person. I can't survive losing him and definitely not losing both of you, so promise me you will watch your ass first."

"I'm not going anywhere," her arrogant Dingo said. "We do have a source who might be able to help us."

Sabrina had opened the door and swung back around quickly. "Who? They can name their price."

"That's the snag. This one can't be bought and Gage isn't keen on allowing her to be privy to what we're doing. She's Nick's secret contact and he trusts her, sort of, but … "

"But it's Nick." That quashed the moment of thrill at a bit of good news. Nick had pulled some amazing tricks to save a mission, but giving him free rein was like being offered a live wire when you were desperate for power.

Too good to pass up, but it came with a hell of a shock that held the potential for disaster.

Chapter 11

GAGE STRODE INTO the war room and took in the bleak silence. No one entered this business without knowing the risks, but he didn't like what had happened to Amanda any more than the rest of them. Good luck convincing this group of that, though.

Since the tip on Sabrina's location had come through his channels, he'd led the team to go after her, and they'd agreed on which Slye Agent to leave with Chatton.

It was either Amanda or Blade.

That had seemed like a no-brainer.

Blade might come across as a low-key personality, but Gage had seen the steel in that agent's eyes when Blade had warned Chatton to start talking or face his tools of persuasion.

In hindsight, leaving Amanda here might have been the better choice, but Chatton was not someone to underestimate. Even grunt soldiers knew that you never let your medic take point on a mission, so rehashing the decision was a waste of energy. Still…

Hindsight sucked pretty much all the damn time.

Sabrina walked in along with Dingo.

She didn't slow or look Gage's way, just kept going until she was on the far side of the room from him. The past twenty-four hours and today's adrenaline overload had hammered this group. Exhaustion showed in their faces, but they would keep going as long as Sabrina did.

And she'd fall on her face before she stopped willingly.

Tanner and Nick took spots on opposite sides of the table. Blade came trudging in and slowed to whisper something to

Sabrina, who nodded in an appreciative way, then he took a spot on the far side of the table.

Gage returned to the rear of the room where he could observe everyone. He leaned back against the desk and curled his fingers along the edge, determined to wait her out. Once she put her house in order and got the team working on how to find Josh, she might let him near her.

If she expected him to apologize for going after her, she wouldn't get that.

Sabrina moved to the front center and leaned back against the wall next to the whiteboard where Dingo's notes were still scribbled. She crossed her arms. Her gaze drifted from one face to the next.

When everyone looked up, she said, "Any agent who's not in the middle of a protective duty assignment for a corporate client is on call and working on obtaining intel from now until I say differently. No one follows a lead without a backup." She took a moment. "This is somehow tied to the Orion Hunters and Orion's Prophecy. That's where we start. I want every bit of intel we can find on the Hunters and anything on the prophecy."

Blade asked, "You think they tried to kill you and grabbed Josh over some ancient story?"

"It may sound like some fairytale story, but the people who believe in this prophecy have proven to be deadly. So we're going to treat this mission as if Orion's Prophecy is a terrorist plan. That way, we won't underestimate anyone or anything and we'll have a better chance at getting to Josh. I understand we have a source who might be able to shed some light on this." Sabrina turned to Nick. "Who is she?"

Nick answered, "I filled in the group about her when Gage first brought Chatton in, but I'll repeat all that now if you want."

"Not yet. I'll ask for what I need." Sabrina arched an eyebrow at Gage. "Where'd you find her?"

"At the parking deck that blew up. She was left there with a dead guy we believe was an Orion Hunter. His arm was scarred with the Orion star pattern that we've seen before." Gage wanted to say more, to tell her that he'd lost years off his life when all he'd found left of her at the blast scene was her purse and blood.

Instead, he held her gaze until she shifted it back to Nick. She said, "Now, I want to know who she is. Just give me the short version."

Nick took his time, explaining, "Chatton has helped us on three occasions that I know of, the last one being in California. She knows the players, maybe all the players in this. A lot more than she's shared with me, but she has given up information she could have withheld."

Dingo had split his attention between the discussion and his laptop, but he stopped typing to angle his head in Nick's direction. "I've been thinking on Chatton. She's the one who gave you the intel when you were laid up in the hospital after the Hunters cut you down at the California safe house, right?"

"Yes."

Gage considered his reply. In California, Sabrina had shared with Gage that Nick either told you the truth or nothing at all.

"Okay." Sabrina nodded, having made some decision. "Bring Chatton to me."

Blade started to stand, but Nick said, "I'll get her."

Nick left the room as Dingo's phone buzzed. He picked it up, scrolled once and frowned. "Shit."

Dingo looked up at Sabrina. "I've got a video. Says it came from Rikker."

Blade asked, "Any chance of tracing it?"

"Doubtful." Dingo was thumbing keys. "I'll give it a try, but I can assure you Rikker is not going to send us something we can trace any time soon." He asked Tanner to toss him a remote from a shelf behind him.

When Dingo pointed the remote at the five-foot-wide monitor on the wall behind him, he moved to the side of the room and watched.

Rikker's face came on the screen, smiling. He asked, "Miss me, Sabrina? Have you figured out why I saved your ass? Oh, and if you've tried to reach Ziggie, I'm afraid he's gone underground where he can no longer take clients. Well, maybe he'll find someone to snitch on in the afterlife. Wasn't all my fault. I got to him after the Hunter left him bleeding from more than one hole. Ziggie had enough breath left to give me the time and place for the meeting in exchange for a quick death."

Gage cut his eyes in Sabrina's direction.

The line around her mouth tightened. She'd probably tried to reach Ziggie from the hospital.

Chuckling at his own macabre joke, Rikker said, "As they say, everything happens for a reason. I needed you to help me orchestrate this moment and you, Sabrina, did your part beautifully. I created this perfect plan as soon as I found out there was a price on your head, then the opportunity arose to make a truly amazing plan. All I had to do was add you to the pot for the coin trade and convince your people that you were on your way to your death. To be fair to your people, you *would* have been dead if not for my well-timed intel leaks that led them in at the last moment. Right now, you have a room full of agents around you and you're probably calling in more, because while you'll sacrifice yourself for the greater good, you won't leave Dingo or Josh swinging in the breeze."

This had all been a setup and Rikker had manipulated Sabrina like a puppet. Gage would not let anything stop him from catching Rikker this time.

Sabrina would never be safe as long as that bastard drew a breath.

"Now that I have your attention," Rikker continued. "Let's skip past all the threats and get right to the point. As you might have noticed, Quon delivered a rare stater that holds great importance to my employer, but the coin is not all I need. That's why the whole point of today was to capture Josh or Dingo. Either one would have sufficed. If you want Josh back alive and undamaged, you will use your vast resources and elite agency to deliver what I'm willing to trade for him."

Sabrina had leaned forward, her entire body begging to know what she could give Rikker.

She'd hand over her life for Josh.

Gage could use everything in his arsenal to prevent that from happening and still not be able to stop her.

No one uttered a word while Rikker continued to hold the floor.

"Upon receiving final directions, you will deliver the following items that are specific to Orion's Legacy. I want the correct Amber Room panel. I'll text Dingo photos of the two that turned out to be duds, leaving you to locate the other two. You'll also deliver the Celtic cross and the Galilean scroll you foolishly handed back to the Vatican. You have a specific time frame. I shouldn't have to tell you which artifacts are the correct ones since you have Soo Jin to explain everything. You will arrive in Mumbai at nineteen-thirty hours local time on Monday for further directions, which will put you close enough to reach your final destination on time if your private jet is fueled and ready."

Not a murmur could be heard in the room as Rikker continued to dictate his terms.

"Once those three exact artifacts have been delivered to the final location, I will exchange them for Josh. If you fail to deliver that list or fail to arrive within the allotted time frame, I will send Josh back to you in small parts over the next month. I'll include proof that it is him and that he was kept alive during the dismantling process."

Rikker reached forward as if he was going to end the video then snapped his fingers. "Oh, yes, one more thing. Soo Jin's expertise is required for this meeting as well. Don't waste your time trying to convince anyone she's dead. Also, if you bring the agency into this, you'll regret it. Talk to you soon."

The agency, as in the CIA.

Gage couldn't look at Sabrina. He'd had a chance at closing a net around Rikker in California, but he'd left it open to try for the bigger fish.

Sabrina had questioned his plan at the time, insisting they grab Rikker and bring him in.

Gage had said no.

She'd never forgive him for not capturing Rikker in LA.

Chapter 12

NICK OPENED THE door to the room where Chatton had been left with one wrist handcuffed to each side of the bed.

She sat propped up in the bed reading a magazine, clearly no longer contained.

He'd expected to find her unshackled. He had a feeling Chatton belonged in a special category of super spooks.

She rolled her head to the side, looking over at him. "Did you get her back?"

"Yes. I need you to come with me." Nick stepped over and extended a hand to help her up.

She looked at it as if he offered her fresh horse manure.

Pushing up off the bed, she stepped over to the bathroom that had no windows and closed the door. When she came out, her hair was pulled back into a slick ponytail and her face had a fresh-scrubbed pinkness.

She leaned against the doorframe and crossed her arms. "I've helped you time and again. This is how you thank me?"

He should have expected this to blow up in his face at some point given their line of work, but he could never have planned on Gage Laughton walking into Slye headquarters with Chatton. "You may not see it this way, but I'm trying to help you."

Her quirked eyebrow came with a large dose of oh-sure look in her eyes. She remained silent, but that was Chatton. She made you talk, which was fine with him. He wanted her to walk out of this place free, and Gage was standing in the way.

Not that she couldn't escape, but she wouldn't leave until she knew what intel they had. He also didn't want her harmed. While she was seriously dangerous and experienced, she was also still healing from the blast and this place was packed with agents out for blood.

Nick explained, "Gage hasn't said a word, but I know he thinks you're here to spy for another country. If I'd hesitated to give them something significant, like a name, they wouldn't have listened to you."

"That would have been Sabrina's bad luck, not mine."

True, but he wanted her to drop her shield enough to allow him to look inside and see just who peered back out. This was the first time he'd ever seen her real face.

The combination of features was unusual. Almost too perfect in places.

Had she undergone cosmetic surgery to alter her appearance? It wouldn't have been out of vanity. Not with Chatton.

She took everything in stride, or at least that was what she wanted you to think. Like right now. She continued to calmly take in everything around her without moving her eyes even a flicker.

"Did you run my prints?" Chatton asked.

"Not me, but Gage will want to put them through our database, and Interpol. Want to tell me what they'll find?"

"Nothing." She smiled.

Evidently he was keeping her entertained.

She stood away from the doorframe. "What now?"

"Things have gone sideways and Sabrina wants to meet you."

Chatton cocked her head. "If she's here, how did it go sideways?"

"One agent is in the hospital, gut shot. Rikker captured another one."

"Why?" Rikker capturing an agent clearly perplexed her.

"I don't know. Makes no sense to me."

"Who'd he take?"

"Josh Carrington."

Chatton stood away from the wall, her interest piqued once he'd given her a name.

Nick asked, "What do you think?"

"Was anyone else at this throwdown?"

"Asian operative who Sabrina said was called Quon."

That really confused Chatton. "What was Quon doing there?"

"Delivering a coin to Rikker that he took in trade for Sabrina and two hits he orchestrated. Sounds like he's the one behind Perdido and Navarro getting killed in their cells last night."

"A coin. As in a very rare coin? A stater?"

Nick nodded, watching her reactions, which screamed that she knew something. "Sabrina said based on what she heard of Rikker's phone conversations, the coin is connected to the Orion Hunters. Would Quon be a Hunter?"

"Yes. In fact, he's a high-ranking Orion Hunter in the US organization, but he's not the one who owned the coin. Just the delivery boy."

Nick's phone vibrated. He lifted it and thumbed the text from Sabrina. *We have Rikker's demands for what he wants in exchange for Josh.* After texting back that he was on the way, Nick asked Chatton, "Who owned the coin?"

She lifted a confident gaze to his and stated very simply, "If your people want to ever see Josh again, they need to start dealing with me on my terms. The person Rikker is taking that coin to believes the prophecy will be revealed this week, which means Josh has very little time. Warn your people to not waste it screwing with me, because saving Josh is not on my back."

Chapter 13

SABRINA CONTINUED TO stand, but it was sheer will and determination keeping her upright. Rikker had given them an impossible option for getting Josh back.

The minute the video ended, Dingo had turned a sick look her way and shaken his head.

Then he'd mouthed *We'll bring him home.*

Yet he still typed furiously on his laptop, trying to trace the text even after admitting that Rikker would never leave an electronic trail that could be easily followed.

Every agent in this room would step up to the plate and into danger for a Slye team member, but Dingo would walk through hell with her for their brother in life.

How was she going to find artifacts others had been searching for long before she came into this mess?

Her stomach lurched with a bigger fear.

How was she going to tell Trish Jackson, Josh's fiancé, that Josh had been captured and they had a tiny chance of saving him?

Nick stepped in and announced, "Chatton's here." Then he moved aside and a woman similar in build to Sabrina entered the room. She had her own share of cuts and bruises, but it looked as though she'd had a shower, so at least Chatton didn't look like a bag lady who had crawled through a fire pit.

Nick directed Chatton to the first seat near the door and she took it.

Sabrina risked a quick look in Gage's direction.

His stare should be drilling holes in Chatton. He must have sensed Sabrina's eyes on him and glanced up. All the hardness there a moment ago faded into concern and sympathy.

She didn't want his sympathy.

She wanted Rikker's throat clutched between her hands.

Dismissing Gage, she turned to Chatton. "You were at the blast?"

Gage spoke up. "She was wearing clothes that made her look indigent."

Sabrina frowned, thinking back. Her memory stirred with the vision of a woman right before the explosion. A woman who had been talking to her about ... damn. She couldn't pinpoint the conversation, but she did remember a woman there.

Chatton said nothing.

Going on instinct, Sabrina asked, "You were talking to me before the blast. What were you trying to get me to do?"

No arrogance or cockiness showed in Chatton's face, but neither was she cowed in the least. When she spoke, her voice had a smooth quality. "I was trying to get you to leave with me before you were snatched. I heard about the contract on you."

Dingo asked, "You were there to snatch her first?"

"Yes and no."

Nick sighed.

Chatton sent a menacing look his way then explained, "I was hunting Rikker when I got word about the contract on Sabrina. Then I heard the Orion Hunters were involved and rumors floated that Rikker hadn't made it out of the country after the debacle in LA. I figured he'd come for Sabrina, but I thought he'd trade her to the Hunters for the scroll." She addressed Sabrina. "Evidently, once I had Ziggie set up the meeting, the Hunters got to your snitch and forced him to give up the details. Rikker saw an opportunity to use you as bait for his master plan."

That drove the knife of guilt deeper into Sabrina's chest. She'd played into everyone's hands because of how badly she wanted Rikker. That bastard would pay as soon as she found Josh and yanked his butt out of wherever Rikker had him.

Dingo stopped typing again, washed a hand over his tired face and said, "Chatton knows a lot about our operations, Sabrina. I told you some of it on the way here, but I'm thinking she knows a name for the person behind the contract that was out on you."

Sabrina gave Dingo a tiny nod, thanking him for helping her out when her brain was still half scrambled.

Nick asked Chatton, "What does Rikker want?"

That's right. Nick hadn't been present when Dingo ran the video.

Sabrina started to just bullet point it for Nick, but Gage suggested, "Run the video again. We may pick up something we missed the first time."

Oh, sure. It wasn't as if that video hadn't been burned into Sabrina's corneas already. But the professional in her knew he was right even if it grated on her to admit it.

She ordered, "Run it again."

Now that the video was in their system, Dingo lifted the remote and Rikker's smiling face came back in full gloating view.

While the video played, Sabrina watched Chatton, who held herself very still, except for when Rikker referenced his employer. If Sabrina hadn't been watching closely, she would have missed the tiny narrowing of Chatton's eyes.

Once the video ended, Sabrina picked up a bottle of water, waiting for all eyes to turn forward again. She asked Chatton, "Who is Rikker's employer?"

Nick made a noise in his throat that Sabrina took to mean she was pushing Chatton for too much.

Chatton said, "I'd rank him as one of the top three most dangerous people in the world. He's not just an employer, he owns Rikker."

"How long has he owned Rikker?" Gage asked.

Chatton tossed him a dry look. "If I'm an enemy spy, why would you believe anything I tell you?"

"Who's saying I would?"

Sabrina was in no mood for banter or power games. She gave Gage a 'stand down' glare that turned him more grim than he'd been. She repeated his question. "How long has Rikker been with this man?"

Chatton answered, "Technically, he bought Rikker when your team was sent to rescue Rikker in the UK."

Tanner asked, "What was the payment?"

"Money and handing over your team to replace Rikker since the broker was giving up a high value asset."

Dingo leaned back. "Is Rikker's owner in the US?"

"No."

The room turned quiet and Sabrina had no doubt that they were all thinking the same thing, which Nick actually voiced, "The person who burned Sabrina's team in the UK wasn't in the US government?"

"I didn't say that," Chatton told him.

Sabrina barked, "Then say what you mean."

Chatton tapped her fingers in a slow tap, tap, tap until she stopped and said, "You need to understand something. I never planned to get involved in anything affecting national security in the US. I have helped your team at times to prevent innocents from being killed. I owe you nothing." Her gaze touched on Nick who showed no reaction.

Everyone glanced at Sabrina, whose attention was solely on Chatton. What else did this spook have to say?

It didn't take long before Chatton told her. "Now that we're clear on where I stand, I want your agreement to release me as soon as I answer your questions."

Gage butted in yet again. "Why should we agree to that?"

Sabrina turned to shut him down before he cost her intel she needed, but Chatton managed it in ten words.

"Because I am your best hope at getting Josh back. Also, I possess the Celtic cross. In a way, it's what brought me into all of this." Chatton crossed her arms and sat back.

Nick's face smoothed into one of appreciation. He knew far more about Chatton than anyone else, but Sabrina was saving that debriefing for when she could get him alone.

Blade asked, "Are you an Orion Hunter?"

"No."

Nick suggested, "Why don't we all get our cards on the table?"

Chatton turned to Nick. "Meaning?"

Nick's dark eyes lifted to Sabrina. "Chatton knows way more than we do about the Hunters and who's behind all this. She may not share everything she knows—"

Dingo muttered, "That's bullshit."

Without missing a beat, Nick continued, "But we need what she's willing to share."

Sabrina had worked with Nick long enough to know he was asking to be given autonomy and if that was what it took to find Josh, that's what she'd do.

She nodded at Nick.

That's all he needed from her, but he clearly had one other person who had to pass her blessing on this discussion.

Nick told Chatton, "I can guarantee your freedom if you'll work with us."

Gage said, "Wait a minute—"

Sabrina cut him off. "Do not interfere."

Gage argued, "She could be a spy for the Orion Hunters for all you know. She's clearly not working for the home team. Are you just going to let her walk out of here?"

He had a point, but Sabrina had no time for debating with him. She'd trusted every person in this room with the welfare of other agents and her own life many times.

She asked Nick, "Do you trust her?"

Watching Nick closely, Chatton's lips twitched. Evidently, she found that amusing.

Nick smiled too, but that could mean anything with him. He said, "I do."

"Then I'll release her once you say we have all that we need." Sabrina addressed Chatton. "Fair enough?"

"Yes."

That ended the negotiations as far as Sabrina was concerned. She'd deal with Gage later, but she doubted he'd interrupt again.

He might just walk out of here and never look back.

She suffered a sick feeling over that possibility, which made no sense after telling him they were done.

Her heart hadn't been on board when she made the declaration, but it would catch up. Just like it had when the woman from social services dropped her off at the group home at seven years old. Her heart had shriveled up, never to feel anything again, or so she'd thought.

Then Dingo and Josh came along and showed her what family could be.

Gage didn't understand that, and apparently couldn't. Maybe it was unfair of her to expect him to grasp her bond with Dingo and Josh when she'd never heard so much as one tidbit about Gage's family or even any close friends. Maybe he didn't have any.

Wouldn't two people in a relationship know those things about one another?

Nick shook her from her thoughts when he started talking again. "I met Chatton while we were in Seattle to stop the terrorist attack by the Banker. Chatton shared intel that allowed us to save one of our own." Nick paused, letting Sabrina make the mental connection to Margaux Duke, a name that could not be said aloud with anyone other than Slye personnel in the room. As far as the world knew, Margaux had died, and Sabrina intended to keep it that way.

Nick added, "I'm pretty sure Chatton gave us a hand on that op in other ways as well, and I'm betting she's been around longer than that." He swung his gaze at the spook. "Right?"

Shrugging, Chatton admitted, "That's possible."

"Now would be a good time to let this group know what else you've done," Nick prodded.

She pushed out a sigh that spoke of irritation. "Fine. Last year, your man Ryder found a briefcase inside his truck while he was keeping surveillance on the shipping docks in Miami. That briefcase led your team to stop Rikker from crashing a commercial airliner on approach to Miami International."

Bodies shifted around the table, sitting up straighter at that.

Chatton continued, "Ryder was arrested for murder after that and I was given intel that he'd killed someone important to me."

"What?" Blade snapped.

Unbothered by Blade's outburst, Chatton kept talking. "But Nick's right. I don't trust anyone these days and neither do I take intel at face value. I determined that the assassin known as Munk had committed the murder. I believe Munk was found not far from where he tried to kill Ryder and the FBI agent Ryder married." She lifted her chin, meeting the surprised gazes around the room. "Let's just say Munk's death benefitted all of us. After researching your operations ... " She paused long enough to look at Gage, letting them all know she included him in that. "I decided Nick offered the best opportunity for occasional collaboration."

Nick grinned as if he'd been given a gold star.

Someone else might be furious with him for withholding information on Chatton all this time, but Sabrina would not criticize him when she had no doubt that Chatton would have avoided sharing intel if it had not been for Nick.

Running a group of skilled operatives meant putting stock in their judgment and taking them as they came, even if their methods didn't fall within a normal operational flow chart.

Plus it sounded as if Chatton had saved the necks of her people more than once.

Nick added, "Chatton got information to me when I was laid up in the hospital that was instrumental in Tanner and Dingo stopping the attack on the aquifer." He directed his next comment specifically to Sabrina. "I'll give you a full debrief later."

"Yes." Sabrina had heard enough. "I get that you've been giving assistance when you choose, Chatton. For that, I thank you. You saw the video Rikker sent. What can you tell us about Rikker and who he works for? The man who you said owns him."

"I've mentioned that Rikker can't return to his boss empty-handed. He would be better off to slice his own throat and take the easy way out. He's tied to a man who is obsessed with Orion's Prophecy and has no tolerance for failure."

"The one you called the Fanatic earlier?" Tanner tossed in.

"Yes."

"Basically, a lunatic," Tanner clarified.

Chatton shook her head. "He is a fanatic, but he's not insane. He's far more deadly because he's committed to seeing that his country comes out on top in the final conflict predicted by the prophecy."

"What if there is no third world war?"

"I can't answer that, but I would not underestimate him."

Dingo interjected, "That makes sense now about Rikker. He was after the scroll in California. Now he wants the scroll, that

Amber Room panel and your Celtic cross. What's his boss going to do with all of them?"

"I don't have that answer. Soo Jin would be the one to know."

Tanner started to speak and Chatton stopped him with a raised hand. "I know she's not dead. I tried to convince Rikker's boss that she was dead, but he wouldn't listen."

"Why would he have been talking to you about her?" Tanner asked.

"Because he has something I want and he offered to trade for her."

Easygoing Tanner looked ready to pounce.

Sabrina hoped Nick could defuse this, but Nick just kept his attention on Chatton, who told Tanner, "Before you think about acting on those homicidal thoughts showing on your face, I *could* have delivered her. I watched you, Soo Jin and Dingo fly out of the Ogallala Airport after you and Soo Jin survived the midair explosion."

Dingo broke the stunned silence by asking, "Why?"

Chatton angled her head at him. "Why what?"

"Why'd you let Soo Jin go?"

"Because Rikker's boss lied to me about Soo Jin and led me to believe I would be helping her. Once I realized the truth, I told him she died in the explosion. He didn't believe it." She lifted a shoulder. "I don't harm anyone who stays out of my way and is no threat to me or mine. Soo Jin can answer your questions about the prophecy. I strongly suggest you figure out how to get her to the artifact gathering—"

"Not happening," Tanner said with brutal finality. Then he looked at Sabrina. "I'll do anything you ask of me and I'm all in on going after Josh, but ... not to sacrifice Soo Jin. There has to be another way."

Since it was clear that they would be wasting breath and time to pretend Soo Jin was dead, Sabrina assured him, "I'm not suggesting we take Soo Jin there, but we are going to find some way to make that part work."

He gave a relieved nod.

At that, Chatton said, "As I mentioned, Rikker's boss is a powerful and dangerous man. He will expect his terms met and those artifacts delivered, as well as Soo Jin, or Rikker will make good on his threat about sending Josh back in pieces. What Rikker didn't tell you is that if you are the reason his boss does not have everything in place when he expects it, he will send people after anyone connected to Josh and this agency. They will keep coming until no one is left standing."

"Who is this man and how do you know him?" Sabrina asked, wanting everything from Chatton.

Chatton deliberated on her answer during a stretched silence. "This man has the ear of a major world leader. He's in league with another man whom I referenced as the Imposter when I explained this to your people. The two of them met before I became aware of their secret little club, which they call the Czarion."

Sabrina blinked at the mysterious name that had surfaced during ops linked to the Orion Hunters.

Ignoring the way everyone became more alert at hearing the word Czarion, Chatton continued explaining, "I'm not sure how the two men actually found each other, but it was because of the Orion Prophecy. They both possessed artifacts when they met."

"Does Rikker know both men?" Blade asked.

"Yes. At times, he's worked for each one, but he truly answers only to the one who holds his life in his hands."

Something Chatton said a moment ago pinged for Sabrina. "Wait. You said they both possessed artifacts. Rikker expects us to find three, but he took a coin with him, which makes four. What's the fifth one?"

"A jade tablet I've never seen, but it's rumored to be about this big." Chatton used her hands to show a rectangle approximately twelve by fifteen inches. "Supposedly, it has words and designs carved into it and one of Genghis Khan's belt buckles is embedded in it."

"What about the other man in the Czarion? What does he own?"

"I said *possessed,* as in past tense. The coin Rikker bargained for belonged to him. The same person who needed Eva Perdido and Maxx Navarro taken out of circulation and who held the contract on—" Chatton tilted her chin in Sabrina's direction.

"You. That's why I came to the parking deck. The contract issued was not to kill you, but to capture you. My guess was that he intended to use you as a pawn to get the Perdido and Navarro hits made."

Sabrina's jaw went slack. "He expected my people to commit murder for me?"

"Knowing this man, that would fit."

Gage had remained silent longer than Sabrina expected. "Who is this bastard?"

"I've told you all you need. Their names are pseudonyms. Knowing them would not only be of no use to you, it would get you and anyone who inquires about them killed. It would also throw a huge kink in my plans. The only people living who know those names besides Rikker and myself will kill anyone who comes stumbling into all of this."

Even Nick had a quizzical expression. "How do you know so much about these two men and their Czarion club?"

She unfolded her arms and leaned back. "Because I'm one of the Czarion and I can be either your ally or your enemy. Getting in my way will make us adversaries. So ... will we be allies or enemies? You choose."

Chapter 14

GAGE EXPECTED NICK and a few other agents to immediately confirm that Slye wanted Chatton as an ally.

He might be the only person in here who could be objective when it came to that spook.

When Sabrina started to answer Chatton, Gage lifted a hand and indicated he wanted to step outside.

That's all it took with Sabrina. She missed nothing that went on around her, especially on her turf.

She answered Chatton, "Of course we want you as an ally, but allies work together. The question is, do you intend to work with us?"

Chatton was in no hurry to give her an answer.

Sabrina said, "Think on it. I'll be right back." Then she left by the door near the front. Since there was a second door at the rear of the room that had been left closed, Gage exited through that one at the same time. He met her halfway, which allowed them to talk away from the doors.

"What is it, Gage?" she asked, her words as cold as her attitude.

He'd expected her to be distant but not the icy anger. "I want to talk to you without starting a conflict in there. Is talking to you too much to ask?"

"I can't deal with you being here."

Whoa. This was worse than he thought. He understood she was pissed at Amanda being hurt and Josh grabbed, but ... "Do you blame me for Josh and Amanda?"

She looked anywhere but his face.

"Damn. You do."

"No." She grabbed a wad of her hair and clutched it in frustration, finally looking at him. "I wanted to be angry with you over what happened, but that was just a reaction from being raw emotionally. Once I left the hospital, I realized who was responsible. I blame myself for all of this."

"Fuck that. Every agent on your team is beyond skilled. There wasn't a rookie in the group and they wouldn't have stayed back if I'd tried to order them, which would have been stupid on my part. As for your part, you got set up. No one in this business is immune to that, no matter how hard we try to avoid it."

She released her hair and held up a hand. "I know. Rikker played all of us on that one. I understand, but ... this is just not the time or place for us to talk."

He considered his options, which were almost nonexistent. If he allowed her, she would shut him out emotionally *and* from this operation.

Shifting gears mentally, he realized she couldn't turn down two things he had to offer—intel and additional assets on the ground. If it meant dealing with her on a professional level to find their way back together emotionally, he'd play that angle.

Gage took a hard edge with his new plan. "I agree. We do need to talk at some point, but I have too much on my plate, and so do you, to waste time on emotional crap right now."

She blinked at the harsh tone and looked as though he'd smacked her.

He'd rather shoot himself in the nuts than hurt her.

In truth, he figured she was surprised more than hurt, but her reaction proved one thing. She couldn't toss him aside as easily as she'd pretended. If his plan to stay by her side worked, he'd get a chance to fix that look on her face.

Give him one minute to hold her and he'd never let her go again.

But right now, he had a role to play. "Look, Sabrina. I want to find the people behind all this as much as you want Josh back, but that's not going to happen unless we reach an agreement."

Her eyes narrowed and she snapped to sharper attention. There was the woman who could stop a wall of terrorists if she was stuck between them and the people she protected.

One day Gage hoped to be included again in the small circle that held her trust.

She cocked her head. "What kind of agreement?"

He had to go all in or not at all with her. She'd know if he hedged even a little. He said, "First, we're either working as a team or not. Which is it?"

She glanced over at the door and he didn't have to do a lot of guessing to know she was thinking about Dingo waiting inside.

When Sabrina turned back, Gage gave her an incredulous look followed with, "Are you really going to tell me that Dingo won't squeeze every possible resource for information to get Josh back? That he would turn down what I can offer?"

Evidently he'd nailed her hesitation, because she looked embarrassed and said, "I just don't want to add stress for this group on top of everything else going on. I still have to talk to Josh's fiancé. Dingo sent a team to pick her up, but all she knows is that everyone connected to Slye is going to safe houses. She thinks Josh is on a mission. I have to tell her all of it."

Watching Sabrina in so much pain was ripping him to pieces inside. He wanted to wrap her up and hold her close, assure her that they'd get Josh back.

If he tried that right now, she'd bite his head off.

Still, he could soften his words this time. "I get what you're saying and I don't want to make this more difficult for you either, but I have to know you're not going to keep me out of the loop if I'm bringing what I have to the table to help you."

Sabrina crossed her arms and pulled in her lower lip like she did sometimes when she was torn on a decision. "I'll do my best to keep you in the loop, Gage. That's as much as I can say with no idea where this will take all of us."

If it was anyone else, he'd push harder and make this deal absolute, but one look at the misery and exhaustion wrapping around her had him easing up. She needed someone to lean on, but if he gave in and treated her like the woman he wanted more than anything, she'd get her hackles back up and question his motives. She'd accuse him of trying to discover Rikker's boss.

She'd be right.

His motives started and ended with whatever it took to keep her safe, but now that also included patching up her heart by finding Josh.

He frowned to shape his face to match his tone. "Fine. If that's the best you can do, then I'll do the best I can, too. No promises." At the astonishment jumping in her gaze, he added, "You can't expect me to be completely on board if you're not, right?"

Always the example of honor, Sabrina said, "No, of course not. I'll take whatever you can give me."

Gage couldn't claim to be nearly so honorable when it came to keeping Sabrina within arm's reach where he could protect her.

He said, "Okay, then let's start with something simple. I'll put people I have on finding any and all Amber Room panels, tracking sales, whatever, but I want Chatton's fingerprints. She's somebody's spook. You may trust Nick's assessment of her, but I have no reason to trust her. Nick admitted he knows little more than what he's shared. While that might sound as though Chatton has helped you out in the past, it could have been nothing more than manipulating Nick and those working with him to do her bidding."

Sabrina wouldn't meet his gaze. "Understood."

He couldn't decide if she agreed with him, disagreed and was trying not to start a fight, or if she was just so damned tired she was throwing in the towel on this round.

She walked away, heading to the entrance at the front of the room.

Gage returned the way he'd come out and took up his same spot again.

She called Nick aside and spoke softly to the Italian.

Sabrina had her back to the room, which meant Gage could observe Nick, who first cocked his head as if he questioned her words, then he crossed his arms. Not happy.

Sabrina folded her arms in front of her and pushed up close, looking agitated as she spoke.

Dingo watched without any expression, but his body tensed. He was ready to jump in if Sabrina needed backup.

She unfolded her arms and held them out as if imploring Nick to understand what she was saying.

He looked disgusted but finally nodded and stepped away, crossing the room to Chatton. He ordered her, "Come with me."

Chatton didn't move. "I shared what you needed. It's time to make good on the terms."

Sabrina said, "I didn't say *when* we would allow you to leave."

Pissed, Chatton stabbed Nick with a look of threat. "Are you sure you want to do this?"

Nick said, "I don't like repeating myself. Let's go."

Chatton jumped to her feet so quickly, every agent pulled a weapon on her, including Gage.

She took in the room and warned, "I'll remember this. Next time you need help, I'll find somewhere comfortable to watch as you live to regret a very bad decision."

She marched out ahead of Nick, who kept his weapon on her.

Everyone sat back and put their weapons away.

Turning to the rest of the group, Sabrina said, "We don't have a lot of time. We need to make the most of what time we do have, but I also need you sharp. Grab some sleep when you can and eat. This is going to be a marathon with no stopping."

She glanced around as heads nodded in understanding, then said, "Everyone travels in pairs as of now. Blade, you contact Ryder. Brief him then give him the list of all Slye agent immediate families. Find White Hawk and tell her to help Ryder move families to safe houses unless the agent whose family is involved has an alternative option that he or she would prefer."

Blade scribbled notes on a pad then his head popped up. "I'm on it and I've already sent a message to White Hawk to pull her in. I'll update her. What about Trish?"

"I'll call her myself. Tell Ryder to say nothing to his wife or Trish until I've had a chance to talk to Trish, because Josh said ... "

Everyone paused at Sabrina's stumble. She kept going. "Josh said Trish had included Bianca in the wedding planning, so they talk to each other."

With their leader showing her steel front once again, everyone returned to their tasks.

Blade kept writing. "Got it."

"Tanner, you get with Soo Jin. Brief her on what's happening. Tell her all the information we have to date on the prophecy and find out what else she can tell us, specifically everything she knows about each artifact and whether she has any idea where the artifacts are to be brought together."

"Dingo, you—"

He lifted his head from where he'd been hunched over his laptop. "As I said, I came up empty with tracing the video, which surprises none of us. I'll work on pulling together everything I can find related to the Orion Hunters and the prophecy. If Soo Jin can give me specifics on the Amber Room Panel, I can start hunting that online, too. Also, uh, Valene will do anything we ask of her."

Gage hoped that didn't set off Sabrina.

Valene had been the person to step up and help Dingo in California twice in the last couple of months. She was also the woman Dingo had gone rogue to protect. And the same woman Sabrina had made homicidal noises about in LA.

Sabrina chewed on her lip. "You should send her to a safe house."

Gage squinted at that. *What the hell?* Sabrina hated that woman. Or she had.

Dingo scratched his head. "That would make sense, but she won't go and we really need her expertise here. You have any problem with me bringing her in?"

"No. Do it. I'm going to grab a shower and I'll be back."

"Copy that."

Gage said nothing, but her new attitude toward Dingo's girlfriend sent up a flag of hope. If Sabrina could change her mind about Valene Eklund, that gave him hope for their relationship once this was over.

He waited silently as Sabrina handed everyone marching orders.

As she started for the door, she looked over at him.

He lifted an eyebrow, asking if she was going to walk away from him yet again.

Not the smartest idea to push her right now, but he was not

going to be shut out so easily after what had happened to her. She looked barely held together with hope and determination after the last twenty-four hours. She never asked for anything and refused to lean on anyone, but she needed support right now and he was going to help her get through this any way he could.

She rubbed her eyes, a delay tactic, and finally lifted her chin. An invitation.

The only one he'd get and he wanted this on her terms.

Gage followed her out of the office and upstairs, trying to prepare for whatever she threw at him next. Only a fool would think Sabrina had stopped fighting him. That woman would battle until her last breath.

Fair enough since he would, too. The hours she'd been in Rikker's hands had brought home every day of the two years that Gage had searched for her. He was not losing her again.

Not that way at least.

Also, they had to talk about Chatton. That spook was not leaving here until he was done with her. He could take time from his duties, but he could not set aside his commitment to protect this country.

Chapter 15

GAGE FOLLOWED SABRINA, who strode ahead of him toward the stairwell, fire and iron will carried on two determined legs. Had to be around nine at night, but it felt like the longest day in history. The Friday night blast that started this was twenty-seven hours ago.

Sabrina needed food and rest. Would she stop to eat or sleep? No.

He'd give her the space she needed around her people, but she couldn't do this alone. Not against the impossible odds she refused to admit.

If she tried and failed, it could break a woman he'd seen bend few times.

She had to know the odds of getting Josh back were so high that no bookie in Vegas would touch it.

When she reached the upstairs, she turned toward the lobby for Slye headquarters, staring at the spot where Amanda normally manned the front of this fort. She'd stood between anyone who came in unexpectedly and Sabrina's private office, which opened into a separate personal quarters for the boss who often spent nights here.

He knew about that area, but Sabrina had never invited him inside this building. The only time he'd entered before now had been one night when he'd breached her security to talk to her alone.

That seemed forever ago.

Sabrina pulled up short before entering her office.

A young woman with Native American facial features and stunning green eyes sat in Amanda's chair. White Hawk. She was a quiet agent with uncanny skills for shadowing someone.

Sabrina asked, "How'd you get here so quickly? Blade said he reached you, but I thought you were on the Feldman project in Birmingham?"

White Hawk's demeanor and voice held respect for Sabrina. "I was. Amanda contacted me early this morning, telling me she'd be working in the field and would like me to cover the desk for her. I was on my way when Blade called. He told me about Amanda. I'm keeping tabs on her through a contact Blade gave me at the hospital. You look ... tired. How bad is all this?"

"It's not good." Sabrina gave White Hawk a quick rundown, minimizing what she'd been through, but Gage could tell that she didn't fool White Hawk. Sabrina finished by saying, "You're assigned to Blade. No one else gives you direction but him unless it's me."

White Hawk said, "Absolutely."

Gage's file on the young Native American woman was thin. Someone had taught her to track and tail *anything* while she remained undetected. She had a way with languages, but Gage's file on her background became sketchy beyond that point. She'd grown up on a reservation. No one there would share much of anything on her with someone outside the tribe.

When Sabrina ended the conversation and walked into her office, Gage followed, noting the suspicious look White Hawk gave him.

He could take the cold looks, but Sabrina's people might as well get used to the idea of having him around.

When he closed the door behind him, he stood back a few steps and waited as she paused at the front of her desk to call Josh's fiancé. Probably afraid to sit down and lose the battle with fatigue.

She already looked ready to face-plant the carpet, but that call took what little wind had been pushing her around, and sucked it out of her sails. Sabrina told Josh's fiancé the truth and assured the woman that she would be kept in the loop via Dingo and Ryder.

With that done, she walked around the right end of her desk and lifted her hand to a mirror just large enough for a woman to check her hair and makeup.

She pulled the mirror away from the wall and placed her hand on the center of a security screen.

A green light flashed in the corner and a door built to look like part of the paneling clicked open.

Gage followed her into her private quarters, where she closed the door behind him. Nothing surprised him about the simple kitchen space with a counter for eating whatever she ordered in or the tidy sitting area on the opposite side.

Sabrina gave new meaning to the word Spartan.

But in walking toward what appeared to be a bedroom from what he could see through an open door, she stopped in front of a narrow bookcase.

He moved closer to see what had caught her attention. She stared at a ragged picture of three scrawny kids. It had been framed with care.

They looked too much like Sabrina, Josh and Dingo to be anyone else.

Gage closed the distance between them and leaned in. "I'm going to help you get him back. Just let me do what I do best."

That must have shaken her from the moment.

She wheeled around. "This isn't going to work. You can't stay objective while you're part of the agency and I can't have you screwing with any resource that might mean the difference in getting him back."

"You mean Chatton."

"I mean anyone. I understand your position, but you have to understand mine."

"I do realize how much Josh and Dingo mean to you. I realized that the minute I screwed up in LA, so do you really think I'd risk losing Josh? Do I want to know more about Chatton? Yes. But I will never intentionally hurt you again. I had my reasons in LA and my concern for your safety was real, but in hindsight I should have deferred to your judgment when it came to Josh or Dingo."

Whatever banged around inside her mind was taking her apart one emotion at a time. She shoved hair off her face. "I know you wouldn't cause me trouble intentionally, Gage, but the rules are off the table for me. I want you to understand exactly where I stand right now. I'm unleashing everyone with only one order and that's to do whatever it takes to bring him home alive, and in one piece."

She took a shuddering breath. "If a questionable opportunity presents itself, I'm willing to go down for this if it takes a bad turn and our government demands my head, but I will not be responsible for putting you or any of my people in that position." She looked him straight in the eyes when she added, "Especially when ... there is no us at the end of this tunnel."

He forced his hands not to fist and give away the anger pushing at him to hurt all the people who had brought them to this point.

Starting with the person who burned her team and ending with Rikker.

If Gage ever got his hands on him again, Rikker would see his last day on earth. Gage had argued against sending Sabrina's team into England when Rikker got grabbed. He argued Rikker was out of control, a serial killer, but no one in the agency would listen.

He'd been given the choice of sending the Slye team or handing Sabrina off to a different handler.

Not a chance he'd have agreed to that.

Telling her might improve his position on that blown op, but only until she hit him up for names again. That would restart the whole war of words. He'd been battling to keep her away from the agency, to keep her from stumbling across whoever had traded her life away once.

The person who did that had to be buried deep inside the government.

"Say something, Gage."

"You tell me you want Josh back but you don't want me involved. You tell me you don't care about me—"

"I didn't say that," she grumbled.

"—but you don't want me to take any risks to help you."

Couldn't Sabrina see how every time she pushed him further away she drove a blade into him over and over? Probably not since he kept his emotions locked inside a bulletproof case.

He lifted a hand and brushed his fingers over her hair. Now

was the time for the talk they'd avoided and to tell her that he would not back away. "I'm officially on leave right now."

She closed her eyes and he wanted to convince himself that she was soaking up the feel of his touch, but she had her own hard shell, and she pulled inside it when her emotions threatened to be more than she could handle.

She said, "You can't operate on US soil whether you're on leave or active. How are you going to live with yourself if Chatton turns out to be connected to a terrorist group?"

"Same way you will if that happens." He was going to do everything in his power to make sure Sabrina didn't rush into anything unprepared. No matter what, he had to convince her to allow him to stay close. He'd lie if forced to and accept her fury later, but she was not going into this mission without him.

He added, "I believe in you and that you'll make the right choice if you find out Chatton is playing for the wrong side."

She grabbed his hand, her grip strong for a woman her size. "Don't bank on that, Gage. Know this. I will do *whatever* it takes to save Josh."

He turned his wrist, breaking away from her hold and cupping her hand in his. He pulled her palm to his lips to kiss.

"Gage." His name came out on a hiss of air.

"Stop shoving me away, Sabrina."

"I can't deal with all of this and you. I can't live with indecision and this ... between us, creates problems I can't allow to take any of my energy right now."

He drew in a long breath and propped her hand against his cheek. "You don't have to do anything. I'm not putting any demands on you. Just let me stay close."

"What if I ... " Her voice cracked with what sounded to him as a brush of hope. She cleared her throat. "What if I do keep you with me through this, then what? When this is done, we're still at the same place we were before. I'm not changing my mind. The last two weeks were torture. Do I want you? Yes. Are we going to continue the way we did before? No."

"Why not?" The words were out before he could stop them, but he just did not get why they couldn't move past what had torn them apart.

"I learned a few things over the past month, but I wouldn't accept them until I watched Dingo walk out of my safe house in LA because he thought I no longer believed in him. I'm not blaming you."

"Yes, you are."

"Okay, truth. I do blame you for thinking you knew what was best for me and stepping over me to say and do what *you* considered the right thing when it was my decision to make. I blame me for allowing that to happen. What I've come to terms with is I can't deal with a clandestine relationship for several reasons, the first being that I won't lie to Josh and Dingo. They are the only real family I've ever known." She didn't look away, not now when he could tell she'd dug deep to give him this truth, the things an agency file couldn't explain. "You and I will never have anything more than stolen moments. That was enough at one time, but now? That's not the life I want."

He struggled to keep everything he wanted to say shoved inside and stuck with, "I feel like a broken record, but I don't understand why you believe we can't ever be together again."

"You once told me that being a CIA agent was enough for you. That's what you'd do until they told you to retire, because no active agent leaves the agency. When I was caught up in missions and we partnered, it seemed nothing could stop us. That you would always be there and I would, too. When Dingo came so close to dying, then almost went to prison when all he'd done was protect everyone he cared for, I realized I would have to live through that every time you left for a mission."

"I know you have a business to run, but can't we find a middle ground of maybe partnering again when we can?" Sure, that was grasping at straws but even if it was on occasion, it would be better than nothing at all.

"No. I'm done with the agency. Also, I don't want to be the one waiting for that day when you don't return. It's not easy being honest about this, but the longer we go on the way we have, the harder it will be to stop again."

Arguing had gotten them nowhere. If he gave voice to how it felt to play tug-of-war over her with Josh and Dingo, she'd shut him out. He didn't want her to give up anyone in her life, just to make room for him.

This was a delicate negotiation and he had one chance for keeping the lines of communication open. His gut squawked over the duplicity he had in mind, but he was a man fighting to stay above water with her.

He released her hand and cupped her face. "If I accept what you just said, will you agree to let me do this mission with you, just one last time? If you don't, I'll end up shadowing you and I don't want to risk accidentally putting you in danger because you don't know I'm around."

When she didn't answer immediately, he tossed in something she couldn't turn down. "You're not going to be on US soil very long based on what Rikker said. You could use my help on any other continent, right?"

Her steel blue eyes had been flint hard in the meeting, but here in her personal space she let her guard down a tiny bit. She looked like a ragdoll dragged through the dirt and stomped on.

He'd given her the perfect opportunity to make a deal.

The logic in his last offer steered clear of emotions.

Drawing herself up, she said, "Okay. If you can dial back the government mentality and agree to support anything I decide to do, I'll be glad to have you on our team."

His noisy gut was warning him he couldn't make good on this commitment and keep his hands off her, but he was out of moves. Either he played this her way, or he was out.

"Agreed." He hoped his commitment to duty wouldn't be tested.

He'd hit his limit of living in hell while she was missing then he'd had to watch her stand defenseless in the middle of a firefight.

Holding her face, he leaned in and kissed her. Oh, man, he'd missed this woman. She tensed at first, as if she couldn't recall what it meant for them to touch each other.

Then she covered his hands with hers and kissed him back. Her body moved toward his, a magnetic force that had been between them since day one. Her hands fisted his shirt and his body wanted to answer that silent call to connect and feel each other again.

In the past, he'd take that one hint as a signal to step up his game and make this interesting, but now ... now was not the time. His body could beg him all it wanted, but the prize was so much more than sex.

He finally held her close enough that he could breathe again, and a moment's release wouldn't satisfy him. Not when he wanted all of her.

Sabrina's moment of giving in didn't last long. She pulled out of his grasp, murmuring about taking a shower. She'd given up an inch of ground in his campaign to win her back.

He'd take it.

This would be an uphill battle, because once Sabrina made a decision she wouldn't back off of it.

If they managed to bring Josh home alive, Gage hoped to have found a place in her world. He'd accept it if, in the end, she still said no, but he knew this woman and she could never just stop caring.

She took on the burden of protecting everyone and put herself last. She feared loss and he got that. Oh, man, did he get that after he'd searched nonstop for her during the two years she went dark.

He feared losing her. If that happened ...

The bulb went off so bright in Gage's mind it could have blinded him. He knew the reason she was pushing him away.

If this mission had a hitch and things went south, Sabrina would never want to be around anyone from the espionage world.

She was that black and white.

Losing Josh would crush her. She might even disappear and, if she did, he knew in his heart he'd never find her again.

Chapter 16

CHATTON HELD HER hand out the passenger window of Nick's sleek Lamborghini Huracan. He had more than this in his stable, because she'd seen another beauty in downtown Atlanta when they first met.

They shared a love of exotic cars.

They might have shared more before this.

Warm night air flowed over her arm. He'd driven past Hartsfield-Jackson Atlanta International Airport minutes ago, heading south. With the Saturday night party crowd flowing northbound into Atlanta, this side of the interstate offered lighter traffic.

She enjoyed the ride while she waited to find out just what was behind this drive.

Living her life one step ahead of death had taught her to enjoy the moment, right down to the second.

Nick had followed her into a room Sabrina had pointed out, then he'd asked her to pull a black bag over her head. Once she covered her head, he'd led her through an area that felt naturally cool and had a gravel floor. She guessed it to be a tunnel from the basement area of their headquarters.

He'd guided her up steps until she could hear jets taking off in the distance.

She'd known Slye headquarters was near the airport, because she'd once inserted covertly into their building to drop off a thumb drive with intel Slye had needed for a mission. She just hadn't known for sure where they'd been holding her since she'd awakened in the basement. Questioning him as they departed had yielded no answers.

Maybe it would work better now that they were on their way. Wherever that was. "Where are you taking me, Nick?"

"Somewhere we can be productive."

Rolling her eyes at his evasive answer she asked, "You aren't handing me off to someone else, are you?"

"No."

"Should I plan to cover our asses when Slye comes after us?"

"No."

She murmured, "My next question will be multiple choice."

His lips twitched.

Once he'd had her inside his car, he'd removed the sack on her head and dug into a small Yeti cooler to pull out a beer for her only.

Then he'd driven off as if they were in complete agreement.

Turning the bottle up now, she took a long pull of the refreshing brew, then returned it to the cup holder and snuck a look at Nick.

She found him interesting. Amusing at times, reckless at other times, but always interesting.

He asked, "You said you had the Celtic cross. Do you plan to show up at the main event with it?"

This felt like a negotiation.

She didn't alter her relaxed position, but she pushed her neurons to start firing faster. "That's my plan."

"Would you agree to let Sabrina claim you delivered it upon her request so that she can meet Rikker's demands for Josh?"

Chatton considered her best answer. "A lot of things can happen in the next two days and I don't make a commitment I can't keep."

He tilted his head in acknowledgment.

She needed some idea of where this was going. "What are we doing, Nick?"

"Talking without any interruption or too many people listening."

Nick had snuck her out of Slye's headquarters, but the bag might only have been to protect the integrity of their security. This was the man who had shown fierce loyalty to his team, even in the face of burning the tenuous bridge between her and him.

He would not be taking her off on his own unless ...

Chatton put it together out loud. "Sabrina wanted me out of that building before her CIA lover complicated her life by pushing everyone to hand me over, huh?"

Nick's mouth quirked with a smile. "That's a possibility."

"Now would be a good time for you to tell me what you really want," Chatton suggested, not willing to ride too far from a major airport. "I could have gotten myself out of your headquarters, so you didn't earn any points to repair the damage you did by handing over the name I use."

His smile dropped a couple watts. "Yeah, I'm sorry about that, but now they're sold on believing what you say the way I do." He paused to toss a look her way. "I believe you'll bring the cross—"

"You hope," she quipped, not entirely joking.

"Sabrina will face a shit storm from Gage over me taking you out of there. I need something to show her she had the right gut instinct about you."

Chatton had been dragged into that building and threatened with torture. They might not have said so, but Gage would have squeezed her body through a pasta press to get what he wanted.

Then Nick came bursting into the room like some avenging angel, weapon in hand and demanding they back off.

A *dark* avenging angel.

The vision made her smile.

He noticed and waited.

Sitting up, she said, "Okay, I'm bringing the cross to wherever Rikker tells Sabrina to show up, because his boss will send the same information to me, and I'll say, yes, that Sabrina can claim responsibility for me delivering it—"

"Perfect."

She raised her voice to finish her point. "—as long as nothing arises that forces me to change my decision. That's the best I can offer. Keep in mind that if word leaks out of my being in Atlanta, and especially of my being with all of you in that building, my agreement is off the table."

"Understood. One more thing. We need information on that Amber Room panel, too, something our people won't find out about it, and I could use some help with the scroll."

"That's two things."

"Math wasn't my strong suit."

She doubted he had a weak suit, but let it go. "Do you really think anyone can pull that scroll out of the Vatican now that the pope knows a group of crazies is after it? If it was at all possible to steal it, Rikker's boss would have gotten his hands on it a long time ago. He can't. I can't. You can't."

Nick drove for a while in silence until he was two counties south of the city and pulled off the interstate. As he slowed the car to take a right turn, he asked, "What about the panel? I'll take whatever you can share."

She quickly assessed the fuel plaza he was headed for and yanked her gaze back to him. "You do realize this is a hopeless venture trying to save your friend, right? A suicidal mission."

"Maybe, but I don't have a lot going on right now. Might as well try to rescue him."

Nick had his own brand of wit.

She laughed, and it came out a low, husky sound. Too many years had passed since she'd sounded lighthearted, but Nick woke that part of her. Every time she was around him, she wanted to run off to a private island and play for a month.

No one to kill. No one trying to kill her. No worries.

He'd pretty much crushed that fantasy when he broke her trust under the guise of helping her and Slye.

She wouldn't give him a second chance to do it. "I'll tell you what I can about the panel."

"Fair enough." He pulled through one of the fuel pump aisles that had been arranged on the opposite side of the property from the bigger ones for over-the-road trucks. Place was full of rigs.

He cut the engine. "I'm throwing some gas in this."

"I've gotta hit the loo." She jumped out, taking a moment to admire the lines of the power ride. Sleek, powerful and deadly at high speeds.

Much like its owner.

He'd been on his way round the car to the pump, but stopped when she met him in front of the grill. His arms hung loose at his sides.

He had a look in his eyes she couldn't read. Another thing that made him interesting, but he had a job to do and she had her own itincrary.

Stepping up, she put her hands on each side of his chin and leaned in to kiss him. He cupped his hands at her waist and lifted her closer, letting her know he had a lot more on his mind than filling up the tank.

Damn, but she'd love to take a bite of what he was offering.

Nick had never turned down a gift and kissing Chatton was Christmas ten times over.

He felt taut muscle through her clothes. This was a woman who stayed on her toes to survive. He'd been honest with her about why he'd shared her name, but the truth was that the name Chatton meant nothing and could be found nowhere.

He'd looked.

No, more than looked. He'd had the best that money could buy hunting for her. Nothing. Had he given a false name and she'd agreed, no one in Slye would have believed either of them.

Someone honked at him holding up the line.

He would have kept kissing her, but Chatton pulled back, chuckling. "Don't want that guy to get his knickers in a wad, do you?"

She'd been using words like that either to convince him she was former MI6 or to make him wonder. Classic Chatton. Keep everyone guessing.

She stepped past him. "I'm grabbing snacks, too. What do you want?"

"Gummy bears."

"Now I know your weakness." She winked and took off for the building. Every male standing at the fuel pumps kept track of her.

Nick stuck the nozzle into the tank receptacle.

His phone buzzed. Sabrina had sent him a text. *All good?*

He knew what she was asking, but he didn't have anything definite yet. *So far.*

There was a limit to how far you could push Chatton and he'd already stomped past that point. Once the tank was full, Nick parked the car off to the side and walked into the men's room.

He used the urinal, washed his hands and walked back to his car where a note had been propped against a bag of Gummy Bears on his dash.

The doors were still locked.

He opened his and slid in, then read the note.

I'll consider letting you off the hook for giving away my name, but no promises. I've listed as much as I know about the Amber Room panel at the bottom of this note, including what I know about the two that Rikker mentioned as duds. If it's at all possible, I'll be there with my Celtic cross. If not, then someone else has gotten his hands on it, which of course will happen only if I'm dead.

I'll warn you again this is a fool's errand. If your team shows up without that scroll, you'll be inviting the wrath of Rikker's boss. You have no idea who you're going up against with him. There is no good outcome to any of this. That only happens in fairy tales.

But I realize you're a man who lives by his own code, so I feel certain I'll see you there.

One last tip. The man who gave up his coin to Rikker handed over his ticket to the party and he'll still need one to attend. Good hunting.

C.

He used his phone to photograph the information in the note about the Amber Room panel and emailed it to Dingo. Then he sent a text to Sabrina. *She's in the wind. I sent Dingo everything she gave me. She indicated you may have to yank it away from another treasure hunter.*

Sabrina replied immediately. *Understood. I hope she remembers this when we meet again.*

He did, too.

He would never have agreed with holding Chatton captive. Sabrina surprised him when she put on a show for Gage's benefit to get Chatton out of the room, but she'd realized just as he had that Chatton would have vanished on her own.

Better to have her exist as an ally than an enemy.

Nick was glad not to be at the office when Gage figured out that he'd been outmaneuvered and lost his opportunity to set a tail on Chatton. Sabrina was definitely playing a no-rules game.

Chapter 17

A SHOWER COULD DO wonders, but it couldn't heal a ravaged heart. Sabrina kept seeing Josh racing off to capture Rikker.

She'd never piece herself back together if she lost Josh.

Neither would Dingo.

She'd tried to tell Gage that she would not allow him to slow her down from reaching Josh, and that she was done trying to continue a relationship.

Gage just didn't want to accept it.

He wasn't fooling her with his offer to stay close as a mission partner, but she didn't have it in her to fight him and the world at the same time. She'd been honest to the point it physically hurt to say the words.

What did he think would happen if he stuck it out around her?

That they'd come home one day and play house?

He was a CIA agent through and through. Gage once told her he was glad their relationship worked, because it was the only way he could have one. She knew he cared about her, but he wasn't changing his life and she would never ask that of him.

One day, he wouldn't make it back.

She'd accepted that at one time, before she realized there was a limit to what she was willing to lose.

Her heart seized at the thought of Gage in a cold grave, but she accepted the risks with their jobs. Or she had until this past few weeks. That had started changing even before Josh was captured.

Rikker would keep him alive, but there were many shades of being alive.

"You will die," she whispered, wishing Rikker could hear her. Her throat closed up every time she envisioned how Josh would be treated.

She'd been hoping to take Rikker down once and for all. She'd gone to the meeting knowing she was putting herself out as bait, which she couldn't admit to Dingo.

He'd have been glued to her side day and night.

It might have worked if an Orion Hunter that wanted to kill her hadn't gotten wind of the setup. That one clearly hadn't been trying to cash in on the contract. But other Hunters were. At this point she needed a diagram to keep up with all the players.

Sabrina twisted a tie around her hair, fixing the ponytail at the nape of her neck, not wanting to look at the bruises on her face. A wave of dizziness hit her. She caught the edge of the vanity with one hand and slapped her other hand on the mirror, blinking until her eyes cleared.

That might be from hunger as much as the residual effect of a concussion. She'd keep putting off facing Gage again if she had the time, but that was a luxury item she couldn't afford any time soon.

Pulling on a lightweight, long-sleeved T-shirt that hid her abused arms, she smoothed it down over her jeans and stepped out of the bathroom.

No one in the sitting area.

Noises escaped the small kitchenette, which along with the bed and bathroom made staying at the office for days at a time acceptable.

Her people had additional showers and bedrooms for down time when needed, just not as built out as this space. If need be, the underground floors of this structure could double as a bunker.

Gage called out, "Hungry?"

She found him sitting at her small counter, which boasted two barstools to provide somewhere to eat. He'd made them ham sandwiches and water.

"I couldn't find any chips. Or cold drinks. Who stocks this place for you?" he asked and took another bite of his sandwich.

"Me."

The only answer she got was a grunt.

She took her seat and ate in silence. Surprisingly, he let her, but then he'd always read her moods when life turned into a hellhole. She'd accept his resources for finding Josh, but she had to find a way to keep him far from her after what Rikker had threatened.

Telling Gage right now would start an argument. She'd save that for when it was time to leave this building and go after what she needed to save Josh.

She dumped her empty paper plate in the trash and washed her hands. A shower had given her a surface charge and the food boosted that. She might fall on her face at some point, but at the moment, she would go through anything that stood in her way.

Gage followed her to the war room without a word.

Guilt nagged at her.

The part of her that expected her to stand firm about parting ways warned her not to show a weakness or he'd touch her and she'd fold.

But the part that owed Gage the respect he deserved made her turn around just before she stepped into the war room and whisper, "Chatton's gone."

"What? How did—"

She put a hand on his chest and forced her fingers not to fist his shirt again and pull him close. "I told Nick to take her out of here."

Gage's expression jumped from surprise to confusion until it finally landed on disappointment when he realized she hadn't wanted him to know she was doing it.

He scoffed. "So that's why I got the invitation to your private area?"

Before she came up with a way to fix this, his all-business mask fell into place. She'd seen him do this many times. He withdrew from everything around him, pulling the human parts of him inside his emotional fortress and functioning as a deadly machine.

She'd just never seen that metamorphosis happen because of *her*. Watching it stabbed a sore place inside of her that hadn't healed since making the decision to let go of him.

But she had no right to his emotions.

Accepting her due, she said, "I thought it would be simpler for everyone to let Nick deal with Chatton. She's a resource I need and she was going to leave anyhow. It's better that she departed under good terms than bad."

"Just for the record, you could have trusted me. You might have been surprised if you'd given me a chance to find out more about her first." Gage moved past her and into the war room.

Her shoulders slumped. She was failing everyone who mattered to her.

Tough. Now was not the time to wallow in self-pity.

Shaking off her personal turmoil, she stepped into the room, which had undergone the change she was accustomed to seeing during missions. Monitors had been uncovered around the room. Dingo could work for NASA with his equipment.

This was how her team protected their country.

Since first deciding to enter the covert business in the interest of national security, she'd prided herself on walking a tight line between getting the job done and making a criminal decision. She'd broken rules in the past and would do it again, but this time there was no rule she wouldn't smash if it got between her and reaching Josh.

This time she might just end up an enemy of the state.

Dingo hammered the keys on his laptop, then he stopped to look up at the screen at the rear of the room where they'd all observed Rikker's video earlier.

Tanner stood just behind him, staying in sync with Dingo to watch the laptop action and the monitor on the wall.

White Hawk and Blade were comparing notes on the other side with both of their laptops open and phones lit up as they sent and received texts.

Someone had brought in a tray of sandwiches, snacks, power bars and cheese. Probably White Hawk, who had become friends with Amanda over the past months and was a quick study.

Everyone noticed Sabrina's entrance first then the collective gazes swept to Gage, who kept walking until he'd taken a position in the rear corner again. He leaned back with his arms crossed.

He wouldn't look at her.

No one seemed to notice but her.

She refused to get off track. "Any word on Amanda?"

White Hawk placed her pen on the table. "No change, but they said she's still stable. They intend to keep her in the induced coma for at least another day."

Basically, nothing had changed in three hours since Sabrina had walked out of the hospital. She gave a nod to White Hawk. "Thank you. I spoke to Trish so you and Blade can tell Ryder it's okay to discuss it with her and Bianca," Sabrina said, referencing Ryder's wife who was an FBI agent. Turning to Dingo, she asked, "Where are we?"

"I've printed copies of the details Nick sent about the panel we need, so everyone can make notes."

This time, Sabrina wouldn't look at Gage, who now knew the rest of the team had already been informed of Chatton's status.

Tanner explained, "I've got Soo Jin set up in a place she can communicate with us." His gaze strayed to Gage, then back to Sabrina as he added, "But I don't want anyone to be able to trace it. Dingo is creating some kind of encryption-free, darknet ... thing ... it's uh ... "

Dingo put his face in his hands. "Just stop talking."

Tanner groused, "I don't know what the hell that deep hacking shit is or does."

"Exactly." Dingo dropped his hands and told Sabrina, "I've got this. What he's trying to say is once I have everything set up, we'll be able to host a video conference with Soo Jin where she'll be safe, but I need more time to come up with a way for her to virtually attend the artifact party."

"Understood," Sabrina said. She didn't need to remind Tanner she would protect Soo Jin with all Sabrina had at her disposal. She needed to talk to her team without Gage at some point, to give them a comfort level about having a CIA spook in the middle of this operation.

Blade lifted a finger to take the floor. "Ryder has all but two families secure."

She had a lot of lives depending on her. As long as her people and their families were protected, she could focus all her energy in one direction.

Blade went back to discussing something with White Hawk in a low voice.

Seeing White Hawk willing to work with Blade took away one stress. The young woman would do anything Sabrina asked, but White Hawk had a hellish background. Sabrina tried to never put her in an uncomfortable position with male agents, which is why she'd paired her with Blade. He didn't need to know White Hawk's history. He had a sixth sense when it came to understanding people.

"*Yes!*" Dingo slapped the table.

Everyone jumped and glared at him.

"Shit. Sorry, mates. I have the final link working. Soo Jin should be up any minute now ... "

There she was on the screen, in front of a solid gray background. The mix of Korean and American blood had produced a beautiful woman, but her normally delicate features had been heavily made up to hide the twenty-five-year-old scientist's identity.

Tanner's gaze flicked to Gage, then he asked Sabrina, "He okay?"

"Yes. We have an agreement."

Tanner accepted that without argument. He turned to Dingo. "Is the camera up here yet?"

"Two seconds." Dingo tapped again and a red light came alive on an audio-video unit mounted next to the screen where it could film the room. Dingo looked up and offered a pleasant face. "Hello, Soo Jin."

"It is good to talk to you, Dingo."

"Did you get the notes I sent on the Amber Room panel?"

"Yes, I am prepared."

"Great." He smiled. "You look like you're ready for Halloween, too."

Tanner thumped the back of Dingo's head.

"Ouch. What's your problem?"

Soo Jin smiled and answered for Tanner. "Tanner made his

sister do this to me. When I showed him my makeup earlier, he tried to tell me I was beautiful no matter what I wear on my face."

She had bright red lips, dramatic eye shadow and curly red hair springing in all directions as if a Korean hooker had tried out for playing *Annie*. Not one bit like the porcelain skin and silky black hair in a video Tanner had shown Sabrina after the mission.

The woman's smile flattened with disapproval, then softened with concern. Soo Jin said, "I am sorry to hear about Josh."

Sabrina answered, "Thank you. I appreciate you taking this risk."

"I am safe. I trust Tanner with my life and always want to help the people who stood by him when he saved me."

Tanner only had eyes for her and the rest of the agents were watching the video with expressions of admiration.

Sabrina said, "We need you to tell us as much as you can on the Orion Prophecy."

"That would take a very long time. I have studied what is known as Orion's Prophecy, also known as Orion's Legacy, since I was seven. I can provide you with specifics on different areas and possibly guide you to find more information."

"That would be great." Sabrina lifted the copy of Chatton's notes that were in the pages sitting on the table for her. "We were told there are four panels, but two have been nixed as not being the specific one. According to our source, a panel belonging to a German collector is not the one and a second panel located in Argentina is not the one."

Dingo lifted his hand, and Sabrina nodded for him to talk. "We have people searching for those two panels all over the world. How do we identify the correct one? How big is it? What does it look like? From what little I've figured out, the Amber Room was covered in assorted panels that fit together like a puzzle."

Soo Jin said, "You are correct. The panels were each unique and not all the same size and shape. However, the correct piece will have small words carved into the amber."

"What words?"

"I have never been able to determine that, but the words will be in Latin."

Sabrina wondered who did that. "Was Latin the language of the original artists?"

"Actually, the indigenous people of Prussia spoke Old Prussian, but during the 13th century they began using the Latin alphabet to write their language." Soo Jin explained, "My research indicated a possibility that a descendant of Galileo carved those words."

Dingo frowned. "You think Galileo is behind *all* this?"

"Not necessarily. As far as anyone knows, he wrote *only* his vision, which is known as the *Profezia di Orione* scroll. Unless he left specific directions somewhere else, which would have been difficult with him imprisoned at the Vatican, it is possible he shared his vision with one of his descendants, who then gave Orion's Prophecy life. That is one theory."

Sabrina put a new topic to Soo Jin. "Our source also said a powerful man has a jade artifact. Do you have any idea who that man is?"

"I do not have a name, but the Orion Hunters who forced me to work for them in North Korea often referred to a man in China as their greatest threat. They said he had one of the artifacts and speculated it was the jade tablet. They also had reports that this Chinese man had tried more than once to gain the Amber Room panel."

The whole room went still at the mention of someone in China. When Sabrina finally looked over at Gage, he said, "Let her finish and I'll find out what I can from my Chinese contacts."

He kept his anger hidden, but she knew it was there. The weight of her guilt over shoving Gage aside and now looking to him for help was what she had tried to avoid. But he'd made the choice to be here.

Allowing him to be present while they spoke to Soo Jin should prove she was trying to include him.

She mouthed "thanks" and he nodded.

Scratching his messy hair, Dingo sat back and looked up at Soo Jin. "What's this deadline we've been put on? What makes this week special?"

Soo Jin inclined her head. "That is a very good question. I have encountered references to a possible time frame, but I have never found a specific date or timeline that would mark this week. Tanner says you must reach Mumbai on Monday with the artifacts, but that you will then have to travel to another location. That would seem correct. I have seen nothing that indicates the *Illustratio* will be in Mumbai."

"The *what*?" Dingo asked.

Nodding politely, Soo Jin explained, "The moment of bringing all these artifacts together is known as the *Illustratio*, which is Latin for enlightenment. It is the moment that the prophecy is revealed. There have been rumors that the jade tablet reveals the location and time for bringing all five artifacts together, but without reviewing that tablet I cannot be sure."

"What's so special about that jade tablet?" Tanner asked, his voice warm when he addressed her.

Soo Jin's eyes brightened, so full of passion for him, the hideous makeup couldn't hide it.

Sabrina envied the two of them. Not in a bad way. She was thrilled to see Tanner and Soo Jin end up together, but she wished for just one minute that she could have what they shared.

She risked a look at Gage and caught him staring at her.

No, he hadn't missed that either.

Soo Jin jumped back in, addressing the question about the jade tablet. "It is believed that Genghis Khan had the jade artifact created, which incorporated a portion of his belt buckle. I've read conflicting stories about what the tablet reveals, but I feel a number of consistent elements are probably true." She lifted a hand and pointed at each finger as she spoke. "First, that it contains the actual time and place for the *Illustratio* or it reveals information that directs someone to determine the time and place. Second, that Genghis Khan passed this tablet down to his descendants, whom he expected to carry on his rule, which never happened. Next, it has a reference to the final conflict—"

"Whoa, what reference?" Blade asked, his head lifting from where he'd been bowed over his notes. "I thought this whole thing about five artifacts was to *reveal* a final conflict."

"That is anticipated by some, but I will not know for certain what all this means until I review all five artifacts." Soo Jin lowered her hands. "With any story that is passed down through time from generation to generation, it becomes much like an image copied over and over. The true image remains, but it fractures in places. You must not look at this information the same way you do information for a mission. You must at some point take a leap and go with your instincts."

Sabrina wasn't feeling too favorable about her instincts after almost getting blown to pieces. She asked Soo Jin, "What do you think is written in Latin on the Amber Panel?"

"Think of these pieces as you would a puzzle that you can shape as you place the pieces. Something from each artifact plays a part in revealing the prophecy. They must be positioned in such a way to force the next step."

Sabrina blinked. "I don't understand."

Soo Jin leaned forward, intent on the subject she knew so well. "The artifacts play an active role in the prophecy. Once they are positioned properly they will share the message."

"You think those inanimate objects are going to speak?" Sabrina said, unable to keep her skepticism from showing.

"I am only explaining things," Soo Jin said, sounding embarrassed.

Tanner turned a dark look at Sabrina.

Crap. She'd made Soo Jin feel like an idiot.

Sabrina waved her hands as if washing away that last comment. "I'm sorry, Soo Jin. I'm trying to wrap my head around what we have to do. I don't mean to imply that you are anything less than brilliant, because we all know you are. I just ... I've never faced anything like this before and it feels like I have to play an archaic video game to find the right door."

Soo Jin's chest moved with a deep breath. She nodded, not speaking for a moment, then said, "To be successful, you must open yourself to the possibility that all of this is real, which means you have to look at this the way those who believe do. If you do not, then you will welcome failure."

Dingo piped up. "Basically, when in Rome, do as the Romans.

I get it. We don't have to believe any of this, but we have to understand how these Orion Hunters think and how deeply some crazy guy in China believes in this."

"Yes." Soo Jin nodded quickly.

Tanner put his hand on Dingo's shoulder.

Everything was good again.

Until Sabrina looked at Gage, who had a thoughtful expression as if Soo Jin had said something Sabrina had missed.

Dismissing that, Sabrina said, "Okay, everyone is on board, Soo Jin. Thank you so much. Please keep teaching us."

Dingo's laptop made a ping sound. He glanced over, tapped once, waited, then tapped again rapidly. "Oh, man."

"What is it?"

He lifted the first look of hope to her that Sabrina had seen in his eyes since they both learned Josh was gone. He said, "I got a line on the possible panel, but it's a stretch. Like only a maybe that this is the one."

"Great. Where is it?"

"Uh ... " He glanced at Gage then back at Sabrina. "This intel comes from someone whose identity we can't share. You gave your word."

She shielded a number of identities.

Who had Dingo reached out to that she couldn't mention in front of Gage?

She turned to ask Gage to step out and he was already heading toward her. He stopped in front of her. A muscle twitched in his jaw. "This isn't going to work until you give them ... *him* a reason to make it work."

Gage was saying she had to tell Dingo and her team that they were working as partners. Did he really expect her to stop everything and have a heart-to-heart with Dingo?

Her hesitation must have pushed him over the edge.

He took a slow look around the room and returned to her. "Can't do it, can you?" He dropped his voice so only she could hear. "You know what? I'm done begging. You know how to find me." Then he walked out.

Tanner followed him out of the room.

Their footsteps faded and she waited to see if Gage would change his mind. When the security panel beeped with someone exiting upstairs, she had her answer.

She tried not to be angry, especially not with Dingo, but couldn't everyone work together just once?

"Who is it?" she snapped and Dingo cocked his head at her, frowning.

Shrugging off her irritable tone, Dingo said, "I put word out to everyone as soon as that video ended, even Logan and his *partner*," he emphasized, letting Sabrina know he was talking about Margaux.

Dingo was right. Even without the trust issues between Gage and her team, Sabrina would not have used Margaux's name. She lived off the grid with an international operator known as Logan Baklanov. She told Dingo, "I'm on the same page now."

"Okay. I figured Logan's HAMR Brotherhood has fingers in places all over the world. His partner put everyone she knew on it and made an offer she said would bring the devil out of hell. She just got a hit on a possible Amber Room panel in Switzerland, but it's thin. We can either wait until someone she knows checks it out, which might take a day or more—"

"No."

"Yeah, that was my thought, too."

"Get me the details. Blade, call up the pilot and get the jet ready." When he lifted a hand, signaling he got it, she said, "I'm leaving as soon as I pull my bag together."

"You need backup. I'm coming with you," Dingo claimed.

"No." God no. She couldn't take Dingo even though he had every right to go. She needed him here to run things, but more than that she didn't want to give Rikker anyone else to take. "Please, stay here and figure out a way to get Soo Jin to wherever I have to go without being there physically." She lifted her hand to stall his argument. "You'll meet me in Mumbai when it's time."

Dingo stared at the table. "You can't go out without someone watching your six. You were the one who said we work in pairs."

"I'll have backup," she lied. She was not dragging more of her people into the crossfire.

Dingo cursed and everyone else tried to pretend they weren't listening to the terse exchange.

Gage was right.

Not about everything, but about giving the team a reason to work with him. She said, "Everyone listen up."

Dingo sat back, arms crossed.

"Gage has offered to help in any way he can. He's on leave and he can't do anything on US soil, but you all know we partnered at one time."

That drew a groan from Dingo.

She sliced a shut-up look his way and continued. "We don't risk any security breach on Soo Jin or the rest of our team, but I trust Gage to help us, which means he's in."

Dingo cursed.

Tanner snarled, "Can it. I don't talk like that around Soo Jin."

Sabrina realized poor Soo Jin had been watching all of this. Addressing the love of Tanner's life, she said, "Soo Jin, please don't hesitate to give us anything you think we need to know. No one, especially me, will think it's insignificant. Everything you've shared is of great value."

Before Soo Jin started talking again, Sabrina told Dingo, "Send me everything as you get it so I stay up to speed."

He grumbled a yes in her direction then told Soo Jin, "Valene is on her way here. She wants to help and she has a background in rare artifacts."

Soo Jin's face bloomed with happiness. "I have missed my friend. Yes, we will work together."

Dingo had been tapping keys and paused to ask Sabrina, "Logan and you-know-who are busy with something at the Kremlin and can't break away. Let me see if one of Logan's guys can be your backup, 'cause Gage left here like he was done with us."

"I don't think that's the case." Lie. That was exactly the case. "But that's a good idea." Sabrina considered contacting Gage to see if he had anyone who could confirm whether this was the correct panel before she got there since he had the ability to reach out to CIA agents and intelligence sources across the world.

But he'd want to go with her and that couldn't happen.

She hadn't wanted him to leave angry, but she hadn't forgotten Rikker's threat to kill him, and she needed to tell him about that. Having Gage leave on his own might be the best way to keep him away from Rikker for now.

She wasn't sure he'd even listen to her once she told him. He'd probably accuse her of using that as an excuse to push him away. She didn't want to think about how close to the truth that might be, but neither did she want him harmed.

Dingo paused, staring at the screen. "Well, shit."

"What?"

He ran a hand over his head as if he hoped to change what he was reading. "Nitro can be your ground man, but he has to disengage from something he's doing for Logan that might run him late meeting you at the airport."

"I'll work with it. Do me a favor and ask Valene if she can get another reproduction of the scroll made up."

Soo Jin spoke up. "This man who holds the jade tablet will know if it is a reproduction. These people, the Orion Hunters and others who believe, are not easily fooled."

"I understand, and that confirms the statement of another resource. I have a backup plan." Sabrina turned to Dingo. "Just ask her."

"I will."

Sabrina walked out with a sick feeling in her stomach. Couldn't she do one thing right? First she let Gage leave on bad terms.

Now she'd pissed off Dingo.

Gage was making a point, that her team would never trust him until she showed her trust in him.

She had no argument for that, but it wasn't the entire truth. She'd put her life in Gage's hands many times and would do it again, just not with Dingo or Josh's lives on the line. Gage believed everyone was expendable when it came to her safety.

She believed just the opposite and didn't want to be put in a position of choosing their safety over his.

"Sabrina?" Dingo called out softly from behind her. The

sadness in Dingo's voice churned her sick stomach, but she turned to him with an open face.

"I'm an asshole."

She smiled and gave him the reply she'd used back when they were kids and he'd been a jerk. "Yes, but you're our asshole."

He pulled her into a hug and she was feeling better until he said, "I never want to hurt you, but you trusted that CIA bastard once and he's still protecting whoever burned us. I need you and Josh both back. Don't let your guard down around someone who's holding back from you."

What would Dingo say if she told him that Rikker alluded to Gage having *three* names he could share. Then again, Chatton had Sabrina thinking the person who sold them out might not have been agency. Who was telling the truth?

None of that mattered. She'd started down this road to stop Rikker once and for all. Nothing had changed. If anything, she was more determined than ever to take him down.

She didn't want any of her people with her when it happened. Not even Gage.

That probably was no longer an issue. Gage could walk into a crowd and never be found again.

Chapter 18

Near Baoding, China

WAYAN SAT AT his desk, a Huanghuali altar table passed down from his ancestors of the Ming Dynasty. He spent his Sunday morning reviewing every detail of the most important step he would ever take in his life. This upcoming week carried too much importance for him to be tied up with any task in Beijing.

The president had granted him six days to spend at his home, a seventy-minute helicopter flight from his office in the capital city. At least it was the capital for now.

After 700 years, leadership wanted to change the location of the capital.

If all went as Wayan planned, that decision would fall entirely to him.

The president believed Wayan required a medical procedure that would be performed in an outpatient facility near his home. All Wayan had to do was mention prostate and the men in his circle immediately understood. They thought he lived as they did.

He would never treat his body so poorly.

As he had never requested a day away from his duties since the age of twenty when he began the climb to his position, the time off was granted without question.

Wayan tuned back in to the man before him, who had been allowed all the leeway Wayan would grant.

If Rikker did not complete his story soon, he might need medical assistance.

Wayan had never been known for patience.

He sat back and steepled his fingers, making no comment or indication of his frame of mind. He merely waited as Rikker attempted to present his failure in America as a success.

Sport coat unbuttoned, thirty-six-year-old face shaved except for a chin beard and dull brown hair styled for a photo shoot, Rikker sat relaxed, confident now that he'd returned to China. He believed the plan he'd formulated to make good on the tasks Wayan had assigned would now protect him from repercussion.

Many proverbs about fools came to mind.

Sharing even one with this man would be a waste of precious breath.

Rikker finally wound down. "Basically, we have what will motivate Sabrina Slye to deliver Soo Jin, the Amber Room Panel and the scroll. Easy peasy."

Had he just said ... *easy peasy*?

Whom did he think he addressed?

Wayan continued to observe Rikker, who killed for pleasure. A trait Wayan valued, as it meant Rikker's conscience would never be an obstacle to overcome.

Settling against his high-back chair, Wayan asked, "What is your plan if Sabrina fails to deliver even one item?"

Rikker's face lost the jovial expression of one who'd been riding an emotional high but who suddenly realized his horse might be lame. "She won't. She'll hand over everything she owns for Josh Carrington, including her own life."

"While that loyalty is admirable, it still does not provide adequate insurance that she will be successful."

Rikker started to squirm.

Wayan had finally gained his undivided attention.

It is hard for a fool to pay attention when enamored of his own value. Wayan said, "The day of enlightenment is not a moment in time that can be captured again. I have not worked this hard and for this long to allow mistakes by others to undermine the plan."

Rikker huffed a sigh of disgust. "I've done everything you've asked of me. All of it. I would have brought the scroll back if I'd gotten my hands on it, but someone was helping that bunch in California. In fact, I'm pretty sure there's a leak somewhere. I had it all under control until Sabrina's team got way too lucky. If you think back, their luck has been running strong this past year. I can do anything you ask, as long as no one on the inside is working against me."

This assassin had proven to be quite useful. Until this incident, Wayan believed he'd chosen well, which forced him to consider Rikker's words.

Sabrina Slye and her people had interfered too many times in the past year for it to be coincidental.

Beyond that, Wayan didn't believe in coincidence.

Had someone who knew him thought to interfere? All things happened according to *someone's* plan. Had that someone perhaps been The General ... or Chatton?

He told Rikker, "I will take this theory of a leak under consideration."

Relief rushed through Rikker's face. He sat forward again. "I'm glad. I really believe what I put in motion with Sabrina Slye will work or I wouldn't have left the US. We're still good on our agreement, right?"

Wayan replied with the chilling edge that let others know he'd been insulted. "I have never broken my word. Just as I stated, if all five artifacts arrive on time, Soo Jin is available to translate the information, and you complete the final task at the appropriate time, you will be free to leave and the money I offered will be transferred into your account."

"Great." Rikker stood up. "I'm going to keep an eye on The General, continue hunting for the Amber Room Panel *and* someone to access the scroll. I'm not finished making good on my part of this just because I'm back and I sent Sabrina after these things."

"Allow no one to know about your prisoner."

"No chance. Carrington is locked up tight."

"You are clear about what I want done with him as long as he is our prisoner?"

"No question."

Once Rikker departed through the private entrance Wayan

required him to use, the air in the room no longer carried the weight of fear. Wayan informed his assistant he was not to be disturbed during the next hour.

His humble home had been constructed during the Han dynasty with elaborate gardens, but none so magnificent as the one which held the small, open-air temple reserved for his private retreat. Working his way through the beautifully maintained gardens, he reached his son, who wore the thirteenth-century robe passed down by an ancestor.

The one whose decree Wayan had dedicated his life to fulfilling.

His son kneeled in front of the shrine with his head bowed in respect. Wayan addressed Temüjin, "Rise, my son. I wish to speak with you."

As Temüjin stood to his six-foot-one height, he towered over Wayan. He bowed and addressed his father with respect. "*Sifu.*"

Family had once admonished Wayan. for not encouraging Temüjin to take up basketball.

Simple-minded fools.

His son carried the blood of the most feared warrior in his genes. It would never be wasted on a foolish American sport.

Wayan asked, "Are you prepared?"

"I am. I feel the power of my great ancestor flow over me as I speak to him. I come as the humble student of his skills and hard-fought victories. I have studied the message on the tablet thoroughly and I am prepared to do my duty."

Wayan's gaze went to the jade tablet he considered the most valuable of the five artifacts required to reveal Orion's Prophecy. Carved into this tablet were the words of the most powerful warrior of all time.

Genghis Khan, born Temüjin, had been visionary in many ways, and ruthless in his plan to rule the world. And his followers had cheered him on.

This world had never seen another ruler such as he.

Wayan had inherited this tablet along with the responsibility to deliver the world the descendant of Khan, who would take up the sword to rule as Khan had. Wayan's father and grandfather had taught him that nothing was more important than duty.

They gave up much to see that Wayan would one day be in a position to fulfill Khan's prophetic words by fathering a leader as great as Khan.

Perhaps greater.

Wayan's father had sustained an injury in battle, and years later, had still suffered. Yet he'd held onto life long enough to see his grandchild, Temüjin, born. Upon hearing that Wayan's son had entered this world on the same day as the great Genghis Khan and in the same way, clutching a bloody clot, Wayan's father had finally released his hold on this realm.

Now Wayan's son would take up the sword and fight for his people just as his revered ancestor had. Wayan had spent his entire life inserting himself deep inside the Chinese government where his word would be unquestioned when the time came.

Where he could pave the way for the next ruler.

That time had arrived. He'd watched his son grow into a man of twenty-three who would be a formidable leader.

The people followed strength.

One look at this powerhouse who stood before Wayan, and the world would know a new leader unlike any other since the days of Khan.

It had been written in the stars that Khan would defeat all enemies, no matter how great the battle.

And Temüjin would succeed where all others had failed to make China great.

Seeing the product of a lifetime of devotion standing before him, Wayan felt the closest he had ever come to being truly humbled.

Turning, Wayan said, "Walk with me."

His son stayed perfectly in step, never forcing his father to hurry his steps.

Wayan said, "Soon all will look to China as the greatest power on earth and cower when this country's shadow falls upon them. I have waited many years as the sign for Orion's Legacy came and went as you prepared. Now is the time for the fulfilling of the prophecy."

Just as the ancient Temüjin's words carved into the jade proclaimed, *When the soldier rises in the sky upon the day of his birth and the moon hides from sight, the final conflict will be at hand.*

Wayan's ancestor had been a brilliant battle strategist whose success had depended upon outthinking his enemies. Genghis Khan had encountered many obstacles, much like those Wayan had faced over the years as he cleared bodies from the path to make way for the new Temüjin.

Two more stood in the way.

Their days were numbered.

Wayan had waited long enough. It was time for Orion's Prophecy to reveal the victor in the greatest war this planet would ever see.

The army of Orion Hunters he had built stood ready to support their new leader.

The blood of Khan would rise again to defeat its enemies that covered the earth.

Chapter 19

SABRINA WAITED NEXT to her car for Darron, one of the crew for her private jet. He handled galley duties just as easily as his 9mm. He walked over to tell her they were close to going wheels up, and took her overnight bag, heading back to the jet.

With another look at her watch and no sign of a returned message from Gage, her hopes of getting his help in clearing her way through Switzerland weren't looking good.

The pilot and crew were busy overseeing last minute details. She'd given her people barely a half hour notice to go wheels up by eleven tonight.

That was as much as she could spare. Enough time for Gage to have returned her call and text by now.

Why should he, after you told him to get out of your life?

She pinched the bridge of her nose and locked the car, too tired to argue with an irritating conscience. Yes, she'd told him that, but it was as much for him as for her.

He said losing her for two years had gutted him.

She'd fared no better while she'd healed her team and suffered through the belief that Gage had tossed her to the wolves in exchange for one of their agents.

Hoisting her weapons bag, she decided to think positively about pulling off the impossible in Switzerland and making it to Mumbai on Monday night. With a little time to plan, she'd clear her own path through each country, but she'd inserted internationally enough to know glitches happened.

She had no time for any snag.

She climbed the steps to her Gulfstream G2 and took a couple of deep breaths to push off the weariness sinking into her bones.

She'd sleep before landing in Zürich tomorrow—that would be around three in the afternoon local time Sunday—but first, she had work to do.

Once on board, with her bags stowed in the aft sleeping area and her laptop set up, she asked Darron, "Would you make a pot of coffee?"

"Right away. The pilot said we're cleared to leave." Darron turned to the galley as angry voices erupted at the steps to the cabin door. He turned to Sabrina. "Are you expecting anyone, Ms. Slye?"

"Yes, she is and you're holding up the flight," yelled Gage from outside.

Her heart jumped to her throat. If she said no, it would start an argument and deny her what she needed from him.

"Yes, you can let him on."

Gage boarded and Darron moved out of the way.

Sabrina called out, "I'm sorry, Darron. Please tell the pilot to give me a moment so we can talk."

Gage shook his head. "Might as well tell him to take off. I'm not leaving."

They had another stare down and she gave in. "Darron, please tell them we're ready to roll."

"Will do."

She waited for Gage to complete the walk to where she sat on one of the sofas. "You could have returned my call."

He dropped his duffel on the floor and plopped down in a recliner next to her. "I could have, but I was waiting on a new phone to power up. I didn't want to call you on my old one."

She got a closer look at his face. His stoic mask hid something that bothered him. What had happened in the short time since she'd last seen him?

Why had he picked up a new phone? A burner? "What's happened, Gage?"

The engines powered up as she waited for him to reply.

He stretched, groaning, then sat back. "I told you I had two people I trusted. One went missing this morning. She was found hanging by a hook rammed through her back. Someone tortured her before she died."

Sabrina waited as Gage got past some dark thought that tore through his gaze. He said, "They burned a set of marks into her face that resembles the scars on the Orion Hunter."

"I ... that's awful, Gage." She considered moving over to take his hand, but she'd be giving him a mixed message. She couldn't expect Gage to understand her let's-not-do-this attitude if she couldn't abide by her own hands-off rules.

But holding back from touching him gnawed a hole in her stomach.

She'd lost track of anything beyond Gage when the pilot announced they were next in line. The jet picked up speed, rushing down the runway and catching air.

Gage dropped his head back in the plush recliner and closed his eyes.

She'd thought he'd fallen asleep by the time they'd climbed out of the pattern and leveled off, but he turned his head to her and said, "The last thing I heard from my contact was early this morning when she sent me a lead on who had you. She's the reason I found you."

Rikker had intentionally fed that information so that it would reach Gage, which could point to Rikker knowing about one of the two people Gage trusted.

She asked, "What about your other one?"

"I heard from my second person while I was at your headquarters. He's the one who alerted me to Perdido and Navarro being hit, but ... I haven't been able to reach him in the last hour. I didn't want to risk any chance of someone following my phone to him. I'll try him another way once we're on satellite."

Sabrina took in the words, trying to make them sound different. Trying to stay upright under the blanket of guilt shrouding her, but avoiding the truth didn't make it any less true. He'd been tapping them to find her.

She started to say, "I'm sorry," but the pitifully inadequate words stuck in her throat.

Gage had once told her, *Don't apologize for doing your job and don't take the burden of someone else's decision. We live in a dangerous world. People die. Unless you killed them without orders or for another reason than self-defense, you have nothing to apologize for. Even if you did, the dead can't hear you and the living won't care.*

He sat there studying her, his gaze neither condemning nor consoling. "I didn't tell you to make you feel responsible, Sabrina."

She believed him, but she still asked, "Why *did* you tell me?"

Gage pushed up until he was sitting forward and rubbed his bloodshot eyes. He propped his elbows on his knees. "I told you because I can't get through to you that this is all bigger than anything we can imagine. No one knew about Contact Victor." He hunched his shoulders. "That's what I called her to protect her."

"Did she know your other person?" Sabrina prompted, curious to see if he'd share more.

"Yes. My second one is Contact Papa. He's been trying to find a connection between the people who knew about your busted op in the UK and the person we're now looking for."

She flinched over the word *we*.

This would be a good time to admit that she knew there were three names, or so Rikker had claimed. Knowing Rikker, he'd only said that to amp up the tension between her and Gage. He could have been talking bullshit.

Gage scowled and shook his head. "Whether you want to accept it or not, I *have* been working just as hard as you and your people to find the smoking gun in all this. It's just as important to me to hang the person in our government who screwed you as it is to you. The more these pieces come together on all this, the more it makes my blood chill."

She didn't realize she'd leaned forward until she could make out every hair in his eyebrow. It lifted into a sarcastic tilt.

He said, "You called. So now you want my help? Me, the person you don't trust until you need me. Oh, wait, you still don't trust me. You just trust my skills and resources."

Bitter much? He had cause to be, but she hadn't meant for things to turn out so badly between them.

She sat back and stared up at the tiny lights concealed along the roof of the fuselage, searching for some way to make this trip less miserable.

No help there.

Dropping her gaze to Gage, she prodded him to be honest. "Tell me you wouldn't have put a tail on Chatton the minute she left if you'd been informed in advance."

He opened his mouth and she lifted her eyebrows, daring him to lie.

"What harm would that have done?" He sounded as angry as he'd looked when he walked on board.

"None, if she didn't make your tail, but Nick believes she would have." Sabrina jumped back to the topic she was willing to eat her pride to get an answer on. "Have you got any ideas on who's behind this?"

"Not yet."

"When you do, will you share?"

He just stared at her in a way that made her want to squirm for asking him to reveal what he had when she'd kept her decision about Chatton from him. But she didn't regret doing that. Yet.

"Have you changed your mind about working together?" That was probably the wrong thing to say to him after she'd tossed up wall after wall to keep them apart, but she was desperate.

He revved up his stare to a lethal one like those she'd once laughed at, daring him to make good on the threat in that look.

Never challenge someone like Gage unless you were ready for the consequences.

Years back, he'd returned one night after no contact for five weeks, and she'd sent him away, in turmoil over her feelings for him. He'd teased her that he could make her beg him to stay.

She scoffed, declaring she would never beg a man for anything.

He'd taken the dare. No torture could have made her fold, but Gage's sensual lovemaking that night had brought her to her knees. Then he'd given her everything she wanted ... and more.

But now? His jaw squared even more with taut muscles. He sucked in a deep breath and let it out slowly, watching her, and holding back something feral that slept in that gaze.

She'd never backed away from him. "Well?" she prodded.

Another slow blink passed as he decided on something. "We

have nine hours until we land in Zürich. I haven't slept in the last thirty-eight. You don't look like you've had any more than I have. I can't think of a thing we can be doing that your team isn't already working on. I'm catching some rest, then I'll talk. I suggest you do the same."

With that he leaned back and shut his eyes.

If she'd had any question of Gage's temper, that answered it. He'd run himself into the ground on missions, but on the few occasions they had rows—and there had been some spectacular ones—he'd always shut down for a short time and tackle the issue once he'd recharged.

She stopped trying to explain it away in her mind and accepted the truth.

He was the one pushing her away this time.

Gage had always been a slow burn. He could kill faster than someone blinked, but he did so with reason, clarity and commitment. She'd always thought that came from his iron control. If he had to hurt someone physically, or use deadly force, he was absolutely sure it was necessary.

Tangling with a cobra would be smarter than crossing Gage Laughton. Trying to outplay him would be laughable.

That he'd shown up in time to leave with her said he would help, in some form.

She needed him to clear the path in Europe more quickly than she could. And if she were entirely honest, she did want a partner on this trip. Gage had been wrong. She did trust him to do what he said and to be there when she needed him.

She just didn't know if she could spend this much time with him and stick to her principles, starting with not touching him if she didn't intend to stay with him.

Of course, as pissed as he was with her, that shouldn't be a problem.

Acknowledging that fact caused her heart to squeeze painfully.

Chapter 20

GAGE CAME FULLY awake in the recliner, orienting to the sounds around him. The engine hum told him he was still thousands of feet in the air inside a luxury Gulfstream G2.

He checked his watch—they'd been in the air forty minutes. Moving slowly, he stretched his stiff neck from where he'd leaned his head over to sleep. It always seemed like a good idea to snooze in one of these cushy recliners, but your spine would eventually let you know it was not happy.

Someone had tossed a blanket over him. He slid it down and sat up.

Sabrina had fallen asleep on the sofa with the laptop open.

Rubbing his face to get some circulation going, he stood, took note of the open door to the bedroom in the back and scooped her up.

She muttered something, reminding him of the sleep of death she'd fall into only around him.

That kind of trust, at least, had never been an issue between them.

Moving around in an airplane, even one as comfortable as this one, was never simple. He slipped sideways into the bedroom and placed her on one side of the bed that looked pretty damned inviting.

Once he had her shoes off, he flipped the light switch off. A string of lights around the baseboard offered just the right glow so that he could see his way around ... and see her.

After closing the door and kicking his shoes out of the way, he stretched out on his side next to her and watched as each soft breath lifted her blouse up and down.

How many nights had he spent just staring at her as she slept? She'd once told him she went into deep sleep only when he was close by.

That hadn't happened in over three years now.

God, he wanted her. Not just the sex, but yeah, okay, he did want that. What man staring at this woman wouldn't?

He wanted her so much it was painful to be this close and not touch her, but things had been difficult enough before California. He got that she'd been pissed at how hard he'd leaned on Dingo out there, but how else was he to determine that someone close to her hadn't been setting her up for a bullet?

His greedy conscience latched onto that and rode his neck hard, pointing out that right before he'd caused the rift with her and Dingo, she'd been willing to try to be together again.

She wanted him, *them*, as much as he did.

It could have happened. *Might* have if he hadn't hammered on Dingo so hard. The minute that Aussie bailed out to protect Valene Eklund, Sabrina began withdrawing.

Just like his sister Sarah had.

A suave German had spent seven months getting inside Sarah's confidence. She'd been an FBI analyst who loved too easily. Gage had warned her he didn't like the guy. She threw it in his face, saying he didn't like anyone and that she'd researched the law student.

That had been the first red flag for Gage.

The German's background had been too clean. Sarah argued that Gage had no reason to criticize who she dated other than Gage's need to be a control freak.

Gage closed his eyes.

He'd lost Sarah by pushing her when he should have backed off, and then by backing off at the wrong time. She'd trained in kickboxing and handled a gun like a pro.

But she also had a knack for destructive relationships.

Beautiful and sharp, she'd kept her emotions locked down just as tightly as Gage did. A year behind him, she'd watched him work his way up in his former agency, the FBI. She'd been determined to prove her own value, when he already thought she was amazing. She'd been every bit that independent since she'd turned ten years old, which was when their parents were killed in a convenience store robbery.

In the wrong place at the wrong time.

When he buried Sarah, he turned his focus to entering the CIA and waited for his opportunity. Once he'd made field agent, Gage tracked down the German *student*. Eventually he'd discovered that the bastard was an undercover operative and contract assassin sent to discover what the FBI knew about his client's US operation after it had suffered busts. Sarah apparently returned home unexpectedly to find her boyfriend hacking her computer.

At that point, the man simply disposed of Sarah as he would any other interference.

It should have felt good to kill him, but it hadn't.

Sarah was still gone.

Sabrina murmured something and his eyes snapped open. She rolled toward him, still asleep.

He reached out to brush his hand over her hair, but pulled it back.

Sarah had told him all the time that he'd end up alone. That he was too much of a cynic to open his heart to anyone. That he'd never risk caring as deeply as she did.

He'd believed her.

Until Sabrina.

The first time he'd been sent to scope out Sabrina, he'd almost told the agency no. He'd been attracted to her from the get-go and had no room in his life for an agent who distracted him. But he couldn't do it. She'd come highly recommended and it was clear that she ran a tight team of well-qualified operatives.

So he'd brought her in—only Sabrina at first—to see how she handled herself in the field. Looking back, spending that much time together had been his first mistake.

He'd been so sure he could maintain the icy exterior he was known for.

Eight months later, they'd barely escaped capture at the hands of a black market weapons dealer in Croatia. They'd been forced to spend two days hiding out while waiting on transportation Gage could trust to smuggle them out.

Two days.

In a tiny hotel room.

During the winter when the power failed.

A monk couldn't have resisted that temptation. He'd known she was not a woman who shared her body easily, which made her all the more desirable.

His gaze swept over her sleeping form, every sweet inch of her.

No longer able to resist the temptation, he stroked his hand over her hair and ran his fingers down to her shoulder, now bare where the shirt had slid off.

Her eyelashes fluttered and slowly opened.

She stared up at him.

He waited, expecting her to snap at him for being here on the bed, touching her. A wise man would pull his hand back and apologize for taking a liberty. He considered it and discarded the idea. A wise man would never have taken a risk that night in Croatia.

If that meant he lost a few IQ points, so be it.

She'd been worth it then and she was worth it now.

"What's going on, Gage?" Her husky, sleep-thickened voice stirred the beast sleeping in his pants.

"Just lying here admiring the most beautiful woman I've ever known."

Her gaze softened and he held his breath to see if the Sabrina he'd missed would come out to play. He smiled, just enough to let her know he was happy to be right here, right now, next to her.

She smiled back, but it drifted off into a sad smile. "I'm too tired to ..."

"What?"

She moved a hand over her eyes. "I'm too tired to argue."

He stopped stroking her arm and said, "What's to argue about? Are you saying you don't want me in here?"

Dropping her hand away from her face, she kept her eyes on him as she sorted through whatever went on underneath all that sinful, black hair.

He loved everything about her.

Loved?

He shook it off. She was far more than just sex, but he couldn't offer her all that went along with the word love. He'd never have that life, but it didn't change how much he wanted to be in her life, and have her in his, in some capacity. She'd said time and again she wasn't cut out for any kind of normal relationship.

Why couldn't they have abnormal?

She didn't want to wait at home for him. *So come with me.*

She'd been willing to meet him halfway until she'd returned from LA, and now this mess with Josh kept driving her further away.

The only way to defeat an enemy was to face it.

Her fear was his enemy and he would win that battle.

Time slipped out of his hands too fast. He would not have a better chance to take another step with her like this one.

He started with a simple negotiation. "Do you want me to leave? Just say yes or no." *Please say no.*

"No."

His fingers had been sweeping along her arm so he kept it up. He had to be careful, but he wanted more. "Do you want me to stop touching you?"

"No."

Two for two.

He considered all the things he could ask and chose the simplest. "What do you want?"

She watched him through soft eyes. "I want a life where my choices only affect me, but I didn't get that one."

"Let's narrow it down." He leaned in closer. "What do you want right this moment?"

Heat smoldered in her gaze. She licked her lips and his cock thumped. Lowering his voice, he urged her, "Say it, Sabrina. Tell me what you want."

"I can't do that to you," she whispered, sounding disappointed.

Oh, please, do it to me. "Why not?"

"It won't change anything, Gage. When we land in Zürich, I'll still be the person I was when I climbed on this plane. I can't ... I *won't* make love with you when nothing has changed about our situation. You have a file on me, but you really don't know me —"

"Yes. I. Do. I know you."

"Not really. You have no idea how far I'll go to bring Josh home."

"And I'll be right there with you." He silently finished, *making sure you don't end up dead.*

"I'm not going to continue a relationship like before." She sounded exasperated with him. "The life I've chosen shaped me into someone who—"

"Dammit, Sabrina." He anchored his hand on her shoulder and kissed her, holding on for dear life. When he leaned over the top of her, his tongue delved inside her mouth, doing a tango with hers.

Man, he'd missed this woman. His woman. Something about her brought out his caveman genes.

She put her hand on his chest with a gentle push. "Wait."

He dropped his forehead to hers. "Why?"

"I care about you, but I don't think—"

"Stop," he ordered and lifted his head to look at her.

"Stop what?" Her lips were a rosy pink from his bruising kiss. Her surprised eyes searched his face.

"Stop thinking. Just feel. I don't give a damn what happens after this airplane lands. I'm with you to the end of this with Rikker and Josh. I'll worry about tomorrow if we're both alive to see it, but this is the first time in over three years that I have you alone. So, let go of your discipline for a while and forget about why we can't be together when we *are* together right now."

Longing filled her face and her fingers clutching his arms tightened.

He brushed his hands over her cheeks. "Give me this moment. No, give this to *us*. We deserve it. Tomorrow will sort itself out."

"Only a selfish woman would take what you offer now with no promise of continuing."

"It's about time you did something for yourself. In fact, I'll be honest. I'm feeling a bit self-centered, too." He grinned and kissed her nose, then her cheek, and brushed his lips over hers. "In fact, I'm leaning toward taking advantage of you in more ways than you can imagine."

He ran his fingers under her shirt and hot damn, she didn't have a bra on. Even better, her nipples were hard little buds. He scraped his finger across one.

She sucked in a sharp breath. "*Gage!*"

"Oh, you're right. I can't leave the other one wanting." He kissed her and shifted his body so that he could cup the other breast and massage it gently, moving his fingers until he almost touched her nipple.

She trembled. "Gage!"

He deepened the kiss, toying with her breast. He lifted his palm and moved it over the tip. She shook harder. Her fingers dug into his biceps and he grunted.

She had strong hands.

His cock ached and rubbing against her was the craziest mix of pain and joy. Grabbing the bottom of her shirt, he lifted it, then dropped his mouth to take in her breast and suck on it with pleasure.

Sliding the zipper open on her jeans, he pushed his hand inside, moving the jeans out of the way, finding lace and silk instead.

He kissed his way down to her panties and pushed them out of the way of the one place he called home. With one lick of his tongue, she shuddered.

"Gage?" Her voice had narrowed to a shallow sound. He didn't care that she could only get out one word as long as it was his name in that pleading voice.

"What, sweetheart?"

"Don't ... "

He paused, suffering the battle going on inside him between needing her and doing whatever she said, even if she wanted him to stop. She hadn't been a tease. He'd pushed this so it was on him, but he would not make it easy for her to turn her back on him this time. He ran his tongue across her folds again and asked, "Don't what, sweetheart?"

"Oh my—" She panted, chest heaving to draw a breath. "Oh, hell. Don't stop."

Two words and his world came into focus.

Instead of saying another word, he put his tongue to better use proving he had no intention of pulling back now. He knew every inch of this body and every hot button pleasure point.

And he planned to find new ones.

He pushed a finger inside while his tongue teased her, pushing her to forget about everything but him. Her legs clamped tight against him and she arched.

Yeah, that. He wanted her to live right now in this moment, to remember how good they were together. How she made his life something worth having, forced him to do whatever it took to make it back to her every time he walked into the mouth of hell to save someone or stop a threat.

He inhaled her sweet smell, watching for the moment the world fell away and she'd soar.

She twisted the sheet in her fists and panted.

Damn, she was driving him crazy. *Come on, baby. Let go.*

Her body trembled. She cried out and he gave half a thought to the flight attendant, only because of her. That guy should be in the galley area where he'd stay until called upon.

Gage never let up until Sabrina's legs fell open, muscles spent.

He kissed his way back up to her breasts. Both of them clearly missed him by the way they perked up. Sabrina groaned, "I'm wiped out."

"You've got more to give."

She lifted her head and eyed him. "Aren't you going to participate?"

"Soon as I find a condom."

"We don't need one."

That's right. In their line of work, a woman would never go into the field without being on contraceptives.

Remembering that twisted his insides.

But she was soft and warm and welcoming right now so he shoved that black thought away and leaned down to kiss her. She dropped her head back on the bed, watching him so much like that first time. Her hungry eyes darkened right before he kissed her.

This woman still knocked him on his ass, just as she had in Croatia. One kiss had ignited a desire that he'd never quench any more than a man staked in the desert could ever have enough water.

He enjoyed the feel of need coming from her.

Damn, he'd waited too long to feel her again. To have her back in his arms.

"Why am I the only one half naked?" she asked, eyebrows lifting.

He peeled his shirt off and she reached for his zipper. He pushed his jeans down and out of the way.

When her hand snuck between their bodies and curled around his hard cock, every muscle in his body went taut with trying to hold back. "Oh, baby, give me a minute."

"Right." She chuckled. She actually fucking chuckled.

Evil vixen.

She stroked him once and he shuddered this time.

Her voice came to him on a dark whisper. "Ready to feel that inside me?"

Holy hell. Sweat beaded across his forehead. "You have to ask?" He reached up and cupped a breast, terrorizing the hard tip with his thumb.

She cursed, which was funny. She rarely cursed and never that lividly. Then she reached further down and cupped his sack. He stopped all movement and gritted his teeth. It had been ... too damn long.

Even when he had no idea that he'd ever see her again, he'd had no interest in any other woman.

Moving back out of her reach, he pushed into her slick folds and eased inside her.

Home. This was the definition of going home.

She gripped his arms and he kept pushing until he bumped her womb.

Heat and chills raced up his chest from his groin at the incredible feel of her clutching him.

He held himself still until he had a grip on his control. Pulling back slowly, he stopped before pulling out.

She was breathing as if she'd just done a two-mile sprint and looking at him with worry in her eyes. "Gage?"

This was the moment he could get her to agree to anything, but he'd never use that power over her. When she came to him, it would be because she wanted to stay with him as much as he had to be with her.

Anything less would not be enough for either of them.

He pushed in an inch and her nails dug in. Then he lowered his mouth to hers, pausing to say, "You are the most amazing woman I have ever known. I want you. I always want you and I'm not letting go."

She stared at him, uncertainty in her gaze, but that was okay. He'd seen it before during their early days together. He'd keep at her until she remembered why she'd made the decision to be with him. Why she needed him the way he needed her.

He drove into her hard and kissed her at the same time, burning for her and damned determined to make it impossible for another man to even attempt to fill his shoes.

Time disappeared. He picked up his pace and she met his every stroke. She arched and clutched him to her, then she reached that pinnacle again, calling his name until she was hoarse. Their damp bodies smacked together and the sweet smell of her release circled in the air.

Gage couldn't hold back any more. Energy coiling inside of him exploded and he let it flow over him until he was light-headed. Hot damn, that was ... incredible.

Better than the first time and that was saying something.

Drained dry, he flopped on his back and brought her with him. Her limp body draped across his chest. How much would he have traded to have her like this in the past three years?

Everything he owned. A limb.

That was not an exaggeration.

Sabrina put her forearms on his chest and lifted up. Her face had the soft afterglow of making love. He didn't have to ask her if it had been good for her. With a little time and more room to move, he'd like to repeat some of the more creative ideas she'd had in the past.

She was the hottest thing on two legs when she wanted to get rowdy and have crazy sex, but once they were finished she hit a whole different level of desirable.

The kind a man fell in love with and had no qualms about admitting it. *Whoa.* But what if?

He regretted one thing most about losing his sister. They'd been raised by a stern uncle too old to be saddled with kids, and the word love hadn't been part of his vocabulary. Sarah accused Gage of being like him.

She'd been right. He'd failed to tell his sister he loved her when he'd had the chance.

But now wasn't the time to try it out.

"Hello, gorgeous," he told Sabrina, happier than he'd been in a very long time.

She propped her chin on her stacked hands. "Hey, you bad boy."

That brought up a chuckle. He'd forgotten how she'd called him that the first time they got naked in Croatia. She'd said he was every mama's worst nightmare and every young woman's fantasy.

A bad boy who wanted to be the star of a woman's dreams.

He'd asked her, "Am I in your dreams?"

She'd smiled back then, sly as a devil cat, then shrugged and said, "In mine, you were more ... imaginative."

He'd known a challenge when it was thrown at him and by the time he had finished with her she'd recanted her words.

In some ways, nothing had changed.

In other ways, everything had changed since then. He didn't care. He lived life each day, taking the challenges as they came. This was one he couldn't afford to lose. His mind might struggle through but his heart wouldn't survive a defeat.

"I missed you," he said. With her in his arms, she couldn't run away.

Turning very still, her face shadowed with disturbing thoughts. He asked, "What?"

"It was a hard time those two years. Even this past year."

Did he hear a door opening into her heart? "Agreed. It doesn't have to be any more."

She smiled and drew circles on his chest with her finger.

He caught her hand and pulled her finger into his mouth, sucking it. Then he released her hand and pulled her up to where he could tuck her head into the curve of his neck. Running his fingers slowly along the long curve of her back, he stroked slowly as her breathing evened out.

For the first time in many months, his mind wasn't a scary place to hang out.

She murmured, "I have to ... check on things."

"We will. Ten minutes. Okay?"

Must have been. He got no reply. As she dropped off to sleep, he pulled the covers over both of them, and wrapped a protective arm across her back. Once this was done, he had to find a happy medium somewhere for this to work.

She didn't want to continue with their occasional relationship.

To be honest, he'd like more, too, but he wasn't ready to walk away from the CIA even if he could. It wasn't as if he could hand in his two-week notice. He'd planned to spend another fifteen years in the field and they needed operatives like him.

The simplest answer to her issue of not wanting to wait at home for him would be for Sabrina to join him again as a partner, but that would mean giving up running her company.

He'd never ask that of her.

There had to be an answer and he'd figure it out once he got her home from this crazy trip.

Gage would give her every conceivable amount of help, from his resources to his expertise, and he'd be there when she reached the conclusion he had. Getting her hands on those three artifacts was unrealistic, which made this mission suicidal.

She would fight him on this, but he had no intention of standing by and allowing her to walk into a death trap alone.

Chapter 21

SABRINA OPENED HER eyes and forced her brain to push past the grogginess of sleeping hard for a short time.

She was in bed.

With Gage.

Using him as a body pillow, to be specific. A very hard-muscled pillow.

Stupid didn't begin to describe this idea.

It hadn't been entirely hers, but she'd been a willing participant.

She could do this. Just get up, shower and not make a big deal out of sleeping with Gage after she'd told him they had no future together.

A heavy arm draped across her back snugged her up close to the warm chest rising and falling beneath her.

"You awake?" he asked. His voice came out rough with that sexy morning gruff, the kind he always had after getting laid.

She planted her hands on his shoulders and pushed up. "How long was I out?"

Gage pulled his wrist into view and his face distorted with shock.

"What?" She cursed herself. Were they close to landing?

He cut his eyes up to meet hers. "Ninety-seven minutes of sleep. Damn, you're such a slug."

She grumbled about wise guys and shoved up to climb off of him. When she caught sight of her overnight bag stored in a corner, she sent a mental thank you to her efficient flight attendant.

Then slapped her forehead.

Gage sat up and propped himself on an elbow. "What?"

Letting her arm fall to her side, she said, "Just thinking about the crew." Not that she answered to anyone for her actions, but she'd intended to keep this strictly professional.

Guess that just flew out the window.

Gage's eyes crinkled with delight. "Tell them we're card carrying members of the Mile High Club."

"Not funny."

"Sure it is." He sighed and muttered, "Or it used to be when you had a sense of humor."

The ring of truth in that nipped at her conscience.

She lifted her bag to the bed and dug out everything she needed to appear respectable again. "I'm grabbing a shower."

Gage rolled off the bed and stood up, right in front of her so that his favorite part thumped her stomach. "Want to save water?"

"There's not room for two."

"That's not why you're telling me no." He waited for her to deny it, but she couldn't.

She placed her hand on his chest. "Gage, I told you—"

He covered her hand. "Stop. I heard you earlier. We'll talk when this is all over, but for now we're a team. Let's just do what we have to do and not make this complicated."

Her eyes strayed to the rumpled bed. "It's already complicated."

"No, it's not. That—" He nodded at the bed. "—was just two people who know each other well enough to enjoy some downtime. I'm here as your backup when you go for the panel. Nothing has changed."

She would not be hurt over his casual attitude after she'd made it clear nothing could come of it, but damn ... that did leave her with an empty place in her chest.

This would be her reality once they returned and he walked away. No, *she* was the one walking away.

She'd better get that straight in her head.

When she remained silent, he added, "I've never pushed you for more than you could give. I'm not going to start now. I know we hit an impasse at your office, but we'll do this your way. Agreed?"

She wasn't sure what her way was, but she had a plan and now he'd agreed to follow her lead. "Sure."

By the time she finished showering, she was starving. Once she made it to the living area again and ordered food for both of them, she linked to the internet and hooked up a Skype visit with Dingo.

The image transmitted from Atlanta came into focus. Was Dingo the only one in the war room? He had the camera focused on him, but he could switch to a wide-angle view of the room.

She asked, "Anything on that fourth Amber panel?"

"Negative." Dingo's eyes wore the grim emotions he kept in check. Dark shadows gave testament to how little rest he'd had. She could demand he sleep all she wanted, but Dingo would do only what Dingo decided.

Staying on topic, she asked, "What about the scroll?"

Valene's voice said, "Working on it."

Sabrina cocked her head. "Who else is in the room?"

Dingo seemed to hesitate, then sighed as he hit keys. The camera lens rotated to open up a wider field of view, which showed Valene on Dingo's right.

Sabrina expected that.

What she hadn't expected was to find Trish Jackson sitting on his left. "Trish! What are you doing there? You should be in a safe house."

Trish turned an angry face to the camera. "I just got here and I'm staying to do whatever it takes to get Josh back. You wouldn't sit in a safe house if you were in my shoes so don't ask me to do that." She sounded irritable, but Sabrina brushed off her terse answer because the woman had every reason to be upset.

Trish had once been an alcoholic before someone tried to kill her and her future sister-in-law. She cleaned up her life and then met Josh when he was investigating her brother as a potential mole in a DEA operation. The mole turned out to be someone else, and Trish had proven her backbone was solid iron when it came to protecting her family and fighting back.

She had grit. Based on what Josh had shared with Sabrina, she shouldn't be surprised to see Trish at Slye's headquarters.

But Josh would kill all of them if anything happened to the woman who owned his heart.

Sabrina accepted that Trish deserved to be involved and said, "I wasn't criticizing you, Trish. You're right. I wouldn't be happy sitting in a safe house either, but I want you to promise me you will not leave that building without an escort while you're there. I fully plan to bring Josh back and I couldn't face him if anything happened to you."

Trish's face changed in a blink. Her eyes glistened. "Sorry. I'm not myself lately. I don't mean to take out my frustrations on any of you."

Not frustration, but fear.

Sabrina wouldn't correct her. "We can use your expertise. Thank you." Sabrina addressed Dingo. "What do we have?"

He'd been watching Trish with a stern gaze, but at Sabrina's question he swung his head in Valene's direction. "Why don't you explain? I'll feed this to the big screen. It'd be simpler coming from you since I'll just end up paraphrasing."

Valene said, "Sure." She wore a mask of calm and grabbed her notes, then looked up to where Sabrina's image would be on the large wall monitor. "The scroll reproduction is in progress. We have someone waiting to fly the final copy here. I expect it to arrive in approximately six hours. I've been conferring with Soo Jin, who is adamant that this reproduction won't pass muster, but it's going to be damned good."

"I understand." Sabrina saw no way that she could show up with all three actual artifacts, and certainly not the scroll. Gage had surprised her by not making an issue of it, or forcing her to admit this mission had no chance.

She'd made a decision upfront to take a reproduction with her and hold it along with the other two pieces—if Chatton came through with the cross—while someone backed her up during the exchange. She'd try her best to locate the real artifacts, but if she didn't she was still attending the *Illustratio*.

With expert backup, she and Josh would leave together.

And alive.

Dingo would deliver the scroll reproduction to Mumbai.

She had until then to decide whether she was taking Dingo or Gage. She would not take both.

Valene cleared her throat and continued, "Soo Jin said the

jade tablet must have the only indication of where the artifacts are to be gathered together, because she can't find any other reference to it. I've scoured the photos of the original scroll and there's no reference to where this happens."

Dingo squinted with a thoughtful look. "So Rikker's boss is the only person privy to the location for this meeting? That's suspect in itself. Maybe there is not a set place."

Trish lifted a hand to interrupt. "Excuse me, but where are you, Sabrina?"

"On my way to find an Amber Room panel we hope is the one I need as part of the trade for Josh."

"Okay, I haven't been here long enough to be up to speed. Thank you," Trish said, clearly trying to contain her anxiety.

"You don't have to thank me, Trish. Every Slye agent and any other resource we have available is tasked with doing whatever they can to help us bring Josh home."

Dingo looked over at Trish and said, "You should tell—"

Trish cut him off. "No, everyone is busy right now and it won't change anything."

"What are you talking about?" Sabrina asked.

"Really, Sabrina, it's nothing. Please, let's just stick to finding artifacts."

Sabrina would ask Dingo later. She felt someone coming up behind her, which could only be Gage. He circled her laptop and sat down on the sofa next to her chair.

In view of the camera transmitting her image.

Dingo's mouth opened and closed. He had the good sense not to say a word.

Sabrina could only imagine how this looked, but she was not going to start explaining with an audience. Dingo would have to give her some space on this. But she did have to address the fact that Gage was here.

She had no choice but to make it sound as if this was all fine with her. "Valene and Trish, this is Gage Laughton. He has considerable international resources available to him that we need. As a minimum, he'll make getting into the countries quicker and beyond that ... he'll be my backup." She looked directly at Dingo when she said that last part.

He didn't comment. She could tell by his face that he got it and wouldn't give her grief, at least not right now.

She added, "He has people searching for the other panel and we absolutely need that one. There's no way to create a reproduction in time so—"

Trish slapped both hands on the table and everyone's gaze snapped to her. She asked in an excited voice, "I just remembered something. Do you know who Czarion is?"

Dingo asked, "They're some clandestine unit of three people with one crazy guy running it. This Czarion bunch is at the center of all this. Why?"

"I've got an idea on the other Amber Room panel. When I fought Leanne Witherspoon in Miami, she made a comment about the Amber Room panel we had on display there, and said it was not the one the Czarion wanted. That's the one we're looking for, right?"

"Yes," Sabrina answered. "Now that you mention it, I remember that being in Josh's report after he finished his Miami operation. I'd forgotten that you were the first one to have any intel on the Czarion."

"Probably because it was only a name at that time and nothing else."

"What are you thinking?"

"I heard that Leanne's father had sold the panel to a broker, which allowed the purchaser to remain anonymous. I don't know if that's the panel you're headed toward or if the one her father sold ended up somewhere else. If we could track down the buyer, we'd know, but ... that will take time." Trish deflated at that thought.

Sabrina asked, "Is there any chance that Leanne's panel could be the correct one?"

Trish shook her head. "I'd say no, but that would depend on Leanne having told me the truth when she'd lied about so much else. I'm very sure she said it wasn't the one the Czarion wanted, because I remember thinking, 'who are the Czarion and what's so special about the one they want?' Leanne said the panel she'd put on display had been in her family for many years. The panel we had was huge, but—" Trish lifted a face so full of hope it hurt to look at her. "Maybe Leanne just didn't know."

"Even if she was telling the truth, it would help to know where that one ended up."

Gage's phone had hummed a few minutes ago. He'd pulled it out and had been tapping keys while they talked. He paused and looked closely at something before shifting that intent face at Sabrina. "I think my people have found the fourth panel."

Sabrina's heart did a high jump in her chest. "Where is it?"

"Italy. A place near Florence."

Now what was she supposed to do?

Dingo said, "Great!"

Sabrina turned back to the laptop camera and frowned. "That *would* be great news if we knew for sure that was the correct panel. I won't have enough time to check out the one in Switzerland first then backtrack to Italy and make it to Mumbai in time for Rikker's text." She hated worrying Trish like this, but she didn't have time to dodge the truth.

Dingo's grin floored her.

He'd been hunched over with a hangdog face since Josh had been captured. Dingo said, "Get ready for a bit of good news. Nick is on his way to Rome and he left just ahead of you. I'll have him alter his flight plans to Florence."

At a loss over this news, Sabrina said, "Not that I'm complaining, but why was he going to Rome?"

"Nick said he was following a hunch about where he believed Chatton is headed. He thinks she's going after the scroll."

That news was both encouraging and disturbing.

Nick must not have contacted Dingo until he was on the way, which fit Nick's MO to a T.

She felt Gage's eyes on her and glanced over. He wasn't happy to hear that either. Sabrina asked Dingo, "Why does Nick think she's going after the scroll?"

"Nick claims Chatton may be the only person who knows enough about all of this to get to it. I asked if he thought she'd hand the real scroll over so you could deliver it and he said he doubted that would happen, but he'd do his best to convince her to work something out if he did manage to corner her with the scroll."

Sabrina had to remind herself to breathe.

If Chatton got Galileo's scroll out of the Vatican, it was at least in play. That would be a decent alternative to showing up with only a reproduction in hand.

Of course, that was a huge *if*.

She didn't want to consider what it would take to breach Vatican security, especially when they were probably on high alert after the incident in California where an assassin had targeted the pope.

What if Nick followed Chatton into the Vatican and got caught?

She couldn't begin to fathom the international fallout.

"We need Nick to hunt down the fourth panel," Dingo said, reminding Sabrina how many balls had to stay in the air in this deadly game of juggling lives.

Gage spoke up. "I've got an address for the Florence panel. From what my people can tell, Harald Fritzl, who owns the villa at that address, is known for buying art through a broker with a shady reputation."

Trish had been typing on her laptop while everyone talked and paused to jump into the conversation. "I found the name of the broker who bought the panel from Leanne's family."

Eyes moving as he read the text on his phone, Gage asked, "Hold up. Was it Mhasalkar Brothers Antiquities out of Mumbai?"

Trish nodded. "Shoot. So the Florence panel is not it?"

"Not necessarily." Gage scrolled his phone. "My people had already found the one that Sabrina and I are heading to see. That same Mhasalkar broker handled both panel purchases." He looked at the monitor. "Without specific details about each one that means either one could be correct."

Snapping her fingers, Trish said, "What about the date it was purchased? Wouldn't that narrow it down?"

Gage shook his head. "The broker acquired both within a month of each other."

Valene interjected, "The broker *could* tell us which one went where, but this is the kind of group that won't risk their street rep for under-the-table deals. Getting blood out of a turnip would be easier than expecting them to share anything on their secret clients. They could have bought both of those panels due to a strong interest circulating in illegal circles, and sold them when the right deal came along."

Trish said, "Then we need someone to make that broker talk."

Sabrina heard a serious threat in Trish's voice. Josh would have a mate equal to his alpha protectiveness. She said, "That would be the best approach if we had plenty of time, Trish."

Josh's fiancé sighed. "I get it."

Gage announced, "I do have someone looking for the person who actually brokered the panels, but his office is not sharing anything. In the meantime—"

Trish hissed and grabbed her side.

Dingo jumped up, but Trish lifted a hand to stop him. "I'm fine. This is perfectly normal." She waved him down and said, "Please keep working. I'll be back in a bit."

Then she stood up.

Sabrina's jaw dropped. "You're pregnant?"

Trish put her hand on her round middle. "Yes. We were waiting until everyone showed up for the wedding to share our news but ... "

"Every damn time you two have set a date, we've screwed it up," Dingo finished.

Shrugging, Trish said, "I knew what I was getting into when I said yes. Josh accepts everyone and everything in my life. I accept everything that comes with his."

Sabrina's skin tingled at Trish's admission. She could not have picked a better woman for Josh.

Trish drew a deep breath and let it out slowly, wincing. "I'm fine. I don't need anyone taking care of me. What I do need is for you to bring Josh home so our child will have a father." She pinched her eyes and everyone knew it was to stem the tears threatening, but Trish lifted her head and shook off the emotional moment. "Now, if you'll excuse me I need to find a bathroom before this little devil kicks me in the bladder again." She smiled, showing how much she loved her little devil.

Just as much as her big one.

With Trish out of the room, Sabrina wanted to wrap this up without giving the poor woman any more to worry about. "What have you come up with for Soo Jin?"

Dingo covered his face with both hands, rubbed his eyes, then dropped his hands to the table. "I have an idea, but it's complicated. If it works, you'll have Soo Jin on site virtually. I have to be able to bounce the feed enough times that it can't be traced for at least thirty minutes. I have to assume that Rikker's boss has unlimited resources for anything he wants to track."

"Agreed. What if it takes more than thirty minutes to do whatever this guy has planned for the *Illustratio*?"

"Then Tanner will kill me, because I'm not sure how long it will take someone to track the feed at that point."

"We can't let anything happen to her."

"I know, but Soo Jin has already made it clear to Tanner and me that she will either do this by remote video feed or she's going to join you in Mumbai on Monday. She says she'll never be able to show her face again if she doesn't help. Tanner looks like he's been kicked in the nuts since that conversation."

Sabrina said, "I trust you and Tanner to figure out the best way to move forward without putting her at risk."

"Got it." Dingo shared a few more things then signed off.

Gage had grown quiet. Too quiet.

Without turning her head to him, she said, "I can feel you thinking. Might as well say it."

He studied her as if she was a new species. "I've finally figured out what your plan is and that won't fly."

She knew where he was going with this, but still asked, "What do you *think* my plan is?"

"You can't get your hands on the scroll, so you're having a reproduction made. You don't know that you'll find the right panel, but I have a feeling you're going to steal the wrong one just to have one in hand. You think Chatton is bringing the cross and you have no idea if any of that electronic hopscotching is going to allow Soo Jin to have any kind of presence at the *Illustratio*. Basically, you plan to bluff your way into a hell zone and hope you walk out with Josh."

When he said it like that, her plan sounded insane, but she wasn't suicidal. "Some of that may be true." Like all of it. "What's your point?"

He stared at her for several seconds. "I was hoping you'd correct me, but you really are going to do that. My point is this. I think you're making a huge mistake by going after Josh without the real artifacts."

"It's my mistake to make."

"I'm not standing by while you throw yourself on the mercy of a madman."

She stiffened at the insinuation that he had any say over her decisions or her life. He'd just given her reason to leave him in Mumbai and take Dingo when she received final instructions.

"One question, Gage. What would you do in my shoes if I was the one captured and you had no artifacts to hand over?"

Darron stuck his head out of the galley and lifted his eyebrows in a "ready?" look. She waved him off and he zipped back out of sight.

Sabrina stood up, needing space.

She looked down at Gage. "Let's get something clear. You have no say over anything in my operation and this is *my* operation. I appreciate the intel on the panel in Florence and anything you can do to get us into Zürich faster, especially if you can get my weapons through. But once we land you have to head back. An operator working with one of my former agents will be in Zürich to back me up."

She turned to step away and heard, "Here we go again."

"What, Gage?" She'd let him vent then leave him to stew.

"I tell you I don't want you throwing your life away on a crazy plan and you push me aside to take yet another person you trust over me."

She spun back to him. "At least these people I trust will follow my orders without question, but more than that? Rikker has guessed at us having a relationship. I tried to convince him otherwise—"

"Should have been easy for you."

"—but he wants to kill anyone close to me and that includes you."

"He's wanted to kill me for a long time. That's nothing new."

Gage was infuriating. She snapped, "Fine. If you have a death wish, don't explore it on my time and you're still not someone who will follow my orders without question."

He stood so fast she took a step back, then crossed her arms, ready to have this out.

"You're right. I'm not one of your people who will jump when you shout. If I did, you'd wonder who I was. Am I wrong to want to keep you alive?"

"That's *exactly* my point. I can't trust you to do what I ask, which could end up getting you and Josh *both* killed because you're so determined to protect *me*."

"I won't do something to get Josh killed, so what's wrong with wanting to protect you?" he asked softly.

If he'd yelled at her, she could have dealt with it. His question asked with tenderness threatened to undermine her resolve about ending their relationship. She shouldn't have slept with him, but she was not about to regret it. She'd missed Gage more than she wanted to admit.

He'd pushed for the intimate moment.

But still, that weighed on her.

She owed Gage the best explanation she could give him and hoped it would be enough. "From the point that I met them when I was seven, Josh and Dingo have been the only people who cared whether I lived or died. They saved my butt time and again when someone would have wiped the playground with a scrawny, mixed-blood brat. They're the reason I didn't end up in some whorehouse to feed myself. We've been more than brothers and sisters since then. I don't know how to explain it to someone who can't—or refuses to—understand. Stop arguing with me about what I have to do and listen when I tell you that no one, and I mean *no one*, will stand between me and going after Josh."

She stared out the windows that were just starting to glow with the promise of sunlight.

"I understand." He lifted a hand when she started to protest and tucked an errant lock of hair over her shoulder. "I had a baby sister in the FBI. She was all I had after our parents died.

I would have walked through the fires of hell for her, but she wouldn't let me. I made the mistake of pushing her away by trying to make her see it my way and the one time she needed me ... I wasn't there."

Sabrina swallowed, but the lump in her throat made it difficult. She'd said they didn't know each other, which had been spot on. He had a fat CIA file on her that couldn't begin to explain what Dingo and Josh meant to her, even though the facts of their upbringing had undoubtedly been in front of Gage many times.

The only information she had on Gage was what little she'd learned from their brief interludes.

She wasn't sure what to do with the emotions this new revelation brought on. She and Gage were supposed to be miles apart, learning how to never see each other again.

Not opening passages into her heart that she had no idea how to close off.

He whispered, "I won't."

What did he mean? She asked, "You won't what?"

"Interfere or try to stop you from getting to Josh. I swear it. All I ask is that you don't push me aside. Let me go with you to get the panel. Don't make me regret a second mistake."

She couldn't continue this conversation. It was zapping what little energy she had. Emotional crap did that. "I appreciate that, but I won't lie to you. I'd rather you didn't go with me."

Two ticks passed then he said, "Why is it that you can trust Josh, Dingo, Tanner, hell, even Valene, and not me? You know I had nothing to do with you getting burned in the UK, but you still hold me accountable in spite of it."

Her anger had been living just under the surface from the minute she woke up in the same room as Rikker. But that anger had been self-directed.

He just had to bring up the UK when she'd planned to ask him once more when they returned. To give him one more chance to come clean. She wasn't even sure those names mattered anymore, but she needed him to be honest with her. To trust her the way he was asking her to trust him. It had to go both ways.

Everything that had happened in the UK had driven her, Dingo and Josh to this moment.

She bit out, "You want the truth? Yes, I hold you accountable because the only person I know who absolutely is guilty of being a part of that scheme is Rikker. And someone else was pulling his strings. I asked him for the name of the person responsible for throwing my team to the wolves and he laughed at me. He thought it was hilarious that you hadn't told me. He indicated the one person who knew everyone in the loop at the agency was you. If you weren't telling me, then no one would."

The tension clouding the air should have forced the walls of the plane to expand.

She was done with this. "You know what, forget it. You stand there accusing me of not trusting you, but—"

"You want those names. Fine. There are three. I'll give them all to you as soon as we get back from this blasted trip. There's no point in me sitting on them to protect you from putting yourself in danger when you clearly don't care enough about yourself, or us, to stay alive."

She had a feeling she'd just lost a battle even though he was going to give her what she wanted.

Chapter 22

SABRINA COULDN'T SAY getting through Zürich customs had been a cakewalk, but thanks to one of Gage's resources in Germany who had a brother-in-law with airport security, they passed through without a hitch.

But without her weapons.

To be honest, she hadn't expected to get her firearms into the country, and Nitro would make sure they didn't go without a means of personal defense, but she preferred her own. Gage explained that he could have tapped his friend for access, but it would have taken ten hours to wait for the right person to be in position to allow their weapons through unchecked.

Josh didn't have any minutes to spare, much less hours.

Her heart ached every time she thought about Josh being in Rikker's hands. Josh had never expected to have someone like Trish and now ... he had a child on the way.

Time to slap her mind back into line.

Thinking about unproductive and distracting things would get in the way—and maybe get them killed.

She needed to slide into her normal op-in-progress mode, shutting out everything except what had to be accomplished. Having a personal stake in this op was making it damn hard.

Due to dragging her carry-on bag, her right hand was doing a clumsy job of typing a text one-handed. She almost dropped her phone.

Gage put his hand on her arm.

When she looked up, he smiled at her as if the sun had risen in her eyes.

Where had that ridiculous thought come from?

She asked, "What?"

His words were only loud enough for her to hear. "We're supposed to be on holiday. You look like you're headed for the guillotine."

Oh, so that was why he smiled at her.

She stretched her neck, licked her lips, catching a heated look from him, and broke out a happy woman look. "Got it."

His eyebrows climbed in a not-sold look. "I know you're worried, but we have to look—and *act*—the part. As a team."

When she said nothing else, he reached over and caught the handle of her carry-on. "At least look like you're happy to have help."

"Sorry." She smiled for real and released her hold on the bag. She didn't have to prove to anyone that she could carry her own luggage, for crying out loud.

Gage led the way toward the exit.

She sent another text to Margaux, who was sharing everything she found with Dingo, who was doing the same. That way, one of them should be able to get through to Sabrina at any time.

That also meant Sabrina could get through to Dingo as well. If luck didn't fall her way and she was physically unable to make the trip with the panel due to being injured, then Dingo would go.

That worked as long as he wasn't dead.

Dingo and Josh would do anything to get to her just as she'd do the same.

No questions. No hesitation.

She hadn't thought Gage could understand, but after his admission about his sister ... maybe he did.

Outside of Kloten Airport, smokers sucked on what might be either their first or last cigarettes. Cars crowded the passenger pickup areas ahead, jockeying for position on a busy Sunday afternoon. Zürich in July proved to be almost as hot as Atlanta.

Gage pulled out his phone. "I'll make a call and—"

Sabrina knew what he was going to say and cut him off. "No. I have someone coming to meet us. We just need to find a place to wait a few minutes until I receive his text that he's close."

"What about tools?" he asked, referencing weapons.

"My person will be prepared. That's why he's not already

here. I'd hoped to bring mine, but since I couldn't he's covering that."

"We got through with no delay. I'd feel better having someone I know who lives here pick us up. He'll have access to a car we can borrow." Gage sounded either tired or irritated. Maybe both.

Sabrina hadn't been bitching about not bringing her guns.

She stopped texting and shoved her phone in her pocket. Then she grabbed a fistful of Gage's jacket sleeve and tugged him to the side.

He managed to pull both bags smoothly across the busy foot traffic without tripping anyone.

Once they were out of the flow, Gage stood the bags to the side.

Sabrina stepped up in his face, smiling her happy woman look for the benefit of anyone watching. "First, I'm not complaining, because I had my doubts about bringing in my hardware. I appreciate all you've done to help so far, including getting us through customs quicker than I could have."

Now he was scowling at her. "I didn't say you complained."

"Happy couple on holiday, remember?" she said, and Gage growled, but plastered a smile on his face. "Number two. I know you hate not being in full control. I also realize we're in your playground, but I'm not a rookie and my contacts are without equal at what they do because they have no allegiance to any one government. I need to know that you can do this on my terms without arguing the whole time."

Something skittered through his gaze, but for once she couldn't read Gage. Not when he made up his mind to mask whatever he was thinking.

He gave her his tough-guy stare. "Got it. You call the shots. You only want to hear from me when I can give you something you need."

Was there a double meaning to his words? "That makes me sound like a bitch."

"I never said that."

He hadn't, but the insinuation hung in the air. She looked around, then returned her gaze to him. "I get that you're edgy over going into a half-baked mission on the fly, but I have no choice."

Every CIA mission he'd given her as her handler had been detailed down to the minute of how he expected her team to execute it. Having that kind of planning in place would be wonderful but planning required time she just did not have.

She offered, "I can't change the situation, Gage, and I do appreciate what you've done, but I didn't ask you to join me. You could have stayed in Atlanta."

"There's no way in hell I would have let you come here without me."

"Let me?"

"Yeah. You want to get pissed, go ahead, but you were not walking into a clusterfuck setup for Josh, or any other reason, with no one watching your back."

She pulled back. "Wait, that's why you're all jacked up?"

He tilted his head, looking at her. His gaze roamed over her face and, as if someone had released the tension in his face, the muscles in his jaw relaxed and his eyes gentled. "I'm not snapping at you for having to make this up as we go, sweetheart, or this being hodge-podge planning. You think flying out at a moment's notice and scrambling to get intel has me worked up?"

"How would I know?" She let out a harsh sigh. "You've been pissed since you found me tied up at that building."

"Damn right. But ... " He chuffed out a sound that could be a chuckle and cupped the back of her head, pulling her to him so he could kiss her hair. When he pulled back, he warned, "This is the beast I turn into when I'm worried about keeping you alive, and yeah I like being in control, but that's not the issue. I'm not going to be easy to live with until you're out of this. You're stuck with the bear ... but with a little honey, I can be contained."

She raised her eyes to the sky, stared a moment, then came back to him. "If you go caveman on me, I'll leave you in the dust. *Tied up* in the dust."

"I'll take that under consideration."

It made no sense, but she was fine now that she knew what had been eating at him.

Her.

She could take care of herself and Gage knew it. This was a side of him she'd only recently experienced, and while it was endearing, it would get him killed. She needed him to watch his own ass. Even that first time they slept together in Croatia, he'd reminded her the next morning that he expected her to hold her own.

And she had.

She swiped hair blowing across her face out of the way and mentally pushed herself back toward the center where they weren't planning to make babies together, but neither were they wanting to strangle each other.

Gage asked, "How long until your ride shows?"

"He knew we'd be clearing customs by three if all went well. He'll text as soon as he's pulling in." Matching his new accommodating attitude, she smoothed her voice. She couldn't even consider losing Josh, but losing Gage too, losing both of them, would ... be unthinkable. "While we have a moment, I want your promise that you won't put yourself between me and a bullet."

"There you go making this difficult again."

"Gage, I'm only trying to—"

He leaned in as if he was listening, then his lips twitched with a smile right before he kissed her, cutting off her words. One of his hands found its way inside her jacket and hooked her waist, pulling her up against him.

He was seriously aroused.

Feeling him so worked up woke up parts of her that had been content since their last kiss on the Gulfstream. She sent her tongue in to play with his and he groaned.

That sound had always gotten to her. He'd show up after having been gone for weeks, climb into her bed and start kissing her. The second she touched him, he'd make that sweet sound of desire and it would turn on every inch of her body.

Like he was doing right now.

His fingers brushed over her suddenly aching breast and she jerked.

Gage eased away, giving her a soft kiss on her cheek, and withdrew his hands. "We can't be doing this right now."

Shit. Now she felt like an idiot.

She pulled her coat together and that friction across her sensitized breasts zipped heat through her core. She might kill him herself.

"From this point on, keep your hands to yourself," she warned in a voice meant to make a man worry about losing some of his favorite parts.

"I was only playing my role, sweetheart."

She arched an eyebrow at that, not daring to say a word.

"I told you we're on holiday. We're being watched from the glass wall behind you. We have to appear as if we really are here for a much needed break." He smiled and brushed an errant lock of hair off her face. "That flushed look in your cheeks looks good on you. If you smile, that will sell it."

Turning around to look would be the height of stupidity on a mission, and it irritated her that fatigue had kept her from catching onto the tail.

But two could play this game.

She did smile and licked her lips, wiping that arrogant grin off his face. Stepping up next to him, she whispered intimately in his ear.

"I'm definitely ready. If only I could feel you inside me right now where I'm hot and aching, it would be heaven." She patted his cheek and smiled at the feral gaze that lit his hungry eyes. "There. Now you look like a lover ready for some one-on-one action. You can thank me later. Just playing my role."

Her phone buzzed and she snapped her game back on. She read the text from Nitro. The man belonged to Logan's HAMR Brotherhood, and was one of Logan's deadly operatives. The text read: *White sedan, dirty, front passenger side fender crunched. Watch windshield wipers.*

She shoved her phone in her jacket pocket. "Our ride is here. Follow my lead."

Keeping track of everyone around her, she led the way to the passenger pickup area just as a sedan arrived and the wipers swept across the windshield one time. The white finish had dulled beneath a layer of dirt. With a dent in the front fender and a pair of sparkling balls hanging from the rearview mirror, it was the kind of car you glanced at and dismissed. Which made it perfect.

Just as Margaux had described, Nitro appeared to be in his midtwenties. He had a scraggly beard that matched his wavy, brown, '70s hairstyle, and he wore sunglasses.

When she let Gage know which car, he stepped ahead of her and opened the rear door. She slid in, surprised at the tidy interior, but not the lingering nicotine odor.

From the look of this vehicle, Nitro had picked it up on the way. It could easily be a local taxi and she wouldn't be surprised if the illuminated crossbar for the roof was tucked into the trunk.

No one said a word while Nitro drove them out of the airport and headed south. His thick shoulders, covered by a loose T-shirt, were the kind that came from serious time on a bench press. He glanced up at the rearview mirror. "I'm Nitro. I'm here to do whatever you need. I have an insertion plan I created with headquarters."

He meant he'd figured it out with Margaux and Logan.

Nitro wheeled the car expertly through traffic, all the time looking like someone's errant college son as he continued briefing them. "It's taken six hours to get everything in place, but we have a plan that has potential."

Gage shifted, but didn't make a sound.

Sabrina had no doubt that Gage would hate whatever off-the-cuff idea Nitro's people had come up with, but she trusted Margaux, who had been one of her best operators before life took a sharp turn and Margaux's identity had to go away permanently. Logan made that happen after a mission where Margaux and Logan, along with Sabrina's team, had saved the state of Washington from disaster.

Sabrina would roll with whatever Margaux and her team had spent the last six hours putting together.

But something in Nitro's less-than-thrilled tone stirred unease in Sabrina's chest. "Is inserting going to be a problem?"

"I don't know that you'd call it a problem so much as tricky."
Gage caught on quick. "What about the exit plan?"
Nitro lowered his sunglasses. "That's what I'd call a problem."

Chapter 23

Rome, Italy

THE GENERAL LEANED back in the surprisingly comfortable leather chair facing a black, lacquered desk. This was the office of a man who pulled the strings on billions in investments. A little heavy with the Italian Renaissance look for his taste, but Ludovico Rosso wanted everyone who entered to know this corner of Rome was his world and all others were here only at his mercy.

Shifting into a more comfortable position for his considerable size and glad his back wasn't complaining at the moment, The General prepared for a meeting he wished he could have taken a pass on.

Rosso topped the list of people who got under his skin. The General normally had those people removed from his world, but he couldn't very well do that with Rosso, could he?

The Rosso family had spread out across the globe, sticking their fingers into shipping, clothing and who knew what else.

In fact, every time someone estimated their combined wealth, the family dismissed the amount as incorrect. Meaning too low.

When asked for a more accurate number, the female Rosso spokesperson brushed off the inquiries as trivial news in today's world. She had a silver tongue and striking face, which she used to quickly shift the conversation to the many philanthropic endeavors the Rossos supported and spearheaded.

The General had no idea who else knew as much as he did about all five of the most powerful families in the world, which included the Rossos. He doubted many knew just how wealthy the dynasties were or how they worked together to maintain a concentration of power.

Whatever it took to ensure their families would always control the world money markets.

"Good afternoon," Rosso said in his suave Italian accent. He refused to use the moniker 'General,' pointing out that only one from the military deserved that rank.

"And to you," The General answered, repeating the same greeting every time. He could think of better ways to spend a Sunday, though.

As the current spokesman for the five families who paid The General handsomely, Rosso epitomized the gracious host, at least to those who didn't know him.

The man could give Satan the creeps.

Of all the families, the Rossos had been the most demanding.

This Rosso made sure The General knew his place in the food chain. Little more than a high-priced servant, which was fine. The General laughed all the way to the bank, when his miserable back wasn't killing him.

He'd had it cut on once already. Damn doctors first said he was fit for forty-nine, then recently they'd told him to lose some weight. Fuck them.

Rosso offered him a Danish cigar, one of a special edition and personalized for Rosso.

Might as well get this party rolling. The General accepted the cigar. Once the rich aroma of fine tobacco filled the air, he asked, "What have you got for me?"

Holding his hand so that he gave his cigar serious consideration, Rosso said, "This is not about a new project. This is about safeguarding the foundation of our industries."

An icy spike of concern wedged itself into The General's spine.

Nothing could ruin his sweet deal any quicker than just one of the families thinking there was a problem with a system they'd been perfecting since the early 1800s. Some had been manipulating governments even before that, but this coalition of families ran in the same powerful circles. They eventually joined together to ensure their families would always have everything they need to remain strong.

To do that, they required people within different governments who would put their interests first. Someone like The General, who was a major cog within the US government, but not so high-profile that anyone would ever suspect him of orchestrating events to favor the families.

He'd often wondered who mirrored his position in other countries, but he pulled his mind back from that mental tangent.

No wandering when he felt as pinned as a bug under a microscope. Maintaining a calm and confident exterior, he gave a slight frown and asked, "What specifically are you referencing? I can think of no issue that has come to my attention."

Taking his sweet time to reply, Rosso said, "Then you find the disaster in California two weeks ago to be of no concern?"

"That's been handled. There's no one left who can cause a problem. Nothing to worry about."

Rosso's face had few lines, probably because he was not known for boisterous laughter. Neither was he ever photographed appearing unhappy, with the exception of a funeral last year.

But he was clearly not happy now.

He put his cigar in a gold ashtray shaped as a hand and shifted a furious black gaze at The General. "You were given resources to put Eva Perdido into office and she would have been elected if the world had seen her as a victim. How was it that she came to have any association with a Mexican warlord?"

Because fucking Rikker screwed the pooch on that one.

The General ground his teeth, mentally searching for a decent spin.

Rosso shook his head and said, "There is no acceptable excuse for this disaster. She was dear to someone who is important to me. I guaranteed him she would be elected."

Oh, fuck. The General felt a stream of sweat working its way down his back. To speak now would only dig this hole deeper than the Grand Canyon.

Sitting back in his chair, Ludovico changed topics on him. "Nikias sent a question for you."

The General hoped it wasn't what he thought.

"He has heard disturbing news and asks if the Greek stater he put in your hands is no longer in your possession."

Shit just kept piling up.

How had Nikias Heron heard about *that* of all things? The General sure as hell couldn't say he'd used that rare coin to pay for Eva's death, not unless he wanted to find out just how dangerous Rosso could be.

Shifting his weight in the chair again, The General leaned an elbow on the desk. "The stater is *still* in my control. I am using it to flush out a threat in China. You made it clear two years ago that China was volatile, especially the man I was sent to befriend. Wayan. I promised you I would not allow that area to destabilize and I haven't. I told you about the former CIA agent Wayan managed to pull out of a tight spot in the UK back then, with my help, of course. I've got that spook working for both me and Wayan, but he's loyal to me."

The General waited to see if that would make the cut.

Rosso said nothing, so The General pressed his slight advantage. "I wanted Wayan to feel confident going into the *Illustratio*. For that reason, I allowed Rikker to deliver it to him, but the stater will be back in my hands the minute that event concludes."

Still the Italian held his thoughts to himself while he took another puff of his cigar and placed it once more in the gold hand.

After a tense minute passed, Rosso sighed. "How will you participate in the *Illustratio* without the stater? You said you needed one of the five artifacts to make contact with Wayan. We produced that. We are not handing you another one."

Relief flowed through The General at realizing that, yes, he was in a bit of trouble over Eva, but at the end of the day this group would always put their financial concerns first.

Sitting up a little straighter, he told Rosso, "I will be at the *Illustratio*, just as I've always planned to be."

"Wayan will give you the coordinates for the meeting without an artifact in hand?" Rosso asked, in a voice loaded with suspicion.

Smiling now, The General lifted his own cigar and puffed,

taking his time. "I plan to arrive with an artifact. There are three still available. I have everything in place to acquire one."

Finally, the stiff-assed Italian cocked his head in acknowledgement. See? All was fine again.

Or, it would be, as soon as The General came up with an artifact. Blood would be spilled.

The blood of his enemies, which included anyone who threatened his secret empire.

Chapter 24

Near Florence, Italy

NICK HANDED THE valet a hefty tip for parking the British green Range Rover his friend Savoir had loaned to him. Savoir's warehouse in Bologna boasted a collection of cars that rivaled Nick's. The art thief enjoyed his toys.

He'd also warned Nick not to return this Range Rover in anything close to the condition of the last one he'd borrowed.

That seemed unfair since Nick had bought this vehicle to replace the one that hadn't really suited Savoir in the first place.

He'd done his friend a favor.

Nick grinned at the memory of returning the first one, though.

He'd flipped *that* limited edition ride six times. In all truthfulness, the Aleutian Silver finish had been a bit of a negative while trying to elude two men at night who were trying to kill him. Savoir should have considered that when he purchased the thing.

A dark green exterior suited a vehicle so much better for after-hours covert work.

He glanced up and paused as the sun threatened to drop out of sight at the edge of the world. Villa GrímR overlooked the stunning Tuscan countryside.

He took a moment to soak it in. He did miss living in Italy, but not enough to give up his way of life. One day, when he was too old to play these games, he'd come back.

If he lived to see that day.

For now, he had an Amber Room panel to steal.

Who'd have thought stodgy Harald Fritzl would be sitting on a piece of art believed lost in World War II? Nick had figured the wily Fritzl, who was known for his extravagant parties, to be more of a Francisco de Goya or Rembrandt fan.

Even more surprising?

For the man to have a hidden art room in this villa. That smacked of illegal acquisitions.

Nick rubbed his hands together. This should be fun.

Time to play his public persona of the worthless Carrera who lived to spend money and indulge in all the beauties striding by him in designer gowns.

Once he entered the sparkling villa where candles were the preferred lighting, he first made the obligatory rounds, speaking to the host and upper tier of society for this region. That done, Nick located a spot where he could stand across from both the stairs leading up and the set leading down. While keeping an eye on both, he nodded at mundane conversation and eyed several delicious ladies.

He made a point of returning their flirtatious attention to keep his sinful reputation in place. He intentionally ignored the one in a bend-me-over-anything red gown for now. She'd eye-fucked him twice already.

Oddly, that hadn't raised any interest for him down below.

He'd gotten these women out of his system in his teens, then he'd become more selective.

His tastes ran more toward the exotic these days, to a different type of woman like Chatton ... who wanted to gut him. He wasn't sure what that said about his psyche, but he started getting hard just thinking about her.

He sent a mental apology to his dick, since it would probably never see Chatton again, much less naked.

The siren in red circled the room again, then slowed as she held Nick's gaze an extra second before giving him the look that said to follow her before she walked away.

Well, look at that.

The opening he'd been waiting for.

She was headed to the downstairs ladies room, while the other women had taken the grand staircase to the second level.

Nick excused himself and took his time working his way to the steps that went to the lower level. He made a point of speaking to a server and asking if there was a men's room below, explaining he had a fear of heights.

A handful of guests noticed when the server nodded quickly and pointed to the downward staircase, then Nick thanked him and left.

The men who had seen him leave would assume he was doing red gown in one of the bathrooms.

A fair assumption based on his past.

When he reached the hall, he found the men's room and kept going. After two turns, he located the room Dingo had decided could be the only access to an underground vault built over seventy years ago. Fritzl would have updated the security, but there was still only one way in or out.

Withdrawing his lock picks while watching the hallway, Nick put his covert skills to use and slipped inside the room. The smell of expensive cigars and aged leather permeated the air. He locked the door behind him and headed for the ten-foot-tall bookcase built across one wall.

Two feet short of the ceiling and with a sliding ladder for access.

Nick took a moment to search the neat desk with a Cartier clock on top. Nothing there and no computer around that might hint at an association with Orion Hunters. Since his priority was to get his hands on a certain panel, he couldn't squander any additional time for intel.

No one would question his disappearance right away. Inquiring about a guest headed to the bathroom was socially unacceptable, but that wasn't his concern.

He saw Ms. Red Dress as the type who would have total disregard for social manners in her quest to find him once she popped back upstairs, disappointed at being stood up.

Security would take note the minute she opened her mouth. The guards would quietly begin hunting Nick.

Unless he missed his guess, she'd wait twenty minutes in the ladies room, spending that time to preen and check herself for any imperfection.

At first, she'd assume Nick had been waylaid.

But twenty minutes in, she'd quit the charade.

As the saying went, the clock was ticking. Three minutes had passed.

His friend Savoir had confirmed Gage's intel on the panel in the best way possible for Nick.

As a professional art thief, Savoir was familiar with Villa GrímR's collection of sculptures and other bulky pieces that he speculated could include a panel from the Amber Room.

If so, the piece was still in place only because Savoir had no interest in nabbing it.

Not even when Nick made him a ridiculous offer.

His friendly art thief had explained that the panel would be too cumbersome for an easy heist, then he'd added that if Nick managed to pull the panel out that Savoir would help him move it on the black market.

What a guy.

Nick couldn't complain too much. Savoir had provided him with all he needed for accessing the vault and, while he snooped, Savoir would run a security loop he already had in hand for their system.

A little bonus from when Savoir had cased the location.

Six minutes had passed.

Nick took a step behind the desk chair, which placed him next to the wall. His heel dipped close to the wall, just as Savoir had explained. Savoir had lived in this area long enough to pick up tips on the villa from old timers who had worked for the owner at one time or another.

When Nick had questioned Savoir on how he knew so much about the security system, Savoir shrugged, admitting he'd spent time mapping out the place for a venture inside before deciding that fencing the art required more effort than he would willingly expend.

Looking down the wall, he could barely make out where the wood had separated a fraction of an inch. Using his fingertips, he eased it open, surprised that the false door swung so easily, then stepped into a dark space before pausing to let his eyes adjust. He used a handle on the inside to pull the door shut.

Now that he could see, he followed tiny, ankle-high lights along the six stone steps leading further down. He'd expected a dank, medieval-feeling area, but this was as pristine an entrance as any gallery.

At the landing for the last step, he viewed the room through a glass door with a security panel next to it, just as Savoir had described. But no obvious laser lights.

Savoir had been specific about Nick being able to see them.

Had his friend jumped ahead to take them down?

Nick stayed to the side of the door while he observed the four security cameras mounted to the walls. After twenty seconds, the tiny red light on the top of each camera lost its glow.

Savoir was on the job.

Nick withdrew the high-tech gadget his friend had camouflaged inside a cigarette pack. He slid the unit out and held it against the security panel.

Just as Savoir had promised, the monitor blinked green and deactivated the lock. Nick stepped inside.

This could have been a bomb shelter if not for plaster walls done in the alfresco style, Berber carpet, subtle lighting and, of course, the perfect temperature and humidity control for preserving art. The room spread out seventy feet deep and twenty-five feet wide. Two columns worthy of a grand entrance stood a quarter of the way into the space and three feet from the walls on the left and right.

Wide enough for someone to hide behind.

Good to know, but not something he would need to take advantage of as long as Savoir had his back. Nick would feel more confident with one of his Slye team members, but Savoir was trustworthy as long as no one offered him more money for the panel than he could refuse once Nick had driven off tonight.

Ten footsteps in, the ceiling domed over most of the room and someone had painted an alfresco image worth a handsome sum.

If a person could figure out how to steal it.

Now Nick got why Savoir passed on this place. Every piece of art would require serious work to remove. How big was the damn panel?

Was that ... ?

If he wasn't wrong, that towering marble sculpture was Michelangelo's *Hercules* that had been missing for four hundred years. Savoir must have hated passing that up. *Hercules* stood in a noble position halfway into the room. Massive framed paintings had been placed strategically to allow each piece its proper space.

Nick paused before passing by the life-size sculptures blocking his view of the last third of the room. In the center and at spots between the pictures on the wall, plants grew inside glass enclosures that misted water beneath the glow of grow lamps.

Large plants that also obstructed his view of the room.

His skin prickled with awareness.

Savoir had warned Nick he'd have seventeen minutes once he opened the door.

That would be a tight time frame if he'd had to wait on the lasers to be shut down, but there were no lasers.

A hinky feeling rode up his spine.

What had happened to the security beams? Savoir said he would turn them off *after* Nick put his gadget on the door panel. Not that he doubted Savoir, but the thief was not one of the Slye agents Nick would put unquestioned faith in.

You work with what you have, he reminded himself.

Nick took a step forward and heard, "Don't."

On the opposite side of the room, Chatton emerged from behind a sculpture. She held a gun on him.

Nick smiled.

Seeing her all amped up to kick his butt turned him on. Dingo would call him crazy. He didn't care if he was, as long as he had someone like Chatton in his world. Life usually bored him, but not when she was around.

Chatton quirked a smile and admitted in a voice laced with humor, "You do fascinate me, Nick, but you're in my way right now."

"Are we here for the same thing?"

"I would assume so. I have a way to transport it."

Really? He hadn't figured that out yet, but he normally came up with something on the fly.

Bluffing, he said, "So do I."

"How?" Her forehead creased with a thought then she said,

"Oh, yes. Your friend, the thief. Did he come up with a plan?"

Nick should stop digging this hole, but he might just pull her in with him. "He's one of the best at what he does."

"Let's keep this simple," Chatton said, going for the bottom line as usual. He did enjoy her no-bullshit, direct way of operating.

She explained, "Your friend is not helping you for your benefit. He has a weakness for baccarat and the man he owes a fat amount to expects to get this panel. If I allow you to leave with it, the panel will ruin your friendship."

"I appreciate the tip, but I'll deal with Savoir."

She sighed. "See, that's the point. I'm trying to help you make the right decision here. You won't have to jeopardize your friendship, because I'm taking the panel."

He'd pretty much figured that out when she made her presence known. "Why? Do you plan to take the panel to the same place I do?"

"Yes, but I have a debt to Rikker's boss. I need this as payment. It shouldn't matter to Sabrina as long as I show up with it."

He considered the pros and cons of her argument while the seconds ticked off his clock. But as long as she was here, they might have more time than Savoir anticipated.

"Here's the problem with your logic," Nick countered. "You weren't able to say for sure that you could deliver the cross you have. I can't risk a second artifact not arriving on time."

She made an oh-well grimace. "We have a problem. Or, I should say, you have a problem." Her gaze lifted to the camera above her that was pointed in Nick's direction.

He glanced up as the camera light barely started to glow.

Nick lunged behind the column and whispered, "The cameras are coming back online. We need to hurry. "

That's when he noticed her sad eyes. "Security can see your corner live, but they can't see me or hear anything yet. And they don't expect to hear something in a silent room full of art. Stay out of my way, Nick." She eased around the backside of the column, going toward the rear of the vault.

She'd obviously shut down the laser beams that crossed the center of the room.

At this point, he couldn't trust her not to turn them on again with him in the wrong place.

Once he determined that only one security camera had been reactivated, which meant she'd overridden Savoir, he mirrored her movements on his side of the room. He ducked and twisted to avoid areas the single camera would pick up.

He *now* sent a silent thank you to some ostentatious decorator for the foliage that offered areas to hide.

Working her way along the wall, Chatton glanced over at him and paused. She snipped, "If they see you here, you'll screw this up."

"Then hurry up and find the panel."

She cursed in Italian, which had to be for his benefit, and kept moving.

Looking over without missing a step, she said, "The *Illustratio* could be a trap. No, correction, it *will* be a trap."

"I expect that. So does Sabrina, but we still have to do what we can to get Josh back."

Chatton gave him an it-is-what-it-is silent reply. She kept moving low to the ground and carefully.

He realized she didn't trust the villa owner not to have another security camera concealed.

That would cap his night.

As she reached the middle of the room, she called over, "I've picked up chatter that an Orion Hunter has put a bounty on the scroll."

That would be through her secret intelligence network, which Nick had learned to accept at face value.

He scowled, but said nothing.

Chatton asked, "Don't you want to know how much?"

"Why would it matter? The Vatican's already on edge about that scroll. The minute they get word of the bounty, and they will, the scroll will be put in a vault you'd need divine intervention just to open."

She swung around to him. "You were going after it?"

"It was worth a shot as long as I was in town."

"You're insane." She propped her hands on her knees that had to be aching from holding that position.

"Me? Are you seriously trying to convince me you weren't going after it?"

"Already did the time on that one. Can't get to it. That's why I need this panel."

Okay, now he understood a little more. He asked, "Think if we show up at the last second with a reproduction even Galileo couldn't denounce, that it will fly?"

Chatton moved past the next sculpture and out of view, but he could hear her. "Rikker's boss is meticulous when it comes to details. He'll have some way to discern immediately if it's the real deal. I can't tell you how, only that it's impossible to get something like that past him."

Nick prodded again as he cleared another sculpture in the rear corner and jerked back out of view of another live camera. "Who is this guy Rikker answers to?"

"If I thought it would help you, I'd tell you. But it won't. If you know who he is, your group might make the mistake of trying to contact him to bargain for Josh. That won't work. In fact, that would end with you never even getting the remnants of Josh's body back."

Chatton added, "Rikker is invested only as far as his boss is involved. Take that person out of the picture and Rikker has no motivation to keep Josh alive."

"What's stopping Rikker from killing Josh?" Nick was thankful Sabrina couldn't hear him. She wouldn't appreciate that thought being given voice, but he reasoned that she would thank him for the intel.

"Rikker is only doing what he's told, which means his boss is holding something over him. Probably what happened in the UK plus all the murders since then, and knowing the man who pulls his strings, Rikker has a deal in play for when this is all done. Rikker can't vanish from his boss unless he has permission, but the man he belongs to is good for his word. Whatever he says you can take to the bank. The only way he breaks his word is if you break yours."

As she spoke, Chatton had reached up to pull the cover off a wall-mounted piece, the only art in this room that had been shielded from view.

Brilliant golden-red colors that seemed to be alive with light covered a panel that was maybe four feet wide and half as tall.

If that wasn't a panel from the Amber Room, the piece had missed its calling in life. It had to weigh sixty pounds or more. Savoir had offered to be close enough to step in as Nick's getaway driver and had a van lined up, but that piece was going to be a bitch to get out of here.

He whispered, "Do you know what the mark is?"

She shushed him and moved her gloved hands lightly over the contoured shapes and edges of the sculpted piece. He'd read up on the Amber Room. That particular amber was created 30 million years ago when amber-bearing conifers ended up at the bottom of what is now known as the Baltic Sea. The wood was eventually buried under the sediment, preserving the hardened wood and allowing the resin to turn into amber.

As he watched Chatton's efficient but unhurried movements, he assumed she was searching for the inscribed Latin letters. She turned to him and shook her head, indicating this was not the correct one.

He believed her, especially since her shoulders had drooped a tiny bit in defeat.

She said she'd deactivated the audio for the security cameras, but Nick still called softly, "Are you *sure* that's not the one?"

Chatton stared back for a moment then waved him toward the entrance to the room again. She rushed back to the front. When he reached it at the same time, she spoke across the opening separating them. "The correct panel has an inscription in Latin."

"I know."

"It also has a leaf fossilized in the bottom right corner, almost hidden by the gold leaf on top. I've got more than one possible size for the correct panel, but it has to have the inscription and the leaf."

He hadn't known about the leaf because no one on the team had that info, but he'd pass along what Chatton had just shared to Dingo and Sabrina once he got out of here.

It might not matter since that left supposedly only one panel. He hoped it was the one Sabrina had gone after.

Then again, where was the proof that only four panels existed?

What if more were circulating? He wouldn't say that to Sabrina. If there were more than four possible ones, she'd never be able to track down another one before going to the *Illustratio*.

Chatton stepped toward the door, which meant the camera above his head that pointed in her direction still had a loop on it.

What about the one watching his exit?

He waited until she reached for the door and asked, "Are you really leaving me here?"

She turned around. "Don't you have an exit strategy?"

"I did until you jumped my claim."

"I'm not even going to acknowledge that."

He still hadn't heard anything to ease the muscles tightening around his neck. "Is this retaliation for my giving up your name?"

She snorted. "No. That was an inconvenience, not worthy of real vengeance."

He lifted a shoulder, wishing he could reach over the distance and touch her. "I was willing to take that risk to get you out of there, but ... I never doubted that you could vanish and resurface as someone entirely different."

She allowed the compliment with her usual stoic acceptance. "If I let you leave with me, you'll follow me to find the cross. I can't have that. For one thing, I can't risk Rikker's boss finding a link to me through you." Looking as if she might say something else at first, she shook it off.

Nick swallowed hard. He had a sick feeling she was pulling away for good. He asked, "What's Rikker's boss holding over you?"

Ever evasive, she replied, "If I solve that by the time this is all done, I'll tell you."

Nick took a stab at the only link he held to her. Every time they met, she'd remind him that he owed her and he'd tell her he wanted it no other way. "Good. Then you'll be ready to collect on what I owe you, right?"

Chatton hedged with, "Possibly."

Everything had changed and it had nothing to do with being pissed about Atlanta.

She'd been telling the truth that this was not about retaliation.

This woman pushed off insignificant issues like a duck's feathers shed water.

She wanted him off her trail for another reason.

He was losing her and he didn't know how to fix it. "What's the real reason you're throwing a wall up now?"

Her gaze remained steady. A little solemn, but determined. "When everyone shows up at the *Illustratio*, we're all on our own. I can't help you. You can't help me, so don't try. You'll be doing your best to walk away from there in one piece if you have only *your* ass to worry about, but if you're there you'll be trying to save Sabrina and Josh."

Her gaze flicked away and returned just as quickly. "I've spent a lot of time studying Rikker's boss, trying to determine what he's up to with all this prophecy business. The man is a die-hard believer. I don't know why, but there's not a more ruthless human being to go up against. Anticipate everything possible and come prepared for any betrayal. That said, none of us might end up walking away."

"Chatton."

She opened the glass door to leave and looked back over her shoulder, "Sorry, Nick. It has to be this way."

Then she was gone.

Chapter 25

IF GAGE HAD been locked inside a cask that had once held scotch, this would still suck, but at least the smell would suit him.

He cursed Nitro that this was the best option for inserting into Sveinn Castle and, while he was cursing, he included the man who'd distilled the first drop of whiskey. Fumes were like termites, capable of inching inside his small air mask.

In fairness to Nitro, it was a decent plan on such short notice. His people had discovered a man by the name of Dirchs invested in single malt whiskies, much as a Wall Street broker invested in stocks. Nitro's people determined this was excellent news as his favored rare-batch alcohol was stored in Madeira barrels large enough to hide a grown man.

Whoever Sabrina's friends were had intercepted a shipment of three massive barrels of the stuff destined for this castle. Two were swapped with identical containers that had been re-engineered with lids that could be removed from the inside. All that had happened in a very short amount of time, which pointed to deep pockets as well as exceptional resources.

Gage's body might never unfold again after being wedged inside the thick oak structure for an hour already. The tight fit at least minimized the chance of making any unusual noise. Nothing kept his head from spinning as the cask rolled down a ramp then over a bump and now he spun on flat ground.

Muffled sounds of Nitro's voice reached him, but not what the guy was saying.

How was Sabrina doing?

She had her comm unit on but he wouldn't risk making a noise, even if no one could hear through the thick wood.

He'd like to say he had confidence in Nitro, but he didn't know him or his superiors. All Sabrina would offer was that Nitro belonged to someone she had ultimate trust in.

Clearly more than she had in Gage since she wouldn't share the person's name.

The rolling stopped.

Now Gage felt a sensation of descending. He had to be in an elevator. Were they going to a wine cellar? The motion ended, then he was on the move again.

He'd rolled over another twenty times.

How big was this place?

The barrel finally stopped and tipped up slowly until the balance of weight shifted and the base planted hard.

Gage stifled a grunt and checked his watch. They'd agreed that he and Sabrina would stay inside the barrel for fifteen minutes once the barrels were turned upright. Extra weight had been added to her barrel so it wouldn't be too light.

Seconds dragged by and the silence folded in on him.

He pushed down the urge to open the lid early. He'd been the one who always said every person on a team had to be depended on to do their part. No one altered the time frame just because he or she thought they could.

But damn it was hard to sit still.

Sabrina would be no better. She never liked surveillance. Give her a high-risk operation and she was golden.

What would it take to get that woman to realize they belonged together even if it couldn't be every day? She didn't believe they could do it in this business, but they'd managed it before. If she'd agree to meet him halfway they could have sometimes as opposed to never. They could make this work. He didn't want her to give up her business or life, but to find a place in it for them. For him.

He'd have been the first to say that two people intimately involved shouldn't partner in the world of covert ops, but he and Sabrina were unlike any other pair.

They had operated as a team and they'd been damned good.

What he couldn't do was watch her continue to go out on her own after people like Rikker.

Which, if he were honest, was exactly what she'd been saying *she* couldn't do anymore. She didn't want to be the one left behind, wondering if he was alive. He wouldn't like to be the one in that spot either.

No damn answers.

His internal clock said it was time. He lifted his watch again, and hit the button to illuminate the dial as the last three seconds ticked off.

When Nitro had pushed the lid down on the cask to seal it, Gage had twisted a series of large wing nuts attached to L brackets that held it in place. Gage unscrewed all those and pushed against the lid.

It didn't move.

He pushed harder, trying not to make any noise.

Not a hair of give. What the fuck?

Putting both hands in the same place, he put everything he had into it and the lid went up a quarter of an inch. Hell, if he couldn't get out, neither could Sabrina.

He touched his comm, turning it on. "Sabrina? Can you hear me?"

Nothing.

Shit. He hit the lid hard again and again, no longer as concerned about the noise as he was about her.

Something thumped on the lid.

He pulled his hands down and listened.

Another thump, then the lid moved up until a tiny slit opened, letting in a sliver of low-level light. *Shit.* It was too early in this op for things to go FUBAR. Stuck in this barrel, he couldn't get to Sabrina. He released the strap on his chest rig that held the Glock 19 pistol Nitro had given him. A flat piece of metal slid in and the lid popped open.

Sabrina smiled down at him and his heart started again. He'd been in this business for many years, so long that his heart rate didn't usually elevate even when he was in a dangerous situation.

But seeing her there, safe and smiling, gave his blood pressure a vicious kick.

She moved out of the way and offered him a hand, asking, "What was the problem?"

He twisted his way up and climbed out. "That lid got jammed tight. How'd you get out?"

"Mine popped up with no problem, but Nitro warned us it was a fast rebuild job on the lids. Yours must have gotten pinched."

"Let's get everything set and put the lids back in place then find our way out of here." Gage adjusted the straps of a night vision setup on his head, but kept the monocular flipped up. He noted Sabrina's was set as well. He tucked their masks and small air bottles into his now-empty scotch barrel.

Nitro's gun fairies had materialized suppressed Beretta 93R machine pistols, the Glocks, and small Kel-Tec 9mm pistols for backup. Gage whispered a prayer that he wouldn't need them as he readied his weapons and took stock of their surroundings. The cellar had a footprint the size of a single-level, three-bedroom house and you could eat off the floors.

He'd bet the lock would be substantial.

The place had a damp, aged smell like what he'd expect in the basement of a castle, but he welcomed the cool air after being in that cask.

When Sabrina stepped up, armed to the teeth and ready to go, he led them through rows of casks of all sizes, and wooden cases that must be bottles. They found a locked glass door that allowed a view of wines stored in a cooling room.

"That has to be to the stairs," Sabrina said nodding to her right.

He strode over to the steel door. "Too bad this place is four hundred years old. Would have been nice to get a working set of plans."

"True." She checked her time. "But I memorized the pictures Nitro scavenged plus some remodeling plans that were done in the past. We should be able to find a gallery, but I don't expect stolen merchandise to be on display." She glanced at her watch. "Nitro should be unlocking this soon."

"If he was able to hack into the security."

"I wouldn't expect this place to be beyond his abilities."

"Still, the security is probably tighter than a bank's, based on the kind of wine and art this guy brokers," Gage qualified. He'd like to have her level of trust in Nitro, but these people were not his people. Too late to waste time thinking on that when they were locked inside a building with two-foot-thick stone walls.

Sabrina stood perfectly still, but she vibrated with contained energy. Her eyes flicked to her watch again. "He'll be contacting us soon."

Gage released a long breath. "With these thick walls and being underground, it might be tough."

"Knowing Nitro, he left some type of boost down here."

Looking around, Gage muttered, "That would be helpful."

Sabrina stepped around to stand between him and the door he'd been studying. She said, "You keep trying to convince me that we can be together and that we could partner this way, but I hear the doubt in your voice even when I've told you my contacts are solid. You can't trust most of the people in your own agency, yet you keep bitching about having to trust the ones I would swear are gold standard. What gives?"

That she'd mentioned partnering at all caught him off guard. He hadn't been expecting that and was at a loss for what to say to her.

She muttered something, more of an irritated sound than words. "Well, Gage?"

He didn't want to screw this up, but he'd never given blanket trust to anyone who hadn't worked with him for a long time. Drawing a deep breath, he said, "I remember the first time we teamed up and you questioned information that I got on the fly from a questionable source. I said it was solid, but you weren't so sure."

She said nothing, which only happened when she didn't have an argument.

"I understood your hesitation back then. I'll say it again. No, I'm not comfortable working with an unknown group, but I'm here, with you, ready to take on anything we face. You can't expect me to like it, and yes, I'm going to question things. But I'm *here* because I'm willing to put faith in *your* people, because I trust *you.*"

She frowned and started to speak, but Nitro's voice came through their comms.

"*Raptor to Badger, you copy?*" Nitro's voice called softly, addressing Gage, but Sabrina would have heard it, too.

"Copy, Raptor," Gage answered. "Got your homework done?"

"*Ten four. Ready for the playground.*"

The door lock clicked and the conversation ended.

Her people were doing their jobs.

So maybe you need to grow a pair and quit adding your control freak trip to her load of burden.

Fuck. Maybe he did.

Sabrina opened the door to ancient-looking stone steps rising two floors. She went up ahead of Gage before he could take the lead. Time to man up. This was her operation. He'd never had a problem following her, and he didn't now. He knew better than to let his need to protect his partner get in the way.

Something had changed though. Watching her walk ahead of him into potential danger was tightening his gut, and he couldn't shut it down.

What was a man who dealt in wine doing with one of the artifacts?

Nitro's group had found out nothing beyond the obvious, but pulling intel on something like this Orion Legacy stuff took more than a few hours. Gage wasn't faulting them for lack of intel, but pissed that this had goat rope written all over it.

At the top of the stairs, Sabrina opened the door slowly, looking around. She pulled it back and turned to Gage, who joined her on the top landing.

Tucking close to his ear, she said, "This opens into a kitchen. Main lights are out. Doesn't appear any meal is being prepared for dinner."

"Let's start clearing rooms looking for the panel."

"Hold it." She stuck her hand in her pocket.

"What?"

"I just got a text." She held her phone up and read the message with no expression as she tapped her finger against the edge. "A friendly shopper found a holiday gift in Florence, but not the one Santa is after." She lifted her head and asked, "Raptor, you copy that?"

"*Roger, Badger.*"

Gage asked, "Is Nick positive?" Damn. If Nick had found the correct panel in Florence, Gage and Sabrina would be looking for an exit point now.

She gave a sarcastic snort and switched off her comm. "Not him. Chatton. He said she was already there when he arrived. She checked it out. Said she didn't have an exact size, but that the correct artifact has the Latin inscription and a small leaf fossilized in the bottom right corner."

That could be encouraging news, but he had no doubt that Sabrina would have been happy for Nick to have been successful so they could head to Mumbai to meet him.

Gage sensed her hesitation. "What else?"

"Nick said Chatton was there because she's hunting the panel to trade Rikker's boss for something. He said she didn't share why, but from the little he knows of her he suspects it has nothing to do with Orion's Legacy. He's guessing it's a negotiation on something personal to her."

"Did he follow Chatton after she left?"

Sabrina typed a quick message, waited, then her eyebrows shot up. She muttered, "Shit." She typed some more and paused again to read before explaining, "Chatton had control of the security cameras. She left Nick pinned in a corner where he couldn't get past the cameras until she'd been gone for eight minutes, then he got a text telling him he had sixty seconds to vacate the premises. She played a loop to cover for him."

"Was that enough time?"

"Nick said it was a challenge, but he managed to leave with no new holes."

Gage said, "That guy's crazy. You know that, right?"

"He's creative and lacks any concern for self-preservation, but he's not crazy."

He admired how she saw the best in all her people, even the ones a half bubble off. No wonder that team loved her. "Anything else?"

"No." She shoved the phone back in her pocket and switched on her comm, then turned to the door that opened into a kitchen built for a celebrity chef. Every possible accoutrement had been installed. Copper pots hung above the massive cooktop, with everything clean and neat.

Gage stayed close on her heels with his weapon at his side.

She opened the door to a spacious dining room that seated twenty, and froze. What the hell?

Then he heard it. A man was talking in the next room.

They stepped over to where Gage could see a sliver of the entrance, where a dowdy woman with a gray blob of hair on top of her head stood holding her purse with both hands as she spoke.

"Benjamin, I am happy to stay late if you think Von Dirchs would like something for a late meal," she offered in a heavy German accent. "It would take no time if you want to ask him."

"No. I'm sure he is fine. He would have told me by now if he had changed his mind. You worry over much about him, which is good of you, but please know it's not necessary tonight." Benjamin sounded Scandinavian.

"If you think so."

"I do. In fact, I am retiring as soon as you leave."

"Oh, I will get on about it then so you may catch up on your cricket tournaments."

Benjamin chuckled. "You know me too well. *Adjö.*"

The door closed, then came the sound of a lock being turned. A slender man in his fifties and wearing a nice suit strode back toward the kitchen.

Hell. Not enough time to reach the stairs. Gage pulled Sabrina into the pantry. He hoped old Ben was not coming in search of serious food or he'd get a good-night tap.

Benjamin opened the refrigerator, withdrew a cold beer and walked out, flipping the under-cabinet lights off as he did, leaving the kitchen in the glow of nightlights.

Bonus. Gage preferred no light, but anything less than bright light was always better.

As Benjamin's footsteps receded, Gage and Sabrina left the

pantry and crossed to the dining room in time to see Benjamin disappear through a door hidden as part of a paneled wall under the regal stairway that curved to the second floor.

With the house still as a tomb, Sabrina moved out swiftly, first locating a downstairs library and a sitting room that each displayed paintings plus pedestal sculptures, but no amber panel. From there, Gage found a movie viewing room with tiered, overstuffed recliners. He shook his head and they backtracked through the downstairs to the stairway for the second floor.

Gage had just made it to the upper landing when the front door lock clicked loudly in the stone foyer.

He waved Sabrina to the left and pulled her against him the minute she was close, and waited.

The door opened and a deep voice spoke in a moderate tone. "No. Absolutely not." Pause, then a shuffle of footsteps, before the same voice said, "Good luck finding a single cask Bushmills for that price. In fact, call me when you do. I can always find room for a steal. Tell your client to come back when he can afford my product."

The one-sided conversation ended, which must have been a phone call. More solid sounding footsteps tapped across the foyer then the sound dulled as he ascended the steps covered in a woven runner.

Gage gave Sabrina a signal to go down to the first room on the left.

They made it inside the dark space that had one slender, vertical window looking out into the hallway. Odd, but it allowed Gage to peek out, which worked for him.

Or it did until the man turned to the left and headed their way, angling as if he intended to come to this room.

Gage pulled his monocular down, sure that Sabrina did the same, then he shielded her with his body as he raised his weapon and pushed them both back from the door.

Chapter 26

WITH HER MONOCULAR in place, Sabrina's world turned gray-green as it came into focus.

She also noticed that Gage had stepped between her and the door.

Was he serious?

Let's be partners, Sabrina. What was she thinking to even consider that?

The doorknob turned and the door opened a quarter inch.

She shoved everything aside to focus on the man coming into the room.

"This is Von Dirchs ... Your connection is terrible. Call me back on my landline. I'm on my way to my office." He pulled the door closed and after ten seconds, Gage stepped over to the tiny window slit.

If not for concern about the castle owner opening the door and exposing their hiding spot, she'd have given him a ration of grief over thinking to shield her with his body.

That conversation could wait for later.

He turned and signaled for her to recon the room while he watched the door and guarded her back.

Stuffing her irritation over this protective side coming to the surface, on an op of all places, she searched the room that sprawled thirty-five feet in one direction. No real furniture beyond tall side tables positioned along the walls between art arranged in groupings. Those tall tables supported sculptures she could've carried in her arms if they hadn't been hefty bronze.

She moved deeper into the room through an opening hung with thick velvet drapes pulled back with sashes.

This back area did offer seating, but even that was two chairs that belonged in a museum for eighteenth-century furnishings. The chairs had been arranged next to each other with a small, porcelain and wrought-iron coffee table, all positioned to face the only item of interest in the room.

A beautiful landscape painting in a massive gold frame.

Disappointment poured into her limbs. It was not the panel.

Where was that thing?

If the owner had it locked away in a secret room, she had almost no chance of finding it without more information.

She closed the distance to the frame and turned around to lean against the wall on the side of the painting so she could observe the rest of the room and ceiling.

He could be hiding it somewhere in here.

Wouldn't he want it to be in his personal gallery?

Or is that just my wishful thinking?

The ceiling had been painted with a Renaissance scene.

Nothing along the walls gave her any indication of a hidden, secret room. No bookcase or fireplace with a lever for flipping around.

She'd watched too many *Pink Panther* movies.

Glancing to her left, she noticed just how deep the frame had been constructed around the painting. It had to be six inches thick.

Straightening away from the wall, she flipped up her monocular and switched on a tiny, red LED finger light. She ran the light along the edge and reached over to push the painting aside.

It didn't move.

She tried to lift it away from the wall. Not budging.

Her whole body went to hyperalert at the possibility swirling in her mind. She searched all around the sides and bottom of the painting.

Still no obvious way to remove it.

She dragged one of the chairs over to stand on. When she stepped up on the arms, the heavy chair stayed put. Shining the light across the top of the frame, she found a C-shaped metal tab.

Gage walked up slowly enough for her to catch the movement,

purposely alerting her that he was joining her. When she glanced across the space at him, his night vision gear had been pushed out of the way and he had his LED light on as well.

He eyed her precarious position. "What'd you find?"

"Not sure yet, but this frame will not move from the wall. I found a latch up here, but I can't see what will happen if I pull it." She kept an eye on the door, just as Gage did.

He got closer and put his hands under the monstrous frame. "I've got it. Move the latch."

She reached over and hooked her finger on the tab and pulled.

A mechanism clicked and thankfully, the whole thing didn't fall, because she had her doubts about one man holding the painting structure.

He pulled on the far side of the painting and it swung open. Soft light spilled over the front of Gage from whatever was behind the painting.

She waited for him to say something. Anything. She finally asked, "What's there?"

"You're gonna want to see this."

Jumping down, she stepped around where he stood holding it open like a door. Gallery lights inside glowed down on the hidden piece.

The painting hid a rectangular panel that was just under four feet wide and thirty inches tall, decorated with intricate gold leaf and the image of a woman in period clothes in the center.

The panel, as in *the* panel.

Under the perfectly set gallery lighting, the resin glowed a color that could only be described as amber.

She gasped. "We found it."

He hooked an arm around her and pulled her close. "I'm damn glad after all you've gone through, but—" Then he burst her helium moment. "We don't know for sure yet."

"Right."

She stepped up and looked closer at the carved edges and contours, searching for the Latin letters. Where were they? Then she remembered what Nick had shared about identifying the panel. They both leaned in to check the bottom right corner.

A small leaf had been trapped in the resin to remain forever.

Gage murmured, "Well, damn. There's the leaf."

Her pulse tripped into high gear and her heart thumped at a crazy rate.

This had to be the one.

"That's encouraging, but you still need to find the Latin text," Gage reminded her before her mind threw a celebration party. "I'll keep an eye on the door."

"Okay." She searched methodically over each side of any raised surface and slowly over the painting in the center. "I can't find it, but this has to be the one."

 Gage suggested, "Maybe it isn't written, but carved. You may need to run your fingers over to feel for cuts."

"I don't want to damage this thing. It's priceless."

"Sweetheart, if it survived all these years of becoming amber, being carved into wall panels and almost destroyed by the Nazis, your soft fingers aren't going to hurt it."

"You got a point. I'll try to feel for something cut into the amber. That's the only thing that makes sense."

Gage pulled out a tiny, Surefire flashlight with a bright white beam and provided pinpoint illumination just ahead of her fingers. She was sure he still watched the door at the same time.

She was running out of places to check when she brushed her finger across the inside of a raised border along the perimeter. Halfway along one side she felt sharp cuts into the amber. "Here."

She moved close enough to see the shapes of letters. She couldn't read Latin, but she'd studied the letters while on the last leg of the flight. Those were the correct symbols.

Seeing her first artifact in hand that could bring Josh home turned her knees wobbly. If only she could call Trish with the good news, but they had to take it out of here first.

She turned to Gage and smiled, then kissed him, really kissed him.

When she broke away, he smiled at her. "I'm not complaining but where'd that come from?"

"Just thank you for helping me find this. Now, let's get the hell out of Dodge."

"I'm all for that, sweetheart."

She stepped to the right side and waited for him to reach the left. Then she lifted it off the wall.

Holy crap, this thing had to weigh at least sixty pounds.

They lowered it together until the bottom edge sat on the thick carpet that smothered the few sounds they made.

Gage hoisted it to his shoulder with a grunt and carried it to the front of the room while Sabrina closed the painting door, flipped her monocular back into place, and slid the chair back where it belonged. No use giving the king of this castle an early heads-up that his treasure had been pilfered.

Once they had the panel positioned to the side of the door, she eased the door open until she could see the office at the other end of the hall.

Dirchs sat behind his desk, going over papers and turning away to face his laptop on occasion, but not for very long.

How long would he do that?

Was he a night owl who slept until noon?

She calculated how long it would take to reach the airport where her jet waited, which meant she could lift off within twenty minutes if they ran into no problems with the air traffic control.

The best she could figure, they had between two to three hours of leeway, with three hours being on the generous side, to reach Mumbai on time.

That was only if they had no issues getting it out of here. Nitro had warned her that the best way out was through the front door. The garage access required lowering a hydraulic floor to the exterior doors. Their other option was a tunnel that had been cleared as an emergency exit but it meant going through the butler's quarters.

The only other known exit points were balconies that overlooked the river.

It was highly likely the castle had additional tunnels that allowed escape, but since there were no plans on file to be raided like there would be with a contemporary structure, finding those would be next to impossible.

Sabrina pushed the door almost closed and turned to Gage.

"We can't waste time waiting on this guy to go to bed, but I don't want to kill an innocent person."

"I've been considering the same thing."

"I'll go first and you cover my back."

"No."

Did he think she couldn't figure out what he was doing, pushing her out of the way? She clicked off her throat mic. "This is another example of why we can't partner."

"Are we really going to have this conversation right now?"

"You know what I'm saying." She released the throat mic so Nitro was included again and turned back to the door, waiting. When would the king of this castle drink enough grog and go to bed? "Like I said, I'll head out—"

"Not happening."

Nitro interrupted. *"Unexpected company inserting."*

She jerked around to the window and Gage's head was right above hers.

A dark figure raced past the glass. Then another.

Shouting erupted in the office.

Gage swapped positions to pull the door open. She dropped low, weapon ready, and peered through the tiny opening.

"Who are you? What do you want?" Dirchs shouted. He stood behind his desk with a weapon pointed at the intruder, who held a Beretta AR70 assault rifle on Dirchs. A match to the weapon his sidekick also pointed at Dirchs.

The intruder replied, "Have you completed the project you were tasked with by your benefactor?"

Dirchs lowered his weapon to rest on the desk. "*That's* what this is about?" He sounded put out. "I could do without all the drama. He knows he can depend on me. I've got everything in place just as he wanted. As long as no one cancels the match, all his dreams will come true."

Who was Dirchs talking about?

She did not need an altercation in the middle of getting the panel out of this place.

Then again, if they all killed each other that would simplify things.

The intruder questioned, "But he doesn't know you've stolen

the piece he's been searching for, does he? I'm surprised that anyone who knows him would risk his wrath."

Sabrina wanted to thunk her head against the door.

No. Fucking. Way. Were these people here for the panel too? Or was this about the castle owner screwing an associate out of whiskey? That would be tons better. She'd hurt someone very soon if they didn't get this finished and move along. If she and Gage stepped out right now, this would turn into a bloodbath.

Time bore down on her shoulders, but she couldn't harm people who happened to be in the wrong place at the wrong time.

Even if they were a bunch of thieves.

Nitro whispered, *"I can leave the nest and put feet on the ground."*

He was offering to come in and cover their sixes. She told him, "No. We need your eyes. We're good."

Good was being optimistic, but she'd still rather have Nitro nearby in the van than caught up in a potential firefight. It would have been better if they'd had the time to set up more observation equipment, because Nitro was limited to the security camera feeds for the castle, which was why he'd had bare seconds to warn her about this pair entering.

Dirchs complained, "I've stolen nothing. How could he question my integrity? I've been one of his most dependable resources for six years." His tone changed from defense to offense. "Just who are you to come in my home and insult me?" His voice went up a notch with a realization. "Wait a minute. Wayan did not send you, did he?"

Wayan? Who was that? She exchanged a look with Gage that said he was just as confused.

"I am Alnitak, and I do not answer to Wayan, but my superior will be pleased that I've discovered that Wayan is up to something. He should have shared it with his associate in all of this. You will now tell me the rest of the details and I will earn a bonus. First, where is the panel you should not have hidden from either one of those men."

Dirchs lost a load of confidence at hearing those words.

To be honest, Sabrina wasn't feeling too perky herself. Who

were the two men this guy was talking about? Was one of them Rikker's boss?

Gage touched her shoulder to gain her attention and mouthed, *Orion Hunters. We need to go.*

She agreed, but not without this panel.

Gage had to be a mind reader, because he looked down at the panel then back to her and, without any question, hoisted it onto his shoulder again. No matter how much he'd fought against her being here, he was still standing by her, which said a lot.

She just couldn't think about them right now.

"I don't have any panel," Dirchs bluffed.

Even without having her hands on the panel, Sabrina could tell he was lying.

Alnitak hadn't been fooled. "Tell me where it is plus the plan Wayan is launching and your death will be quick. Otherwise, I will twist your nuts off one at a time with pliers."

"Even if I had the panel to give you, Wayan would hunt you down like a jackal starving for something to eat."

"Fine. I'll save a bullet just for him."

Gage pushed the door to and whispered, "I'll carry the panel. You cover my ass. No arguing."

Since he could out-bench-press her, Sabrina said, "Copy that."

He said, "The minute they make a move to subdue Dirchs, we make a run for it and hope like hell they don't have more men waiting below."

Sounded good until she opened the door a little and Dirchs jerked a gun up to shoot his intruders, who unloaded on him.

Gage pushed out a hushed, *"Now!"*

Sabrina stepped out and stayed close to the wall, watching Gage's back as he slipped past her to the stairs. She followed, swinging around at the last second to race down the steps.

The gunfire above had quieted. Dirchs was either dead or would be once Alnitak finished with him.

Nitro's calm voice said, *"Two more guests coming. Abort alpha exit. Go with bravo plan."*

Plan B was through the butler's quarters where the entrance was under the stairs.

Damn. She was right behind Gage, who had one step until he reached the main floor where it faced the castle entrance.

The front door opened with the barrel of a weapon leading the way.

Chapter 27

GAGE SUFFERED THE worst fear of his life when a man carrying another Beretta AR70 pushed through the castle's front door.

Sabrina stood above him, completely exposed.

She ripped off two suppressed rounds, the thunk-thunk so quiet that he heard the pistol cycle just as he felt the bullets zing past his left ear. Time slowed, the way it always did for him in these moments until he heard the crisp ping of 9mm brass as it ejected onto the tile floor.

The man dropped like a stone. She'd double tapped him in the forehead. Gage had forgotten what a crack shot she'd always been.

His partner would hold back only a few seconds, then come at them.

Not wasting a second, Gage cleared the last step and swung around, running softly to the butler's door under the stairwell. Sabrina was there to open the door and close it quietly behind them, squeezing his shoulder so he knew to keep moving.

Gunshots rattled in the foyer, then the shouting started.

With just a tiny bit of luck, Gage would find a way out of here before Alnitak figured out how whoever killed his backup had escaped.

Gage raced down steps lit by sconces. He could barely hear Sabrina right behind him, but as he reached the bottom landing, he caught the heavy thumping of music on the other side of a door just down a hall.

Sabrina swept past him and opened that door slowly.

The short hallway must serve as a sound buffer.

As soon as she opened the door, the music got crisp and louder.

He strode ahead, checking once to see that Sabrina had shut the last door and was catching up to him.

She tried the doorknob to what had to be the butler's apartment. It turned.

When she pushed it open, headbanging heavy metal music slapped him in the face. That meant Benjamin couldn't hear a damn thing.

Sabrina led the way with Gage close on her heels.

At the entrance to the kitchen, they found Benjamin in a T-shirt and his boxers, singing away.

More like screeching to the music as he prepared a meal.

He turned halfway to his refrigerator and jumped when he saw them. Anyone would jump if they found a man toting a rare piece of art on his shoulder and a woman pointing a gun at him.

Benjamin froze. The plate in his hands slipped loose and crashed against the slate floor. His jaw would follow next.

She shouted, "Where's the emergency exit?"

"Wh-what?"

Sabrina tapped her ear and sliced her finger across her neck. Benjamin got the message and grabbed a remote. The music dropped about a million decibels.

Sabrina said, "Your boss is dead. Men are on their way to kill you. *Run!*"

He understood that, at least. He took off like his butt was on fire and he had to find the nearest mudhole.

Gage shifted the panel and they followed Benjamin through the apartment to a built-in bookcase he pulled from the wall, then ran through an opening behind it. Gage turned and squeezed through into a tunnel that belonged to a cave.

Flipping his monocular into place, he had to hand it to Sabrina. Her warning to Benjamin had been much more effective than trying to get the butler to make any sense with directions. "Good way to get him moving."

"Thanks." Sabrina shut the door and locked it, but they both knew that would buy them only a little time once someone knew where they'd gone.

She hurried ahead, shouting, "Follow me. I can hear him running."

Nitro's voice popped in Gage's ear. *"Shit. Traffic coming in from two directions. One group heading around the structure. Don't exit without checking first. I'm going mobile."*

"Copy that." Gage's gut squeezed into one twisted ball of worry for how to get her and this panel out of here. He hated underground with no idea for sure how to get out.

When Sabrina reached a choice between going straight and turning left, she took the turn.

Gage got there right behind her and could just make out the butler, who had come up with a flashlight. He probably kept one down here just for an emergency. The light bobbed up and down for a moment, then it stopped.

Was Benjamin at the exit point?

Sabrina picked up her pace, probably to warn the guy not to rush outside.

Benjamin shined the light on a door.

Bullets tore through the covering, slamming into the butler, who danced like a puppet being yanked around.

He fell backwards on the damp cave floor.

Had to be dead.

Sabrina skidded to a stop six feet in front of Gage and swung around, racing back the way they'd come. She passed him to take the lead. He backtracked behind her to the turn where this tunnel had forked off from the first path.

The sound echoed as their pursuers hacked through the wood covering the exit behind them.

There was only one direction they hadn't been, which meant taking a left into a pitch dark hole that could be a dead end.

Fuck.

More shots were fired. Probably shooting out whatever lock stood in their way.

She said, "We can't go back toward the butler's quarters. We have to go left. You go first. I'll cover our rear."

He took the lead, because much as it sucked that she'd face two groups of guns coming for them, this was the best strategy.

She stayed close enough for him to hear her footsteps.

They were trapped. He couldn't shake that sick feeling.

If they got out of this ... he'd think about it later. The only thing he knew was that he never wanted her to be in a situation like this again.

Fuck being partners.

He wanted her safe at all costs.

This miserable panel would end up getting her killed.

The tunnel curved and started to rise every ten steps. Gage pressed on, forcing his legs and body to pick up speed in spite of the extra weight.

It seemed the further he went, the more he banged his arms against the walls. This passage was getting narrower.

He had a bad feeling about this exit strategy.

A ping reached his ears.

A bullet hitting the stone walls? "You good?"

"Yeah. Keep going."

He climbed steps and ran around a curve to more steps going up. Maybe this was winding them back to the upper floors. What was the chance of finding a way out up there?

He ran out of tunnel and barely stopped before hitting a dead end. Fuck.

He turned to Sabrina, who had just realized the same thing.

She looked to her right at a shadowy alcove and smiled. "That way."

"What's that way?"

"You can't feel that breeze? It has to be coming from the outside."

"Let's do it."

She scrunched down and he could finally see where she was going. Hell, they might get stuck and be easier to shoot than the ducks swimming the river that ran past out back.

She turned to him. "It's about ten feet before the opening. They're close behind us. I'll take the panel with me and go first."

If she went first with the panel, he'd be able to use his weapon, but she'd be the first one exposed to whoever might be watching that exit for a kill shot.

Hell, no. There was no telling how much these men knew about the castle.

Bullets pinged, but not deep enough to reach them yet. There were two curves to get around before this point and no one wanted to step out and be exposed.

But that wouldn't hold back determined men very long.

On the other hand, if they were after the panel, they wouldn't want to damage it.

Gage told her, "I'll go first, then you scoot inside and pull the panel in last. They don't want to shoot that thing."

"That's right. Good idea."

Damn. Nice to win one with her on occasion.

One of the men chasing them shouted, "Stop shooting you idiots. That's the panel." The same deep voice called into the tunnel. "Leave the panel and I'll let you live."

Yeah, right.

Gage would buy oceanfront property in Iowa before he bought that lie.

He lowered the panel to the ground and turned around, backing into the hole feet first in case he had to drop down to a ledge. He didn't want to go anywhere face first.

Once he made it four feet in, he told Sabrina, "Get your ass in here and let's go. They aren't sitting out there waiting for an answer. They're figuring out how to incapacitate us."

She wiggled her way into the hole until her boot heels were next to Gage's face. He could see that she had the panel with the backside flat on the ground to pull in the narrow end behind her.

She got it six inches inside the tunnel and it stopped.

Ah, hell.

He waited for her to admit the obvious.

Sabrina strained and pulled on it. She tried to turn the panel to find the right combination that would allow a square peg to fit in a round hole not big enough for it.

She had yet to see what Gage had found out deeper.

He said, "It's not going to make it, sweetheart. I'm at a point where my shoulders are tight, because it's at least an inch more narrow back this way."

"No." She slapped the ground with her fist. "I have to have this."

"Even if we could break off three inches, which we can't, the artifact would be ruined. It might be worth nothing to Rikker's boss if we damage it."

Someone from the group hunting them shouted, "Last chance or I'm throwing tear gas."

A firefight in a tunnel against men with rifles was a losing proposition already, but gas was the trump card. Gage growled and warned her, "If you die here, you can't save Josh."

Sabrina let out the sound of a trapped animal who'd just realized the only way to freedom was to chew off a limb. She released the panel and whispered, "Go."

"Secure your weapon so your hands are free." He worked his way backward as fast as he could, then his feet pushed out into nothing but air.

Her boot soles were staying close.

"Slow down a second," he told Sabrina. He shoved his body further. If his body made it through this opening, hers would for sure. The alternative was getting stuck here with no way to go forward unless they wanted to die. When his hips passed the last solid spot, he kept going until the toes of his boots dropped to touch a downward shaft.

That shifted his weight. He started sliding away.

Slapping his hands out to the walls, he pushed his elbows against the rock to slow his descent, but his hands were slipping over the damp stone. He shoved his boots to each side. They slid.

The sound of a metal can hitting the rock echoed through the space.

"Tear gas coming at us," Sabrina said into her comm.

If he had no way to look where he was going, it would be better to go there without being disabled by tear gas.

He said, "Straighten your arms."

Trusting her to do just that, he made a quick move, jerking his hands from the walls to grab her ankles a second before he would have dropped out of reach.

He yanked her toward him with an extra tug as his body shifted backwards.

She coughed.

The tear gas was fingering its way to her.

Without another word of warning, Gage pushed his legs out for leverage and gave her one more yank, then he gripped his knees together and gravity took over.

He shot backwards down the shaft, dragging him with her.

The second his feet lost contact with any structure, he shouted, *"Keep your body straight!"*

He fell out of a hole into nothing but air.

Chapter 28

SABRINA HAD JUST figured out Gage was in a shaft that sloped severely downhill when Gage pulled so hard they went flying backwards.

Then there was nothing but air.

One thousand one. Body straight, she kept her feet together with no chance to look down.

Please be water below.

One thousand—

She plunged feet first into icy-cold water, not as straight as she'd have liked but it hadn't broken anything so far.

Black water swallowed her and the cold leached into her body, freezing her. She twisted, trying to get her bearings.

The current dragged her around.

Waving her arms, she slowed her descent and paddled her feet hard. With no idea whether she would be diving into water instead of trees or the ground, she hadn't gotten a good breath of air at the last second.

Her lungs screamed for oxygen.

She strained, fighting panic. *Keep paddling,* she told herself. *Tell me I'm going up.*

Where was the surface?

Everything looked the same.

Inky blackness surrounded her. Her chest ached. Her lungs burned.

If she took in water, she'd drown.

Her head burst through the surface. She heaved in deep breaths, dog paddling while she tried to catch her breath. She still had her monocular, but it was wrapped around her neck. The current continued to move her along.

She kept turning around and called in a hoarse voice, trying to keep it soft. "Gage?"

Through a break in the trees, she saw lights shining on the upper levels of the castle, much further away than she'd expected to be.

"Gage!" she hissed out again, not wanting to draw the attention of Alnitak and his friends.

Catching a deep breath, she paddled her feet harder, which took all she had to give. Her soaked boots were dragging her down like weights. She pulled her monocular up on her face. The lens dripped with water but she could make out the bank on the castle side of the river and swam hard.

A limb swatted her head. Land ho.

She grabbed it and pulled herself up, struggling until she could sit on the ground and suck in air.

Where was Gage?

She'd lost her comm unit. Panic kept trying to find a claw hold. She whispered, "Gage?"

Still nothing.

What if he'd been knocked out when he landed? How would she find him?

Or his body?

I am not thinking that way, she scolded herself mentally. She propped her elbows on her knees and dropped her head into her hands.

She'd lost the panel.

The scroll was out of reach.

Chatton might or might not show with the cross.

Shaking her head, she muttered, "I can't lose them both. Gage can't be dead." She had no idea how long she sat there, muttering that to herself when she heard, "Damn right, I'm not dead."

"Gage?" She lunged up, turning in the direction of his voice. He caught her to him and all the misery she'd kept locked inside spilled out with her tears.

"Take it easy, sweetheart," he murmured, clutching her as tightly as she held him. "I've got you."

She'd never had to lean on a man to make it through life,

but she leaned into Gage, so glad for the strength of his arms holding her close.

He kissed her hair and her face. "I surfaced and you were gone. Longest minute of my life."

She caught her breath and asked him, "How'd you find me?"

"Nitro's still tracking both of us."

"You didn't lose your comm?"

"No. I figured yours was gone." He held her face between his hands. "I refused to believe I had lost you."

His mouth descended on hers, kissing her with a ferocity that said just how much he'd feared her drowning. When he paused, he put his forehead against hers. "I couldn't call out without drawing fire to you, but I called quietly until I was hoarse. Then I got to the bank and tapped my comm. Nitro's made contact and he said your body ... *you* were down river from me."

Her heart felt ripped in half.

Thrilled to have Gage alive.

Sick over losing the panel ... and the best hope she'd had for Josh.

Chapter 29

GAGE CARRIED SABRINA'S luggage into the hotel room Nitro had rented just south of Zürich. Nitro stopped at the door and held out a key. Gage took it. "Thanks."

"No problem," Nitro said. "I'll be back in an hour. We have to leave then to get you to the airport by zero-three-thirty for the flight to Mumbai. That allows you about thirty minutes of leeway. I'll be on watch until you're ready to go. Just cut the light and I'll come up to cover you."

Glad to have had Nitro on his team tonight, Gage shook his hand. "Thanks. For everything."

Nitro dipped his head. "Any time."

Sabrina had already walked in. She dropped her night vision gear and weapons on the bed.

Gage placed his on the dresser and locked the door. "We've got an hour to shower before Nitro gets back. Why don't you go first?"

She stood there staring down at the bed. "I don't know who has that panel or what they're doing with it."

"Maybe they're selling it to Rikker's boss."

When she turned around, Gage took in the devastation she struggled to hide. He walked over and brushed his hand over her still-damp hair. "It's not over yet."

That got him a sharply arched eyebrow. "This from the man who has tried to make me accept that this entire mission was hopeless?"

"That was before you hit me with what I'd do if it was you. If I had to go there empty-handed to get you back, even knowing that it meant a death sentence, I'd do it. Do I wish you weren't going to be in danger? Yes. Will I try to stop you from going? No. And I'll be right there beside you."

Her lips parted. No snappy comeback. "You can't, Gage. It's insane. I won't have even one artifact in hand."

"Then that's the way we'll roll, because I'm in if you're in. We came here as partners. We leave here as partners."

"Josh is my responsibility, not yours," she argued.

"Your safety is mine. We've just lost five minutes of our hour. Hurry up and shower."

"You first. I need a minute to call Dingo and find out where we are with the scroll reproduction."

Gage cupped her cheek and kissed her softly, then walked into the bathroom, pushing the door half closed. He shed his clothes and stepped under a scalding shower, then leaned an arm against the back wall. He kept hearing the empty silence after calling for her in that river.

He'd been terrified she'd hit wrong and was unconscious. That she had drowned.

Anything was possible when a mission went sideways.

He fought the sick concern over her walking into that meeting with no artifact, but he'd told her the truth when he said he'd do no different if she were captured.

She was going after Josh and Gage would be right beside her.

But when this was over, they had to talk, because he'd changed his mind on one thing. There was no way they could partner together as he'd once thought.

He never wanted to go through that feeling again.

To know he couldn't protect her. She was a hell of an operative, but she was no longer someone whose safety he could be objective about on a mission.

That made *him* a liability.

She'd been right the first time when she told him this wouldn't work.

That didn't leave a lot of options. He wasn't ready to walk from the CIA, and more importantly—the agency wouldn't allow him, not in his prime. Even if Gage could figure out some way to do it and go far enough away to live in anonymity, Sabrina wouldn't go. She'd built a life and wanted it.

Gage would not take that from her.

The shower curtain moved aside.

He turned his head to find his beautiful woman naked. Without a word, she stepped into the small shower and put her arms around him. He pushed off the wall and twisted around to wrap her up close and hold her warm body as water sluiced over them.

Her lips started at his neck and moved around to his waiting lips. He was hard and throbbing for her.

No apologies. He wanted her twenty-four-seven.

Always would.

She lifted a leg and he hooked his hand under her knee, holding her up, and dragged a finger through the soft curls between her legs. He pushed it inside her.

She moaned. He captured her mouth with a kiss and plunged another finger inside. The leg he held shook. He kept the motion slow, pumping his fingers in and out. She arched up against him.

His body burned for her and only her.

Withdrawing his hand, he caught her other leg and lifted her. She locked her legs behind him and rubbed her heat up and down his erection. His muscles clenched, holding back the surge threatening to burst from him.

Swinging her around, he put her back to the wall, freeing his hands to reach for her breasts. She was firm and her nipples now taut buds waiting for attention. He gave it to them, brushing his thumbs over each one.

She keened high and gripped his shoulders.

Her body arched. She lifted against him.

Catching a hand on each side of her waist, he eased her down, feeding his length into her. She called his name over and over, driving him to the edge of oblivion.

His body shuddered with holding back, then he pushed up, all the way.

She hugged him to her and bit his neck, meeting his strokes and pushing down each time.

He clenched her sides, struggling to hold on. "You're so

fucking hot." Reaching between them, he went right for that spot, the one he knew so well that would snap her control.

"Gage ... oh, yes ... yes ... "

That stopped her slow torture up and down his cock.

She clamped her muscles tight and he drove into her over and over, ready to fill her up. He found the sensitive nub and began to torment her until she let go. Didn't take much.

She lurched, arching back and calling to him.

Her breast was right at his mouth. He nipped it gently with his teeth and she yelled, shaking as he forced her to keep giving up all she had.

When she finally slumped in his arms, he held her there. As bad as his cock wanted release, he needed to hold her more. To have her in this moment when he had no idea if he'd ever have this again.

After a bit, she roused, kissing his cheek and moving around. Her husky whisper of, "Don't stop," was all the prodding he needed. He pulled out and eased back in, shuddering at the feel of her.

He wanted to take it slow, to make it last, but she ran her teeth across his shoulder and demanded, "More."

Roger that, sweetheart. Driving harder, he held onto his own control as long as he could.

She clenched him again.

Tension tightened and snapped all at once, turning loose the flood of energy he'd been holding back. He roared, clutching her to him as the orgasm drained him.

When his breathing finally slowed, he could feel her heartbeat thunder in sync with his.

He held her and she had him wrapped up, unwilling to let go.

If only life would be so simple.

Chapter 30

Near Baoding, China

"WHAT HAPPENED?" That sounded like a simple question from Wayan, but Rikker's palms dampened, and no mission had *ever* given him sweaty palms. He'd been looking forward to a nice lunch until he'd gotten word from Zürich. Now his stomach was trying to turn inside out.

No one made him feel this way and lived.

He'd moved way past hating this Chinese prick, but he was too close to walking free to blow it now.

Rikker admitted, "My people found the panel, but by the time they got to the location everyone was dead."

Wayan stood at the window in his office with his back to Rikker.

That bastard had better give me what we agreed to or his brat will die along with him. Now more than ever, since the day Wayan purchased Rikker from the UK broker two years ago, Rikker hated him. But he'd had no say in the deal when he'd realized the CIA had not pulled him out of the UK. Wayan had.

Not a man to question a potential gift horse, Rikker had jumped in to make the most of this new arrangement once he realized what had gone down.

He had no love lost for the agency that had been giving him more shit every year, especially once that prick Gage Laughton put a target on his ass.

Wayan turned to him. "You assured me all the artifacts would be at the *Illustratio.*"

"It hasn't *not* happened yet, Wayan. I'm still working my

contacts. You can't accuse me of failing unless the other three artifacts don't show up. I got my hands on The General's coin when no one else could have. Let me finish doing my job."

During the tense pause, Rikker mentally tabulated what he had in a Swiss account. Not enough to live the way he'd prefer for the rest of his life, but with some cosmetic surgery he'd be able to pick up wet work for another ten years.

All he had to do was get away without this piece of shit Wayan catching him.

"Very well, Rikker. You shall have your time, but you will remain here until this is done."

Rikker had figured on something like this, but he was way ahead of Wayan with his exit plan. "I've got no problem with that as long as you don't need me to go somewhere."

"You sound confident, but remember that our agreement has always been total success or nothing."

"I haven't forgotten that. I know my contacts. They'll come through. That's why I sound confident." Not really, but Wayan didn't need to know Rikker had banked money for years just in case he needed a backup plan, like he did now. "You'll have everything you need for your *Illustratio*, but it would help me to know where it's going to be. What if that panel turns up on the other side of the world? I can't snap my fingers and get it here without knowing where it has to be."

"You will know when the time comes. Until then, have the panel delivered to Mumbai at the same time we have given the Slye woman to be there."

"Understood." Rikker checked his watch and lifted his head. "I'm expecting one of my people to be in touch in the next ten minutes ... unless you have anything else to talk about."

"No, you are free to go."

Rikker had made it to the door when Wayan said, "One last thing."

Rikker muttered, "Give me a break," but not loud enough to be heard. He turned with a what-else-can-I-do-for-you expression plastered on his face. "Yes?"

Wayan rarely changed his emotionless expression, but damn if it didn't look as though he wanted to smile. If he did, Rikker would start looking for someone's head being delivered to Wayan. Nah, that probably wouldn't even make him smile.

Wayan said, "I have located the account in Switzerland that contains just over sixty million dollars."

Rikker had never been so shocked he was unable to form words. But he couldn't get a sound past his lips.

"Correction," Wayan said as if telling him dinner would be ten minutes later. "The account *contained* that much. It is empty now. I will return it along with the money I have agreed to pay you when all the artifacts are delivered."

That fucker. Rikker's exit plan just got bloodier.

Chapter 31

Mumbai, India

MINUTES TICKED DOWN closer to half past eight in the evening. Sabrina had watched each minute tick off since they'd arrived in Mumbai just under an hour ago. She hated walking into an unknown situation and without any of the genuine artifacts. Was the *Illustratio* going to be today?

If so, what was so special about this Monday?

Staff at this private airport near Mumbai had all been exceptional in offering Sabrina and Gage a comfortable place to wait.

If only she could relax, but she kept checking the time on her phone as she typed messages to her team. She murmured, "Dingo's flight has landed. He'll be here soon with the scroll."

When Gage didn't answer, she glanced over at him.

He'd said little since they departed the hotel in Zürich last night and flew thirteen hours to Mumbai. Even now, he tapped just as nonstop on his phone when he wasn't talking to someone. For the half hour they'd been sitting here he'd said nothing to her.

When he finally met her gaze, he said, "We're good. Everything we need is on your jet. It's fueled and your pilots are ready the minute you say go, and Dingo will walk through the door any second now. What's wrong?" He gave her a half smile. "Besides the obvious?"

She'd left coming up with body armor and any other toys Gage could scavenge for this next leg to him. He'd done everything she'd asked without argument. Sure, he grumbled some, but she'd known Gage a long time. He would throw himself into the path of harm to protect others. Seeing her in danger evidently brought out his dark side.

Once she got over the urge to strangle him when she'd thought he was discounting her ability, she'd found a comfort in his arms that no one and nothing else had ever been able to offer her.

She wouldn't fault him for the way he showed that he cared.

Not when he intended to walk into a death trap with her.

For her.

"You'll be walking into Rikker's hands. If you stayed here, I'd have someone to come back to if ... this doesn't go well."

He put his phone down and turned to take her hands. "I already told you. Rikker has wanted me dead since I pushed the agency to take a closer look at the kills he was making. If he hasn't taken his shot at me before now, he has a reason for waiting. And if this trip doesn't go well, that means neither you nor Josh will make it home." He rubbed the backs of her hands with his thumbs, stalling, then he said, "Do you really think I could sit here and wait to find out? I said I would support this even though I don't see a good ending to it. We do this together no matter how it goes down."

"I just don't understand—"

"No, you don't. I doubt you ever will, but this is me caring about you. I can't help what the rest of the world has done to make you doubt everyone but Josh and Dingo. I can only do what I say I will."

Gage's eyes tracked to the side. He released her hands and murmured, "Company."

"G'day, mates," Dingo greeted, but it lacked enthusiasm. He took a seat and placed his laptop on the flat arm of his cushioned chair, effectively destroying the moment.

Gage gave her a look that said he'd table their talk for later.

Would there be a later?

Sabrina sat up and turned to Dingo. "Where is it?" *It* being the reproduction of Galileo's original scroll.

"I stashed the tube on your jet before I came in." He put his laptop on his knees, flipped it up and started working.

"Good thinking." Sabrina would have to thank Valene when

she saw her again, and not just for getting the reproduction created. No, she had to thank the woman who had brought peace to Dingo's wounded soul. If, by some miracle, they all survived this, Sabrina would make sure Valene knew that she was truly happy for Dingo to be with a woman like her.

Things changed in California when Dingo walked away from everyone to protect Valene, and she'd taken risks to protect him as well. They deserved each other.

Sabrina took a long look at Gage.

What did he deserve?

Better than she'd been able to give him. When they were first together, they had both been content to live on the edge with a day or two here and there. She'd been comfortable with him, far more than with any other man in her adult life. So much that she'd welcomed him into her bed, but something had changed along the way.

When she barely escaped the UK with her team bleeding and battered, she'd turned two years of anger toward a single target—the CIA and Gage.

They'd become one in her mind.

During the past year, Gage had shared intel with her several times. He'd obviously been trying to keep her and her teams from walking into traps. In hindsight, she recognized that as his attempt to show her he was not just an agency man and prove he hadn't thrown her out with the dirty bath water.

But she clearly had done that to him.

He'd batted away every excuse she brought up for not going back to what they had before. She was running out of time to admit the truth. She was a coward.

She should tell him. She couldn't go back to the way things were before because she'd gotten so attached to him she'd lost herself. The only way she'd found to pull all the broken pieces back together, to be the strong woman her team needed, had been by forcing her emotions too deep to get in the way again.

Those pieces had no glue without Gage in her life.

She'd been falling deeper for Gage all along.

Was this love?

That word had been twisted too far out of shape early on for her to speak it with any honesty. But Gage had taught her his version, one that transcended words. He'd shown her his own brand of caring in all the things he did for her.

Now she understood what Dingo had gone through in California when he'd gone after Valene to keep her safe.

Sabrina couldn't stop the painful need to be with Gage and keep him safe, too. Maybe this had been the real thing all along.

If so, he deserved to know, but what would she say? *I love you.* Her heart beat out of sync with her body at the fear of uttering words that had brought her so much pain as a child.

She forced herself to calm down.

If she was going to tell Gage how she felt, then she had to be prepared to partner with him when the opportunity arose so they could have some kind of life together. Otherwise, how could she tell him how much he meant to her, then do to him what everyone but Josh and Dingo had done to her, and walk away?

Dingo's phone hummed and they all tensed while he opened and read the text just loud enough for Gage and Sabrina to hear.

"Rikker here. It's show time. If you leave your current location immediately and have your pilot file the attached flight plan, you'll be on time with maybe fifteen minutes to spare. Do not come armed or you'll be turned away before you can board the helicopter. Don't pull anything foolish or you know who will suffer. At the moment, your boy is still in decent enough shape to get married. I'm disappointed in not getting an invitation but to be honest, I don't have time for a tux fitting. Have a nice flight to Taichung."

Flying to Taiwan would take at least eight hours.

Sabrina jumped up. "Let's roll."

Dingo finished rapid typing on his phone. "Pilots have the plan." He grabbed his laptop. "With the time change, we should reach Taichung by zero-seven-hundred hours Tuesday, give or take fifteen minutes."

Already at the door two steps ahead of her, Gage had once again turned into the icy machine she'd known during past operations. The three of them moved as one person and were airborne in no time.

Gage opened the box that had been delivered to the jet while they'd waited for Rikker's text. He handed out equipment. "Everyone suit up. This is the lightest body armor made and it's damned tough, but nothing is foolproof."

Sabrina was already pulling the vest on over her body-fitting tank top. Just putting on this bulletproof shield brought home the cold reality of what they faced.

This would be of no use with a headshot.

Once they were ready, Sabrina went over the plan with Dingo. "I'll carry the scroll. You carry the faux panel." Her gaze went to the rectangle that Trish and Valene had joined forces to create just so Sabrina would have something the right size to take with her, but it would never pass muster once someone opened the box.

"What about me?" Gage asked.

Dingo's eyes flared before going flat as he locked down his reaction.

She understood that he still didn't trust Gage and wanted no part of the CIA handler she'd once said she'd kill on sight. So much had struggled to pass under the bridge since that time for her, but not for Dingo and Josh.

That was her fault and she'd start fixing it now.

She answered, "I want your hands free so you can cover our backs, Gage."

If Dingo's hair could stand up, it should have. He bristled without moving a muscle. "I'll cover your back."

"No. We do this my way all the way, Dingo."

Dingo had been staring spikes through Gage and flipped his attention to Sabrina. His eyebrows lifted in a WTF look.

Gage had not left her at any moment during all of this. He'd been good for his word. She couldn't keep judging him by someone else's yardstick. "I trust Gage to be where he needs to be and to do what he needs to do."

Dingo's face wrinkled with disgust, but he nodded.

She couldn't ask for more, and to be honest that was a lot, coming from him.

Gage studied her silently, but he didn't comment on her show of faith. Instead, he asked, "What's the plan for Soo Jin?"

She nodded at Dingo who explained, "It's going to be a long

shot, but what else is new on this op? I've got a system in place that will allow her to do her part from a distance. I'll use this camera ... " Dingo paused to pull out something the size of a tube of lip balm that he attached to his phone with a short cord. "The quality is three times that of my phone lens and it needs almost no light. As we show her each piece, she'll walk us through the meaning of the artifacts."

This was really going to happen. Or not.

Sabrina had a phony scroll, a really phony panel and no Celtic cross. She wanted to throw up, but she hated throwing up and it wouldn't help in any way.

Minutes flew by faster than she'd ever known on a flight this long, and before she knew it she was strapping in to land. She'd instructed the pilots to refuel and leave as soon as they had a new flight plan filed.

She would not have them sitting here when she had no idea when she'd return.

If she did make it back to Taichung, Gage could find transportation, or Logan and Margaux would come up with something.

A jet helo sat waiting for them, similar to the ones used in corporate transportation back home. When she stepped down out of the plane, two armed men waited next to the helicopter.

What if they wanted to inspect the artifacts before allowing her to board?

Chapter 32

GAGE'S BOOTS HIT the ground. He walked past Sabrina and Dingo, heading for the goon twins guarding the helo. Sabrina silently thanked him for allowing her an extra moment to pull her thoughts together before they climbed on that bird.

Was the *Illustratio* happening in Taichung?

Gray skies hid the morning sunshine as if this moment wasn't grim enough.

A movement at her left pulled her attention from the guards waiting on them to a man jogging over from a nearby hangar.

Gage stepped back to ask Sabrina, "What's Nick doing here?"

"I don't know." She looked to Dingo who said, "Who knows with Nick? I sent him a message that we were on our way to Taichung and that it looked like the *Illustratio* might be going down today, but he never replied. I figured he was somewhere he couldn't talk or text. Looks like he's got a briefcase locked to his wrist."

"Caught you." Nick slowed to stop in front of her, catching his breath. He lifted a metal case that appeared to be a thin, but oversized, briefcase and handed Gage a key.

"What's going on, Nick?" Sabrina couldn't believe Nick had gotten the Celtic cross, but that case wasn't large enough to hold the Amber Room panel.

They all knew where the scroll was sitting.

Nick said, "Patience."

Once Gage had Nick free of the case, Nick turned the locked side of the case to her and Gage. "Both of you place your index fingers on the black panel."

She placed her finger on it and Gage put his next to hers.

A snick sounded.

"This is now keyed to your fingers. I give you the scroll." Nick opened the case and inside, an ancient parchment had been sandwiched inside a non-glare, clear case with tiny bolts screwed in all around the perimeter. Someone had marked each bolt with red paint, or wax, dripped in a small puddle then stamped with an odd spike-shaped icon she didn't recognize. In the extra two inches across the bottom that didn't interfere with the scroll text, technical looking information had been written on a label. The label had a number stamped on it, and had been covered with a clear sheet. Holographic images appeared in the sheet if you turned your head just right.

Her hand shook when she pointed at it and looked at Nick. "The *real* one?"

"Yep."

She handed him her tube with the fake scroll, not believing what he'd pulled off. "How could ..."

Nick grinned. "Just bring it back and in the same shape or I'll end up royally screwed."

That didn't sound good. She tried to keep it light, which they could all use right now. "What? You'll go to purgatory if this doesn't make it back?"

He lost his smile. "Worse. I made a deal that if the pope loaned the scroll to me it would come back intact, and that I would use it to ensure we would not have World War Three, or I end up living at the Vatican for a year."

Sabrina couldn't make any promises, not even about a world war starting, heaven forbid, but she'd do everything within her power to make good on his commitment. "If I make it out of this alive, I won't leave without the scroll in my hands, Nick."

"That's good enough for me."

No matter what anyone thought of Nick's methods, he always came through, but she would have never bet on this.

And would never be able to repay him the value of holding this scroll at this moment.

Dingo shifted the box in his hands. "Those guards are waving us over. Our fifteen minute leeway is about done."

Nick said, "Good luck."

Sabrina had the case cuffed to her wrist and was turning to

leave, but paused to asked Nick, "I'm never going to question you again, but how *did* you get the pope to hand this over?"

"I didn't. My godfather, and I mean it in the literal sense of the word, grew up with the pope. My godfather doesn't expect me to return it and thinks it would be funny for me to spend a year at the Vatican with no outside contact. Please don't do that to me."

A godfather, huh? So Nick did heel to one person in this world. "Thank you so much for this, Nick. Take the jet. It's going home as soon as they can get cleared."

"If you don't need me."

"I want no one here, to be honest."

Nick gave her a finger salute and trotted over to her jet with the tube in hand.

At the helicopter, one of the guards held up his hand with two fingers. "Only two go with us. Choose. We leave immediately."

Shit. She turned to face Dingo, who held the box, and Gage, who waited for her to send him away. She'd sworn to herself that she wouldn't take both into a death trap, and now Rikker was forcing her to choose.

Her heartbeat amped up at the rate of a cardio work out. Seconds were ticking off. She looked at Dingo, who shook his head, trying to ward off what she was about to say.

"Please go back and watch over Trish, Dingo. I'm taking Gage. We talked about keeping our locals in the loop." She referenced Margaux and Logan who were not local to Taiwan, but they had more reach than anyone else if she needed help. "Please do this for me."

Dingo growled, shoved the box at Gage, and hugged her. "The camera for Jin is in the box with the panel. We are so talking about this when you get home."

She hugged him back. "I know. Please stay safe no matter what."

"I'm good. You better come back or I'm going after Rikker first, and Gage next."

Oh, boy. She pulled away and Dingo gave Gage one last loaded glare, then strode over to her jet.

Now the guard said, "Give me your phones."

She and Gage had emptied their phones of any history before landing and they were both burners that Nitro had provided. They handed those over.

She warned, "My partner and I are the only two who can open this metal box and we have to be together to make that happen."

"That is not my responsibility. I am only transport for you."

The other guard said, "I will check for weapons."

She held her arms out, though one dipped with the briefcase. He gave her a clinical pat down and nodded to his partner, then put Gage through the same check.

Then he directed them to climb aboard. Once she found a seat and Gage had joined her, the guard who patted them down handed her and Gage black bags. "Put over your head."

She gave one last look at Gage then covered her head. She hated the lack of light, but willed herself to stay calm and alert.

The guard tied the bottom of the bag and she forced her hands to stay down when her training pushed her to reach up and attack him.

In the next moment, she heard someone else cursing as he got on board. He sounded American when he ordered, "Be careful with that!" After some noises of moving something around, the man said, "Who's under the bags?"

The guard answered, "I am not at liberty to reveal anything that is not obvious on this trip."

"That's bullshit. Forget it. I'll find out soon enough."

The loud humming of the rotors, then the whump of the blades as they changed pitch, let her know they were on the way somewhere. She gripped the edge of her seat as the bird lifted off, then warm fingers covered hers. Just that touch and she felt safe for the moment. It was only an illusion since she and Gage were at everyone's mercy, but she'd always remember this minute.

After what seemed to be close to an hour ride, the sound of the rotors shifted again, and the helicopter bumped down.

The guard ordered her and Gage to leave the bags on their heads.

She waited while the other traveler departed, then someone

untied the string on her bag. She jerked it off, making a half-assed swat at smoothing her hair off her face.

Gage led the way to the steps and down, where she took a scan of the landscape. It didn't take long.

Nothing but water surrounded the three-hundred-foot luxury yacht. She didn't even know which direction they'd flown from Taichung.

Chapter 33

A GUARD ARMED WITH a Chinese QBZ-03 assault rifle ushered them down to the main deck, where they were checked again for weapons and bugs. Sabrina kept tabs on everything she saw. Flanked by two guards, she and Gage descended two levels through the largest yacht she'd ever stepped on, and continued down a hallway.

The lead guard directed her into a theater room offering comfortable chairs next to short sofas, with low tables in front of the arrangements. Three elevated levels had areas for sitting on the left and right sides.

A twelve-foot by six-foot oval table had been placed between the first seating level and an impressive movie screen that covered two-thirds of the front wall.

When the guard said, "Take a seat," Sabrina turned and paused.

Sitting on the top left side of the viewing area was a large man in his forties and fit for his size, with coffee-brown skin. Were sunglasses and a fedora meant to keep him incognito?

Had this been the other person on the helicopter?

His lips parted slightly at the sight of her.

Or had it been when he'd looked at Gage? Or the box Gage carried?

The man knew one or both of them, but she had no clue to his identity.

Gage stepped up to the top level and waited as Sabrina took a seat on one end of the sofa then he sat in the chair next to her. They'd have a view of everything this way, with their backs to the wall.

One more person entered, pulling Sabrina's gaze to the door.

Chatton stepped inside and sent Mystery Man in the fedora a tart look. When he scowled at her, she seemed satisfied with his reaction and walked to the far side of the room, where she stood in a spot that allowed her a wide view.

She had a briefcase attached to her arm.

When Chatton leaned against the wall, she finally caught Sabrina's eye and gave a subtle nod.

Sabrina took that to mean Chatton had brought the cross.

That and the authentic scroll would have to be enough.

Sabrina was not handing over the real-freaking-Galileo scroll unless they gave her Josh. Then she'd have to figure out how to get both of them, and Gage, out of here before they demanded to see the panel.

Josh had to be on this boat, or at least she hoped so, but this op still had zero chance of success.

She nipped that thought in the bud. Negative thinking was never productive.

Chatton looked up at the man in the corner. "Did you introduce yourself to our guests? You should tell them you and Wayan are the mighty Czarion."

Chatton had said that for Sabrina's benefit.

Wayan was the name tossed around at the castle where the Amber Room panel had been hidden. Had this man in the disguise been behind those killers?

Mystery Man snarled, "Don't start on me, Chatton. I'm in no mood."

"Do you have a plan for getting off this ship?"

He gave her a dark grin. "Me? I'm good. You're the one who was never part of our club. Not really."

Sabrina thought she saw a tiny slip of surprise on Chatton's face. Why would that be if these two were both Czarion?

What was going on?

The movie screen began rising into the ceiling, revealing Rikker standing at a podium behind it.

Two monitors had been mounted on the walls, one on each side as high as his head.

His eyes glittered with excitement, which made him insane in Sabrina's book. He'd found a home with this bunch. He said, "Welcome everyone to the *Illustratio* for Orion's Legacy. This is a very special day. On this day, the Orion constellation rises upon the birth date of the next world leader. The same day the greatest warrior of all time was born. The mighty Genghis Khan."

Sabrina split her attention between Rikker and Chatton.

She was particularly interested in anything that surprised Chatton.

Rikker continued, "More on the new world leader once this is finished. I'm sure you all want to do this as quickly as possible. For this to be the most efficient, you will answer my boss's questions when they show up on that terminal." He pointed to his right, Sabrina's left.

Mystery Man asked, "Where is he, Rikker?"

"Where he chooses to be," Rikker replied.

Gage cut his eyes at the man, then Sabrina, clearly thinking along the same lines as Sabrina. This man knew Rikker and his boss, aka Wayan, who was possibly the powerful Chinese man Soo Jin had mentioned. Gage would have also noticed how this man had looked at them when they'd entered the room.

Conclusion? Mystery Man could very well be the one who had Perdido and Navarro put to death and issued a contract on Sabrina. That would make him her number one suspect for the leak in the US government and maybe even the person behind the debacle in the UK.

"It's time to put our artifacts on the table," Rikker announced. He kept glancing at Sabrina and Gage, but he directed his first question to Chatton. "Where's your ticket to the party?"

Chatton said, "I've got the Celtic cross." She lifted the briefcase into view.

Rikker turned to Mystery Man. "Regarding the Amber Room panel ..."

"You know I brought it, Rikker. Move on."

Rikker spared a moment to unleash a load of hate for the Mystery Man with his next glance. "Do not interrupt me, General. This is my show."

The man called General grunted. "Then have the guards bring in my panel."

Rikker spoke into a radio, but not loud enough for anyone but him to hear.

The door opened. A stocky guard carried the panel Sabrina and Gage had almost died retrieving. He placed it long ways in the center of the table so that the top of the panel was pointed at the podium, then he left.

Gage pushed the box out of the way and muttered, "This is of no use."

The General and Wayan. Sabrina had two names for the Czarion. Three actually, when she included Chatton.

Rikker's gaze glided over to Sabrina.

She loathed this man so much it hurt to speak to him, but she intended to get this done.

He asked, "What happened, Sabrina? I thought you wanted Josh back." Rikker spoke with false bravado. She could see a small layer of perspiration on his forehead.

She replied, "As you can see, the Amber Room panel and the Celtic Cross are here."

"You didn't bring them."

"You did not specify how these artifacts were to arrive, only that they had to all three be here."

Rikker's jaw muscle ticked. "I know about only two at this point."

She lifted the briefcase and said, "I brought the scroll, so my part of the agreement is intact."

Rikker's jaw slackened and relief speared his gaze. "I have to see the scroll."

"I have to see Josh."

"You aren't in a negotiating position. You still have two items left to deliver."

The scroll and Soo Jin. "Fine, I'll show it to you." She had Gage place his finger next to hers, unlocking the briefcase. While she carried the case down to where Rikker could see it, he spoke into his radio again.

An elderly man walked in. His face had a combination of features she'd pin as Israeli, including wary brown eyes filled with contempt when Rikker said, "There's the scroll. I need an absolute yes or no authentication."

The old guy walked over and pulled a jeweler's loupe from his pocket. He gave the seal a thorough study then stood up. "This is authentic."

"You sure?" Rikker questioned.

"This has been documented by the House of Zosimus, then secured using the *Probatur Per Manum* system they patented. They are above reproach and they specialize in authenticating Vatican treasures. I am telling you that their seal is genuine and unbroken. It states in Greek and in Latin that this is the *Profezia di Orione* scroll. Not even Galileo would argue with those credentials."

Rikker accepted his statement and Sabrina slapped the case shut.

"What are you doing?" Rikker snapped.

"Holding onto the scroll until you show me Josh." She walked back up and sat next to Gage who said, "Well played."

"You can't leave without handing it over," Rikker said, taunting her with the power he held.

She warned, "You can try to take it from me and open it using our fingers, but you can't do what I did to prevent a security device from destroying the scroll."

Nick hadn't said anything of the kind, but this was her power card, so if there ever was a time to bluff her way through a game, this was it.

Who could prove her wrong without risking the scroll?

"Sit down." After dismissing Sabrina, Rikker told Chatton, "Time to ante up."

She opened her briefcase on the opposite end of the table and revealed a slab of stone that would cover Sabrina's palms placed side by side. Somehow, she'd thought it would be an actual cross shape, but she'd read where the original crosses were carved into stones.

Just how old *was* that artifact?

Rikker directed, "The artifact has to come out of the case and be placed next to the top left corner of the panel." He pointed at a spot.

"Is that your rule or Wayan's?"

"You have to ask?"

She shrugged and pulled out a pair of gloves. Placing the cross on the table, she closed her carrying case and moved back to lean against the wall.

She asked, "Where are the stater and jade tablet?"

Rikker produced his own little carrying case just large enough to hold a laptop. He stepped around the podium to the table where he unloaded both items, putting the stater at the bottom right corner. He lifted a jade rectangle with carved words and a gold emblem in the center that might be a belt buckle, and carefully placed it at the bottom left corner of the panel.

Once his antiquities expert had passed an eye over everything, he said, "As far as I can tell without elaborate tests, these appear to be authentic as well."

With the exception of the scroll, it wasn't a leap to believe the rest of the artifacts were bona fide since members of the Czarion had delivered those items.

What would be the point in bringing fakes if they really wanted to find out about the prophecy?

With the expert out of the room, Rikker took his place behind the podium again. The monitor on his left came to life with an Asian man's face.

Chatton said, "Hello, Wayan."

That was the infamous Wayan? Rikker's boss?

Wayan angled his head and a camera above the table swiveled to point at her. "You surprise me by coming to this."

"I've always told you I would deliver the cross. Like you, I'm good for my word. Besides, I wouldn't miss this for the world. I'm just as interested as you and The General are in finding out who starts the war ... I mean who wins the war, right?"

"I find your attempt at humor trying."

Chatton popped off, "I find your hospitality lacking. No one has offered me a drink."

Wayan's face didn't change, but Sabrina sensed his slow blink was the same as a sigh. The camera made a whirring noise and Sabrina guessed it was taking a wider shot of the room.

When the camera was still again, Wayan inquired, "Where is Soo Jin?"

One look into those cold eyes and Sabrina knew he was not a man to be bluffed.

She lifted her chin, ready to sell this to the megalomaniac. "Where is Josh Carrington?"

"He is much closer than Soo Jin appears. I will allow you to retain the scroll until the time comes, but I thought Rikker was clear about delivering Soo Jin."

Sabrina countered, "Soo Jin is not *physically* here, but she is on standby to review all the materials. To have brought her out in the open would have risked her life, since not all Orion Hunters in the world know her value or are truly invested in this *Illustratio*. Had she been killed, she would not be available to translate all this. I felt it prudent to do whatever it took to keep her safe. Don't you agree?"

Wayan said nothing and Rikker glanced over at the monitor, waiting for his boss to speak.

Sabrina shrugged. "All you need is her expertise. I gave you enough credit to assume you would have satellite access for this, but if I was wrong ... "

Wayan just stared out at her. Damn him.

Please don't tell me this is going to be the snag that unravels everything we've done to find Josh.

Chapter 34

SABRINA HELD HER breath, because she was out of moves. If Wayan didn't accept Soo Jin attending virtually, things were going to fall apart quickly.

Maintaining his robotic, even tone, Wayan said, "I will accept Soo Jin's expertise in that manner as being in the spirit of the agreement. Rikker will arrange for the connection once all is in place, but now you will place the scroll into position if you wish to have your man returned."

Rikker visibly calmed the minute Wayan agreed. So he wasn't too keen on the man holding his leash, huh?

Sabrina returned the open case to Rikker, who took the framed scroll and placed it next to the top right corner of the amber panel. She gave Rikker a URL that would connect Soo Jin to Rikker's satellite setup.

He typed it into his computer.

She warned him, "That URL will not go live until I give you the login."

While she returned to her seat, Rikker spoke into his radio again. In the next minute, a guard led Josh into the room with flex-cuffs on his wrists.

She wanted to stand, but had no faith in her knees staying locked.

Until this very second, she hadn't wanted to think about it, but deep down she'd worried he'd either be dead or so badly tortured he'd never heal physically or emotionally.

Josh had dark shadows under his eyes, but he didn't look beaten or tortured, as she'd expected. Not that she wasn't thrilled to see him whole and safe, but her suspicions shot through the roof.

The guard cut the cuffs, freeing Josh, who met her gaze with a confused one of his own.

It was all she could do not to race down and hug him, but now wasn't the time for an emotional display. They weren't out of this mess yet.

Josh climbed the raised levels and sat down on the short sofa next to her, leaving Gage on her other side.

She put a hand on his arm.

He whispered out the side of his mouth, "It's a trap."

She said, "I know."

He gave Gage a cursory glance then asked Sabrina, "Is … *she* okay?"

Sabrina knew he meant Trish. "Yes. She's safe."

The tight lines in his face eased. He rubbed his wrists.

Wayan instructed Rikker, "If the artifacts are in place, proceed."

Rikker thumbed keys and a camera mounted on a hydraulic arm descended from the ceiling. It moved over the table and Wayan had to be receiving the feed based on the way his eyes moved in sync with the camera.

When he appeared satisfied, Wayan said, "Now the questions."

Sabrina slashed a look at Gage, who caught it and lifted his shoulders a tiny bit, letting her know he was just as thrown at the way this was going down as she was. Josh, too, seemed at a loss, but in truth, she wouldn't have expected his captors to share what was happening with him.

The General grumbled, "Get a move on."

Wayan called out, "I have waited many years for this. Do not cause me to regret your presence."

"Whatever."

Rikker tapped buttons on his remote and the camera filming the room pointed specifically at Gage. Rikker said, "I didn't expect to see you here, Laughton, but I had a feeling Sabrina was lying to me when she said you two weren't working together. Working together, sleeping together, it's all the same, right?"

Gage gave him a look Sabrina had seen right before Gage killed someone trying to harm an innocent.

Rikker laughed. "Hey, it's good to be back together. Sort of like a CIA reunion, but you can't screw me this time."

Calm as a jaguar waiting to attack, Gage said, "Don't be so sure about that. My reach is wide and far."

"Yeah, yeah." Rikker stepped down to the floor and positioned himself so that the monitor on the left was just above his right shoulder. He addressed the room. "Remember, the faster you answer these questions, the sooner this will be finished."

The first question that appeared was addressed to Sabrina. *Did you deliver Galileo's authentic scroll?*

"Yes. I said I would." She mentally thanked Nick for coming through, but what was the point in this questioning?

The next question went to The General. *How did you acquire the panel, General?*

"How I do what I do is no one's concern. Only that I come through."

"Got it." Rikker pointed at the monitor and looked at Chatton. The question to her read: *Are you still interested in finding the person who killed your family for that cross?*

Chatton visibly stiffened. "Yes. Believe me when I promise to make everyone involved pay."

The General said, "Why are—"

Rikker snapped his hand with the remote down to his side. "You don't answer unless you're asked a question. If you interrupt again, we'll have to start over."

Everyone groaned.

Returning to his job, Rikker pointed at the monitor, which again addressed Gage: *You were not expected to be here. Do you intend to interfere?*

"No."

The next question was for Josh. *A war is coming. How do you plan to protect your wife?*

Josh leaned forward and answered with no hesitation. "Kill anyone who gets too close."

Sabrina tapped his leg and Josh eased back, unclenching his fists. She understood the need for action, but Wayan and Rikker had not shown their hand yet. She'd like to think Chatton was neutral, if not an ally, but she had no idea who this guy in the corner was or what he did.

Plus, these questions had to be some part of Wayan's insane game, whatever that was.

Hydraulics whirred as the camera above the table moved higher, which allowed Wayan or anyone else like Soo Jin to view the whole table.

Rikker lifted his sat phone and murmured a few words then ended the call. He stepped in front of the camera filming the room and sent Wayan a thumbs up.

Then Rikker asked, "How do I contact Soo Jin, Sabrina?"

Josh tensed and Sabrina moved her fingers just enough to let him know that Soo Jin would not be in danger. She gave Rikker the login credentials to open the URL.

While he typed, Sabrina added, "Any attempt to track the signal will result in a severed connection."

Wayan said, "There will be no attempt to track her. Soo Jin is of no use to me after this."

That sounded like the man Chatton had described—a man who would have snipped a loose end like Soo Jin without a second thought to her death.

When Rikker appeared to have it all set up, he muttered, "There's no video."

"You don't need to see her. You only need audio," Sabrina said, then raised her voice to ask, "Soo Jin?"

"I am here, Sabrina."

"They have a camera that will focus on each piece for you to review."

"I need only a quick look at the cross and scroll to confirm what I expect to find. I know what is on those from information I studied while in North Korea and from ... more recent resources."

That shocked even Chatton.

Sabrina had to hand it to Soo Jin, Valene and Trish. That was a hell of a trio when it came to digging up buried information on ancient artifacts.

Soo Jin said, "I must have a close examination of the stater, the Latin on the Amber Room panel and the entire jade tablet."

Tension spiked the air as the camera moved slowly over the panel first, and paused for several minutes on the slate.

Wayan ordered, "Speak the truth of the next powerful leader to rule."

Soo Jin was quiet a moment, then explained, "Based on the writings I have reviewed from historians of every era who speculated on Orion's Legacy, the artifacts have been placed appropriately to circle the Amber Room panel. The Greek stater shows Athena wearing a Corinthian helmet on what is considered the head of the coin. The scroll is a journal of Galileo's vision, which shows his fear of what he sees in the future. The Celtic cross inscription is in Ogham, an alphabet from medieval Ireland, which translates to 'my enemy of today is the seed for tomorrow ... plant wisely.' The Amber Room panel's Latin states *memento et stellas*. The jade tablet, which holds the belt buckle of Genghis Khan, speaks to descendants of Temüjin, his birth name."

Sabrina had watched Wayan the whole time and her skin pebbled when his eyes took on an unholy look of delight the minute Soo Jin mentioned Temüjin.

"I would caution everyone to not rush to conclusions," Soo Jin warned. "This legacy has been anticipated for many centuries, which means it has had time to gather myth and misinformation around it as one would pull on a comfortable coat. For example, many believe this legacy predicts a great world war to come and the country that will be the victor, but now that I see all the elements together I do not believe that is the message intended."

Wayan's eyebrows drew tight in a frown as he listened.

She continued to state, "The Amber Room panel translates to 'remember the stars,' and that is the start of the legacy. It is believed the phrase on this panel means we are to remember how small we are in this universe. The stater's image of Athena points to a goddess of wisdom and military victory. The Celtic cross indicates how today's decision will affect the future and to choose wisely about what seed to plant—war or peace. Galileo's vision clearly frightened him. He states that a great war is on the horizon, but he also says he who gives it life will hold all responsibility for the outcome of his destiny."

Without slowing, she went on. "After reading everything and reviewing the jade, I feel I have the last part of the puzzle that I had not been able to decipher before now. The jade tells of a warrior who will lead all the people in his world."

Wayan smiled and spoke up, breaking the trance-like moment Soo Jin's voice had created. "Yes." He lifted a fist next to his face. "The great Khan will rise again and rule this world unlike any other warrior before him. Nations will bow to his power."

Okay, that just stepped off into the deep end of the crazy pool.

Sabrina didn't move for fear of drawing Wayan's unwanted attention to her trio. Better to allow the fanatic to show what the hell he was all about first.

"I respectfully disagree," Soo Jin said, snapping all gazes to the table where her voice flowed from the audio above it.

Sabrina noted that the shock on Wayan's face surprised both Chatton and Rikker.

So this was not Wayan's normal MO?

A chilling darkness spread through Wayan's gaze. "How dare you contradict me? You are here only at my behest."

"I understand that you are not happy with me but I was trained from my childhood that when this moment came, my duty was to provide nothing but the truth. That is what I have done. There is a message revealed by these artifacts. The simple message I have gleaned from this is that the one who starts a war between countries will die before he has a chance to win. That is the prophecy. It makes no reference to who will win a conflict. Galileo's journal states that he fears a great war will happen when men lose the ability to talk. The tablet does state that when a new warrior steps up to lead, he will take over at the right moment and the people will follow, then their world will be a greater place. Not that he will conquer the world as Khan had attempted. You cannot rearrange the truth to fit your desire."

"You are a liar."

"I do not lie."

Sabrina had told Dingo to make sure Soo Jin understood to share exactly what she discovered. A lie might kill them all as quickly as the truth, so better to go with the truth and figure it out from that point.

Seeing Wayan's reaction, she might have been better off to give Soo Jin different advice. Still, it wouldn't matter if Wayan had a way to start a war.

Over a freaking prophecy?

Wayan pulled himself together and returned to the emotionless crazy guy. He said in the calmest voice, "Terminate the feed, Rikker."

"Yes, sir."

"I do not need a disbeliever to twist the truth. I know it as I have since eight years old. Heed *my* truth. It was predicted that I would be the catalyst for a great leader. I gave my sacred blood to a son who will become the next ruler today. Just as his ancestor Genghis Khan took his first breath while clutching a fist of blood, so did my Temüjin on the very same day of the year. By tomorrow, his path will be open and those who fail to bend to him will die."

Sabrina sat forward. "Is this masquerade over?"

"Shut up," Wayan said in a deep voice that sounded like a pit bull speaking. Quite a change from the refined voice he had used earlier.

The General hefted his wide body to his feet, groaning and holding his back. He glanced over at Sabrina. "You've been a pain in my ass for the last time. You and your Slye agency." He shifted his head enough to address Gage. "You turned out to be a huge disappointment. We could have used more like Rikker."

Gage watched him without saying a word.

When Gage stayed this quiet for this long, it should worry everyone.

Guards entered the room with their weapons raised. The General started down the steps.

Chatton moved to the table and lifted her slab of rock, which she stuffed in the briefcase before taking a step toward the door.

One of the guards pointed his weapon at her.

She looked around at The General, then back at Wayan's image. "Wait a damn minute. If the General goes, I go."

When The General finished his limping steps to the bottom

landing, he turned to her. "You never got it. You can't be a part of the boys' club without a dick."

Chatton held her composure, reminding Sabrina of a cobra sitting up to access her strike zone. "Hell has a place for you."

The General chuckled. "Save me a seat."

Once he was gone, Wayan said, "You miscalculated, Chatton. You hold no value for me. The General, on the other hand, will be useful when the time comes during the war. One must always look toward the future. You should have handed over Soo Jin. I would have told you who hunted your family."

She slowly turned to the monitor. "You don't know. You're just screwing with me."

"That challenge does not work on me. I will not be baited. But I do wish for you to know the truth so that you may take it to your grave. You have been on the right path for the person who killed your family members, but for the wrong reason. Just as with your false interest in Orion's Legacy, you were shortsighted in your pursuit of the one who killed your family, and you stopped questioning whether the motivation had changed over the centuries. Now, you will never know satisfaction. Think on the fact that you have not lost a family member in quite a while."

Chatton didn't answer as she stared off in a thoughtful gaze. Then she sucked in air as if she'd taken a punch to the solar plexus. "You fucker."

"I have never underestimated you, Chatton, but you have been so sure of yourself that you missed what was right under your nose. I will be glad to have you out of the way. You've been interfering with my plans. There will be a great conflict. My army of Orion Hunters will be given the truth that *I* know."

Ah, now Sabrina got that Wayan needed his people to believe in the charade so that they'd fight for his cause.

Only, it didn't appear to be a charade to him.

Pure insanity.

He continued boasting, "Once the first trigger is pulled and countries come forward to rattle swords at one another, it will be necessary to show who is really behind the conflict. You, the Slye woman, Laughton and Carrington will become notorious celebrities in a video Rikker will release when the time is right. It will show how the four of you played roles in all this."

Gage muttered, "Shit."

"Once the United States steps in to protect its ally, they will face a political apocalypse as the country who organized the death of a world leader they wanted replaced. First I will step in to pave the way, then my son will take his rightful place."

Chatton stood there, letting him get it all out. "Just couldn't wait for us to find out in real time, Wayan?"

Wayan said, "I would have much preferred that, but you will not live long enough to see this played out. You will receive notoriety posthumously. Rikker."

"Yes."

"I gave my word everyone could retain their artifacts. Pick up the stater, jade and panel. The General traded the panel to me."

Gage stopped Wayan with, "One last question."

He paused, staring calmly into the lens recording his image. "Yes?"

"Who in the US government traded a CIA contract team in the UK for Rikker?"

Wayan's mouth twitched as if he might actually smile, but no. He said, "You just watched him walk out."

Sabrina couldn't stop the roaring in her ears. Two years of watching Josh and her team recover from that op. Two years of hell while blaming Gage.

Her stomach rolled. The whisper slipped past her lips the second she thought it. "I'm so sorry."

Gage covered her hand and just said, "It's okay. Focus."

He was right. They had to get out of here and it didn't look promising, but they couldn't do it without her full attention.

With two guards to cover his ass, Rikker had no concern about being overpowered. He waited for Wayan's monitor to go dark, then he grinned at Sabrina and Josh who were now standing with Gage. "Wayan says to never let your enemy know everything, but he got his chance so this is mine."

"What video is he talking about, Rikker?" Josh asked.

"Oh, I'll leave it playing for you. Once I get off this boat with my men, it'll be your last movie before the Titanic goes down. Shame to lose this baby, but like Wayan told me, we're too deep for an insurance company to go snooping. First this goes down, then I get to make the hit to take the old guy and his kid out of Wayan's way. This whole plan is fucking beautiful. But shit, I have no one to share it with. What's the point of all this when I can't tell anyone?"

Sabrina curled her hands, wanting to snap his neck.

"Enjoy your last hour. I would shoot you and take you out of your misery, but I fucking love the idea of you sinking with this thing. The CIA and other alphabet agencies will spend years harassing everyone you know to find you. I told you. Fucking. Beautiful. The agency was never this creative."

He walked out and the two guards backed out behind him.

Then the door shut and locked.

A video went live on the movie screen dropping back into place. The camera panned Sabrina, Gage, Josh, The General and Chatton, all relaxed as if they'd come willingly to meet.

The General had no idea that he had a starring role, too.

Rikker's voice rang out asking Sabrina, "You said you could have feet on the ground when the attack happens. Are you still ready to follow through?"

The camera focused in on Sabrina. "Yes. I said I would."

Rikker asked, "How are you going to keep everyone in the Pentagon in the dark?"

The lens turned on The General next who said, "How I do what I do is no one's concern. Only that I come through."

And on it went.

Rikker had been weaving in previously taped questions that they'd answered like puppets. She'd known he was doing something, but this was ... scary, because Rikker and Wayan were going to pull it off.

Gage said, "Enough of that crap. We've got to get out of here."

Chatton held up a finger and pointed to the roof.

The subtle sound of a helicopter powering up came through. Now chewing a piece of gum, she sat down and started unzipping her boot.

Josh ran down to the door that had no interior handle, just a round lock plate for a key, and tried to bash it open. Gage joined him, using a chair. If everyone knew this boat was going down, the guards weren't wasting time outside.

An explosion rocked the boat, and it listed to one side.

Chapter 35

GAGE HIT THE door to the theater room in tandem with Josh, but it didn't budge. He refused to watch Sabrina, or any of them, die here.

But damn, he really regretted not doing what Sabrina had wanted for so long in going after Rikker. That had to wait right now.

First he was getting everyone out of this floating coffin.

Chatton had been unzipping her boot a moment ago. She walked up and ordered, "Move."

What the fuck? Gage backed up and checked on Sabrina, who was pulling her earrings off. Good. One of the earrings functioned as a sort of EPIRB, a transmitting device that normally sent out a distress signal to be picked up by a worldwide service for search and rescue. The radio beacon from this transmitting unit had been modified to specifically alert Sabrina's people watching for it.

That would be useful only if they made it off this sinking boat.

And if her people were in a position to send a rescue team.

Gage stood back with Josh.

Chatton held a small rubbery tube the size of lipstick that she twisted in the middle. Then she pulled the gum out of her mouth and stuck the tube to the round lock face and backed away.

The little device popped like a miniature firecracker, leaving a hole where the lock had been. Gage got there first and used his shirttail to reach in and yank on the lock parts still in place.

The door opened and another blast shook the yacht, rocking it from side to side.

Gage looked for Sabrina, who had grabbed the case with the scroll. "That doesn't float."

She marched straight ahead. "It's going."

Chatton carried her case, too, which had to weigh even more with that rock in it.

They rushed out of the room and into the hallway where the stern area had begun dipping. Water poured in from the stairwell.

"Going to the bridge and check the radio," Josh yelled, taking steps two at a time.

When Gage surfaced on a level with fresh air, he said, "Let's get as high as we can and start searching." He rushed around to a walkway that led to the next set of steps going up.

Chatton warned, "Wayan wouldn't leave any lifeboats."

"I wouldn't expect it. That's why we go for the next best thing."

"Which is?"

"Anything that floats."

On the mid-deck level he found a pool, but the accessories were nowhere in sight. That bastard Rikker would have made sure they had no lifejackets either.

Sabrina was on the other side of the pool looking through a window into a room. She shouted, "Over here!"

Returning from the bridge, Josh showed up as Gage and Chatton reached Sabrina. He said, "Every electronic has been destroyed."

The yacht listed more to starboard, but not as much as the stern was dropping.

Gage said, "Need something to break the glass."

Chatton was gone. Where was she?

He couldn't worry about her if she'd gone to save her own ass.

Josh came running up and when the boat rocked again, he almost fell in the pool before he launched a fire extinguisher into the glass window on the door. It shattered.

Gage had his shirt off and wrapped the material around his arm to reach inside and unlock it, then he rushed in.

Sabrina and Josh were right behind him. She grabbed a floating chair. Josh lifted a double lounger and Gage snatched a life ring and length of rope coiled for throwing it.

The boat shifted hard and they all fell against a wall, then fought their way up to push out of the room, which contained all the latest in pool furniture.

While Gage and Josh took the floats to the low side of the deck to start stringing the pieces together, Sabrina called out, "I'm looking for more supplies."

She came out a minute later with an armload of beach towels, which might help keep hypothermia at bay, and another floating chair.

Gage caught movement and swung around.

Chatton strode up with a mesh bag filled with water bottles and snacks sealed in plastic bags. She wore a backpack that drooped with the weight of the briefcase. Better than having it on her arm.

She told Sabrina, "Give me your case."

Sabrina handed it over without a second thought.

He revamped his opinion of Chatton. Sabrina had chosen to trust the woman from the start, and Gage had done his best to get in her way. *Just like you did with Dingo.*

Not anymore.

All at once, the stern started dropping faster.

Gage shouted, "Let's get to the edge."

Chatton grabbed a corner of the hodgepodge flotilla and tied the mesh sack in place. "I'm not giving this cruise a high rating."

Gage reached the wall of the deck that should be thirty feet above the water. The sea had gone from a gentle, five-foot swell to eight or nine feet at times, just from the yacht fighting its way down.

The water was within ten feet of the deck. He ordered, "Grab your float and hold on. It's going to yank hard the minute we hit."

Sabrina stood six feet to the side of him and he had a flashback moment of that sick feeling when he thought he'd lost her on the river.

The boat groaned and the bow started up.

If it slid down too fast, they'd get pulled under with it.

Gage shouted, "*Three ... two ...*"

The yacht did a backward slide into the water, shuddering as it picked up speed.

"Now!"

He grabbed his pool lounger and jumped backwards so he could watch for Sabrina. His heart tried to fight its way out of his chest.

She was airborne with the deck coming straight down above her. He hit the water and it yanked him sideways. He kept his mouth shut, fighting to keep a grip on the float.

A wave crashed over him.

He held on, praying this damn thing would find the surface.

It did. He popped up, being pulled back and forth in the water. "Sabrina!"

"Here."

And there she was, smiling and clinging to her crappy pseudo-lifeboat.

Josh and Chatton's heads rose with the next wave. They'd made it. The bow of the boat vanished in seconds. This churning water would calm in just a bit.

Gage looked to the east, where a thunderhead was brewing up a storm. Fuck. Could they not get a break?

Fighting the waves, they pulled their floats within arm's reach of each other, and tied them in a circle with each facing out.

He pushed Sabrina up on hers so it wouldn't flip over on her. Josh was doing the same for Chatton. Then the women held the loungers as Gage and Josh climbed on.

He dropped his head back and fought to give his lungs the air they wanted.

As the minutes passed, the waves settled into a slow roll. He reached over and caught Sabrina's hand. "Still got the EPIRB?"

"Oh, yeah." She carefully pulled the earring from where she'd attached it to her bra, probably the only reason she still had it.

She yanked the wire stem out, setting the specially created unit to send out a signal only her people could track, because they hadn't known where they'd end up.

Dingo's work.

Now he was thinking they might've been better to take their chances with a standard EPIRB, which would've reached out to the first boat that could get to them.

Chatton passed bottles of water around.

Gage asked, "Who do you work for?"

He didn't think she would answer, but she surprised him. "No one in the past three years. Let's just say I'm not your enemy. If I was, you'd have all been dead by now."

Josh looked at her. "Sure about that?"

Chatton gave him a smile that held no arrogance. "You've heard about the Yaawt Seven Thai terrorist cell, right?"

"Yes. Seven of the deadliest contract killers to come out of Thailand. Four were brothers. They died in a bloody battle and no one has ever taken credit."

"That's because people in our line of work do not do it for the publicity. Well, unless you're Rikker."

Gage recalled that takedown. "Whoever killed them took trophies."

"Not trophies, but the head of MI6 had built a relationship with a man in charge of the Royal Thai Armed Forces. The Thai commander asked for a favor and requested that MI6 deliver undeniable DNA proof that those seven were dead."

"Damn," Gage muttered. "That's a ghost story no one talks about. That was you?"

"Yes. I wasn't fond of the contract." She shrugged. "It was not my place to question orders at the time—"

Gage said, "But you had to know what they did to those Thai girls."

"Yes. I choose what I do, how I do it and to whom I do it, which they knew when I came on." Shifting her attention back to Josh, she said, "Anyhow. The seven had kidnapped a pair of twin sixteen-year-old girls and demanded money from their wealthy father. He was willing to pay. Money was delivered and the two girls were left naked, sitting on the side of a street. They'd been raped repeatedly and in ways that a child should never suffer."

No one said anything. That image would be permanently pasted inside his mind.

Lukewarm water washed over Chatton's feet, nudging her back on course with her story.

"The girls spent two weeks in the hospital and another two under care at home. Their parents doted on them. Counselors were brought in. The first day the teens asked to be left alone so they could talk to each other, everyone thought that was a good sign. They slit their wrists. The note they left behind said they could never live with the shame they had brought their family."

Sabrina whispered, "Oh, dear God."

Wiping his mouth as if the story was so rank he could taste it, Josh said, "How does the government get involved with a civilian situation?"

"The seven had become notorious for looting and giving a lot of the money away to the poor. A sick group of Robin Hoods. The government feared a major backlash if they touched them. The Thai government wanted someone to come in and clean house, plus make it obvious it was not a government job. That way, they could posture and make noises along with the people, then let the whole sordid mess fade away as old news does."

Sabrina asked, "Did you go alone?"

"Yes. When the seven lay dead, I left a warning note that made it clear anyone who stood up for these men would receive a similar visit. The writing had a feminine stroke and it was in English on linen paper that could be traced to a Mumbai stationery manufacturer, but anyone investigating would question it being a woman and any tie to Mumbai as diversion."

She stretched to get in a better position. "The reason this drew the attention of the government, Josh, was that those two teenage girls had been the only grandchildren of that Thai commander. His daughter was an only child who had undergone years of infertility treatments to have one child. They'd protected those kids like royalty, but the Yaawt Seven still managed to grab them. He wanted blood."

When a spell of silence passed, Gage asked, "Who is The General?"

"He's an advisor of some sort. He's buried deep inside your government, but he has an office in the Pentagon and his real name is Nathaniel Lonker."

Sabrina asked Chatton, "Wait a minute. Do you know if *he's* the one who screwed my team in the UK?"

"Yes. He is, but I'm sure Wayan carried the lion's share of that operation on his end."

"Fuck," Josh snapped.

Sabrina sat back hard and looked at Gage with a sick expression.

He reached over and squeezed her arm to let her know he understood how she was thinking of twenty-four months they'd circled each other over finding the person who did this to her.

What he wouldn't give to get his hands on Lonker right now. "I need more on him," he told Chatton.

"I'll think about it."

Just when Gage was starting to warm to Chatton, she pissed him off. "Why the hell not?"

She sighed loud enough to reach his ears. "It's complicated."

Didn't matter. Gage had a name. That was enough to find Lonker if he ever made it back to the states. He'd just wanted more on what she knew.

He switched topics. "We have to figure out what Rikker and Wayan are up to and find a way to stop it before the shit hits the fan and we're left holding the bag."

Josh snorted. "Have you not noticed that we're like, floating in a fucking sea and we don't even know which one?"

Gage waved off the comment. "You have something better to talk about?"

Chatton said, "I figured out in the beginning that Wayan wanted a war, but the man currently leading China will not start a war."

Twisting toward Chatton, Sabrina asked, "Who exactly is Wayan?"

"He's one of the president's closest advisors, and they came up in power together. Wayan knows that the president will posture and issue all kinds of warnings, but does not want to start a world war. However, if one erupts, China wants to be the one who comes out on top after it's over. They'll wait to see who the players are before choosing a side. If they chose today, clearly Russia is their favorite play partner."

"Agreed," Sabrina said. "But Wayan isn't going to wait for a war if he has a son he intends to put into power."

"No," Chatton replied. "Wayan and Rikker are going to kill the president and his son."

Gage kept a check on the building squall. He couldn't stop it, but they had to be ready.

Josh finished off his bottle of water and stowed it in the net bag. "I don't see how he's going to pull this off. I thought the Communist Party ruled China. Does Wayan think they won't notice he killed their president? And a popular one at the moment, on top of it."

Chatton said, "He won't be that bold. Wayan has planned for too long to leave any chance of this coming back on him. I didn't know about his kid, because I have never seen his son with him anywhere. I had no idea Wayan had this mad idea of raising the next Khan."

She leaned back and poured water over her face.

Josh suggested, "You may want to conserve that."

Gage scratched his head now that the saltwater was drying. "We aren't going to be here long. Sabrina's people are watching for that EPIRB signal. Let's just hope they can make it before that storm."

The other three turned to see what he'd been facing.

Chatton settled back down. "Wayan may very well be a descendant of Genghis Khan. If so, he inherited something that designated today as Khan's birthday when all I've ever found was that Khan was born *around* 1162. Sounds like Wayan's son was born the same way as Khan with a blood clot in his fist, so that might have been all it took to push Wayan into Fantasyland." She lifted a hand to shield her eyes and added, "I just can't figure how Wayan intends to get rid of Zhou Tai Peng's son, Chao, plus Zhou himself. I do believe Wayan has amassed an army, many of whom are probably Orion Hunters. He may have people in place to silence everyone who could interfere, stage a coup, and make his fantasy a reality."

Sabrina's hand slipped off Gage's arm and he grabbed it.

She looked over, gave him a smile that turned his heart into a dance machine, and leaned back.

The only thing better had been seeing her alive after the castle escape.

Shit. Gage said, "We were trying to get the Amber Room

panel out of a castle that belonged to a guy who knew Wayan, but was hiding the panel from him. The General sent men to get the panel, and they killed the castle owner. But before that happened, he said something like all Wayan's dreams would come true as long as the match wasn't canceled."

Josh frowned. "Match like a sports match?"

Sabrina mused out loud, "Wayan said they'd release the video once everything was in motion. Wonder if it's whatever match this is? With Wayan hosting the *Illustratio* today, I don't see that match being a long time off, like days, if it's a catalyst to his plans. If he's killing Zhou's son, then we should start with finding out where his son is going to be."

Chatton said, "Chao is a competitive kickboxer. No. Not kickboxer, he's a—"

"Mixed Martial Arts fighter," Josh supplied, then slapped his head. "That's it."

Sabrina looked around. "What?"

"Zhou's son has a fight coming up in Kaohsiung tonight ... *if* I'm right and today is Tuesday in Taiwan."

"It is," Chatton confirmed.

"Shit," Josh muttered. "Lot of hype going on about it. Trish's martial arts instructor has been talking about this match for weeks."

Sabrina sat up. "We've got company."

Gage had been watching a ship, not sure it was headed their way, but it appeared to be now. The size and bright white appearance reminded him of a coast guard cutter.

That could be good news, or bad, since it sure as hell was not a US ship.

He said, "I can't tell if that's Chinese or not, but I speak Chinese. This might be our ride home."

Since Chatton faced in the other direction, she had to angle her body around as far left as she could without tipping over. She still wore the soaked backpack. As the ship drew closer, she said, "Don't utter a word of Chinese."

"Why not?"

"That's a Taiwan Coast Guard ship."

Sabrina groused, "If we're anywhere near Spratly Island, this could get difficult." She asked Chatton, "How did you reach the yacht?"

"Wayan had a helo for me in Taiwan but I had to wear a black head sack."

"How's your Taiwanese Hokkien?" Sabrina asked.

Gage hoped for a positive answer since that was the language spoken by seventy percent of the population.

Chatton frowned. "Depends." She paused and met everyone's gaze. "Do any of you speak it?"

Head shakes all around.

"In that case, mine is the best on this flotilla, but no guarantees. I know enough to insert into their country, deal with a problem, and leave, but this is going to take some sensitive negotiation."

The ship slowed then the crew lowered a tender that motored over to them, splashing through the waves.

Two armed men pulled near and threw a rope that Gage caught.

Chatton spoke quickly.

The men exchanged a look and one replied.

Gage asked, "What'd you say?"

"I said we were kidnapped on a ship that was sunk and we're requesting aid."

Josh muttered, "You told them the truth?"

"Better some truth that can be confirmed than an entire lie that can't."

Sabrina climbed into the tender, then Chatton, Josh, and finally Gage. Once they were transported to the ship and brought aboard, the crew had them lined up shoulder to shoulder.

When a man who appeared to be in charge addressed Chatton, she replied in a calm voice and with facial expressions meant to encourage someone to believe her.

But the man interrogating her pulled back as if she'd insulted him.

Gage murmured, "Shit. What'd you say this time?"

"He asked the name of the ship. I told him I didn't know and I asked to speak to the captain."

The man she'd addressed rattled out words so blunt and acidic, it was obvious that this could not be good.

Sabrina whispered, "What'd he say?"

"He said he needs passports. I told him ours went down with the ship."

Josh said, "Mine's back in the States."

Sabrina said, "I have additional passports for you, me, and Gage on the jet, but I have to call it back here."

If Gage could get to a phone, he'd come up with passports or get them into an embassy.

The Taiwan crewmember Chatton spoke with got a suspicious look on his face and rattled off something sharp.

Chatton sighed. "I'm paraphrasing, but he said interrogating us was above his pay grade and the captain can't be bothered right now."

The next thing Gage knew, his hands were tied behind his back and Chatton interpreted that they were being led down into the hull. He eyed Chatton's watch.

If the fight was tonight, they had maybe six hours to stop Rikker from killing the Chinese leader's son, keep the US out of a war, and make sure that video didn't get released.

Chapter 36

SABRINA HAD NEVER been seasick, but she couldn't recall being closed up in a ship's hold smelling engine odors and the soured stench of clothes still damp with saltwater. She swallowed a bout of nausea when the ship rose and dropped into another deep trench before evening out to rock side to side.

They must be heading into the squall.

The boat plowed on.

Sabrina practiced techniques she'd been taught for torture, but no one had ever addressed *this* kind of water torture. She had doubts about keeping down the water she'd drunk before being *rescued* twenty minutes ago.

Gage sat next to her on the bench. He leaned over. "You going to be okay?"

She looked at him, but could only nod. If she opened her mouth this would get ugly quickly.

He cursed.

Josh sighed for the fiftieth time and Chatton sat beside him on the other side of the room, still as a mannequin.

Sabrina kept her voice down, but Josh and Chatton would be hard pressed to hear her over the engine rumble. She swallowed against her sour stomach and angled toward Gage.

He missed nothing and came alert, staring at her with a question in his eyes.

She'd been waiting until this was all over to sort out her emotions, but there might not be time to figure things out later. She said, "I've been sitting here since we got locked up, asking myself what I would have done differently if I'd had a chance."

"Sabrina, don't do this to yourself. We're going to survive this."

"What if we don't?"

"I can't consider that possibility." His eyes had always shielded his emotions, even from her, but she saw the fear in them and knew it wasn't for himself. He said, "There is nothing in this world for me without you."

She'd spent so much energy trying to do the right thing and end this doomed relationship that she'd wasted time she could have spent with Gage. "I'm sorry."

"For what?"

"For making you pay for the sins of others. For not trusting you when you wouldn't give me the names in the CIA. For pushing you away and making decisions for both of us. I've finally realized what the real enemy was in all this."

"What, sweetheart?"

"Me. I couldn't face losing you again and I wouldn't own up to it."

He got that fierce look in his eyes. "I'm not letting you go."

"I know, but Rikker threatened to kill everyone close to me. I've been terrified I'd get Josh back only to lose you. That's when I was forced to face up to the truth. I've never gotten you out of my—" She swallowed and breathed shallow breaths.

"Your system," Gage filled in, his eyes twinkling.

"No, I never got you out of ... my heart. You're so deep inside my soul, I don't know where I end and you begin. I don't care anymore. I'm tired of fighting every day of my life. If we survive this, I want whatever life we can carve out. I have no idea what that will be, but I'll make Josh and Dingo understand that this is what I want. I want to be with you somehow, some way."

She'd need some time to think on how to rearrange things, but if they lived to see that day, she'd make the time. "I'm not sure how we'll make this work, Gage, but I want it to. I don't want to be the one at home wondering if you're alive. I want to be with you ... I don't have a life without you either."

Gage had just heard the words he'd wanted Sabrina to say days ago, but now he was the one who couldn't do it.

He'd told her the truth when he said he wasn't letting her go, but there was no way they could work together as a team.

He'd just survived a sinking ship with her and now they were prisoners of the Taiwan government. He couldn't get up every day with the possibility of watching her die by his side.

She smiled at him and leaned over to kiss him.

He met her halfway, hungry for any touch.

The boat motion changed drastically to less severe.

Chatton called over, "We're stopping."

The motors idled.

Josh sat up from where he'd leaned back with his eyes shut and grumbled, "What now?

Gage said, "We could be stopping for them to board another craft."

"How long is this trip going to take?" Josh asked no one in particular, misery eating at his tone.

"Too long," Chatton said, sitting forward as if getting ready for something.

Footsteps pounded down the metal steps outside the room where they were being held.

Josh tensed and met Sabrina's gaze. She gave him a nod that Gage took as their silent acknowledgement to prepare for whatever came next.

The door opened and several men came in. They each had a T75K1 9mm holstered at their hips. One held an M16. Next, a man came in wearing a uniform different from the others. His had more decorations on the shoulders. He removed what Gage guessed was his captain's hat and tucked it under his arm.

He spoke to Chatton, whose face morphed from resigned to interested. She nodded slowly and replied to him, then stood. She kept her eyes on him when she spoke to Gage, Sabrina and Josh in English, "I don't know who is here, but the captain is handing us over to someone else. Just get up and let's go with it."

"Could be Rikker," Josh suggested.

"Doubtful," Chatton argued. "But that doesn't rule out someone from another unfriendly camp."

Gage stood with Sabrina. One of the crew uncuffed each of them.

The captain led the way up to the deck where the loud whomping of a helicopter roared. Above them hovered a Taiwan Coast Guard Black Hawk with a rope ladder being lowered.

Frustration punched Gage's chest.

He didn't want Sabrina in that helicopter any more than he wanted her here, but their choices came down to climbing the ladder or jumping overboard.

Chapter 37

TWO CREWMEN GRABBED the flapping rope ladder as the helo blasted wind down on the ship.

Gage was tired of his group being at everyone's mercy while this situation showed no signs of improving.

He might be commandeering that chopper.

Chatton said something to the captain, who gave her a terse nod, then she stepped up first to climb. Josh waited for Sabrina to go next, then he stepped up before Gage, obviously watching Sabrina's back.

Sabrina, Josh and Dingo were three peas in a pod.

After finding her in that river that swept her away from the castle, then suffering the terror of trying to get her off a sinking ship, Gage now said a silent thanks for her having two surrogate brothers. He could have died anywhere during this trip. Where would that have left Sabrina?

I don't want to be the one left behind.

Her words haunted him. If he couldn't be there for her when she needed someone, he didn't want her alone, which she eventually would be when the time came that he didn't come home from a mission.

And even if they made it out of this, he'd have to leave her again, because his offer to partner with her was off the table.

Oh, he'd kill to keep her with him in any other way, but not working in the field together.

The minute he rescinded that offer, she'd castigate him for changing his mind and pull back into her shell. He wouldn't blame her. He'd pushed her hard, when she'd been right to say partnering wouldn't work. Now he was the one backing away.

He might as well face the truth.

There would never be a time for them.

Furious prop wash lashed at him as he climbed up to the helicopter and inside where seating was along the walls. He waited for Sabrina to turn around from where she and Josh crowded near the cockpit. Sabrina was speaking to the pilot.

Wait a minute. She didn't speak Taiwanese.

Chatton held on to a handgrip and watched in confusion, too.

When Sabrina did spin back to him, she put a headset on and handed one to Gage, saying, "We're good. Talk when we land."

Josh passed a headset to Chatton.

If they were good, why couldn't they talk now? Gage didn't ask.

The pilot announced in English, "Everyone buckle up."

Sabrina backed away to sit against the far wall.

The crew chief came back long enough to close the hatch. He looked just like the Taiwanese crewmen on the ship.

Gage strapped in as the helicopter lifted and banked away, kicking it in the ass to get moving. There would be no private conversation since he'd bet everyone was on the same channel.

Sabrina smiled and mouthed, *It's okay.*

They landed in Taichung forty minutes later. That's when the pilot stepped into the passenger area as everyone unbuckled harnesses. The rotors were still spinning but slowing down.

Pulling the headset off, Sabrina stood to meet the pilot and introduced him to Gage. "This is Logan, a friend of mine."

They shook hands. "I'm Gage. Are we among friendlies?"

Logan gave him a not-really grimace. Clearly not Taiwanese, Logan was a big guy with Slavic features who might be Russian, but he was someone Sabrina trusted and that worked for Gage.

As the noise of the helicopter died down, Chatton and Josh moved close, listening.

Logan thanked his Taiwanese copilot and crew chief, waiting on both to leave, then he turned back to the group, keeping his tone low. "On your flight from Mumbai here, Sabrina filled me in about being sent to Taiwan. I got to Taichung right after you, but had to wait on the signal you activated to come find you. I pulled strings to get this helo and pick you up, but those connections have a limit. I have an associate who is involved in national defense for Taiwan and told him I had friends tracking a terrorist who needed to be brought in. When you boarded, Sabrina filled me in that Rikker and his boss got away before the ship sank. If you don't find them, and *stop* them, before that coast guard captain goes off duty and hands in his report, I put my connection at risk and it will be far more difficult to get out of this country."

"We need a few things," Sabrina said.

Logan didn't look excited over that. "Like what?"

"We think Rikker is going to kill Zhou Tai Peng's son tonight, then Zhou at some point after that, but the minute we try to convince anyone of an assassination attempt with our questionable status, it will blow up in our faces. I'll give you all the details later, but we've discovered Rikker's boss is planning a coup and he's launching it by taking out Zhou and his son. We need access to the big MMA bout tonight where Zhou's son is fighting."

He cupped his chin and his eyebrows tucked in tight. "Damn, this is huge. The main fight will probably be on around nine. That gives us eight hours to pull together everything you'll need to insert. I can make a couple of calls and get you into the match."

"What about an exit plan?" Gage asked.

Logan huffed out a harsh blast of air. "If you catch Rikker there and stop him, my friend in the defense department will step in to handle it at that point. If you don't catch Rikker, getting out will be dicey, but I'll be your ground man ready with transportation once you're out of there."

Sabrina clearly didn't like that. "What if you're caught here?"

"I won't be."

Gage liked the confidence behind that. He asked Logan, "What about getting me to Beijing?"

Sabrina wheeled around on him. "Why in the hell would you do that?"

Chatton told Gage, "Zhou isn't known for mercy with his own people, much less foreigners."

"I know," Gage said. "But someone has to catch Wayan before he figures a way around all of this. With his position, he probably has a backup plan that will work." Gage hated to leave Sabrina here hunting Rikker, but he was not taking her with him. She'd be with Logan, Josh and maybe Chatton, putting better odds on Sabrina getting through this safely.

Much better than taking her to China with him.

He said, "If Logan gets you into the arena and out, then regardless of what happens, you have to get out of this country when you're done."

Sabrina argued, "I'll go with you as backup. Josh and Chatton can handle this."

Chatton cleared her throat. "I can't stay."

Logan asked, "Why not? How are you leaving?"

"I've got my own contacts. I have a situation to handle."

Sabrina scowled. "Something more important than catching Rikker?"

"No, but you and Josh can handle that without me, because Gage isn't taking you to China." Chatton fished Sabrina's scroll briefcase out of her backpack and handed it to Josh. "Thanks for the ride."

With that said, Chatton descended the steps and walked away. Gage shook his head at the woman. She just might *be* the ghost who took down the Yaawt Seven.

Sabrina huffed out a noise. "Josh and Logan, would you give me a minute?"

Logan said, "That's about all we can afford to hang around here."

As soon as the men stepped off, she started in on Gage. "What the hell? One minute you're talking to me about being a partner and the next you go off on your own."

He scrubbed a hand over his face, rubbing his tired eyes. When his vision cleared, he said, "We didn't get a chance to finish that conversation on the boat. We don't have time to go into it here, but I was wrong to think you and I can work together in this business. I can't handle you being in danger. It's killing me to consider leaving you here hunting Rikker, but I'm banking on Josh's overprotectiveness toward you as well as Logan being good to his word and getting you both out of here. The two of them can keep you safe."

She put her hands on her hips and got in his face. "I don't need anyone to watch out for me. I can keep myself safe. So now, after I finally agree to do this, you're backing out?" She shook her head in disgust. "Just like every other man in my life when things got real."

She turned to leave.

He grabbed her arm. "No, I'm *not* like the men who walked away from you, dammit. I'm just as dependable as Josh and Dingo."

"Josh is staying here and you're leaving. Looks the same from my side right now."

Pulling her to him hard, he kissed her and his chest ached at having to let her go. He kept up the kiss, begging her silently to understand, until she joined him in the connection. This was more than a kiss. This was him telling her so many things words couldn't convey.

When someone outside shouted, "Let's go!" Gage pulled back, feeling as if his body was being yanked in four directions. Couldn't hurt any more if it was.

Holding her close, he said, "You have no idea what you mean to me."

She put her fingers on his lips. "Don't say it. I don't want to hear words. Not those words."

He knew she meant not to say he loved her.

It didn't take much to figure out someone, or more than one someone, in her life had uttered words of love, then betrayed her trust. He did love her. He knew that now, but this wasn't the time for trying to convince her.

He could have handled her anger, but she was hurt. "We will talk when I get back."

"If you get back." She lifted her chin, daring him to swear he was returning.

"If I don't, will you miss me?"

Her eyes got shiny. "No."

"Liar."

He kissed her again, but softly. "This is not goodbye."

"Feels that way." She turned and descended the steps.

He refused to think they would end this way, but he finally

saw this from her side. He didn't want to live without her, but he couldn't keep her close and safe.

What kind of life was it for her if he ended up in a Chinese prison, or beheaded?

He shoved all that into a place that didn't interfere with what he had to do next.

Logan stepped up to him as soon as Gage reached the ground. "You aren't going to China."

"Why not?"

"Zhou is in Taiwan for tonight's match."

Chapter 38

SABRINA PREPARED TO step from the sedan delivering her and Josh to the Kaohsiung Arena on the southern end of the island. The arena held fifteen thousand patrons, one of the largest event centers in all of Taiwan.

She took in Josh, who could make any tux look good, even the rented one he wore. He'd been grim for the last three hours, so he had no problem stepping into his role as her irritated date for tonight.

Josh hadn't spoken to Trish yet, but Logan had sent an encrypted message to Margaux who would pass it on to Dingo, Trish and team that Josh was safe for the moment. Logan wouldn't risk even a burner cell for calling out of Taiwan regardless of his local friendlies.

In his mind, the less chance anyone had of picking up non-local chatter, the better.

Sabrina agreed.

Now, if she could stop Rikker and get everyone safely out of Taiwan she'd be content. Almost.

Damn Gage. He had his own plan, one he wasn't sharing with her other than to say he intended to speak to the Chinese president. No backup.

This is what I said I couldn't do with him.

He'd turned her head into a cage match between fearing what he was up to tonight and wanting to rail at him for making a decision for the both of them that he had no right to make.

She'd finally been willing to give what they had together a shot.

Gage had stomped that idea into the ground without any room

for conversation. Served her right for doing the same to him in Atlanta, but she'd told him that had been fear talking.

He didn't get a last say.

They were discussing their future as soon as this was behind them and he would listen to her. She didn't open up her world for anyone, but she'd been willing to do it for him and take a chance that he was the man she could have some kind of life with, even if it was just fragments of time.

Josh murmured, "Show time." Then he was out of the car and circling the back to her side.

She grabbed a bottle of Japanese whiskey, poured a little into her hand and flicked it all over her.

The driver opened her door and Josh pulled her to her feet, then took the bottle from her and shoved it at the driver, who gave him a sympathetic glance.

She turned to the raucous sounds of MMA patrons happy to watch two men beat each other to a pulp.

Logan had some impressive contacts, and not a one of these had anything to do with national security.

Far from it in some cases.

That worked for her. Some of her best contacts were people who lived in the shadows and worked out of the backends of acceptable businesses.

Josh stared straight ahead and tugged her forward. She stumbled and he caught her arm, yanking her upright.

He looked every bit a man who was put out to be dragging her along as his inebriated date.

Sabrina played the pretentious arm candy, dressed in skin-tight black shorts and a shimmering, red silk cover up that reached her waist and swirled like water when she walked. Her brunette hair was streaked with cotton-candy pink and flowed in a pile of messy curls spotted with glittering bits of silver, gold and copper.

She wore a wide choker of polished silver that had been embedded with black pearls and copper flecks. She thanked her mixed heritage for eyes that could turn exotic with a little creative highlighting.

The vacuous smile had taken practice.

She pooched her deep red lips while waiting for the security to run a scanning wand over Josh.

No alarm went off.

He moved over with his arms crossed, waiting impatiently.

Stepping up, Sabrina struck a sexy pose and lifted her arms in a playful way as if to say, "Come on, boys, take a look." Then she winked and smiled.

Her wrists were covered in bold bracelets similar in style to the choker.

A female security agent lifted a wand in front of Sabrina and the alarm screeched.

Josh snapped at her, "I told you not to wear that."

She gave her best effort at looking hurt and frowned at him, then she smiled at the crew of four security men who had converged to look her over. She told them, "Just ignore him." She dismissed Josh with a flip of her hand and wobbled on her platform shoes, flailing her arms.

Everyone wrinkled their noses.

Eau de Hibiki was doing its job.

Sabrina pouted in Josh's direction. "You loved this outfit when we bought it." She drew out her words and let them slur a bit.

Security exchanged glances.

Josh stepped closer and dropped his voice to a threatening level. "You didn't say you were going to wear it to test security scanners. If you hadn't run us late putting all that on, you could have changed."

"I'm not changing. I'm perfect. You said so."

He pinched the bridge of his nose.

An older man whose face held lines that said he'd seen it all and had yet to be impressed by anyone, stepped up.

The other security backed away in deference.

This had to be the boss.

She held up a finger, asking him to wait a moment. Then she pulled off her red shawl top and tossed it at Josh, who barely caught it. "See?" she told the old guy, showing off her assets above a corset of steel boning. "Wave it here." She pointed at her tits.

He wasn't amused, but he took the wand from the woman and waved it over Sabrina's body.

It screeched and he stared at her.

She shrugged and started untying the front of her corset.

That bulged his eyes. He said, "No."

"Okay, doe-kay. I thought you needed to check everything."

His movements jerked with anger when he lowered the wand, which stopped screeching at her knees, then started up as soon as he waved it past her boots.

This would be the real test.

She twisted her leg, showing off the platform boots that had three inches of sole. This was the most ridiculous outfit, but she trusted Logan, who trusted his people.

Crabby old man said something that she didn't understand.

She sighed loud enough to let everyone know this was not what she expected, and leaned down to start unlatching each steel toggle that ran down the side of her boot.

There was a collective intake of air from the men facing her backside.

She lost her balance and wobbled to the left.

Josh cursed, doing such a great job of sounding like a furious boyfriend that she glanced up and said, "Come on, honey, no harm in them looking."

She got her balance and winked at the old guy.

That must have been all he could take. He barked out an order and one of his men said, "No more, miss. Is good. Just go."

"Really?" Sabrina grinned. It took two tries, but she clipped the toggle back in place and stood up looking around with an empty-headed expression. "We good?"

The man in charge waved her away.

She smiled at them. "Thanks."

Josh turned and strode ahead of her as if he couldn't get far enough from his PIA date.

She caught a look at her watch.

Sixty-eight minutes until Zhou's son came out to fight.

Josh bought them each a drink on the last level before the box seats. That drink turned into a loud fight.

She started crying.

People turned away, too embarrassed to watch.

She covered her mouth and made sounds that came right before someone barfed.

Even the staff backed away. Josh growled, "Ladies room?"

Everyone pointed to the same side and he dragged her away. Perfect.

When she left the bathroom after making more hideous noises and crying loudly, she clung to him as she staggered to the private box seats where Josh opened the door and hurried her inside.

Staff on that floor pretended not to notice her, but one well-dressed male patron took the time to send her an appalled glare.

As soon as she stepped inside their private room, Josh closed the door and locked it. She went down the three steps of the tiered levels to the front row and pushed the curtain aside just enough so she could peek through a tiny sliver.

On the far side of the auditorium was the box full of Chinese security where Zhou was expected to watch his son fight.

What are you doing, Gage? she asked silently.

Josh said, "Fifty-two minutes."

"Got it." She let the curtain fall shut.

He shrugged out of his jacket and dropped to the floor to look under the long serving table loaded with hors d'oeuvres, cheese, fruit and shrimp.

She lifted the filmy cape over her head and tossed it aside, then sat down and unbuckled all the toggles on her boots. She withdrew her feet, then reached in and tugged out the ballet-type flat shoes that had been inserted in a larger size boot.

She called up to Josh, "Knife."

He flipped her a butter knife from the table. She used it to pry the boot heel from the shoe foundation, exposing the pistol frame for a field stripped Kel-Tec PF9 9mm, along with a loaded magazine. The Kel-Tec was small, but it could do the job. The other boot concealed the slide, barrel, and a suppressor for the gun.

Eight rounds better be more than she needed.

By the time she had the boots put back together, Josh finished finding the clothes one of Logan's people working as staff had brought in with the food.

The two of them were on their own until they stepped out of this building. There were limits to what Logan could do with so little time to plan. His inside person couldn't get involved if Josh and Sabrina were caught in the wrong place at the wrong time.

Or if Gage's secret plan didn't work.

Sabrina wished she knew his freaking plan.

Logan might know, but he wasn't talking. Just that fact kinked her insides. Gage didn't want her involved.

He was treating her like a rookie.

Her heart took up his defense, arguing that he was treating her like a woman he didn't want to see harmed.

She forced her mind back on the job at hand.

Josh deposited new clothes for Sabrina on a chair near her, then returned to the area around the table.

They turned their backs on each other, just like they used to do in the group home. Josh had beaten manners into a couple of boys who had pretended to turn, but hadn't.

Sabrina flipped the corset around to view the inside of the steel boning. She freed a knife blade hidden inside one rib and a hilt from another rib, then pushed the blade through the handle until the wider, blunt metal on the other end wedged it in place. Now Josh had a blade with a handle.

When she finished dressing, she called out, "Ready?"

"Yep."

She climbed the steps to Josh, who now wore dark blue coveralls with the arena's logo. He had a ball cap on his head and a full beard in place, plus half-glasses sitting on his nose, which now looked much wider.

He eyed her change of clothes to a uniform of black pants with a simple black jacket over a white, round-neck shirt. "I thought that first outfit and hair was over the top, but except for makeup overload you don't look a thing like the screeching Barbie who staggered in with me."

She handed him the knife. "Give me a minute."

After washing the heavy makeup off at the bar sink, she came back, glad to have ditched the jewelry and wig. He handed her a pair of square, black-rimmed glasses, which she slid into place.

Josh said, "Between that and your braid, you're set."

Her black hair fell in a single braid to the middle of her back.

Though taller than the majority of female servers in the arena, Sabrina wasn't the tallest now that she walked in flats.

The noise level outside was getting loud. The first match would be starting soon.

When this curtain did not open, she hoped they believed Josh had gotten fed up and left. Everyone would be talking about the American man with the slut date.

She hoped.

"Forty-four minutes." He handed her a small electronic piece the size of an iPod Nano. The casing was black and one side had a spring-loaded tab for pressing to make a click. One double click, pause ten seconds and another double click meant either she or Josh had found Rikker.

Two successive double clicks with no pause meant one of them had found no one and was leaving.

"Test it." She adjusted the ear bud hidden by hair covering her ear.

His double click came through clear. They couldn't use a radio inside here with no idea how many channels, or what frequencies, security might be monitoring.

She reached up as if she were checking her button and clicked hers.

He gave her a thumbs up. "Don't be late."

"I won't." She considered how they'd never left each other and reminded him, "You stay on time, too. Don't change the plan. No matter what happens, if you find Rikker on the other side, you send me the signal and wait for me to come over. I'll do the same. If you don't find Rikker, send those clicks and get out of here the minute the main fight is over, and find Logan."

Josh couldn't hide the sick look in his face. "We're not leaving without you, Sabrina."

"I plan to be there, too, but ... " She had to take a breath and make him understand. "I'll send you a heads up the minute I locate Rikker, then you come back me up. I'll follow the plan if you do," she lied, not intending to leave without Rikker's head.

She had to get him to remember what waited at home for him. A life. A family. She caught Josh's arm. "If for some reason I fail, don't waste what we did to get you back. You and Dingo are the world to me. I wasn't much for Valene before, but I can see that she's good for Dingo, and Trish is waiting for you. You two have a family to raise." She wanted to be there to see Josh's first child, but she wanted him there more. "This will end the threat to all of us so you can finally have a life."

"What about your life?"

She had no answer to that. "I can't talk about this right now." Turning for the door, she touched the handle.

He said, "Dingo will be okay with Gage."

She swung around, "What are you saying?"

"We talked while you were ... missing, and I told him if he wanted you to respect his choice in Valene, we both had to do the same for you. Gage was on that ship for you, but he also stuck his neck out for me. Dingo and I will support any decision you make. Your choices matter to us, too."

"Thanks." She meant it, but Gage had already kiboshed her offer to stay together.

The audience roared.

She opened the door and looked out to find this hallway empty. "We're on the clock. Make it count."

Chapter 39

GAGE HAD CONVINCED Logan to get a message to Zhou, which Logan wouldn't do until Sabrina and Josh cleared the entrance.

Sabrina had pulled off crazy girlfriend like a pro, but watching her walk inside that building had reinforced his decision to keep her out of his world.

Not that he could make that woman do anything, but he could try his damnedest to convince her that staying as far as possible from his world was the best way to prevent Josh and Dingo from ever being at risk again.

That should do it.

She sure as hell wouldn't do it for him. Not after he'd flipped the tables on her and turned down his one chance at being together.

He ignored the ache in his chest and accepted that he'd rather live without her than suffer her death.

Speaking of which, Logan had warned Gage that his plan sounded like a one-way ticket to hell. Sabrina would not be happy with anyone if he didn't come out of there alive.

Gage had no choice.

He had to ensure that Sabrina, and even those two hardheads she thought of as brothers, had a chance at being happy and safe. None of that would happen if she didn't get out of here alive.

Gage walked between four armed Chinese guards marching him to Zhou's private box.

Logan might have called this one.

The message Logan had sent to Zhou through Logan's friend who had loaned him the helicopter informed the Chinese president that he had a traitor inside his trusted advisors. The note included a photo of Gage and said Gage would explain, but only to Zhou in person.

Even that little bit of information was a gamble if Wayan or one of his followers found out. A man in Zhou's position suspected traitors all the time.

Gage was banking on Wayan's minions not being inside the president's personal guard and Zhou's confidence in his security allowing him to indulge his curiosity.

Telling anyone except Zhou could end with Gage in a dark prison and with no chance of speaking to anyone.

When they reached the box, Gage was kept outside with two weapons pointed at him.

The guard he'd been communicating with stepped inside.

Seconds ticked away, taunting him with his lack of time. His gaze lifted to a nearby television camera where Zhou's son would soon step into the bright lights. If Zhou gave Gage ten minutes, he believed he could convince the man of Wayan's subterfuge as well as get Zhou to withdraw his son from the match.

Gage trusted Sabrina and her skills.

He didn't trust Rikker.

If Gage could take the target away, Rikker would end up waiting longer than he intended, which would allow Sabrina and Josh to take him down or not find him and leave.

For now, he'd rather she didn't find Rikker, but if she did, she had the element of surprise. Rikker thought they were all dead. Gage prayed that confidence would make the bastard cocky and careless.

The guard Gage had been speaking to returned and spoke this time in English. "The President said he will speak with you after this event and that you should use this time to consider the position you are in. If I decide you are a threat, I am authorized to take you back to China to stand trial."

Gage said, "What if I tell you someone is here to kill Zhou's son."

"I would tell you we receive threats against him daily. Chao is a revered fighter." He looked at his men and rattled off an order in Chinese that said to stick Gage's ass in a room downstairs.

Fuck.

The guards hooked a hand on each of Gage's arms and pulled him around to take him away.

Zhou wouldn't even give him a chance to state his claim? This bunch would drag him to a country where he would never leave a dark prison cell ... unless it was to be beheaded as a spy.

He couldn't protect Sabrina from there. The whole point of this gamble was to stop the fight and have Logan's man coordinate getting all three of them out of Taiwan.

Gage tried one last time. "You don't want your president to figure out later that I needed only two minutes. Zhou is too intelligent to allow this information to slip away before he can act on it."

The guard said, "You should have told me when I asked."

Could this man be trusted?

What if he worked for Wayan and hadn't even said a word to Zhou?

Chapter 40

SABRINA FOLLOWED THE plans she'd memorized and found the entrance she was looking for. It led to the upper level access that ran around the top of the arena.

At the next garbage can, she dumped the small tray with two empty drinks and a black napkin she'd used to cover the weapon she wanted close. She made a turn at the end of the hall into an alcove with a locked door. White Taiwanese writing on a red sticker probably warned her not to enter.

If she'd known she would be on a mission here she'd have studied enough of the language to know for sure.

Pulling two lock picks, supplied by the tailor, from inside her bra, she shoved the small 9mm into a pocket and unlocked the door, opening it slowly.

Spotlights flooded center ring far below.

All the lights up here were out, but the ambient glow offered enough light for moving around.

The preliminary match had ended and the muffled roar filled the air.

The sound of a rabid crowd rocked the top of the arena.

Sabrina might lose her hearing, but that noise was covering any sound she made.

Zhou's son would be on soon.

The crowd noise and announcements coming now sounded similar to those she'd heard just before the first match, except far louder.

She and Josh had pinned down the best places on each side of this arena to snipe a fighter and get out.

But this side had offered the highest potential.

Please tell me I'm not guessing wrong and letting Josh walk up on Rikker.

She had her doubts about Josh waiting for her, or walking away if he found nothing. Rikker was the nightmare they'd shared for almost four years.

She ran through all the reasons this side had been the best hunting ground. She, Josh and Logan had handicapped this while Logan's people created costumes and props for a deadly play.

Searching ahead, she sized up every location as an assassin who would be searching for the perfect perch. Nothing up here fit the description for ideal.

Wait, she saw it.

An area that formed a T off of the narrow walkway she'd been using and was also floored with the expanded metal used on this catwalk.

She didn't see a body in a prone position.

Large light canisters were mounted on each side. Maybe he had tucked between them.

As she eased up closer, the crowd noise settled down in anticipation of the big show.

She risked a glance at the match area to see the two men being introduced.

Leaning to the left, she took another step and saw ... the stock of a gun. A sniper rifle.

The crowd shouted, calling for blood.

She whipped around, searching for Rikker.

He dropped onto her from above, knocking her hard enough that she went down on her back. He pulled a knife into view and landed on her, pinning her to the catwalk. She caught his knife arm with both hands.

He pushed up on his legs to get more leverage. "You bitch. What are you doing here? You need to die and stay dead."

She shoved up hard between his legs, but he blocked at the last second and that threw them both off balance. His knee slipped off the catwalk, landing his other one on her chest.

Her grip slipped and the knife stabbed her shoulder.

Pain screamed at her to do something. She shoved the heel of her hand at his nose, breaking it with a solid crack. He shouted, but no one would hear him screaming with the crowd getting into the battle going on downstairs.

He threw his weight back over her, gaining ground again.

She saw her weapon lying three feet away on the catwalk.

His gaze followed hers. He lurched for the gun.

She jumped on his back, catching his arm between his body and the catwalk. She grabbed his forehead and yanked back. "Give up, Rikker. It's over."

"It's never over." His words sounded screwed up with his nose bashed and her holding his head back.

"Is he dead?" Josh called from her left.

She turned to him and shouldn't have. It allowed Rikker to twist the gun free and aim.

Josh had nowhere to go but down and he'd never beat a bullet.

Sabrina wrenched Rikker's head so hard it yanked his body as his neck bones cracked, but it worked. The suppressed shot went wide.

His arm dropped.

She let go of his head and it flopped down. His eyes had frozen wide in shock.

Josh got to her and helped her up. He looked at Rikker. "There's your fucking beautiful plan, you miserable shit."

She was shaking at the thought of losing Josh and grabbed him. "I should strangle you."

He held her to him. "You know I just couldn't leave you here to face Rikker. Shit, you're bleeding. Let me take a look."

"Not here. It's not deep." She hoped. Burned like hell. "But thanks."

"Dingo's going to be pissed he wasn't in on taking Rikker down."

"He was," Sabrina argued. "Everyone played a role in this, even Chatton. I'd like to know where she is right now." She stepped back and looked down at Rikker's silent body that would no longer threaten the world, or her family. "He's dead. Zhou's kid is alive. Logan's Taiwan defense contact may be just as good as Logan thinks, but I say we leave and let his contact sort out the body on his own."

"Agreed." Josh ran his hand through his hair. He'd lost his cap. Someone would probably be looking for the owner down below. "You need a medic, but we got lucky."

Looking down at where the Chinese president sat watching his son, she said, "Yes, but what about Gage?"

Chapter 41

THE GENERAL WIPED perspiration off his forehead, ready to get back to the hotel. He hated the heat, even with the so-called cool breeze after dark on this private island in the Indian Ocean. His blood pressure, normally under control, had spiked out of sight during that whole fiasco with Wayan. He'd just made it back to Taiwan when he got a call to climb on another fucking airplane.

Wayan had caused him too many problems recently.

If Wayan wasn't so high in the Chinese government, The General would put his name at the top of the people-who-were-breathing-too-much-of-his-air list.

That little prick better be good for his word and not stab me in the back the first chance he gets.

"I apologize for keeping you waiting," Rosso said when he walked into the hut. Sure, this place had a romantic flair and high rollers would spend too much money to visit, but in The General's world, anything built of local materials on an island was a hut.

"No problem." The General tried to sound sincere, but his ass had been on airplanes nonstop since getting off that yacht.

Rosso carried arrogance as his calling card, but the families he represented kept The General's Swiss bank account full of money. After this last year, he was seriously considering retirement. He had enough cash reserve. All he had to do was get his back surgery done before he left his measly, low-paying government position. They owed him that much.

His back had started complaining on the flight from Taiwan and the pain had gone from a four to a ten. If not for needing to stay sharp around this Italian bastard, The General would have taken a pain pill.

"I'll get to the point," Rosso said. "When I took over speaking for the families, I was told they had a particular concern."

"Oh? No one mentioned it to me."

"That's because you were part of their concern."

For the first time in hours, The General stopped thinking about his back. "What do you mean? What did I do?"

"It's what you haven't done."

Now he was angry. "Like what?"

"You were given a rare stater for the purpose of building a bridge with your China contact. We all agreed you had a good idea."

"I did build a bridge. I just got back from meeting with him." That son of a bitch had barely allowed him to walk away, but with Wayan that could be considered a bridge.

"Why were you seeing him?"

"You know he's an Orion Prophecy nut. I had to go for the *Illustratio*."

Rosso gave his reply consideration then waved a hand in dismissal. "Yes, yes ... we were aware of this event *and* of the timing."

Thank goodness. Now they had no reason to bitch at him.

"But ... " Rosso said, causing hair on The General's arms to stand. Rosso put his fingers together, forming a steeple and looking so much like Wayan did at times, it got under The General's skin.

The Italian leaned forward. "You did not take the stater to the *Illustratio*, and now it is gone. You traded it for your own purpose."

"Now wait a minute," The General started. "I already explained that I did that for the good of everyone. I work in your best interests. When Eva Perdido and Maxx Navarro were going to spill their guts, that would have led to me and, in turn, to you." He pointed at Rosso and said, "I was watching out for all of us."

Rosso didn't comment on that, but dropped his hands to his knees before standing. "Something new has come to light as well. The families have agreed that if you can straighten out this issue, then you may continue in the same way."

Relief hit The General so hard he had to grip the table next to him to keep from sagging. "Sure thing. Let me have a few days to catch up on rest and I'll make a full report on everything that went on with the *Illustratio* and how I will ensure the stater is returned. I have a plan. Never doubt me." He smiled, ready to patch things up with the man he'd be stuck doing business with for another two years.

"Very well. Get in touch with my assistant." The Italian walked to the door.

The General pushed himself to stand. "What about the issue you want me to straighten out?"

"Oh, you're clever. I believe you will find it on your own."

What the fuck? He'd flown all the way here for this? The General let Rosso get a full two minutes ahead of him, then made his way to the door. He'd had enough of that guy's crap.

Cold air conditioning and a comfortable bed waited for him.

When he stepped out into the night air, the breeze swept by and he had to admit this place wasn't as bad as he'd thought, but it was still too damned remote for his tastes.

Ten steps through the soft sand and cold metal touched his neck.

"Did you really think I couldn't get off that yacht?" a deep, feminine voice whispered close to him.

Chatton? No fucking way. The General asked, "What do you want?"

"Answers."

Way. That was Chatton. He couldn't begin to fathom the fallout if that whole bunch had escaped. Damn Wayan and Rikker. The General calmed his breathing.

Chatton was psycho, but that was her style. He said, "Okay. What's the problem?"

She said, "It took me a while to figure out what happened."
"With what?"

"My family dying off. I failed to put it together until we were all on that yacht waiting to die, that the deaths of my family members had stopped as soon as I joined the Czarion."

What was she getting at? The General said, "What'd you put together?"

"I thought it had to be you or Wayan, because I'd researched Orion Hunters. One group of Hunters answers to you and the other two answer to Wayan. One of you had sent killers after my family's Celtic cross. Wayan was the best suspect, but he'd have kept going until he had it from me. He knew that you'd sent someone searching for the cross three years ago."

Yes, but that had been one time. Not multiple. What was she getting at? "I sent someone looking for your cross way back then, but I got my hands on the stater and called them off."

"You know your Orion Hunters would not give up so easily."

He'd hoped not at first, but once he got the stater he didn't care. What the hell had they done?

Sweat poured down the sides of his face and soaked his shirt. "Okay, Chatton, this is clearly a matter of a misunderstanding."

"Murdering my family is not a misunderstanding."

Fuck. That was the wrong approach with her. He said, "Let's deal. I didn't want to have anyone killed, but I was in a tight spot. I answer to five families and they—"

"—have apologized for the damage created by their beast," she finished. "They had no idea what other business you were running in their name. They never asked for any artifact. You asked *them* for the stater when you saw a chance to expand your dirty little empire. You used the American Orion Hunters to do your wet work. All you had to do was come up with intel on other artifacts as the reason and point them at what you wanted done. Who would care about the families impacted? Right?"

"People know I'm here, Chatton."

"No, they don't. Oh, wait, yes, they do and they don't want you to return to their world. Just as you played God with my family and so many others you killed for your own benefit, I am your judge, jury and executioner."

Chapter 42

SABRINA CLIMBED INTO the van where Logan waited for them. She and Josh had escaped through a service stairwell and a complicated route that she'd begun to think was a maze. They'd stepped through an exit at the loading dock as Zhou's son won his match.

The crowd was shouting his name. They didn't do that for a loser.

She asked, "What's going on with Gage?"

Logan turned to her. "You gave me a heart attack sneaking out."

"That's how we roll. Now, about Gage."

"I haven't seen any activity since he went in." Logan turned back to the bank of monitors where he'd linked into security cameras and television feeds from inside. She leaned forward and her shoulder complained.

"Why don't you tell me what's going on?" Sabrina asked.

Josh sat down hard. "Yeah, what's the super agent up to?" He gave Sabrina a smile when he said that.

Logan kept an eye on the monitors where patrons in the arena seemed happy about the win. "Gage has had dealings with a couple of China's former State Council members. He wants to alert the president to Wayan. He couldn't just send a message or it might get snagged by one of Wayan's people who are planning the coup with Wayan."

Sabrina grabbed Logan's arm. "Are you telling me Gage went in there himself?"

"Yes."

"What if the president doesn't believe him?" She released his arm and sat back.

Logan gave her a consoling look. "Stopping Rikker might be all it will take, because Gage went in planning to tell the President that his son was under threat. He wanted to get Zhou to pull his son from this match."

Josh shook his head. "He can't. No fighter would want to be embarrassed, but calling off the match and losing face would be unthinkable for his son because of their culture and his father's position."

"Right. I pointed that out."

Sabrina thought it through. "What if his son had died?"

"That wouldn't have gone well for Gage. Zhou would have struck out at the first person he saw and Wayan would have released that video of all of you on his ship. That's what I'd do in his shoes."

She dropped her face into her hands. "It could have gone so badly tonight if we hadn't stopped—"

"*Shit!*"

"What?" She jumped up.

"No, no, no," Logan moaned, tapping furiously on his keys. "Zhou's son was killed on the way to his father's limo."

Josh murmured, "That's not possible."

Sabrina's skin chilled. "It is if Rikker had a backup plan."

Chapter 43

WAYAN WALKED THROUGH the elegant Kaohsiung hotel with the calm of a man who had been born to lead. He was flanked by six of his men.

Not Zhou's men, but his.

The ones who would form the inner circle of his private guard once he took control. A year down the line, his son would be experienced and ingrained in the palace, which would be restored as a seat of power.

China respected power.

The people wanted a ruler who would demand that the world kneel at their feet. Khan had once ruled the greatest empire of all time, and would again.

At the presidential suite, Wayan prepared himself to finish what Rikker had started. That miserable ex-CIA agent had vanished after the hit without his money. The fool. Probably because Zhou's son had not been a clean kill. Chao had been flown home to be treated by Zhou's personal physicians.

Zhou had sent Wayan a message that his son was on life support and he needed to see Wayan before Zhou left Taiwan.

Wayan would be expected to find out who was behind the attack. This was perfect.

The door to the suite opened and Wayan strode in, giving the proper greeting to his leader. He looked at the room crowded with guards and asked, "I humbly request a moment to grieve with you before we discuss how to retaliate for this brutal attack."

Zhou sat in a large chair, looking much as a king would, but appearances could be deceiving without power to back it up.

Once the men walked outside, Zhou waved his hand for Wayan to sit down.

Wayan would never be below anyone ever again, except his son when the time came. He wanted to be standing when he called his men in to kill this obstacle to his son's rule.

He paced and said, "I would beg your forgiveness that you allow me to remain standing. My recent surgery forces this sometimes."

Zhou nodded and watched him with dark eyes.

"I have served you for many years," Wayan started.

"As did your father and grandfather," Zhou agreed.

"I am sorry for your son. I heard the wound was grave and, as a father, I can understand the pain of losing a son."

"He is not dead yet."

Wayan had to give credit to Rikker's planning. For some reason, Rikker had not been able to take a shot in the arena and had been forced to go with his second option.

Wayan said, "I fear that sadly it is only a matter of time for your son based on the report I received."

Silence stretched, but Wayan was ready to end this blithering and start a new rule.

Zhou commented in a dark tone, "You have a confident stance."

Now was as good a time as any to take control.

"A ruler should never appear weak," Wayan countered.

"No truer words have ever been spoken." Zhou stood. "Chao, come to me."

Wayan swiveled to see Zhou's son walk out of the bedroom looking a bit bruised, as if he'd fought, but not as if he'd been shot. "What ... "

Another door opened and Gage Laughton stepped out. "I am so glad the president gave me a chance to share who planned to kill him and seize power. I understand it was Zhou's personal yacht you blew up after your people took it out to check a phony maintenance issue."

Wayan had never felt faint, but his head spun. He reached in his pocket and pressed the button he refused to call a panic button. He considered it a call-to-action alert.

A ruler did not panic.

There was a knock at the door.

Wayan shouted, *"Enter!"*

The door swung open and the head of the president's guard stepped in. One of Wayan's men lay on the floor behind him. Groans followed him in.

Zhou said, "Take this prisoner back to China where he will stand trial, as will his son, for treason."

Wayan turned to Zhou, wide-eyed. "You cannot do this. Temüjin is the rightful ruler. Not you." Stars shot through his gaze as strong hands grabbed him. He mumbled, "This is ... no. This is wrong."

～

Gage waited until Zhou's guard gave Wayan a thump on the head that silenced the lunatic without killing him.

When it was just him, Zhou and the young fighter, Gage said, "I revealed a traitor and protected your son." Technically Sabrina and Josh had stopped Rikker from killing Chao, at least he hoped so, but Gage had protected this man's son by preventing Wayan's backup plan from being executed.

Once Gage had taken the leap to tell the head of Zhou's security what was going on, Gage and a squad of guards set up a fake attack with a guard playing the role of Zhou's son hidden inside his hooded robe.

That was possible because the head of Zhou's security had found the second assassin and dealt with him quickly. Rikker had been forced to use people he might not have known as well as he should.

"Yes, you have performed an honorable service," Zhou agreed, then stood. "I will deliver on my part of our agreement ... in Beijing."

That hadn't exactly been the deal, but then neither of them had spelled out all the terms Gage had hoped to finalize in Taiwan. He took in Zhou and the head of his security, not trusting them entirely, but this deal had been made on a handshake.

This time, he wanted a clear set of guidelines. "For how long?"

Zhou gave his question a drawn out moment of consideration. "As long as the task requires."

Gage could ask to check in with his people, but he'd surrendered his phone to gain Zhou's confidence and been told not to alert anyone. Clearly, he had a ways to go to gain the man's trust in spite of protecting his only son.

Fear settled in his gut and it had nothing to do with traveling to Beijing with Zhou's guards.

No, his only concern grew out of not being able to reach Sabrina, who would point to this and tell him she would not spend the rest of her life with no idea every time he left, whether he was coming home.

He had no argument for that and it hurt to admit it.

Chapter 44

SABRINA SMILED UP at Josh and Trish, who had paused to speak with a handful of their wedding guests. The newly married couple had just changed out of their wedding attire and into jeans to enjoy a twilight reception in progress five hundred feet away on Miami Beach.

Couples still remained scattered around the hotel gardens where Trish had made a beautiful bride in her vintage dress.

It had been altered for her obvious baby bump. She and her BFF bridesmaid Heidi had walked down the tall steps from the hotel, then between guests seated in rows of white chairs to reach the quaint gazebo where Josh waited to marry Trish.

The whole thing had been as fairytale as it got.

Sabrina tipped her champagne glass up for another sip, enjoying the moment of peace, and waiting to give the happy couple her real wedding gift.

The one that wouldn't end up on a shelf.

A young woman walked past who reminded Sabrina of Amanda, and made her heart squeeze. Her assistant was recovering physically, but the loss of being able to have children had been difficult for Amanda.

Sabrina had spent a long time with her before flying to Miami. She wanted Amanda to know she was part of the Slye family and could depend on all of them for anything she needed.

Trish and Josh disengaged from the conversation, then Trish turned a searching gaze on the garden area. She waved at Angel Jackson, Trish's sister-in-law, who waved back. Angel and her husband, Zane, were each holding a hand of their little girl, walking the toddler along a path that led to the beach.

Trish looked around then her face lit up when she saw Sabrina.

Damn. Sabrina's eyes stung with the threat of a tear.

She squeezed them shut to shake off the silly reaction and looked back up to find Trish yanking on Josh to pull him down the steps. Josh frowned, but that was him being in hover mode, protecting his baby mama. He'd already stopped her once from moving too quickly because of her condition.

Trish wore a pretty blue silk top over her maternity jeans, but it was the smile and glow in her face that dazzled everyone, Josh most of all.

He'd never been so happy. Sabrina would attest to that. He had changed so much from the vagabond warrior of their youth.

Just as Dingo had.

Searching the grounds, Sabrina found Dingo tucked into a private spot with Valene, who had smiled with pride as Dingo stood next to Josh in an elegant tux.

Trish waved at Sabrina as soon as her foot touched the last step and Josh stopped fussing. Well, he'd probably *never* stop fussing completely, and that made Sabrina proud of him. When they reached her, she got a hug from each one.

Sabrina stepped back. "Your wedding was ... special."

Liquid pools shimmered in Trish's eyes and every tear announced her happiness. "Thank you for bringing him home."

"You're welcome. You did your part, too."

Trish shrugged off the compliment.

Josh butted in, reminding Sabrina, "It's not like you're never going to see me again."

"Not for a month. Stay out of my hair that long and get moved into that house you two built." Sabrina hadn't realized how much Josh had been juggling around helping her at Slye. This was his home now and she wanted him where he'd be happy.

Time for Sabrina's final wedding gift. "When you're ready, give me a call so I can come down here to talk, Josh."

"Why?" He gave her a confused look. "You don't want me back in Atlanta?"

"You're always welcome there, but I'll need someone to run the south Florida division of Slye."

The look he gave her was worth all the sadness she'd suffered when she decided not to bring him back to Atlanta. Seeing him today just reinforced the decision she'd made to carve out a niche for him that would be safer.

Sabrina accepted his hug and smiled when he whispered, "Thanks."

She glanced at Trish, whose eyes had widened. His bride wasn't entirely sold on this new plan, even if she had plastered a polite smile on her face.

Sabrina finished explaining, "This division will be exclusively corporate security." She looked at Trish. "Nothing else. No more black ops missions. I need you in management more than I need you in the field."

Trish burst into tears and Sabrina backed up one more quick step, saying, "I'm sorry, I didn't meant to upset you."

Still blubbering, Trish grabbed her in another awkward preggy hug and said, "Thank you, thank you. I am not upset, just so damned happy. Thank you for the best wedding gift ever."

Sabrina patted her back and smiled, fighting off tears of her own again. Damn, she had to cut this out.

To diffuse all this emotion, Sabrina said, "I know you'll take care of him, Trish, and he'll take care of you. I can't wait to meet your child."

Trish moved back and looked up at Josh, nudging him with her arm. "Now would be a good time."

He grinned. "Excellent idea." Then he told Sabrina, "We were trying to find a chance to ask you if you'd be our baby's godmother."

Fuck. Tears ran down Sabrina's face. She wiped at them. "I, uh, I... "

Trish seemed surprised. "You don't want to be?"

"No, I mean yes, I do." Sabrina used the napkin she'd been holding to wipe her eyes. "I'm just shocked." She took a breath. "And flattered. I don't have any experience ... "

Waving off her comment, Trish said, "You'll be great."

"I'll do my best, so, yes. Thank you for asking me." Sabrina would approach being a godmother just like any other mission. She'd do her research. "This goes down as one of the best days of my life starting with watching you two get married. I'm sorry your wedding got delayed so many times."

Dingo walked up, pulling Valene along by her hand. He said, "That's just how we roll at Slye. You gotta roll with us to be part of the family."

Trish let out a watery laugh. "True. I figured that out right off the bat when I delayed it the first time when Ryder ended up in prison."

Ryder and Bianca had arrived just in time for the wedding, thanks to his father loaning them the Van Dyke private jet. They had disappeared after the ceremony and were probably sitting together, watching the waves roll in and the sky slowly darken into a deep blue with night coming on.

Josh scowled. "We waited on Ryder to get out of prison then he got married without *us*."

Laughing, Trish said, "Only the first time, and I can't fault him and Bianca. It was such a romantic wedding."

Josh stared down at her and asked tenderly, "More than ours?"

"Not even close." She winked at him and he let out a sigh.

Valene chuckled. "You two are nauseating but adorable."

Trish nodded. "We are, aren't we?" Then she put her hand on her stomach and frowned. "Crud."

Everyone looked at her middle with panic and said, "What?"

"This kid is using my bladder for bongo drums. I have to go pee."

Josh put his arm around her. "I'll go."

"I can find the bathroom by myself, Josh."

He leaned down and whispered something that turned her cheeks deep pink. "Done."

They walked off with Josh holding her arm as they went up the tall steps into the hotel.

Valene smiled as the couple disappeared and murmured, "I wish Tanner and Soo Jin could have been here."

Dingo scoffed. "Tanner's not ready for Soo Jin to be out in the open yet, but we'll go see them soon."

"Good."

Dingo turned to Sabrina and asked, "Heard anything?"

"Not a word." She knew he was inquiring about Gage. She would not let on how much it hurt to admit she'd had no contact from Gage. Logan had gotten her and Josh on a cargo flight back to the US three days ago.

She hadn't wanted to leave Taiwan, but Logan couldn't stay and he didn't trust anyone with her and Josh's safety once he left. The clincher had come when Logan discovered that Gage had departed Taiwan with Zhou's entourage, though he couldn't determine under what conditions Gage had gone with the Chinese president.

Or what had happened to Wayan.

Dingo had his arm around Valene's waist. He said, "I'm not going anywhere until we know something for sure."

Sabrina arched an eyebrow at him. "Not that I don't appreciate the concern, but why would you care if Gage ever came back?"

A warm glow lit his face. He glanced at Valene when he said, "Because my life is a better place with her in it." Shifting back to Sabrina, he admitted, "I finally realize Gage means just as much to you. He went with you to get Josh. If you trust him, then I will."

Coming from Dingo, that was a major stamp of approval, but she had already accepted that she wouldn't have a relationship or life like Dingo or Josh's. She had only herself and she'd have to make the best of it. "Thank you, but ... I don't think there's going to be anything else between us."

"Why?" Valene asked. "If I'm not prying."

"You're not. I haven't had a chance to talk to you, Dingo, but I'm shutting down the war room in the basement of Slye and moving ahead with full-time corporate security."

"Really?" Dingo murmured then cleared his voice. "You sure about this?"

Sabrina nodded. "I'm tired of that life and I can't watch you or Josh step into danger like that again."

"Holy smokes," Valene said. "I never thought that would happen and I was prepared for Dingo's way of life, but let me be the first to say how ecstatic I am over this decision."

But what about Dingo? Sabrina cocked her head at him. "You okay with that?"

He beamed her a smile that came from deep inside. "Yeah, I like it. Josh and I grumble all the time about boring security work, but that was before we both had someone we wanted to come home to." He shot Valene a heated look and hugged her close to him, adding, "I'm good with playing bodyguard to suits and tracking down electronic criminals in the security world."

Valene's gaze tracked past Sabrina, then her pretty eyes rounded with surprise. "Well, we may need to find something to drink."

Dingo grinned at her. "You thirsty, babe?"

"To be honest, yes, but it looks like things are about to get interesting and we might be in the way."

Dingo's gaze followed Valene's and he swore softly.

Sabrina noticed the light chatter had died down, leaving soft music to fill in the quiet gap. She turned to find what had drawn everyone's attention.

Gage walked toward her, looking gorgeous in a smoking black suit and crème knit shirt.

Four days and he just walks up? Not a phone call, text, smoke signal, nothing?

He'd better hope bloodstains would come out of that outfit.

Chapter 45

GAGE DRANK UP the vision of Sabrina in a wispy, cinnamon-red dress that dipped into a deep V in front then tucked in at her narrow waist and fell to her ankles in the back. The hem swooped up in the front to show off her sexy calves.

Diamonds shimmered at her ears behind strands of black hair falling loose over her shoulders.

She was exquisite, so beautiful inside and out.

Perfect. All except for the hurt and anger simmering in her gaze.

Worry had banded his chest for the past four days while he barely slept as Zhou held private trials for the traitors aligned with Wayan. Gage had been called upon to give testimony. The vote was unanimous on Wayan's guilt and all of those connected to him were sentenced to die.

Zhou's party leaders had agreed with their president that it was in their country's best interest to put down this coup attempt as quietly as possible. No point in sharing details that might aid another attempt.

In the end, Zhou handed over what Gage had requested in trade for saving his son.

That would have all been perfect if not for having to maintain zero contact with anyone, including the CIA, while Gage was being detained.

He'd had no chance to call Sabrina until six hours ago when he'd found out she was in Miami for Josh's wedding. He hadn't wanted to disturb the event. Plus, he wanted a chance to fix this and that wouldn't happen over the phone.

By the time he'd crossed the hotel grounds to reach Sabrina, conversation had died to whispers.

He noted Dingo and Valene walking up the steps to stand with Josh and his new wife, who had just appeared at the entrance to the hotel veranda.

Sabrina didn't move a muscle as he closed the distance to her.

Gage had sucked it up to deal with Zhou's demands, then spent a long-ass flight home with his CIA superiors after Zhou's people had alerted them to come retrieve their honored guest.

Yeah, that had shocked the agency, and ruffled their feathers, *and* shot their suspicions out of sight.

Through it all, Gage kept going. Nothing had mattered except getting back to Sabrina.

He stood in front of her, straining to keep from reaching out. "I do have an explanation."

The disappointment that washed through her expression lashed pain through him, but he would not be easily defeated. He said, "Can we step out of the limelight and talk?"

She glanced around and everyone suddenly found something else to look at except for Josh and Dingo, who now had their arms crossed and expressions tuned to suspicious.

Sabrina sent them a fierce look and lifted her chin.

That must have been a stand-down message.

The couples walked down the steps and took the path that led past Sabrina on their way to the beach.

Dingo got there first and told Sabrina, "Be sure to show up in time for the cake to be cut."

She had a twinkle in her narrowed eyes when she retorted, "Not a problem. Don't cut it until I get there."

Trish smirked. "I can arrange that." Then she tugged on Josh who said, "Just a moment."

Josh stepped over to Gage and extended his hand.

Gage started to ask if this was trick, but the change in Sabrina from death glare to doe-eyed, made him think twice. He took Josh's hand and shook it.

Josh said, "Thanks for coming with Sabrina to get me, and for everything you did to bring an end to all of the threat."

"You're welcome. You deserve thanks for your part of it, too. Congratulations on your wedding and new family."

Trish stepped up to offer her thanks as well then told their foursome, "Our guests are partying without us. Let's go so you can drink my share and do stupid things while I make videos for later when I need to blackmail you to babysit."

Valene laughed, a full body sound, and said, "I thought we'd have to fight for our turn."

Trish and Valene hooked arms and walked off, headed to the beach where the party was now rolling hard if that music drifting in was any indication.

Josh waited.

Dingo eyed Gage for a moment then said, "Good to see you, mate. Don't fuck this up." Then they walked off, hurrying to catch up with both women, who were hooting over something they found funny.

Probably their overprotective men.

Once everyone was out of hearing range, Gage took Sabrina's hand, surprised when she allowed it. He guided her away from the sidewalk and up to the gazebo that had a soft glow inside from hurricane lamps placed in stands surrounded by ribbons and flowers.

When he stood in the center, he turned to her and took her other hand.

"Please don't do this, Gage."

That put a knot in his throat. "Don't do what? Explain why I couldn't call you since we separated in Taiwan?"

"No. I know how our work functions and that you would have contacted me if you'd had a choice. But that's the issue. There is no choice in this business, not when you're trying to stay alive in the middle of a dangerous situation." She squeezed his hands. "I'm never going to deny that I care for you, but that's why I can't do this. I've finally realized I'm tired of the business."

He waited quietly as she watched him for a reaction to her wanting out of the clandestine world. He was here to act, not react.

She kept explaining. "I don't have it in me to sit home and wonder every time you leave if you're going to come back. Maybe if I'd never lived in your world, I might have, but I know how slim the chances are for returning from *any* operation."

A salty breeze lifted tendrils of her hair and tossed them around her face.

He released her hands, smoothed her hair back, then slid his hands to her shoulders. "I died a thousand times over when you went missing for two years."

She pulled her bottom lip in, biting lightly on it. "I know."

"No, you don't. I swore if you ever showed up again that I'd never let anyone harm you or live if they did. That's why I was so stubborn about handing over the names."

"You were right. I wouldn't have gone off to kill anyone, but I wanted someone to be at fault. You tried to tell me it wasn't anyone in the agency. I might have unintentionally harmed someone innocent."

"You would never make a dishonorable choice. It isn't in you. You'd throw your life out there first. That's why I was willing to stand firm on investigating on my own, because I needed to limit the threats to you if I poked the wrong person." He forced himself not to pull her in close when his body begged to feel her next to his.

Holding back was worse than any torture.

She lifted a hand and wrapped her fingers around his wrist. "I'm sorry for the pain I caused you."

"It wasn't your fault."

"Not during the two years, but ... it is once I returned and knew you were not behind the blown mission." She glanced away for only a moment, hesitating before she asked, "Is it done? Is everyone here really safe?"

Always worried about her chicks.

Sabrina would pick up a weapon and march back into battle tonight if she thought any of them were in danger.

He tried to smile, but his heart still hurt too much over the possibility of never being near her again. "Zhou held a secret trial to prevent anyone from knowing all the details. He doesn't want to give another group any ideas. And that allowed his people to quietly begin tracking down the Orion Hunters in league with Wayan."

"Really? That would disable two of the Hunter groups, but what about the Orion Hunters here?"

"I struck a deal with Zhou. I asked if I proved to him one of his most trusted advisors had a coup planned and intended to kill his son as well as him, would he give me everything I need to track down the Orion Hunters in the US?"

"Did he?"

"Yes, but he required that I join him in Beijing first while he dealt with Wayan. I was not allowed any outside contact. Wayan was a genius when it came to gathering intelligence. He had a file on everyone who had ever shown interest in the prophecy and those who had joined the Hunters. Zhou had Wayan's office and home computers confiscated. His guards brought in Wayan's son along with all the Orion Hunters waiting for Wayan's orders to attack. The trial and executions were ... brutal, but both China and the US realize how close everyone came to a war that would have destroyed much of this world. The right people are talking now."

Gage moved his hands, bringing Sabrina a tiny bit closer as he did. "Once the trials were over yesterday, his people called mine. The CIA flew a team to pick me up. It included my superior. I spent the trip home debriefing and showing them how to track down everyone associated with the Orion Hunters."

"What about that General? Nathaniel Lonker."

"Wayan gave up even more on him. Lonker was a high-ranking intelligence specialist in the Pentagon. No one had ever paid him any real attention up to now, but a photograph of him dead arrived at the Pentagon with a warning to do a better job watching their people."

Gage had received a note that said The General would never be a problem for anyone who mattered to him or Sabrina again. It was signed with a C.

MI6 should have held on to that one.

He'd tell Sabrina all of that later, if there was a later.

Sabrina dropped her forehead to his. "I try to remember why we do what we do." She lifted her head and said, "Or what I did. I'm sorry I got so angry with you in Taiwan when you changed your mind about us being partners."

"Sabrina, listen ... "

"No, hear me out. I really meant it when I first said I'd try out your plan to work together, but bringing Josh home alive made me accept that I couldn't ... " She swallowed and her voice got thin. "I couldn't go on a mission with you and bring your body home. I can't do that. In fact, I'm not taking on any more missions for the government. I'm out of that business."

She could have knocked him over with a feather at the announcement.

She sniffled and pressed fingers against her eyes, then took a deep breath and stood back from him.

The smile she gave him had the lowest wattage he'd ever seen from her.

She said, "I wish it could be different."

"You're killin' me," he muttered. He gave up and pulled her into a kiss.

She came willingly, but he knew it was only because she planned to walk away as soon as it was finished. His mouth took over hers, playing tongue to tongue. He ran a hand into her hair and cupped her head, holding her right where he wanted her.

Forever.

When he wrapped an arm around her waist and pulled her to him, she had to know how much he wanted her and he wasn't apologizing for being hard as stone. He wanted this woman with every breath. Wanted her with him *for* every breath.

The kiss pushed away time and space.

There was nothing but the two of them.

Sabrina slowed her side of the kiss, but wrapped her arms around his neck. He could feel her heart thundering.

It was now or never. He couldn't keep putting off finding out if they were over.

He said, "I have one question. I want a truthful answer."

Her reply came muffled against his shoulder. "What is it?"

His heart pounded. "Do you ... love me?"

She begged, "Don't do this to me."

"I am doing this."

Pushing back from him just enough to face him with damp eyes, she said, "I can't say those words when I know where this is going."

"No you don't." He saw the love in her eyes and trusted that, just as he trusted her. "Here's the other half of this. I love you in a way that is beyond words and nothing will ever stop me from loving you."

A tear ran down her face. "I told you, Gage, I can't do this."

"Do what? Admit that we love each other?"

"I can't do this when we both know it won't work."

He put his hands on each side of her head. "We can make anything work as long as we love each other. I'm leaving the agency. I. Choose. You."

"What? You can't do that!"

"Yes, I can, and did."

"You can't trust them to let you walk away."

The tightness around his chest eased.

He smiled at her. "Those four days without any ability to contact you were a hell I never want to suffer through again. But I had the time to think through everything that has happened and with the help of my new friend Zhou, I came up with a plan."

Her eyes widened with a spark of hope that sent his heart cartwheeling.

Gage had to get this all out. "Zhou holds details of a long list of atrocities The General committed against China and other countries. Thanks to some unknown informant whose initial is probably C, those details were delivered to Zhou who is tucking them away somewhere safe. Between my part in all this and negotiating a peaceful end with Zhou, plus an unspoken threat to use those details if anything happens to me, the CIA has decided that I'm a national fucking asset. Not only am I to *never* be harmed, there's a group tasked with watching my back."

"That means..." She lifted a hand that trembled.

"That means you and I can be together and no one from the government would dare touch either of us. I'll never have to go undercover again ... unless it's at home with you."

She leaped into his arms, hugging him and kissing him.

He swung her around and around, feeling like a young man again who had a whole new life before him.

Or rather, held his life in his arms.

When he set her down, he moved in close, nose to nose, and said, "You still haven't answered my question."

She gave him a genuine smile. "Already you've lost your touch for getting intel?"

"Sabrina," he said in a warning voice, but smiling the whole time.

"I do love you and I've never uttered those words to anyone."

His chest relaxed all the way. "While you're in an agreeable mood, are you going to marry me?"

"Depends."

"On what?" Yes, he sounded shocked, but what the hell?

She kissed him and said, "On whether you're going to help me run Slye's corporate security division."

"As long as I can sleep my way to the top, babe."

"We'll have to negotiate positions."

Thank you for reading my books. If you enjoyed this story, please help other readers find this book by posting a review.

To find out about new releases, sign up for Dianna's private newsletter list (emails are NEVER shared) at
AuthorDiannaLove.com

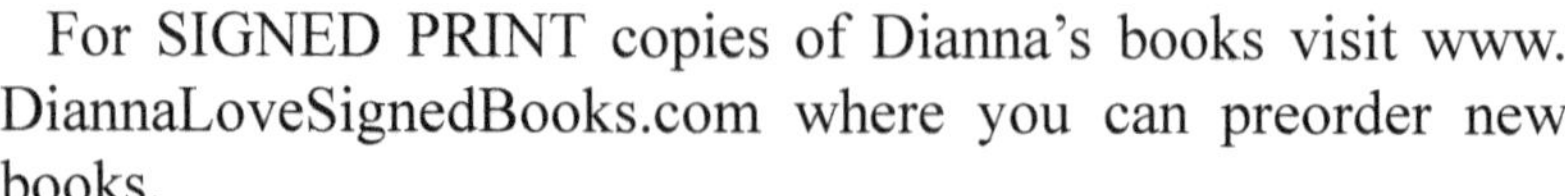

For SIGNED PRINT copies of Dianna's books visit www.DiannaLoveSignedBooks.com where you can preorder new books.

E-book and international fans:

You can also order a set of signed bookplates for your print books and/or signed cover cards just for the cost of postage at www.DiannaLoveSignedBooks.com (click MORE)

This is the last book in the Slye Team series, but Dianna is working on a spin-off series, which will include Slye Team characters who have not received their HEA. Sign up for her newsletter at www.AuthorDiannaLove.com to find out first about new releases.

Keep reading for a sneak peek at **WRECKED**, book one in the HAMR Brotherhood Black Ops Romantic Thriller series

Trained for dangerous situations, Hallene risks everything to save her sister who has been kidnapped as a pawn in to ensure a deadly attack happens. Sam's future with the HAMR Brotherhood as a black operative is hanging by a thread when he saves Hallene during a blown op, which was not his mission. She offers him a chance at redemption, putting all that matters to him on the line because he can't tell anyone if he accepts her deal. This enemies-to-lovers romance is loaded with wild twists, sizzling romance, and an unexpected ending.

HAMR BROTHERHOOD
ROMANTIC ACTION ADVENTURE
FALCA TEAM

WRECKED
Sam "Partyman" Leclair

DIANNA LOVE

Chapter 1

SAM HAD HIS NVG monocular flipped out of the way so he could see everything in natural colors as he died.

He kept waiting for this old-as-hell helicopter carrying his HAMR Brotherhood FALCA team to sputter and crash into the waves below. An early evening storm pounded the fuselage as if the chopper needed help nosediving.

An August to remember.

Thick foam rolling along the Venezuelan coast would be a stunning photograph for tourists.

The only sight he cared about capturing was W in cuffs and leg irons. Few international terrorists had eluded security forces and military in every country the way W had for five years.

Sam would never forget the bloody images of citizens, especially children, killed in the attacks. In his mind, he still saw the eyes wide open and body parts missing. One teenage girl who had looked so much like Sam's sister kept visiting his nightmares with her half-blown-away skull and eyes wide open in fear.

Had his sister looked as terrified when she'd died?

Bile ran up Sam's throat. He forced his mind back to the here and now. Stick to the mission.

He couldn't screw up on this one, not after the last mission where he'd made a misstep. Logan, leader of all HAMR Brotherhood teams, understood what his men faced, but he expected everyone to stick to their duty and keep the team strong.

Sam still felt justified over rushing through enemy fire to save a woman being dragged away. Sam freed her and handed her off to another woman then rejoined the team.

Nitro had chewed him into pieces. Yes, Sam had no one to cover his six for those seconds, and yes, she could have been hiding a weapon, but he'd seen true terror in her face and had a plan to return safely.

The fact that his plan had worked failed to spare him from Nitro's wrath.

Sam would do the mission tonight by the book no matter what crossed his field of vision.

No one wanted to lose a spot in HAMR Brotherhood, and Sam lived for operations with his FALCA team.

His seat dropped suddenly in an air pocket. Muscles in Sam's gut clenched even though it was only inches.

Having spent an hour helping the forty-something pilot get this bucket-of-crap-parts running, Sam had up-close knowledge of the flying death trap.

He didn't mind flying at night and low to the ground. That was perfect for a stealth approach when he had faith in his ride.

Nothing fazed Pablo, their intrepid pilot, not even lightning streaking across the sky and rain hammering so loud Sam should be deaf by now. Sadly, he wasn't. Was Pablo even the pilot's real name? Thick, curly hair sprang out in every direction. He wore flip-flops and one of those Hawaiian-print shirts with a string of seashells around his neck as bright against his deep tan as the white around his dark eyes.

Didn't matter what he looked like so long as his reputation as a former hotshot Army pilot held up.

The team medic, Blade, sat in the co-pilot's seat, but he couldn't fly this thing if Pablo fell out the opening on his left. As the largest of their four, Blade had to ride shotgun. If not, somebody would have been hanging off the side of Pablo's OH-6A chopper, a Vietnam-era relic like the one his revered Army colonel father had flown.

The LOACH, which pilots and crews had nicknamed this chopper, had the exact attributes needed for tonight's mission. It had flown in low, fast, and quiet to flush out the enemy during the Vietnam conflict. When the speedy little helo took on enemy fire, a larger, noisier, and deadlier Cobra AH-1 hanging back on their ass would sweep in and break up the party.

But that had been sixty freaking years ago.

"You enjoyin' the ride, Partyman?" Nitro asked, his voice coming through Sam's headset. The leader of their FALCA team found most things amusing until show time. Right now, his eyes gleamed with amusement as if they were on the way to a bar.

That would be the day. For Sam to go barhopping would surprise all of them.

Sitting between the two of them, Angel's lips curled, but the Spaniard stayed out of this.

Positioned behind the pilot and with an open door on his left, Nitro was not one to show any concern. Always cool on the outside. Of course, Nitro would find flying in this rattling bucket of bolts funny if Sam gave the least indication it got under his skin.

Not happening.

Sam wanted no one on this team to question his commitment at any time, but especially tonight. He would nail his part without bitching. He grinned at his leader.

Nitro smirked, not buying the grin one bit.

Angel, one of their snipers and the master of impossible stunts, held his HK 416 assault rifle in a relaxed grip. Sam, Nitro, and Blade held identical weapons. They all carried Baretta M9 handguns with suppressors as well.

Sam had thanked Esteban for damn good weapons, ammo, NVGs, and tactical gear. Sam had vouched for Esteban when Logan needed an in-country arms supplier close to the target on short notice.

Hard not to vouch for someone who helped Sam survive being a prisoner in a Libyan drug-running and terrorist camp three years back. Trust ran both ways after Sam took a shot to save Esteban's life during their escape.

The chopper engine groaned and skipped.

Sam gripped his rifle, muscles kinked in his shoulders. He silently asked to not go diving into the black ocean. He had no idea if they were so close to the beach that they'd hit too shallow and break into a thousand pieces or sink a hundred feet the minute the chopper smashed into water.

Blade's neck muscles flexed. Yeah, he didn't like this either.

As if sensing tension, Pablo held up a hand and spoke into their headphones. "Not long now."

Sam ground his teeth to keep from yelling at Pablo to put both hands back and keep this thing airborne. They could have used Slider on this mission. He could fly a tin can with two wooden wings and orange juice for fuel.

Pablo leaned forward quickly and tapped at a gauge.

Blade's head whipped to the left, sharp eyes watching him.

The motor coughed and sputtered.

Ah, shit. Sam moved his boot closer to the opening, preparing to make a quick jump and get out of the way for Angel.

Pablo's flying dinosaur dipped for the longest second of Sam's life before the engine caught again, blades whining at full power once more.

Pablo grinned and pumped his fist. "She's old but solid."

Sam cursed. He couldn't be the only one holding his breath until they landed. He'd made HALO jumps from thirty thousand feet that were less dangerous than this.

Angel cursed lividly in Spanish.

From the team daredevil?

Oh yeah. Bad sign there.

If they landed at the designated spot, they had to hike five klicks. On the other hand, if the motor cut out one more time, Sam was ready to set this chopper down immediately on the nearest strip of beach and hike the additional distance.

Lightning crackled and fingered into jagged zaps of power.

They had been flying straight into the rain, but Pablo banked sharply toward the coast. Hallelujah. Sam gripped the side of the fuselage. Water bullets drilled into his body, battering the right side as the chopper continued angling west. He didn't care. Wind buffeted him, lifting and pushing the egg-shaped cabin around.

The helicopter neared a narrow strip of beach and raced across it, closing in on the drop point.

Nitro clicked into mission mode, reminding Pablo what time to return and to not land if he did not see a flashing signal from the team. They either made it in and out on time, or something had gone FUBAR.

Sam flipped his NVG monocular down and lifted his rifle to his chest, ready to get rolling.

Pablo slowed the beast then hovered only seconds and touched down as softly as if he had been carrying dynamite.

Bailing out first, Sam's boots hit solid ground. Relief.

Now they had control of their mission.

He strode from beneath the rotor wash with Angel right behind him.

They met up with Nitro and Blade on the other side as the chopper lifted off, flying away toward the coast.

Rain fell in a heavy drizzle, soaking Sam until he felt at one with the dark Venezuelan forest they entered. He didn't give a damn about bad weather.

It came in handy sometimes.

His first concern was always keeping his team safe as they extracted the package—a kidnapped US senator.

This op had been pulled together with plenty of talent but rushed. Opportunity rarely cared about time when it knocked. No one to date had been this close to nailing the international predator known only as W, who his FALCA team believed held the high-value hostage in a reclusive location.

This was not a kidnapping that required a monetary payment.

If W did indeed have the senator, there was no amount of gold that would save the politician. Senator Turner had publicly vowed to bring W to justice. Special Force teams were already following other leads in multiple countries. One of Logan's intel specialists turned up intel pointing at W possibly being in South America.

Hell yeah, Sam had wanted to go for many reasons the minute he knew the plan, not just to cement his position with FALCA moving forward.

Moose, another FALCA member, one who handled intel gathering for multiple teams, had hit paydirt while searching for anything on the senator's kidnapping.

Logan had activated FALCA immediately.

They all wanted W. None more than Sam. The word *crimes* failed to describe the hideous murders and destruction committed by that sick monster, W.

They went wheels up knowing every detail could not be flushed out.

No op went exactly as planned.

Sam kept waiting for the mission calm to settle over him. He lived for that moment when his world made sense, but he could not shake the foreboding sensation of spiders with sharp claws crawling up his spine.

Chapter 2

HALLENE SQUINTED TO see ahead where an endless darkness waited and paused to listen for any sign she'd been discovered. If they caught her in this dirt tunnel, she had no chance of outrunning bullets.

Her jeans and long-sleeved black T-shirt had been soaked by the time she parked the BMW 1200 GS motorcycle built to be used on or off-road. She'd been fortunate to even find a dual sport bike to ride, which could handle dense woods as easily as the highways in Venezuela.

Money solved most problems in a foreign country, but only if a product was readily available.

She breathed slowly and had to push away claustrophobia needling her, then strode forward on the hard-packed dirt path. An LED light hidden in a ring she wore bounced over the hard-packed ground with an occasional thick root bulging up across the path. Roots in the wrong place could compromise an old tunnel like this built centuries ago without engineering plans.

Dirt in here smelled of old wood and damp mulch, two things that deteriorated. If this tunnel caved in, she'd die here, and no one would ever know. *Nice, Hallene. Why not think about running into a slumbering anaconda and being strangled to death?*

She had hacked at vegetation for over an hour to reveal parts of the crumbling shack that had collapsed over the closest access point to the ocean for this underground passage.

This tunnel would likely not be the only one along the northeastern coast of Venezuela from back when pirates stashed their stolen goods.

She didn't want gold and jewels.

She was here to save a seventeen-year-old girl then beat the crap out of the kidnapper who had dragged her here.

According to her intel techie, a big-time pirate historian and enthusiast, this seventy-hectare, or two-hundred-seventy-acre location had once been a sugarcane plantation. But time changes everything. The plantation had been left in ruins for almost a hundred years. Then two years ago, a US businessman who had lost his entire family acquired the decaying mansion along with twenty acres the government allowed him. He spent nine months remodeling the structure back to its glory days and kept the place up without any domestic help. A loner who raised his own food as well as goats and chickens.

A sophisticated hermit.

A dead hermit by now.

She shook her head at someone who looked at a reclusive South American location and thought *sanctuary*. The government might have no interest in him so long as he paid taxes when they came due, but cartels were another story.

The person her intel indicated was currently squatting in the mansion for two days. He would not fear cartels nor be here long enough for a tax collector to show up.

Kidnappers frowned on paying taxes.

She only needed this world-class scumbag to be here one night. Just for a few more hours, in fact.

She'd been mentally counting steps in groups of fifty and bent a fourth finger into her palm. The tunnel exit leading into the basement of the remodeled mansion should be before she tucked the fifth finger.

Her head bumped something hard. She cursed and rubbed her head. She'd hit a rare crossbeam installed for support. Damn pirates. She was five-nine. Had the men back then been that much shorter than her or just too lazy to carve out a taller corridor? Ducking her head, she kept moving.

Wouldn't a taller tunnel have made carrying trunks of gold and jewels easier?

She would not go through this hell tonight for all the lost treasures in the world.

Only for Phoebe, a seventeen-year-old girl with a bad attitude who had been a pain in Hallene's backend since Phoebe's birth.

Still, no girl deserved the fate her half-sister faced.

Hallene rarely had regrets in life, but she now had a few when it came to Phoebe.

Without missing a step, she peeled open the Velcro cover shielding her black watch face turned to the inside of her wrist. Closing in on half past nine at night.

Two and a half hours should be enough time if she had a team with her, but doing this solo felt as if she cut it close. Her plan required inserting and extracting Phoebe before midnight. The infamous Collector never spent more than seventy-two hours at any location once he had a captive. He'd arrived here at midnight two nights back.

Now that he'd been located once, he could be found again, but that didn't mean Phoebe would still be in his possession or alive by his next stop.

Her intel resource had gained a tip when the Collector stopped in South America and traveled to the remodeled home. Her techie told her there was a high probability the Collector was headed to this mansion.

If that was true, Hallene would never tease her friendly hacker about his obsession with pirate lore again.

She pushed her legs harder.

Everything about this half-assed plan went against her sense of preparation. Worry climbed across her shoulders at the fear she'd make a mistake and either die before she could free Phoebe or get them both killed.

Discovering the location of El Coleccionista, aka the Collector, had been too good to pass up or to wait on backup, which she no longer had. Hacking the computer of Phoebe's father sealed the deal when Adam Kovac received a message about an unspecified task he had to perform once details were delivered if he ever wanted to see Phoebe again.

Resources were everything.

Her tech also supplied information to UK military such as SFSG, Special Forces Support Group, where Coop had been a respected member. His buddies had been nice to her after Coop's death, but she'd told them nothing about this or they would have hauled her away and taken time to recon the area before any insertion decision.

An excellent idea if time had any part in this equation beyond running out too quickly.

Any interference would blow her chance at rescuing her half-sister.

She'd trusted Coop to a point. He'd been an elite operative after all, but Coop would not approve of her being here. She understood. Without rules, there would be chaos in his line of work.

Phoebe didn't have time for someone to bless this. Coop's team sure as hell wouldn't bless her take-no-prisoners plan.

Hallene's fingers curled into a tight fist with the urge to make the kidnapper pay. She hadn't decided the exact definition of making the Collector pay yet, but it had to be more than sticking him in a jail cell where he'd find a way to slither out.

Monsters could not be rehabilitated.

She'd reached forty-five steps.

Her blood pressure jumped. Where was the end of this tunnel?

She clicked the light in her ring to the lowest setting, a bare glow that should not give away her position by leaking through an opening to the mansion. She just hoped some entry point still existed. With her eyes adjusting to the ambient light, she took one step then another, always reaching forward.

Her fingers bumped something solid hanging away from the wall. Lifting her ring, she had a tiny thrill at finding an old wooden ladder. This was where things got dicey.

Her heart thudded.

Would she have a welcoming party?

Sweat drizzled down her face and neck even in the cool temperature down here.

How many times had Coop said, "In the world of special operations, hesitation gets you killed."

So would a bad decision, but sometimes that was the only option.

Climbing carefully and praying the wood was not rotted, she

made it up six steps, constantly feeling above her head. Her fingers hit a solid surface. She moved her hand over the texture and found parallel lines in the rough surface.

Wood planks.

She pushed. Nothing moved.

Hooking her leg over a rung, she used both hands to push up.

She grunted from straining until the covering began to give. Dirt rained down on her face. She closed her eyes and spit out debris, pausing to listen. No light bled through from above. Demanding more from her arm muscles, she gritted her teeth and shoved harder. The trapdoor began lifting.

Her vision blurred from perspiration stinging her eyes. She kept going until she had the wooden covering a foot high and paused to swing her light around quickly to search the opening.

No one stood there pointing a weapon at her.

It took some maneuvering, but she managed to ease the heavy covering over to one side before hoisting herself through the hole.

She sat there breathing in and out as quietly as she could until she'd regained her energy and pulled her legs up, turning to kneel. That gave her leverage to lower the cover. It fit perfectly back into the floor, but with a snick of sound.

Heart thumping, she waited.

No voices. No footsteps came her way.

Sweeping her light over the cover, she could see where thick dust had been undisturbed for many years prior to her opening the hatch. She had just enough room to turn around in the space without hitting a wall.

Where was the way out? She ran her hands everywhere until she touched a thick piece of wood that had been slid through two wooden loops. Yes!

She removed the heavy board that felt hand-hewn and tugged on a loop, inching the door inward. It squeaked. She held her breath. Chills ran up her arms.

No one attacked her. No bullets flew by.

Only dark met her on the other side.

Her ring light could stay on longer.

She squeezed through as soon as she had enough room and

pulled the door back in place. It fit into the wall in a way that camouflaged the access.

She sniffed, expecting the musty smell. What else was she picking up?

The room stank. Body odor and something worse.

Then it hit her. Dried blood.

She pinched her nose and breathed through her mouth as she swept her light to inspect the closet-sized room. Her foot bumped into something that didn't move. The body of a man in khaki pants and a white cotton shirt was lying in a dried pool of blood from his throat being slashed.

He'd been dead more than one day.

Very likely the hermit owner.

That meant any options were on the table to get Phoebe to safety, even burning this house to the ground to send the Collector's security running to find the threat.

But only if she located Phoebe and knew she could free her.

Moving around the body, Hallene found a walk-in door, which opened to a larger room ... the basement she'd been hoping to find. Disappointment slammed her in the chest at the silence.

An empty room.

Phoebe was not here. No one was.

As much as Hallene wanted to hammer the Collector into the ground, she'd hoped to find Phoebe kept in the basement. If so, she'd pass on any payback to spirit the girl away to a safe place then send law enforcement to look for the property owner.

She walked around to determine all exit points. Only one besides the tunnel route. A set of stairs led way up to a landing easily thirty feet up.

That had to be higher than ground level.

She pulled out a lipstick camera and found a place to put it near the exit to the tunnel then headed for the metal stairs.

She climbed fifteen steps, then turned and climbed another twenty steps along the wall to a landing when the stairs turned left.

A modern-looking light fixture had been mounted at the side of a door she hoped opened into the living area. Rushing across the landing on her soft-soled shoes, she paused to carefully open the door and peek out.

Yet another closet. Big one.

Passing through that ten-foot-long by six-foot-wide space, she opened the second door into a grandiose ballroom.

The distinct smell of lemon polish replaced the stench clogging her nose.

While the tunnel appeared to still be a secret, the basement was not, but access to the basement had been somewhat hidden.

Where would they have put Phoebe? In a bedroom?

Where were guards set up to patrol?

She lifted a powerful stun gun from where it had been hooked on her belt. She'd brought it into South America broken apart with pieces hidden in her luggage contents, a camouflaged set Coop had created for her.

This gun was not even on the market yet.

Coop had always been getting his hands on the latest and greatest but warned her to stay in top shape. Never depend on the stun gun for more than gaining a moment's edge in a fight.

She stuck to that rule.

She pulled off her shoes and continued in her socks. Any sound could get her killed.

Her pulse quickened. She hurried into the ballroom where she found only two other doors on her right. The farthest one opened to reveal a long set of steps going down.

She'd save downstairs for last. Bedrooms were normally upstairs. That seemed a logical place to hold a captive.

Closing that door carefully, she moved to the other door, which opened into a small kitchen. Vintage cooking utensils were hung on a wall rack and stuffed into a ceramic vase sitting on a long prep counter with white cabinets below. More white cabinets were above a porcelain sink. The small refrigerator and free-standing gas stove with two small ovens all appeared clean and just as old as the cooking utensils.

Nothing appeared to be in use, which made sense for a single occupant. Probably a larger kitchen downstairs.

Could this have been the servant's access to upstairs living quarters for the domestic staff at one time?

Crossing the galley kitchen, she opened another door to find a long walkway overlooking a wide foyer. She inhaled fresher air here, thankful not to find the copper penny smell of fresh blood.

No sound came from below in the foyer. At the end of the walkway, a curved set of stairs with a polished wood railing descended to the main floor.

Deep breath. Then another.

Go time. She stepped out onto a wood floor and glanced over the railing, patiently waiting to locate a guard before moving into the opening.

A man dressed in dark fatigues and carrying a high-powered rifle finally walked by outside beyond the tall glass windows on each side of wide mahogany double doors. Exterior lights spaced along the walkway tossed beams across the marble floor inside where a circular table held a vase of dead flowers.

Her heart squeezed at the poor guy who had come here and worked so hard.

As soon as the guard went out of sight, she lifted her stun gun and moved quickly across the carpet, staying close to the wall on her right. Once she passed the staircase going down, she stopped at the first door. No lights shined out from beneath.

She opened it carefully and kept her voice low. "Phoebe?"

No one answered. Closing it softly, she opened the next door.

Someone gasped in a high-pitched voice.

Hallene whispered, "Phoebe?"

Loud sniffling, then Phoebe begged in a trembling voice, "Go away. Leave me alone."

Hallene's heart broke at the terror in the girl's voice because Phoebe couldn't see who entered. Still, her heart pounded, excited to have found the girl.

She took a step in, quietly saying, "Stay calm. It's me—"

"*Nooo!*"

Something hard slammed Hallene in the side of her head. She went down to the sound of Phoebe screaming.

⚬⚬⚬

Buy as signed and personalized copy of WRECKED at
www.DiannaLoveSignedBooks.com

***

The Slye Team Black Ops
romantic thriller series is 'completed' (great for binging!)

Prequel: Last Chance To Run
Book 1: Nowhere Safe
Book 2: Honeymoon To Die For
Book 3: Kiss The Enemy
Book 4: Deceptive Treasures
Book 5: Stolen Vengeance
Book 6: Fatal Promise

Want more romance with suspense?
You might like Dianna's new shifter romance series:

The League of Gallize Shifters books are stand-alone paranormal romances written in an larger urban fantasy style world.

Book 1: Gray Wolf Mate
Book 2: Mating A Grizzly
Book 3: Stalking His Mate
Book 4: Scent of A Mate
Book 5: Wild Wolf Mate

Dianna Love and Mary Buckham created the sci-fi/fantasy, time travel Red Moon Trilogy, stories appropriate for Hunger Games readers.

(You can order signed/personalized print copies at
www.MicahCaidaSignedBooks.com)

Book 1: Time Trap
Book 2: Time Return
Book 3: Time Lock

Author's Bio

New York Times **Bestseller Dianna Love** once dangled over a hundred feet in the air to create unusual marketing projects for Fortune 500 companies. She now writes high-octane romantic thrillers, young adult and urban fantasy. Fans of the bestselling Belador urban fantasy series will be thrilled to know more books are coming after soon with the new Treoir Dragon Chronicles. Dianna's Slye Team Black Ops sexy romantic thriller series wrapped up with Gage and Sabrina's book–Fatal Promise–perfect for bingers! She has new League of Gallize Shifters paranormal romance series. Look for her books in print, e-book and audio. On the rare occasions Dianna is out of her writing cave, she tours the country on her BMW motorcycle searching for new story locations. Dianna lives in the Atlanta, GA area with her husband, who is a motorcycle instructor, and with a tank full of unruly saltwater critters.

Visit her website at *www.AuthorDiannaLove.com*
or *www.DiannaLoveSignedBooks.com*

A word from Dianna...

No book is possible without the support and love of my amazing husband, Karl.

I fall in love with every story, even when the characters *won't act right* (as we say down south) and the story keeps trying to race off in the wrong direction. It's a battle all the time, but one I can't wait to go back and tackle again because I love to tell stories.

Thank you to all the readers who send me encouragement, leave reviews and take the journey through each story with me. Everything I write is for you.

I can put my all into every book because of my support team, starting with Cassondra who reads early, middle and last, plus she keeps me on track when I'm so focused on writing that everything else would fall through the cracks. Thank you to Judy Carney who is always ready to read every line and watch for those pesky errors that need a fresh set of eyes. I so appreciate former Special Forces elite soldier Steve Doyle for the time he carves out to read my books. He advises me on how to coordinate a black ops mission, which weapons to use for specific situations and then he catches things that get missed even after 2-3 reads. Joyce Ann McLaughlin somehow manages to find time to read no matter what is happening in her world. I also want to give a shout out to former Marine Sharon Livingston Griffiths who is another early reader. She shares a love of romantic suspense and riding motorcycles with me. And a big hug for Leiha Mann who has saved me a lot of time and energy by compiling electronic things. She saves me from using a sledgehammer to turn my computer into tiny pieces.

Thanks to my fabulous cover designer, Kim Killion, whose talent always bowl me over, and to Jennifer Jakes for sorting out the pile I send her then turning it into nicely formatted pages. Thank you also to Candi Fox for always stepping in to help with the Street Team and promoting my books on many venues and to Xiamara, another talented artist I call friend.

Thanks also to Manuella Robinson, who was one of my very first readers *before* I was even close to being published. I hope you enjoy this last Slye Team story, but the HAMR Brotherhood will be a spinoff series. You met them in *Kiss The Enemy.*

I want to give a shout out to my Dianna Love Reader Community who visit with me on our Facebook group page by that name (all readers are welcome to join us). *waving at you*